THE MALICE BOARD OF DIRECTORS
PRESENTS

MYSTERY MOST TRADITIONAL

Malice Domestic 17

WILDSIDE PRESS

Published by Wildside Press LLC

www.wildsidepress.com

First edition

Cover art by Wildside Press

This book was professionally typeset on Reedsy.
Find out more at reedsy.com

Contents

Acknowledgement

The editors would like to thank John Betancourt at Wildside Press for his constant and unwavering support to Malice Domestic and these editors.

The editors would also like to express their special thanks to the selection committee—Edwin Hill, Cynthia Sabelhaus, and Tonya Spratt-Williams. As a result of their hard work and dedication to excellence, we present for your reading enjoyment *Malice Domestic 17: Mystery Most Traditional.*

Malice Domestic Anthology Series

MYSTERY OF THE MIDNIGHT FIRE

By Cynthia Sabelhaus

Muriel came into the carriage house as Jack folded the last of the newspapers to deliver before school. The sun was barely above the horizon, but she could make out the headlines:

1932 PRESIDENTIAL ELECTION IN THREE WEEKS
HERBERT HOOVER or FRANKLIN ROOSEVELT?

"Hey, sprout, what 'ya doing out here so early?" Jack said. "School doesn't start for another two hours."

Muriel dropped an armload of books into the woven basket on the front of her shiny red ladies' bicycle—a birthday gift when she turned eleven the previous week. Jack had received the blue boy's version in July for his twelfth birthday. "I think we might have a new case," she said.

"What? Did somebody lose another cat? Hey, maybe we can make ten cents—five for you and five for me."

Muriel flinched. It was true, their detective agency hadn't been doing so well lately, but she was sure things would pick up. "Mrs. Wixom called last night. I'm going to see her before school. She needs our help."

Jack frowned as he loaded the papers into his bag. "Then how come she only asked for you?"

"She asked us both to come, but I told her about your paper route. I'll find out what's on her mind and fill you in tonight." She hesitated. "You still want to be part of our agency, don't you?"

Jack stood and lightly touched Muriel's shoulder. "What? You think I'd let you take all the glory on our next big case? Not going to happen, baby sister."

Repeating the word *sister* to herself, Muriel grinned. *I never thought I'd have a family again after Mama died and Papa left town to look for work. Old Mrs. Wixom was nice enough to let me work for her and live in her attic, but now I have a real home and a brother.*

* * *

The day was rapidly warming by the time Muriel arrived at Mrs. Wixom's. She wiped the sweat from her face and admired the ocean view from the old mansion's side porch. October wasn't usually so warm in Rhode Island. Indian Summer had made a surprise appearance, and the ride to Mrs. Wixom's was all uphill.

Inside, Tillie was working in the kitchen. Muriel tapped on the screen door.

"Miss Muriel, you come on in here. There's no need for you to knock."

Muriel stepped inside and noticed there were already plates drying in the dish drainer. "Mrs. Wixom must be up early."

Tillie nodded. "Ever since her friend, Miss Darcy, came to stay, the two ladies are wanting breakfast before the sun comes up."

Mrs. Wixom's voice carried from down the hallway. "Is that Muriel I hear? Come into the sitting room, dear. I have a little problem to discuss with you."

Muriel shrugged at Tillie and answered, "Yes, ma'am."

She found the two old ladies sitting in matching high-backed chairs near the fireplace. The marble-topped occasional table between them held a tea tray, and each balanced a delicate porcelain cup and saucer on her lap.

Mrs. Wixom nodded. "Muriel, I'm glad you could come. This is my old friend and fellow retired teacher, Miss Darcy."

Muriel smiled at the woman. "I'm pleased to see you again, Miss Darcy. I was in your first grade class."

Miss Darcy grinned. "Of course. You were one of my best students, even if you did ask so many questions." Her smile quickly disappeared. "I was so sorry to hear about your mother, dear. She was a fine woman."

Muriel was used to people expressing their sympathy, especially older people, but it still brought a painful stab. She thanked Miss Darcy, quickly took a seat across from the women, and turned to Mrs. Wixom. "You mentioned a problem?"

Mrs. Wixom glanced at Miss Darcy and cleared her throat. "You may not have heard about the fire out on Cox Road. It was only three days ago, so it hasn't been in the paper yet. Miss Darcy's house burned down."

"Oh no." Muriel turned to Miss Darcy. "I'm so sorry that happened, but I'm glad you're okay."

Miss Darcy nodded. "Yes, I was lucky. There'd been a big scruffy dog coming around looking for handouts. He barked that night and woke me from a sound sleep. I was on my way out to chase him off when I saw the smoke. Otherwise, I hate to think what might have happened."

"And now you'll be able to build a new house," Muriel said.

Miss Darcy shook her head. "I thought I could rebuild. I kept the insurance paid up, even in this terrible depression. But the inspector for the insurance company went to the house the day after the fire. He said he found gasoline splashed near the building—evidence of arson."

"Arson?" Muriel said.

"That's when someone starts a fire on purpose," Mrs. Wixom said. "They're saying Goldie, um, Miss Darcy started the fire herself to collect the insurance money." She thumped her cane on the floor next to her chair. "We need to prove them wrong and make sure Goldie can rebuild her house."

Muriel saw a tear roll down the side of Miss Darcy's nose. "Don't worry. Jack and I will begin our investigation after school."

"What can we do to help?" Mrs. Wixom asked.

"I'll need the address of the house and the name of the insurance company. Then, I can ask Aunt Thea whether there have been any complaints." Muriel looked at Miss Darcy. "Aunt Thea isn't really my aunt. Her name is Althea Robinson, and she works at the courthouse. She was my mother's best friend. You probably had Jack in school, too. Aunt Thea is his mother, and I

3

live with them now. Jack's my partner in our detective agency."

"Well, I can't think of two better detectives to have on the case," Miss Darcy said. "It'll be just like having Nancy Drew and the Hardy Boys solving the mystery of the midnight fire."

Muriel took notes as the two women provided the information they had. When the mantel clock chimed, Mrs. Wixom said, "You'd better go, Muriel. School starts in fifteen minutes. Come by tomorrow afternoon and let us know what you've found out. In the meantime, Goldie and I will make some calls. If this company has cheated people, we'll find out."

* * *

After school, Muriel decided to bike past the burned house, maybe stop for a quick look. Aunt Thea wouldn't be home for another hour or more, and Jack had a meeting at the newspaper office.

Miss Darcy's house was on the other side of town and on top of a different hill than Mrs. Wixom's. The ride took twenty minutes. Muriel parked her bicycle off the road and walked up the steep gravel drive. The damage was worse than she imagined. The chimney still stood, and part of the front wall was upright but leaning inward. She walked to the rear of the house and discovered the roof and back walls were gone. Charred rubble lay where the house should have been. Whatever furnishings Miss Darcy collected over her lifetime were now black and gray ash.

Muriel checked the rest of the property. A wooden shed remained intact at the back of the lawn, although its green paint was blistered in spots. Nearby trees and bushes were singed, and a few puddles remained where the firemen sprayed water to stop the fire from spreading. A small red gasoline can lay at the edge of the lawn where the trees grew thick. She shook her head. *This is such a sad place now, but I don't see any clues. I might as well go home.*

As Muriel started down the driveway, she heard a noise behind her. She jerked back and scanned the yard but saw nothing unusual. When she turned to leave, the noise started again. Scratching and a high-pitched whine. *Was some animal trapped in the shed?*

Muriel hurried to the shed door. The noises grew louder. "It's okay," she said. "I'll get you out of there."

Not even thinking about what kind of animal might be inside, she twisted the door handle and pulled. Nothing happened. She pulled again, but the door remained shut. *It must have warped with the heat and water.* The scratching behind the door grew frantic. Muriel put one foot on the side of the shed and strained against the door with all her might. It gave way with a screech and popped open, slamming her into the shed wall. She stayed there, unmoving, not knowing what kind of animal might come bounding out. Instead, the noises ceased, and nothing moved.

She peeked around the door and saw a large, matted pile of fur on the shed floor. *I think it's a dog. Maybe it's too weak to stand up. It's been three days since the fire.* She crept toward the animal. "It's okay. You'll be all right now."

The dog's eyes were closed. Its breath sounded raspy. Clumps of fur were missing from its back, and the skin looked blistered. *It must have been near the house when it burned. It could be the stray that saved Miss Darcy.* Muriel caught the unmistakable smell of gasoline on the dog. She pilfered a saucer from beneath an empty flowerpot and filled it from an almost empty watering can. The dog could barely lift its head, but Muriel held the saucer under its nose, and its tongue came out and lapped a bit of it.

Muriel sat down, held the dog's head in her arms, and stroked between its ears. *This feels so familiar.* Under the dirt and grime, she could barely make out the white streak around its nose and between its eyes. "Bernie?" The dog looked up at her and whined. "Oh, no! Papa said you were at a farm. He said we couldn't afford to feed you anymore."

The dog closed his eyes and settled into Muriel's warmth.

Let's get you to Doc Amy. Muriel eased out from under Bernie. She knew she couldn't carry the dog far or ride her bike with him. When he lived at her house, he weighed over 70 pounds. Now he was thinner, but he was still huge. She spotted a wheelbarrow standing on its end, the front edge of the red metal tray resting on the floor, the handles propped against the back wall. *That might work. It's downhill all the way to the doc's office.*

Muriel lowered the wheelbarrow to the floor. With its wide metal front wheel, it was easy to roll it toward the dog. When the tray was close to Bernie, she lifted the handles and stood it on end again with the tray's front edge on the floor next to her dog. Next, she pulled a bale of straw from the side of the shed and used it to hold the wheelbarrow upright. Then, she walked to Bernie's other side, got her arms under him, and stood up, pulling the dog with her. "That's it," she said. "You can do this."

After getting most of Bernie onto the wheelbarrow, she ran to the opposite side and kicked away the straw bale. The wheelbarrow slowly sunk to the ground, and the dog slid further into the tray. She repositioned his legs and head and threw an old tarp over him. Then, dreading the trip down the steep driveway, she hoisted up the wheelbarrow handles and took one small step and then another.

* * *

By the time Muriel reached the veterinarian's office, her face was bright red, and she was breathing hard. Bernie hadn't budged. She left him, ran to the door, and rang the bell.

Doctor Amy Hale, who specialized in small animals, stepped onto the porch. "Muriel. What's happened?"

Muriel pointed at the wheelbarrow. She wiped tears from her eyes. "It's Bernie. I found him stuck in Miss Darcy's shed. He's sick, and I think he got burned in the fire. Can you help him? Please?"

Doc Amy stepped onto the porch and gave Muriel a quick hug. "Let's take a look at him."

Muriel followed her down the steps to the unconscious dog. After a brief examination, the vet called toward the house. "Adam, I need your help."

Her husband, a veterinarian who worked with large farm animals, came out and carried Bernie into the examining room. Doc Amy followed him, and Muriel waited on the porch. It was getting dark when the vets returned.

"Muriel," Doc Amy said. "Bernie's in bad shape, but with meds and rest, he'll pull through. Do you know what happened to him?"

Muriel told the Hales about finding Bernie in Miss Darcy's shed. "I don't know. When Papa had to leave town to look for work, he gave Bernie to a farmer outside Lexington. Miss Darcy mentioned a big stray had been coming around her place for food. Do you think Bernie has been trying to find his way home? He saw the fire and just knew it wasn't right, so he barked until Miss Darcy woke up. I don't know how he got stuck in the shed."

Doc Amy patted Muriel's shoulder. "Would you like to come in and see Bernie? I think he'd like that."

Muriel jumped up and grinned. "Yes, please! I've missed him so much."

"We gave him some medicine to make him sleep so we could clean his wounds, but he should be waking up soon," Doc Adam said. "I bet he'll be happy to see you."

Bernie was lying in a big wire cage. A pole holding a bag of clear liquid stood next to it, and a tube snaked through the wire side and was taped to one of Bernie's legs. The door to the cage was open, and Muriel sat on the floor as close to Bernie's head as she could get. She stroked the white patch between his eyes and told him again and again how happy she was to see him. His tail gave a slight wag, but he didn't make a sound or open his eyes.

"Can I stay here with him tonight?" Muriel asked.

Doc Amy shook her head. "I think it would be better for Bernie if you let him rest tonight. You can come back in the morning. I called Althea, and she's driving over to pick you up."

"Oh," Muriel said. "But I have to take the wheelbarrow back to Miss Darcy's and pick up my bike."

"You can leave the wheelbarrow here tonight. I'll drop it off in the morning when I make my rounds," Doc Adam said.

Just then, Aunt Thea stepped into the room. She leaned over and gave Muriel a hug. "I'll take you to get your bike on our way home. How's Bernie doing?"

The adults talked a while longer, but Muriel hummed to Bernie and wasn't even a bit curious about their conversation.

* * *

After dinner, Muriel explained to Jack and Aunt Thea about Miss Darcy's fire, the insurance problem, and finding Bernie. She knew she should be concentrating on the case, but one thing kept popping into her mind: *Will Aunt Thea let me keep Bernie?*

"Why did you name him Bernie?" Jack asked. "Seems like a snazzy name for a dog."

"He's a Bernese Mountain Dog. They come from Bern, Switzerland, so I named him Bernie. The breeder gave him to papa for free because he has too much white on his legs. Usually, the white stops at their toes, but Bernie has white all the way up to his...knees, I guess you'd call them. *Oh, please let Aunt Thea say I can keep him.*

She didn't realize she'd spoken out loud until Aunt Thea said, "Of course you can keep Bernie. He'll be a fine addition to our family."

Muriel hugged her. "Thank you."

Aunt Thea cleared her throat. "Well, now that's settled, what are we going to do about the insurance case?"

Muriel looked at her notes. "Can you check at the courthouse to see if anyone's complained about the insurance company not paying up?"

Aunt Thea nodded. "I can do that."

"What about me?" Jack asked.

"Jack, would you ask the other paper carriers whether there have been any fires on their routes?"

"Okie-doke."

Muriel studied her list again. "I'm going to stop at the Hales' before school to visit Bernie. I want to sketch his injuries. I think they might tell us something, but I'm not sure what. Jack, Mrs. Wixom asked us to visit her after school to talk about the case. She's going to be doing some snooping of her own."

"Aces!" Jack said.

* * *

The following day, Muriel left before Jack started his paper route. The vets' office was about halfway to school, and she wanted to spend as much time as she could with her dog.

Luckily, the Hales were early risers. Doc Adam's truck was just pulling away from the house when Muriel rode up. He stopped and rolled down his window. "Good morning, Muriel. You can go on in. Amy's tending to Bernie's wounds, and he's more alert now. He should be going home in a couple days."

Muriel grinned. "That's great news. Thank you. I'd like to draw some pictures of his wounds if that's okay. I think it might be important to a case we're working on."

"Ask Amy to take a few pictures for you. She has a Brownie camera she uses to document her patients' injuries."

Muriel nodded. "Thank you. I'll ask her."

Bernie was on his feet drinking water from a metal bowl when Muriel walked into the examining room. The line and bag of fluid were gone. As soon as he saw her, he came over and rubbed his big head on her arm. She gently patted him while she told him she was never letting him go again. She asked Doc Amy about the photos and then held Bernie in various positions for the pictures.

Muriel could still smell gasoline when she hugged Bernie. She ran her hand over his flank. It felt oily. She sniffed her fingers. *Gas.*

"I know he smells bad, but I think we should wait a while before we bathe him," Amy said.

* * *

After school, Muriel and Jack raced their bikes uphill to Mrs. Wixom's. Tillie greeted them with cookies and milk while they waited for the ladies to wake up from their naps. At four, Muriel and Jack helped Tillie bring a tea tray and more cookies and milk into the sitting room where Mrs. Wixom and Miss Darcy waited.

Muriel got out her notebook while tea was poured and plates were filled.

She took another cookie and chewed while she waited for the meeting to begin.

Mrs. Wixom patted her lips with her napkin and looked at each member of the team. "I've been on the phone practically every minute since yesterday morning. I found out there have been seven house fires around town in the past two years. I called each owner and found four of them were insured by Town and Country Insurance, the same company Miss Darcy used. Of the four fires, two had only minor damage, and the insurance paid up with no problem. Those happened over a year ago. Then six months ago, a barn burned to the ground out near Chelsea Road. The insurance company's inspector said it was arson, and the company refused to pay. Another fire, this time in a house near downtown, happened two months ago. The kitchen was gutted, but the rest of the house was undamaged. This time the inspector said the fire was caused by lightning, and the company refused to pay because it did not cover 'acts of God.' The homeowners claim there was no lightning."

Muriel made careful notes and then looked up. "Do we know the inspector's name? Was it the same one who inspected Miss Darcy's house?"

Miss Darcy set aside her cup and got up. "I'll get the inspection report. We can see if the inspector put his name on it."

She came back with a stack of papers. "There's no name on the report."

Mrs. Wixom took the papers and paged through them. "There's a place for the inspector to sign the report, but there's no signature."

Muriel told everyone about her trip to the house, finding Bernie, and using a wheelbarrow to transport him to the vet. "He had burns on his paws and back," she said, "so he must have been in the yard when the house was burning. I'd like to know who trapped him in the shed and how the can of gasoline ended up in the woods."

Miss Darcy sat up straighter. "I keep a can of gasoline. Sometimes I use a little to light the trash fire when it's damp. It sat at the back of the shed. I don't know how it could have gotten into the woods."

After the meeting, Jack had an idea. "Let's ride over to the fire station. I have a couple of questions for the captain if he's still there."

* * *

The big doors at the firehouse were open when Muriel and Jack arrived. Captain Mike was rolling up a long fire hose. He stood and smiled. "Muriel, Jack, are you out for a bike ride this fine evening?"

Muriel looked at Jack, and he stepped forward. "We have a couple of questions about fires and gasoline."

Captain Mike shook his head. "You never want to use gasoline to build a fire. It's dangerous because the vapors from the gas are what catch on fire. When a fire source like a lit match gets near gasoline vapors, they explode, and that sends fire all over the place."

"Thanks," Muriel said. "Could you come over to Mrs. Wixom's house tomorrow at four? I think we'll need your help on our case."

As soon as Captain Mike agreed, Muriel grabbed Jack's arm and rushed him from the fire station.

Jack jerked his arm away. "What are you doing?"

"We've got to get over to Doc Amy's. I'll explain when we get there."

* * *

Muriel and Jack raced to the Hales'. There were no patients, and Muriel called out to Doc Amy.

"Muriel," Doc Amy said as she wiped her hand with a towel, "I was just filling a tub to give Bernie a bath. Do you want to help?"

"No," Muriel said. "I mean, I don't want you to give him a bath. I think that gasoline on his fur will prove that Miss Darcy didn't burn down her house."

"The pictures we took this morning are being developed."

"Good. Could you bring them over to Mrs. Wixom's house around four tomorrow afternoon? And could you bring Bernie, too?"

"Sure. Can you tell me what's going on?"

"Not yet, but I think we're pretty close to solving the case."

* * *

That evening Muriel, Jack, and Aunt Thea talked about the case. Aunt Thea said she would try to get Walter Ridgeway, Miss Darcy's insurance agent, to come to Mrs. Wixom's.

Muriel called Mrs. Wixom to let her know about the meeting.

* * *

By 4:05 the next day, everyone was there. Doc Amy was the last to arrive. Muriel met her outside and asked her to leave Bernie out of sight.

Mrs. Wixom welcomed everyone and then spoke directly to Mr. Ridgeway. "We're here to discuss the matter of the fire at Miss Darcy's house."

Ridgeway chuffed through his wimpy little mustache. He was a red-faced, corpulent man. "Now see here, Mrs. Wixom," he said, "the investigation found evidence of arson. Miss Darcy is lucky Town and Country Insurance is not pursuing criminal charges. She's the third arson case this year among our insured homeowners. It's a—"

Mrs. Wixom interrupted. "Let's save the conclusions, Walter, until you've heard what our guests have to say."

"Yes, but—"

This time Mrs. Wixom thumped her cane. "Miss Darcy was awakened by a barking dog sometime after midnight last Thursday. When she got up, she discovered her house was on fire. Is that correct, Goldie?"

"Yes," Miss Darcy said. "I rushed outside, but the dog was gone. So, I ran to the neighbors to call the fire department."

Mrs. Wixom smiled. "Captain Mike, can you pick up the story?"

The captain described fighting the fire.

When Mrs. Wixom didn't ask another question, Muriel did. "When the fire was out, could you tell how it started?"

"Not really. When we arrived, it looked like it may have been an electrical fire where the service drop came into the house. There was a lot of charring around the box. Later, after the back wall fell in, the box ended up under

12

roof debris."

Muriel asked, "Did you happen to see a gas can at the edge of the lawn? And did you smell gasoline anywhere near the house?"

"No, I did not. I could have missed seeing the can in the dark, but I doubt it. If there'd been any odor of gasoline, I would have noticed."

"Now, Muriel, tell us about going to the property three days later," Mrs. Wixom said.

Muriel told them about meeting with Miss Darcy and Mrs. Wixom and then riding her bike to the house. "I noticed the red gas can at the edge of the backyard. Then I heard noises from the shed, and I found Bernie, my dog that I thought papa gave away. Bernie was trapped in Miss Darcy's shed, and he was hurt. So, I took him to Doc Amy."

Amy stood. "May I bring Bernie in? It will be easier if I can show you the injuries."

After Mrs. Wixom nodded, Muriel jumped up. "I'll get him."

Muriel walked Bernie slowly into the parlor. *He smells of smoke and gasoline.* She patted his head and held onto his lead.

Amy walked around the animal. "You can see the raw skin across his back and hindquarters. These areas had second-degree burns and were starting to get infected. Now, look at this patch on the top of his head." She brushed up the fur between Bernie's ears. The hair stood on end. "This fur is oily and smells of gasoline."

Captain Mike rubbed Bernie's head and smelled his fingers. "Did you find any sign of gasoline near his burns?"

Doc Amy nodded. "Yes, there were small spots of gas on the burns. It looked like it had been drizzled over him after the fire was out."

"I agree with Amy. The dog came in contact with the gasoline after the fire was extinguished. Otherwise, it would have burned," the captain said.

Aunt Thea looked at Mr. Ridgeway. "Who is your inspector? He did not sign the report on Miss Darcy's house, and I've talked to two other owners of homes you insure. Both had fires at their properties, and your company refused to pay their claims. They told me the inspector in each case did not introduce himself and did not sign his report."

Mr. Ridgeway cleared his throat. "What are you saying?"

"I can tell you who he is," Captain Mike said. "He's a fella named Hugh Henry. He has to file his reports at the fire department. Although he seemed proud of his work and even bragged about getting bonuses from Mr. Ridgeway, he wasn't happy about signing his name."

Ridgeway stood up. "I pay bonuses when the reports are thorough and filed quickly. I would never bribe an inspector to falsify a report."

"Maybe not," Mrs. Wixom said, "but it appears your inspector thought he'd be more likely to get that bonus if his report let you get out of paying the claims. Did you ever give him a bonus when the insurance company had to pay up?"

"I don't know. I'll have to check our records." Ridgeway started toward the door, then stopped. "If the inspector thought we'd only pay bonuses for findings that let us off the hook, well, he misunderstood. That's not how we do business. From what I've heard today, we'll be paying the claim on your house, Miss Darcy. I'm sorry for the misunderstanding. You'll have the check next week."

Miss Darcy said, "That's fine, Mr. Ridgeway. But it's not enough."

"What do you mean?" Ridgeway glared at Miss Darcy.

"To get to the truth about the fire, I had to hire detectives. You'll give Muriel and Jack the same amount you paid your inspector for staging the gasoline and writing a false report, including the bonus. And you'll pay the vet bills for Bernie's injuries since the only person who could have gotten gasoline on the dog and stuck him in the shed was that inspector."

Ridgeway nodded. "It's fair. I'll do it. Now I've got to go fire Mr. Henry and look for another inspector."

* * *

Two days later, Aunt Thea was sorting through the mail when Muriel and Jack got home from school. She opened an envelope from Town and Country Insurance and held up a check. "This is made out to the two of you."

Jack snatched the check, looked at it, and began jumping up and down.

"Two hundred dollars!"

Bernie, who was now clean and healthy, ran to Jack and joined in the jumping game.

Muriel grabbed the check and looked at it. "We'll have to take out at least twenty dollars to pay the vet bill."

Aunt Thea held up another check. "Nope. There's a check here for the Hales, too."

Muriel looked at the check again. "I think Bernie deserves a reward. Without him, we would never have solved the case. So, I'd like to buy him a new collar and a tag with our address and his name: Bernie, Private Investigator." She looked at her dog. "Does that sound good to you?"

"Whoof!"

THE BUTLERS' ANTI-DEFAMATION SOCIETY

By Chris Chan

"Are you aware of how offensive that phrase is?" I asked.

DCI Manvers didn't look the least bit contrite or embarrassed. If anything, he looked a little amused. "All I said was 'It looks like the butler did it. But which butler'?"

"Sir, you are contributing to an atmosphere of contempt and suspicion with that remark. It's exactly the sort of comment that the Butlers' Anti-Defamation Society is trying to eliminate."

"Yeah...about that. Mr. Rummage—"

"Just Rummage, sir."

DCI Manvers looked me up and down. "You're really dedicated to your job, aren't you?"

"True, but I'm not sure what you mean by that, sir."

"You're all dressed up like a traditional butler. I've never seen anybody wear an outfit like the one you're sporting since *Downton Abbey* went off the air. You're standing up so straight that I think you use a protractor to measure your posture. If you don't mind me saying so, you're acting more like a butler stereotype than a real human being."

"I can assure you, sir, that aside from providing quality service to my employers, I have devoted my life to battling negative stereotypes about members of my profession."

"Right...about that, Rummage. You're the president of the...." DCI Manvers consulted his notes. "The Butlers' Anti-Defamation Society?"

"Yes, sir. I have had the privilege of holding that position since the organization's founding five years ago."

"Who founded it?"

"I did, sir."

"And how many members do you have in your little group?"

"Eighteen dues-paying members, sir."

"But only four of them attended today's meeting, including yourself."

"Correct, sir. The rest of them are busy with work."

"Uh-huh. Have you seen much of an impact due to your efforts?"

"I believe that I have persuaded several prominent individuals that a certain degree of care and respect is necessary to improve the negative impressions of members of my profession that have become ingrained into our public consciousness. The perceptions that butlers are uniformly stuffy, humourless, and hidebound, for example."

DCI Manvers didn't even attempt to conceal a snort. "Yeah, I wonder where people get those ideas. And, of course, you want to stop people from automatically considering you the most likely suspect in a murder, right?"

"Are you aware, sir, of how many butlers have been convicted of murder in England in the past century? Hardly any! Yet thanks to widespread bias, we're always treated with more suspicion than people in professions with a far higher percentage of murderers amongst them."

"Truly, you butlers have it rough," DCI Manvers snorted. "Have you or any of your friends ever been suspects in a murder before?"

"No, but it's our greatest fear."

"And today, that fear came true. Your employer, the Earl of Brownslate, was stabbed in the back this afternoon."

"Yes, sir, it is very distressing. But I resent the implication that either I or one of my colleagues was involved."

"You four were the only ones in the house. Did your employer mind you holding your little meetings in the basement of his home?"

"The late earl had no complaints about my using my butler's pantry for our monthly teas. As long as we didn't bother him and paid for the refreshments we consumed, he allowed our monthly meetings of the B.A.D.S."

"Hmm. How many butlers usually attend the meetings?"

"This was a light afternoon, sir. Eight is the average, though six is also a common number."

"So, fourteen absences isn't suspicious?"

"Certainly not, sir! As I told you, we are busy men who make a point of sacrificing some of our precious spare time in order to protect the reputations of our brethren."

"Well, it's lucky for me that the suspect list is so small," DCI Manvers shrugged. "The rest of the family is vacationing in Scotland, and the rest of the staff had the afternoon off. Do you recognize the weapon that was used to kill the earl?"

"Yes, sir. That letter opener's proper place was on his desk."

"Well, as he was found in his study, face forward on his desk, it stands to reason that someone came up behind him, picked up the letter opener, and stabbed him. The carpet's very thick. It's unlikely that anybody would have heard him coming. Now, between you and me, Rummage, which of your fellow butlers do you think is the most likely killer?"

"None of them, sir!"

"Oh come now, Rummage, don't prevaricate."

"I assure you, sir, that neither I nor any of my colleagues could have done this. We were all in the pantry from four to five, when the earl rang for me. We all saw the earl at four when he called down to us and told us not to disturb him until he rang. We were just wrapping up our business when I heard the bell, and when I made my way to the study a minute later, I found him dead. None of my colleagues left the pantry during that time. In any event, Ulrich is ninety-five and long retired. He is arthritic and hasn't the strength to stab a man with a fairly blunt-edged letter opener. Renly has a deep-seated phobia of blood and would never have used a knife. His phobia cost him his job with a fox-hunting family, sir. And when I discovered the body, I noticed the angle of the fatal blow came from a right-handed person.

Gerrard is left-handed, sir. In any event, none of them knew the earl at all, and none of them had any motive to kill him."

"So that just leaves you, doesn't it, Rummage?"

All of my muscles stiffened. "Sir, you have my word as a gentleman's gentleman that I had nothing to do with my employer's death. It would be contrary to all of my principles. In any case, if I had been responsible, why would I have just now made a point of explaining why nobody else could have committed the crime?"

"There's something in that," DCI Manvers conceded. "And yet...if you didn't commit the crime, who did?"

"It's possible that someone else entered the house, committed the crime, and left. The late earl kept going inside and outside, and he often forgot to lock the doors behind him."

"The rambler says that she didn't see anyone approach the house during that time."

"The rambler?"

"Yes. A young woman. Rowena, that's her name. She was hiking along the public path, and she had herself a little picnic between four and five. She was on her way when she saw the police cars coming. She says that she saw no one else coming to the house." DCI Manvers paused. "Could a member of the household have remained in the house and hidden somewhere?"

"I suppose it's possible, but I saw the other servants leave and drive away today, and the same goes for the family members who left yesterday."

"Is there anybody who might want to see the earl dead?"

"I know of no one who would wish to murder him."

"What about his son? He stands to inherit the estate."

I felt my jaw tightening, despite my determination not to show annoyance. "He's devoted to his father, and in any case, he inherited a small fortune from his late great-uncle."

"What about his wife? Countess Brownslate? By the way, why is the wife of the earl called a countess? I get a count's wife being a countess, but wouldn't an earl's wife be an earless?"

"It has to do with various language and historical issues that are too complex to go into here."

"I'm not that interested, anyway." DCI Manvers sighed. "Look, you don't strike me as a killer. But right now, you're pretty much our only suspect. Unless...are you sure the countess didn't hire someone to do it? I've heard rumors that the earl had an eye for the ladies and no self-control."

I drew myself up to my full height. "I never gossip about my employers."

"The rules about discretion don't apply to murder investigations."

"I can assure you that they do, sir."

"Well, whatever. We've removed the body. Would you care to take another look around and see if anything's amiss?"

He led me back into the study, and I scanned the room, looking for missing objects or anything that shouldn't be there. When I'd last been in the room, I had been distracted by my employer's body. Now, I was a bit calmer and more observant.

"What's that?" I crossed over to the windows, my attention caught by a tiny brown dot towards the bottom of the blue velvet curtain behind the desk. DCI Manvers warned me not to touch it, and after a bit of fiddling with tweezers, he extracted a little burr from a fold of cloth.

"It's a little burr," he informed me.

"These curtains were cleaned earlier this week. That shouldn't be there."

"It's small and easy to miss."

"I tell you, that wasn't there before. It must have been deposited there recently." I looked at the burr more closely. "That's from a common burdock plant. It doesn't grow anywhere near the house, but it does grow along the rambling path."

"Are you sure?"

"Positive. If I were you, sir, I would go have another word with that rambler. I suspect she unknowingly picked up that burr on her clothes while walking on the property, and as she came in through the open window, the burr transferred to the curtain."

"You think Rowena committed the crime? A young woman you've never properly met? That's quite an accusation."

"It wasn't an accusation, it was a suggestion. I really would advise that you talk to her about it, sir."

After a bit of hemming and hawing, DCI Manvers questioned Rowena further, and when asked about the burr, she brushed her hair out of her face, and he noticed a little bloodstain on the cuff of her shirt that he hadn't seen before.

It didn't take much more to crack her resolve, and she swiftly confessed. Apparently, the earl had taken liberties with her sister, who was now in a condition that would produce a scandal even in this permissive day and age. The earl had cut off all contact with the sister, and Rowena had come by to confront him. She'd seen him in the study and decided to come in through the window so as to avoid knocking on the front door and being patronized by a servant telling her the earl was not at home. The earl had been rude and turned his back to her, sitting at his desk. Enraged, Rowena had grabbed the letter opener.

I hated the thought of a scandal affecting the family, but if Rowena was offered a plea deal, the matter might be kept fairly quiet.

As DCI Manvers led Rowena away, he smiled and told me, "Well, Rummage, at least you don't have to worry about one of your brethren embarrassing the profession, eh?"

I allowed myself a small smile. "Indeed, sir. I must say, I was quite anxious over the possibility of the newspapers all running the headline, "The Butler Did It!" Thankfully, we've avoided that embarrassment. Goodbye, DCI Manvers. Goodbye, Miss...I don't believe I know your surname, Miss."

Rowena glared at me, and then she smiled in a way that sent chills down my spine. "Maybe you won't like the headlines after all. My name is Rowena Butler."

DINNER FOR SIX

By Kerry Hammond

"The police never solved the case," said Ginny, sipping her tea and looking across the table at her friend with a cat-who-ate-the-canary grin. She adjusted her glasses, a habit that came out of hiding whenever she was pleased with herself.

"Then how do *you* know who murdered Ron Harper?" said Anne. Anne was Ginny's oldest and dearest friend, but she wasn't the sharpest knife in the drawer, and Ginny couldn't help but feel superior as she regaled her with the story, which came by way of her Aunt Ida.

Aunt Ida was like a second mother to both Ginny and Anne, who had been friends since the third grade. Ida had never married or had children, so she had taken the two girls under her wing, whisking them off to her lake house every summer and giving them advice when they needed it.

"Because Ida was good friends with Sara Finnegan, the owner of Finnegan's Inn. She was there when Sara died, and it was something Sara said on her deathbed."

"Sara confessed to the murder?" said Anne, her eyes wide as saucers.

"No, silly," said Ginny. "You're not listening. Sara didn't confess, but she said something that revealed the identity of the murderer to Aunt Ida. She almost took it to her grave, but Ida suspected that Sara needed to get it off her chest before she died.

"Ida had followed the story of the murder, heck, the whole town had. She knew instantly what Sara's comment meant. The problem was, that's all it was, a comment. Made by a dying woman, no less. There was no way to prove anything, and besides, twenty years had passed since the murder, and Ida didn't think there was much use in bringing it all up again."

Anne refilled her teacup, waiting for Ginny to continue. She loved it when Ginny told Aunt Ida stories, it took her back to their childhood and all of the fun they'd had together.

Thunder rumbled outside, and Anne stole a glance out the kitchen window. She hated thunderstorms; the noise always made her jump. Worried that Ginny would tease her, she tried to ignore the storm and concentrate on her friend's story.

"Okay, I'm getting ahead of myself," said Ginny. "Let me start from the beginning. In its day, Finnegan's Inn was the only place in town to get a room." Ginny launched into her story.

* * *

Sara stood at the window of the Inn and watched the torrential rain lick the picture window of the small Inn. The storm was unseasonal for their little area of New Hampshire, and they hadn't had much advance notice. The weather reports originally said that the storm would miss New Hampshire, but it clearly changed course. She and her husband, Jack, stocked up on food and supplies for themselves and their guests just in case, and it was a wise decision.

She expected cancellations, but none came. Perhaps no one had time to change their plans. Each of the four available guest rooms in the old Victorian was occupied, the fifth was out of order for a plumbing repair, which meant that eight people were stranded there during the storm, including Sara and Jack.

She and Jack had owned Finnegan's for six years. Sara inherited the property from her grandmother, and she and Jack immediately came back to run the business after her death. Sara grew up at Finnegan's and always knew she would one day own it. She spent every summer here since the age of eight, and her grandmother taught her everything she needed to know to run a successful business.

When she met Jack in her senior year of design school, it was the first place she took him on their hometown visit. Her parents died when she was only twenty, so her grandmother had been all she had left. Her grandmother, and Finnegan's.

"Wow, I can't believe it's still raining so hard," said a voice behind Sara, breaking her out of her memories and bringing her back to the present. It was Patricia Moore, a fifty-something actress who was staying at the Inn while visiting her parents, who lived in a retirement community nearby. At least Sara assumed Patricia was in her fifties, but she knew that it was hard to pinpoint an age for anyone who lived in Hollywood. She hadn't seen Patricia in anything and suspected that the actress was what they called a character actress, holding only supporting roles to larger stars.

"They're predicting another five inches overnight, but it's supposed to let up by tomorrow afternoon," said Sara, trying to offer her guest a light at the end of the tunnel. It seemed to work, and Patricia gave a short nod, as if in agreement. Sara noticed that her eyes remained watchful.

"I'm sorry you haven't been able to visit your parents, but the highway patrol is saying that it's not safe. The roads are flooded, and even vehicles with a high clearance have been warned not to try it."

"I heard the same report when I passed through the sitting room," said Patricia. Mr. and Mrs. Steadman were listening to the weather report on the radio. There's really nothing we can do but wait it out."

"Dinner will be served at seven," said Sara, looking at her watch. "We're having roast beef, and if you'll excuse me, I should probably go and check on it. Jack and I are playing cook and server tonight since our staff couldn't make it here in this weather." She nodded to Patricia and slipped out of the room, leaving the actress staring out into the darkness.

Sara found Jack in the kitchen peeling potatoes for the side dish. He seemed quieter than usual, and she wondered if he was worried about the flooding. The Inn sat on a small hill, so they were usually safe when a storm hit, but this was the worst they had ever seen, and she worried that the water levels would rise to meet the Inn.

"I don't know if you saw the lights flicker," he said. "But the power went out, and the generator kicked in. I'm not worried about running out of fuel, this storm can't last that long, but I still think we should turn off the lights we're not using and make sure the fires are stoked so the furnace doesn't have to run as much. The temperature just dropped to 48 degrees, so it's a cold rain."

Sara was comforted by her husband's nonchalance and trusted his assessment. He was a great handyman and took care of the maintenance at the Inn. She didn't know what she'd do without him.

Seeing that Jack had the potatoes under control, she left the kitchen to turn off unwanted lights and inform the guests that they were running on generator power and should be mindful of their usage.

When she approached the sitting room, she heard raised voices. Two men were arguing, but she couldn't make out what they were saying. As she rounded the corner, she heard Mrs. Steadman say, "gentlemen, please, do we need to discuss this now?"

As Sara entered the room, she saw Mr. Steadman, a burly man with snow-white hair and matching beard, facing off against Ron Harper, who was also largely built, but a good ten years younger than his adversary. Mrs. Steadman, a petite, frail-looking thing, was standing between the two men, one hand against her husband's chest and the other in midair as if she wanted to push Ron away but was afraid to lay her hand on him. Both men were red in the face but stopped speaking at Sara's entrance.

Sara was confused, she had sworn that the Steadmans told her they had never been to New Hampshire. How they could know Ron Harper, a local businessman staying with them while his home was being renovated? She couldn't imagine what could have angered two strangers so much in such a short period of time.

"Is everything okay," said Sara. At first, no one spoke. The two men stared each other down, and Mrs. Steadman looked back and forth to each with a pleading look on her face.

"Everything's fine," said Ron, with a tone in his voice that said everything was anything but fine. However, he backed off and turned to leave the room.

As he was about to turn the corner toward the staircase, he suddenly whipped back around, pointed his finger at Mr. Steadman, and said, "This isn't over." Still staring, he slowly turned back toward the doorway.

As he entered the hallway, Patricia was coming the opposite way. He grabbed her by the arm and bent down until his mouth was next to her ear. When he spoke, his voice had an edge to it, but the volume was too low for Sara to hear any of his words.

A flush started in Patricia's neck and flooded through her entire face as she pulled her arm from his grasp. She glared at him, but was silent. Ron let out a loud, fake laugh and continued toward the staircase.

After he was gone, Patricia looked into the sitting room at her audience of three. She looked like she was playing out a scene in her own movie.

Mrs. Steadman broke the silence by fussing over her husband and asking him to stoke the fire. Sara watched Patricia, who smoothed back her hair, tugged down the shirt sleeve where Ron had grabbed her, and turned to go back the way she came. Sara wondered what Ron could have said to upset her.

Sara turned back to the Steadmans and told them about the generator and dinner. As she did so, she realized she hadn't gotten a chance to tell Ron about the generator before he accosted Patricia and made his exit. She would wait to tell him at dinner.

That only left Mollie Sabastian. Sara hadn't seen the young woman since breakfast and assumed she was in her room. She didn't like to disturb the guests when they were in their rooms, so she decided that telling her could wait.

On her way back to the kitchen, Sara passed the library and poked her head inside. She found Mollie sitting in an armchair under the glow of a reading lamp. A book rested on her lap, but she wasn't reading. She was staring into space and didn't even notice Sara enter the room.

Sara cleared her throat softly to make her presence known, and Mollie jumped in her chair and put a hand to her boney chest. "I'm sorry, Mollie, I didn't mean to startle you. I just wanted to let you know that we're currently using generator power and ask that you keep electricity use to a minimum.

But it looks like you're already doing that, can you even read by that light?"

"Oh, I'm not really reading," said Mollie. "I was just thinking. Can I ask you a question, Sara?"

When Sara nodded, Mollie continued. "If you had information about someone that you felt should be told, but the way you obtained that information put you in a less than flattering light, would you still feel compelled to tell?"

"I'm not really sure how to answer that," said Sara. "I guess it would depend on what the information was and how crucial it was that it come to light."

Mollie laughed half-heartedly and waved her hand in the air like she was slowly swatting a fly. Her long fingers were graceful, and Sara wondered if she'd been a dancer. "Never mind, it was stupid. Just a hypothetical, that's all. Just ignore me."

"Are you sure?" said Sara.

"Yes, really, I'm sure. Thank you for humoring me."

Sara nodded, "Sure, anytime."

When Sara got back to the kitchen, Jack was just coming down the back stairs from the second floor. "Jack, did you see that letter on the hall table addressed to me? The return address was a law firm in Manchester. It was there this morning, but now it's gone. I didn't recognize the firm, but I'm afraid it has something to do with the property dispute."

"No, sorry, sweetie, I didn't. I haven't had a chance to look at the mail from yesterday."

"If they sue us, I'm not sure what we'll do. We can't afford to hire a lawyer, and if they win, we could lose the Inn. I know my grandmother owned the entire lot this building sits on, why that company is claiming she didn't is beyond me. But in order to challenge them, we would have to spend thousands of dollars in legal fees. It makes me sick to my stomach just thinking about it."

Jack came over and gave her a hug. "Then don't think about it. Things will work out, you'll see."

Jack always knew what to say to make her feel better, and Sara decided that she had enough to worry about with the storm outside and guests getting on each other's nerves. She leaned into his embrace and closed her eyes.

One by one, the guests entered the dining room at seven. There was very little chatter. It seemed that the weather was affecting everyone's mood. As usual, Jack had put out place cards for the guests. They found that if they let people choose their own seat, there was less dinner banter. People often sat next to someone with whom they felt comfortable and quickly found out they had nothing in common. But Jack and Sara knew a little bit about each guest that stayed with them, so they made sure to seat people next to someone with a common interest or connection. It had proved successful, and dinners at the Inn were always lively and fun. Until tonight.

Mr. Steadman seemed to still be agitated from his run-in with Ron Harper, and Mrs. Steadman was fluttering around him like a mother hen. Patricia looked troubled and kept glancing over at the window as if she was trying to see something beyond the blackness. Only Mollie seemed in good spirits and had turned to chat with Jack as he set the food down in the center of the table. They would be eating family-style tonight.

It was Sara's habit to wait until all guests had served themselves before she filled her own plate, and Ron Harper still hadn't come down. She would have to break her own rule and go up and knock on his room door.

Excusing herself, she left the dining room and climbed the stairs to the second floor, where all of the guest rooms were located. As she approached Ron's room, she saw that his door was ajar. She called out to him as she got closer. "Mr. Harper, it's Sara. Dinner is ready."

There was no answer, and she tapped on the door as she called again. "Mr. Harper, it's," she stopped in mid-sentence when she looked inside the room. Ron Harper was lying on the floor on his back. He was still dressed in his suit and tie. A knife was sticking out of his chest.

* * *

"It was 24 hours before the police could get to the Inn to investigate, and by the time they got there, they had no idea who had trampled over the crime scene or what evidence had been lost." Ginny leaned back in her chair, the teapot long empty. "Everyone clammed up. The statements they did make were all suspiciously similar. So much so that it seemed like they had spent the evening getting their stories straight.

The police looked into everyone who was at the Inn that night and found that they all had a reason to kill Ron Harper, so rather than not having *any* suspects, they had *too* many.

Mollie Sabastian had been Ron Harper's personal assistant about three years ago. She had had an affair with him and found out he had been falsifying tax documents. The problem was, Ron told her in the heat of, um, let's just say in the heat of the moment. He knew she would keep her mouth shut because he threatened to tell her husband about the affair if she breathed a word."

"What about the Steadmans?" said Anne. "What did he have over them?"

"Mr. Steadman was Ron Harper's former business partner. They bought and sold several apartment buildings together before Mr. Steadman found out that Ron Harper was paying contractors to sign off on repairs to the buildings that were never completed. The problem was Mr. Steadman had trusted Ron, so he signed the closing documents at each sale that stated that the repairs had been completed. Trying to take down Ron Harper would mean that he would go down too. His hands were tied, and he wasn't happy about it.

Now, Patricia Moore, that was personal. Her first husband was the love of her life. He went to college with Ron Harper, and after graduation, they got together yearly for a guy's weekend camping trip. On one such trip, Patricia's husband died in a freak accident. They were hiking, and he fell off a cliff in a national park. Ron was the only one hiking with him, and he said he tried to get help, but Patricia suspected foul play. Ron had been pestering her husband to invest in a business deal, and her husband had finally decided to consider it. Before he wrote a check, though, he had Ron investigated. Let's just say he didn't like what he found out and told Ron in no uncertain terms that he had no intention of investing a dime in his business. I think even you can do the math on that one."

"Wow," said Anne, ignoring the dig. "Three strong motives, four if you add Mrs. Steadman to the mix, assuming she would back her husband."

"You're forgetting the owners of the Inn, Jack and Sara." Ginny smiled slyly. "They also had a motive to want Ron out of the picture. Ron owned the company that was suing them over their property. He was claiming that the Inn was built on his land and threatening to force them to tear it down or pay up. At the time of Ron's death, though, the law firm he hired was the only one to make contact with the Finnegans. The police were never able to prove if Jack and Sara knew that Ron was behind their legal troubles, but they strongly suspected they knew.

"So you see, one corpse, too many motives, and no evidence. The knife used was one from the kitchen, an area that all guests could have easily accessed. There were no fingerprints on it. No fibers were found on the body. There wasn't even a bloody footprint next to the body. If this were a television crime show, you'd at least see one of those things. The police were stumped, and the case went cold. They were never able to figure out who killed Ron.

"But they never closed the file, they never do with murders. When Aunt Ida told me the story, she made me promise to never tell a sole as long as she lived."

"But your Aunt Ida died five years ago," said Anne.

"I know, dear," said Ginny patiently. "That's why I'm telling you now. The Inn just sold to a corporation that is going to tear it down and put up a condo. Jack and Sara are long gone, and they never had any children, so there's no one left that can be hurt if the story gets out."

"So, who did it? Who murdered Ron Harper?" said Anne.

"How about I tell you what Sara said to Aunt Ida on her deathbed and see if you can figure it out." Ginny knew she was being a bit cruel, but she relished her role as storyteller and having a secret that no one knew. She wanted to draw it out as long as possible.

"What she said to Aunt Ida was, 'the table was only set for seven.'"

Ginny smiled at her friend. She thought she'd give her a few minutes to think it over, but knew she would have to explain it in detail to her.

"Oh dear," said Anne. "Oh my, I see."

"What is it you see?" said Ginny with a condescending smirk.

"I see that Jack killed Ron Harper. Clearly, it was to save the Inn, something that meant the world to both Sara and himself."

Ginny stared at her friend, her mouth hanging open and her eyebrows knitted together. "How in the world did you guess it?" she said.

"It was simple, really. Jack always set the place cards out for the guests at dinner. There were eight guests at the Inn that night, but Jack only set out seven place cards. He only set the table for seven because he knew Ron wouldn't be coming down to dinner. Because he had killed him. It took the police 24 hours to get to the Inn, so by that time, dinner had been cleared and the place cards destroyed. So the police wouldn't know that Jack hadn't created one for Ron."

Ginny looked incredulous. She couldn't believe her friend had figured it out. "Let me get us some more tea," she said and got up from the table in a huff.

Anne put her elbow on the table and rested her chin in her hand. "That's a great idea, dear, I'd love some more tea." She smiled as Ginny turned her back and walked into the kitchen. "You weren't the only person Aunt Ida confided in," she thought. "I can just keep a secret better than you."

HOME & GARDEN GOTHIC

By Jean Macaluso

Elegant Tudor Revival on 10-acre Wooded Lot
Historic Charm Preserved in Thoughtful Upgrades
Ocean View w/Exclusive Beach Access. No Neighbors!

For once, the ad copy didn't exaggerate. Set inland from the Pacific Coast Highway, and surrounded by dense forests of fir, spruce, and hemlock, the listing's location epitomized seclusion. Survivalists trading live fire in the bordering wilderness would be unlikely to disturb its residents.

Most travelers whizzing along the Oregon stretch of US 101 between Astoria and Cannon Beach barely register the turnoff. Eagle-eyed adventurers, thinking it a lark to explore the interior, would reconsider on beholding the chunks of basalt edging that section of highway. Even hardcore off-roaders might be deterred by the rough terrain, not to mention frequent signposts warning interlopers that they're on private land and violators "will be prosecuted." Some wag (or radical recycler) had amended the final notice to read "will be *composted.*" Anyone foolish enough to venture beyond would face a rusted, over-sized chain sagging across a mere semblance of road.

This driver didn't hesitate. Wheeling around the chain's left stanchion, she rammed her Tahoe through a hedge of tall grasses, bursting back onto the alleged road with little more than a few stalks caught in the undercarriage. Leafy boughs resettled behind the vehicle, leaving scant evidence of penetration...and an undisturbed chain. After a teeth-juddering 20-minute ride, the woods opened to a clearing. The big SUV rolled to a stop.

On the passenger side, Elinor loosened her death grip on the door handle and shook her "braking" foot to restore circulation. Directly ahead, a granite wall encircled the property, its stonework softened and largely camouflaged by swathes of creeping fig. Above the wall, she dimly glimpsed the upper reaches of a grand edifice, whose towering roofline loomed gray and forbidding. *Dearest Edward. What the hell were you thinking?*

Swirling mists nudged the scene from monochromatic into melodramatic. The car inched forward, halting at a substantial wrought-iron gate. The driver immediately launched into her real-estate agent's spiel. "If you look between the ornamental bars, you can see that the back yard is beautifully landscaped, with lots of charming elements." Poor visibility belied her words.

Tapping the windshield with a fake fingernail, the agent directed Elinor's attention to a foggy metal-and-glass confection. "The gazebo was designed to be an outdoor party room; it's been reglazed and weather-proofed. Inside there's a slate fireplace and a fabulous wet bar. On chilly afternoons you can make s'mores for the kids, while you and your husband sip martinis." She coyly lifted an eyebrow, hoping to elicit her prospect's marital status. Not for one minute did she believe that her handsome client was this woman's brother.

Elinor winced at the pushy real-estate agent's sally. She'd learned to mask her youthful shyness with bland detachment. The habit revived in adulthood at particularly stressful moments. It was infinitely harder lately to stay aloof; a casual remark, catching her off guard, could pierce her heart.

Surely Edward informed the agent—here she peeked at the business card in her lap—Stacie that he wanted his *sister* to be shown the house. It wasn't the first time that she and Edward had been taken for a married couple. Where the notion came from, she couldn't fathom, unless it stemmed from Edward's occasionally over-solicitous manner.

He'd been the one fixed point in her universe since they were orphaned in their teens. Elinor had idolized her father; his disappearance was devastating. When their mother died a few years later, it hurt dreadfully that her father's formerly cordial family had declined to attend their daughter-in-law's funeral. Edward's oft-repeated mantra, "It's the two of us against the world," continued to both console and sustaine her.

Elinor's gaze swept the regimented beds of yellow bearded iris, blue agapanthus, and orange daylilies limning the outer base of the wall—stabs of color where the mist had dissipated. The contrast between the cultivated beds and the shadowy woods around the 'fortress' (the word popping up unbidden) was striking. And unsettling.

Then, as if some celestial housekeeper had flipped a switch, the massed clouds overhead parted dramatically, and sunlight reigned. Inside the gates, the gazebo preened like a debutante in the radiance. Elinor could also discern a curved glass conservatory jutting from the rear of the house, flashing its bottle-green panes at circling seabirds; a terraced patio; a spurting fountain. Then she spotted the lone western red cedar rising majestically in the middle distance, its roots mantled in purple ajuga.

A woodsy, resinous wisp of olfactory memory floated up from childhood. In the family's sprawling southern California home, her mother had stashed cedar chips in all the closets to ward off insects. Elinor warmed a bit to the property. No wonder Edward had urged her to come here. He'd been lingering stateside for longer intervals; perhaps having satisfied his wanderlust, he was ready to settle down.

Elinor bit her lip. She'd yet to see the house, but gardens like this, despite their 'natural' appearance, required significant upkeep. Overall the place seemed far too splendid for either of them. Certainly she lacked sufficient assets to afford it on her own.

Elinor had never inquired into Edward's finances, but he managed their estate, and she assumed he'd inherited their father's financial acumen. Dad's personal investments had been long-term and blue-chip. He only risked OTM (other people's money)—invariably making his clients rich... and richer. Edward was generous to a fault, his gifts frequently *too* lavish. Unless he's replenished the coffers materially, their inheritance wouldn't last forever.

Maybe being a photojournalist was more profitable than she thought. Edward always had a camera slung round his neck. It would be gratifying to think his talents were amply rewarded. For her part, Elinor was content with her fairly spartan existence. She hadn't touched her share of the family money once she started working, preferring instead to build up her savings and 401k. She resolved to be more assertive with Edward about regular financial updates.

Stacie droned on. Something about a multilevel HVAC system. Elinor shrugged her off. She seldom dredged up the past. Today it was crowding in on her.

Elinor had happily filled her days heading up the reference section at the downtown branch of Portland's Multnomah County Library, sharing occasional meals or outings with Edward. Her nights were spent crafting modern versions of genres popular in eighteenth-century fiction. Jack was an investigative reporter researching a local building code scandal, with her indispensable assistance. His exposé garnered widespread attention and accolades. Over a celebratory dinner, they fell in love; by the third date they were discussing a future together.

She had decanted the Chambertin an hour earlier. Edward often brought a case of wine back from France. He'd given her the bottle—a full-bodied red from the Burgundian region—as the consummate pairing for a special meal she'd planned for Jack.

"It must *breathe*!" Edward had discoursed at length on 'presentation.' She'd listened attentively, smiling and nodding. She'd drawn the line, however, on double-decanting; her and Jack's palates would never know the difference. She'd relate this mild sibling rebellion to Jack over dinner, and he'd share gentle amusement over her doting-but-fussy brother's ways. Then Jack would tell her about the current story he was chasing. After dinner, they'd pull out their calendars and pick a wedding date. The cassoulet simmered in the oven. Elinor had finished lighting the tapers in the dining room, and was admiring the effect, when the police rang. She hasn't made cassoulet since.

"Three fully equipped garages run along this side of the house." Stacie put the car in gear and slid through the yawning gates, amplifying the volume of her monologue.

Jolted out of her reverie, Elinor started guiltily. She owed it to Edward to stop tuning out. She straightened in the seat and inhaled deeply, channeling innate powers of observation, enhanced by early exposure to the Sherlock Holmes *oeuvre.*

Stacie had somehow triggered the gate remotely. As they breached the ramparts, Elinor saw a metal box mortared into the inside wall abutting the hinges. A compound like this was bound to have a security system, she reasoned. The gates whirred closed behind them.

The back yard was larger than expected. They followed the paved driveway to the garages. From there, a covered walkway gave onto a double-doored rear entrance—kitchens, Elinor surmised. No service structures had been visible from outside the gates, and they were situated out of sight line of the conservatory as well—a nicety for rich folk, but it left Elinor feeling wary. Just as the rear approach to the house had felt wrong, even sinister.

This could be a bootlegger's mansion! It's beachfront, after all. Caves are common along the craggy Oregon coastline. It's an ideal setting for nefarious deeds committed sub rosa. *I'd never lack for plots if I lived here!*

Stacie maneuvered the Tahoe into position athwart the shuttered garages. "We can park here and walk around to the front," she announced, brooking no demur. "The tenant is long gone and no one will complain." She briskly led the way on highly inappropriate stiletto heels. As Elinor rounded the corner, "... sunsets to die for!" wafted back to her.

An emerald lawn dipped gently to a broad promontory, beyond which the Pacific bobbed in ultramarine glory. Edging closer to the bluff, Elinor leaned over gingerly and looked down. There was no guardrail, just a rugged staircase winding down to a secluded cove, where seafoam spread like icing on sugar-cookie sand. Savoring the warmth of the sun, tasting the salt air on her lips, Elinor felt herself unclench. *When did I become so edgy?* The mildly disturbing 'fortress' effect evaporated.

"It's stunning, isn't it?" Stacie waved grandly. "Completely private.

No access—except by water, of course...and air. Your nearest neighbors along the beach are miles away, but..." she confided, "they tell me that helicopters used to buzz this headland." Before Elinor could interrogate her about previous owners, Staci added, "The concrete apron in front of the garages would make a perfect helipad!"

Elinor's hair lost its mooring pins and whipped across her face. She tossed her head back, turned away from the ocean...and gasped when she beheld the front of the house for the very first time.

Peaked roofs—steeply pitched, with lapped shingles and rolled eaves, an excess of gables, and taller-than-normal chimneys—rose above a whitewashed stucco façade studded with fieldstone. Leaded windows were haphazardly placed, as were parapets, arches and alcoves, and the occasional gargoyle. A turret room projected from one corner of the house. White and mauve roses spilled from *faux* balconies and sprawled with abandon over the large purple vases flanking the front steps. It dazzled the senses.

Despite the Tudor touches, this was really a Storybook house. Popularized in the 1920s, the Style was inspired by Hollywood film-set versions of medieval European dwellings. Elinor had been enchanted by Storybooks from an early age. Many fine specimens of the Storybook Style were tucked into the well-heeled neighborhoods of Pasadena. Sunday drives through that patrician Los Angeles suburb, followed by an ice cream treat at Fosselman's in Alhambra, were among her most cherished memories. Edward must have remembered her partiality to the eccentric art form.

Elinor couldn't wait to get inside this magical Hansel-and-Gretel house. She hurried after Stacie, who was already unlocking the iron hardware on the Gothic-arched front door. Relieved to observe this spike of interest, the agent gladly let Elinor precede her.

The ground floor rooms, albeit musty and sorely in need of lemon oil and greenery, showed well. They featured dark wood ceilings with crossbeams, wide-planked hardwood floors and woodwork, and antique ivory plastered walls. Most rooms had stone fireplaces or hand-painted murals (or both). It was not quite open concept, but spacious nonetheless. From every window, the vista was spectacular. The women wandered from room to room through arched pass-throughs. Stacie quieted. The house spoke for itself.

An oak-paneled library, complete with sliding ladder, captivated Elinor even before Stacie revealed its secret. A concealed door in the wall-to-wall shelving led to a suite outfitted like a traditional men's club. The new bronze safe in the corner struck Elinor as jarring, but Edward might find a use for it. The windowless bathroom would make an ideal darkroom for him.

The unpretentious morning room sealed the deal for Elinor. The coffered ceiling, cream-colored woodwork, and overstuffed chairs were instantly welcoming. Her mother's Queen Anne desk would fit exactly under the corner window. She'd write for a few hours, then take a long walk. There would be trails through the woods, some of which no doubt led down to the sea. All that was needed to bring her bootlegger fantasy to life was a secret passage through the house to the anchorage below. A story idea glimmered.

Stacie interrupted Elinor's creative process to drag her up zigzagging staircases to view several cozy second-floor bedrooms with slanting walls and Deco-tiled *en suites*. Well before they got to the kitchens and outbuildings, Elinor had fallen in love with the Story.

She thought Edward would appreciate the home's proximity to his latest project. He first gained international prominence through his knack for making French vintner's *terroirs* look even more romantic than they were. Now he roamed Oregon's coastal ranges, capturing the zeitgeist of America's rare temperate rain forests—fast becoming the eco-intelligentsia's chosen chronicler of the Pacific Northwest aesthetic. He probably found this architectural gem on one of his forays.

Elinor had been inconsolable after losing Jack in a hit-and-run less than a year ago. Edward had spent all his free time with her (as he had after her ill-fated college affair). Forgoing his penchant for overseas travel, he initially aimed his prized Nikon D7 closer to home. Occasionally he'd take her on a shoot with him.

In particular, they frequented the International Rose Garden in Washington Park, in the hills above Portland. During World War I, the city's rose aficionados read about the fiery bombings in Britain and elsewhere—and fretted over the many unique plants being destroyed forever. They created a special "test garden" as a safe haven for rose hybrids in danger of extinction. To this day, conservationists around the world sent *at risk* roses to the Park. While Edward shot in tight closeup, Elinor contemplated the sky across thousands of tiered rose bushes—and grieved for Jack.

Stacie dropped Elinor in Seaside, at the weathered bed-and-breakfast where she'd parked her car. This spit of land on the Oregon side of the Columbia River didn't have much upscale retail. If Elinor and Edward purchased the Storybook house, they'd have to drive to Astoria, near the Washington border—or to Portland, a good hour's drive along the Columbia River—for serious shopping. A walk-in freezer that came with the house should tide them over between times. Fortunately, Elinor enjoyed cooking; Edward claimed she was better than their mother.

As she and Stacie bumped along on the return trip to the 101, Elinor visualized herself in safari gear, manhandling a Jeep through the bush. She'd miss her old green Miata—convenient for buzzing around the city, but hardly up to these ten acres.

* * *

Edward's coffee table book on European roses saved by Portland's 'rosarians' came out last month. He dedicated it to "My Mourning Rose," a gesture that touched Elinor profoundly. The more so, because she knew Edward had never really liked Jack, though he denied it.

Around that time, Elinor and Edward's last living relative in England passed away. Aunt Prudence, their mother's only sibling, had kept track of her sister Martha after her marriage to an American had led to parental estrangement.

A teenaged Elinor had caught her mother pocketing an airmail letter with a Queen Elizabeth stamp. When her mother died soon thereafter, Elinor had searched for the letter. If their mother was in surreptitious contact with the Brit side, they should be apprised of her death. Edward thought this inadvisable. Besides, the letter never surfaced.

39

It astonished them to learn that Aunt Prudence had made them her heirs.

* * *

Elinor and Edward have been living in their Storybook house for nearly six months. Edward is in Tillamook, reshooting a few photos for his new *magnum opus* documenting the reforestation efforts following the Great Burn of old growth forest in the 1930s.

Elinor's first novel is already on the shelves in hardback, being promoted as "An exciting 'Pacific Northwest Gothic'—a tale of mystery and mayhem, à la *Jamaica Inn*." A sequel is in the works.

She sits at her mother's desk in the morning room, now her study. She stares unseeing out the window, absently fiddling with the ribbon holding back her hair. She's been feeling restless, unable to settle. Today, she resolves, she'll unpack the rest of the boxes she's brought from Portland.

The rawness of Jack's loss has transmogrified into solace when recalling their time together. But Edward wants her to put all thoughts of Jack away in a casket and bury them. She's careful not to speak of him to her brother, yet she resents the constraint. *As if sadness has an expiration date!*

By mid-afternoon, Elinor has shelved all her books and added a studio portrait of her parents. She'll relegate Jack's pictures to her bedroom, on the wall above an antique hope chest—as soon as she finds them. She can't imagine how she's lost track of them.

Unlike Edward, she's not compelled to record every moment on film, but she regrets not having more pictures of Jack, especially the snapshot of the two of them arm-in-arm in front of Portland's Keller Fountain—taken shortly before Jack died. Plus the one from the Pearl District.

Meanwhile, she'll surprise Edward by unpacking the last of his boxes. If she sorts the contents into piles, he can catalog them whenever he's in the mood. It's wonderful having enough space for all their possessions. Elinor's apartment in Portland was a good-sized two-bedroom, but Edward's *pied-à-terre* was a tiny studio, so he stored most of his belongings in the basement of his building.

It's nearly dark by the time she retrieves the final box.

Elinor sits cross-legged on the floor of the spare bedroom, next to the upended black metal container labeled "Misc. Receipts," examining the mementos she's laid out.

In one pile are her father's carved briar pipe (still smelling faintly of Prince Albert tobacco), his Bank of America checkbook, and an old wallet. When the LAPD investigated her father's disappearance, foul play was considered because none of his belongings were missing—except his wallet, which he'd naturally have carried on his person, and his Mercedes (and its keys). But he had no known enemies or shady business entanglements...and neither body nor car was ever found. Eventually they concluded he'd left voluntarily.

Her mother refused to believe it. "If he had run away, his pipe would be missing, too." She pointed to the briar pipe on the mantel. "He took that silly thing with him everywhere," she told the detectives. "Just find him," she sobbed brokenly. Days later a large check was cashed at a San Fernando Valley branch of BoA. Case closed. The pipe had vanished.

Elinor riffles through the checkbook. Carbon duplicates confirmed that this was the checkbook her father was using when he disappeared. The Valley check and its duplicate had previously been removed, presumably by him. Holding the wallet, Elinor inhales the musky smell of old leather. Inspecting the compartments, she finds two square school pix, one of her and the other of Edward. Lodged under the stamp flap, her father must have missed them when he supposedly transferred items to a new wallet. *But no wallet was found among his belongings. Where has it been all this time?*

A second pile holds a three-month supply of her mother's thyroid prescription, a bottle of heart pills, and a contraption that a quick internet search reveals to be a "pill former." Elinor and Edward had been attending their respective sophomore and senior classes when their mother drove off the Arroyo Seco Bridge. Witnesses reported she was driving erratically. Autopsy findings indicated "inappropriate" levels of her medications—either she hadn't been taking them as instructed, or she'd confused the two in some fashion and become disoriented. Elinor still dreams of her.

A third pile holds the elusive photo of Elinor and Jack in the Pearl

District, Portland's refurbished warehouse quarter-turned-foodie haven and cultural landmark. In a Chinese gift shop, Jack bought a jade turtle for Elinor. The friendly proprietor offered to take their picture. As they were leaving, he joined their hands and pressed on them a silk pouch of what he called the Five Immortality Herbs. He bowed and wished them long life and happiness. Elinor had assumed that, in the depths of mourning, she'd mislaid the keepsake. But here it is—along with the herbal concoction in the silk bag. *Edward has had them all this time?*

Wait! What's this? She uncovers a stark shot of Jack lying on his back, head propped on the curb, legs splayed in the street. *Why would Edward have a crime scene print of Jack?* Quivering, she slams it face down.

In the final stack are old letters between their mother and Aunt Prudence. *I was right. They were in touch!* She frowns; the later ones are between her *brother* and Aunt Pru. *Edward corresponded with Aunt Pru?* Elinor reads the most recent, wherein Aunt Pru thanks Edward for his "delightful visit." But it is the British Airways ticket in Edward's name—round trip to Heathrow, dated a month before Jack was killed—that forever realigns Elinor's perspective.

Like a kaleidoscope, fragments of what Elinor knows and what she *thought* she knew collide/converge, until the final pattern slots into place. Disparate thoughts, niggling questions, discrepancies. *It all makes sense now.*

"You've found my cache, I see," Edward says pleasantly, as he enters the room and pulls over a hassock to sit near Elinor. He touches her rigid shoulder; she doesn't turn. He reaches down for the briar.

"You seem upset. Don't be." He turns the pipe in his hands, sniffs the bowl. "I did it for us, you know." Elinor doesn't respond. "You must have suspected. No? Well, well. It doesn't matter." Elinor turns and glares up at him. He flicks the pipe in her lap.

"I had no choice. Dad kept telling Mom that I was obsessed with you...that it was 'unnatural.'" Elinor gapes. "How absurd," he scoffs. "It was the most 'natural' thing in the world. But Dad kept at her."

"It was quite easy to forge Dad's signature," Edward muses, pride lurking in his tone. "I just traced it from a carbon." Elinor fights for air. "Darkroom supplies were expensive, but every time I asked Dad for money, he lectured me...and accused me of...*things!*" Defiantly, "It's not as if he couldn't afford it!" Sniggering, "That's why I kept his Merc' for a couple years before scrapping it."

"What did you do? Where is he?" she rasps, barely able to speak.

"Don't ask, don't...." He scowls. Then snapping his fingers, eagerly counteroffers, "But I could show you the Polaroid I took of Dad before I...."

"Oh, God," Elinor moans.

"Look at the bright side. Once Dad was out of our lives, we all did fine...for a while." She makes a strangled sound. "Well, we *did!*" he says indignantly. "But then, Ellie, you, uh, you just *blossomed.* Mom suggested I was 'sick' and 'needed help.'" Edward's voice rises. "Ellie, she was going to send me away to military school, then take you to England to visit Aunt Pru. She wanted to separate us...forever!"

"Mom, too?" Elinor says, aghast.

"Yep! I ground her heart pills into powder, then shaped it like her thyroid tablets. Saccharin pills in the heart bottle, heart tablets in the thyroid bottle. Hey, presto!"

Elinor muffles a whimper.

"Remember how hostile Dad's relatives had become...." Elinor cocks her head and waits. "Well, Mom was heartbroken; she couldn't understand it. One day I found her rummaging under my bed; she guessed that I'd *created* that rift and was looking for proof. Boy, when she went after my emails, I had to move fast."

Neither spoke for long seconds. Then Edward adds, "We didn't really need anyone else by that time, Ellie. It was you and me against the world."

Elinor's pupils dilate and darken.

"Think, Ellie. We had the house to ourselves; we got our degrees; we moved to Portland; *and* we kick-started our careers!" Edward counts the wins on his fingers. "Good thing Mom never shared her concerns with Aunt Pru." He chuckles. "And why would she? They were totally groundless. You're my sister!"

"What about this?" Elinor snatches up the frozen-in-time obscenity of

Jack *in extremis*, and thrusts it at Edward. "*You* took this photograph; not the police! The blood... Edward, you were there! You might have saved him."

"That's where you're wrong," Suddenly cold. "Jack said I had an unhealthy fixation on you. How dare he! He was going to take you to Connecticut after you married!" Edward visibly struggles for control.

"I was there, all right, because...because, *I* was the *contact* he was supposed to meet! Jack was a strong guy, you know; I needed the element of surprise so he'd stand still in the road long enough for me to..."

"No, no, no..."

"He was investigating me, Ellie. *Me*! He had the nerve to claim my travels covered up a sideline in smuggling! Hmph. Little did he know it was much more than a sideline. I was damned clever about it, too. Those Frenchmen have fortunes stashed in their cellars; some of those dusty old bottles are a hundred years old. One or two of the rarest would pay for this house ten times over!"

"I was so careful," he whines. "I probably shouldn't have mentioned this house. That might be what tipped Jack off. Turns out the erstwhile owner of this little fairy tale castle was pretty high on Interpol's list. He was into artwork, drugs, guns—whatever he could get for a song and sell at a premium."

"Edward!"

"Listen, Ellie. All I did was palm the occasional rare vintage and a couple minor impressionist oils that were 'hanging around' the local bistros. Get it?" Edward pauses to admire his pun. "At least, that's what I told Jack. But, damn him, he'd already notified the FBI about *Mister Big*."

"By the way, that's how I 'anticipated' this house being on the market." His machinations exposed, Edward wants Elinor to fully appreciate his brilliance.

"Too bad about *Big's* accident; but I really wanted this house for *you*. All it took was a cut brake fluid line. Except, now I have to find another 'import/export specialist.' Really, it's most inconvenient!"

He returns to his original grievance. "But Jack didn't care that I wasn't into the bad stuff, like *Big* was. He swore he'd turn me in if I didn't stop immediately. So, I 'stopped' Jack."

Elinor is incandescent with rage. There is no room for grief, or even fear. Loathing will have to wait, as well. Instinctively she tamps down her reactions, ensuring that only shock and surprise surface. Edward expects and understands such emotions.

He leans over and takes the photo of Jack's last moments out of her unresisting hand, and drops it on the nearest pile. "Come now, haven't I always taken care of you. What about that lump of a fiancé at Berkeley?"

"What *about* George?" She'd never believed he was guilty, but he had firmly terminated their engagement for *her* sake. An expensive diamond parure had been stolen from a wealthy alumna during Homecoming. The necklace and earrings were found in George's locker (the brooch was never recovered). He lost his scholarship and was expelled for theft.

Edward points to the diamond-and-ruby clip on Elinor's sweater, his birthday gift to her last month. She covers it with her hand. He is amused.

"It suits you."

Elinor reels from the enormity of this latest revelation.

"Aunt Pru's inheritance came right on time." He resumes his litany of accomplishments. "Honestly, if I'd known she was that rich, I'd have paid my visit sooner," he giggles.

Edward's moods are cycling rapidly.

"C'mon. Leave all this stuff. I'll deal with it later." He clasps her hand and pulls her to her feet. She sways, but remains upright, and calmly withdraws her hand. He studies her critically, then slowly unties the ribbon at her nape. "You have beautiful hair, Ellie. You should always wear it long and loose—like Rapunzel."

"Now, what's for dinner, hmmm? I've got a '64 Dom Pérignon. Does that work for you?"

Elinor smiles tremulously, and Edward relaxes. His sister always acquiesces in the end. Tonight, will be no different.

* * *

Slippers in hand, Rose descends the servants' staircase on tiptoe. Alone in the world, but blest with wit and courage, she has contrived her escape. She must remain undetected as she makes her way to the hidden passage, cunningly disguised behind shelves in the kitchen larder. She is relying on the parvenu Squire's unfamiliarity with how stately homes are organized below stairs. She has watched him, and is confident he knows naught of the route used by his predecessor (the late, unlamented Lord Hellston) to smuggle contraband in and out of the cool, dry caves beneath the manse, thence through tunnels to the sea. Goods of all style and type can be stored there in absolute safety, prior to selling them for a fine profit in the City. The local gentry have no notion how much furtive activity takes place under cover of innocuous revels in the Great Hall. Nor does the constabulary suspect they are in such close proximity to illicit swag when they share a cuppa with the housekeeper. Only a few more steps....

THE PARLIN FORK LETTERS

By James L'Etoile

When Bill McDonald turned up dead, the people of Parlin Fork turned out to make sure it was true.

I found out first because his body was propped up against my bookstore door. Another long night on the town was my first thought. There isn't much else to do in Parlin Fork, and it wouldn't be the first time Bill passed out on his way home from tying one on.

I nudged him with my knee because I was trying to unlock my front door with one hand while balancing a cardboard tray of coffee in the other. Bill fell over on his side, leaving a bloody swath on my door from the gash on the back of his head.

My coffee tray fell when I recoiled away from Bill's dead form. I'm no medical examiner, but even I knew he was dead based on his gray pallor and the spot of purple lividity on his back peeking out below his grimy mail-carrier uniform shirt.

After struggling with the key in the lock, I threw open the bookshop door and ran to the phone on the counter. A landline was a must-have in Parlin Fork because the cell signal was notoriously unreliable in the dense redwoods.

I punched out 911 and turned around, half-expecting Bill's corpse to reanimate. Note to self: stop reading paranormal stories.

"Nine-one-one, what's your emergency?" a familiar woman's voice said.

"Connie? It's Tim Barnes. You gotta get Sheriff McCauley down here. It's

47

Bill McDonald. He's dead."

"You sure? He's been known to sleep one off in town."

"I'm sure. What am I supposed to do?"

"Okay, Tim. Sit tight, and I'll get the sheriff out there. Try and keep people away, would you?" Connie's normally calm voice became tight.

After I hung up, I ventured back outside, hoping I'd been wrong about Bill. Nope, still dead.

A slight breeze blew down the street, and I spotted a scrap of yellow paper tumble away from Bill's clenched fist. I stooped to grab it, and the wind carried it away, around the corner of my store. Catching up to the paper, I snatched it and discovered it was half of a yellow-colored envelope, torn so only the return address was readable. A Post Office Box number in Parlin Fork.

A few feet beyond the corner, Bill's mailbag lay upended and the contents strewn on the asphalt. Letters, junk mail, and small packages spilled around the stained canvas bag. I knelt, stuffed the torn envelope in my pocket, and gathered up as much mail as I could before it scattered in the wind. My mail was rubber-banded together, and Bill hadn't shoved it through my mail slot before he dropped dead on my doorstep.

"Don't touch that, Tim."

Sheriff McCauley stood behind me with his hands resting on his black Sam Browne utility belt. The leather crinkled as he moved.

"It's gonna all blow away," I said.

"I'll take care of it," he said while pulling on a pair of latex gloves.

I backed away from the mailbag with only my mail in hand. "I'm sorry I didn't mean to screw up anything."

"You're fine. I'll need a statement from you later. I'll control this mess. Go see if you can help Deputy Miller keep folks away. Seems like the Parlin Fork gossip network got hold of Bill's demise already."

I returned to the front of the store, less than ten minutes from my 911 call, to find Deputy Sheila Miller. Her hands outstretched, attempting to herd a small knot of townsfolk away from Bill's final resting place.

"Sheila, you need a hand?"

Sheila didn't answer but rolled her blue eyes, her frustration showing.

"Let's give Bill a little respect, huh?" I said, urging the small gathering back.

"What do you know, Tim? Bill was a no-good drunk," said Ruth Ann Willow, the owner of the only cafe in town. Red hair and a red temper to match. She was probably Connie's first call after I hung up.

"Come on, Ruth Ann, he wasn't all that bad," I said.

"What do you know? You're new around here," Sandy Owen said, decked out in her flour-coated apron from the bakery across the street. She looked fresh from the kitchen with clear plastic gloves and sticky dough on her cheek.

Five years meant nothing to a town with more inbred, questionable cousin marriages than I could count. I've been an outsider here since the day I opened the bookstore.

A few more people pressed as close as Deputy Miller allowed.

"Go to hell, McDonald!" someone shouted.

"About time," another said.

The Parlin Fork Fire Department's only ambulance pulled to a stop in front of the store, red lights flashing. The EMT on the passenger side waded through the crowd until he cast his eyes on Bill's crumpled body.

"Huh, had to see if it was true. Good riddance to bad news," the EMT said to Sheila.

He and his partner made quick work of Bill's body, stuffing him unceremoniously into a black plastic zippered pouch.

"Don't you need to, like take photos of the crime scene or something?" I asked.

Sheila turned to me and said, "What crime scene? A drunk falls down and hits his head. That's no crime."

Once the EMTs hefted Bill into the rear of the ambulance, the crowd began to disperse. I spotted a few high-fives and heard a handful of disparaging comments about the dearly departed as they went back to their lives.

The EMT closed the ambulance door. "Hey, Sandy. Can I get a dozen of those poppy seed muffins?"

"Sure thing, Ron. Got a batch in the oven. Fresh from winning a blue ribbon at the Mendocino County Fair." Sandy stood a little straighter, the pride in her award-winning confections showing.

Sheriff McCauley rounded the corner with Bill's postal bag slung over his shoulder. "Sheila, I best get this over to Miss Tapson at the Post Office. She'll know what to do with it."

The sheriff hefted the bag and headed off in the direction of the post office, but my eye drew to a yellow envelope sticking out of his back pocket. It was identical to the torn envelope I found near Bill's body. He'd stuffed this one envelope in his pocket, and my stomach tightened when my mind put the two together. Sheriff McCauley was hiding something or was covering up a murder.

The thought of a murder committed on my doorstep was unsettling. Worse was the realization one of Parlin Fork's good citizens was a killer.

Stunned, I watched the ambulance pull away with the dead man, and no one had expressed the slightest kind word about him. Granted, I've known Bill to be a drunk and a lazy mailman who was likely to give you someone else's mail. He'd complained about how I ran my store, but the entire town was cold to his passing.

I caught Sheila before she got into her patrol car. "What gives? No one ever heard about not speaking ill of the dead?"

She leaned on her open car door and sighed. "Bill McDonald wasn't a nice man."

"So he was a little rough around the edges."

"He was all edges." She lowered her voice. "Rumor is that McDonald blackmailed some of the folks around here over secrets they had. You know how small towns are; there are more secrets here than Houdini's closet."

"Blackmail? You think he was killed over it?"

Shelia got in her car and started the engine. "All I know is Sheriff McCauley told me this was probably a drunken accident before we ever drove up."

She got in her car, and before I could respond, she said, "You best get that cleaned up before it dries." My mind raced over her comment. I knew she meant Bill's bloodstain on the bookstore door, But the term "cleaning up" struck a nerve. The Sheriff calling this an accident. That's something a killer would say to clean up behind themselves. My stomach turned to lead at the thought.

I dropped off my mail, retrieved my cleaning supplies from inside the store, and used two pairs of rubber gloves to avoid touching the viscous reminder of what happened in this place. Based on the send-off from the townsfolk, I wouldn't be surprised to see a brass plaque commemorating the spot where he died mounted at my door.

Sheila was right, the blood was starting to set, and it took a bit of scrubbing to get the red swath off the door. I think I'll always see it there, really. Some things you can't wipe away—like human life.

I took a sponge to the last errant blood drop on the concrete sidewalk next to a wooden bench installed by the local scout troop. There, behind the back leg, I spotted a flash of something out of place. Dropping to my knees, I immediately recognized it for what it was—another yellow envelope.

With double-rubber-encased fingertips, I pinched the cover of the envelope and pulled it to me.

The plain yellow paper bore the same post office box address as the piece in my pocket. And it looked to be identical to the one Sheriff McCauley stuffed in his. This letter was addressed to Ruth Ann Willow at her cafe address.

Maybe, I'd personally deliver this wayward letter and see what the fuss was about. First, though, I wanted to track down the post office box and who sent these letters.

I figured the sheriff would be finished dropping off the mailbag by the time I cleaned up and got over to the post office. The Parlin Fork post office wasn't exactly a thriving hub of activity. The post office took up one side of the gas station office, and a white line had been painted down the floor to operate the two spaces. Rumor has it that the Postmistress grew tired of bumping into car tires and oil cans.

Along the wall allotted for the post office, fifty bronze four-by-four inch doors were arranged in five rows of ten. I was looking for box 38, the return address on the letter in my hand.

It was easy to find because it was the only box with the metal door hanging open. The scratch marks on the soft metal and the warped door meant someone pried this open with something sharp.

Letters, bills with red, overdue stamps, and junk mail catalogs lay strewn on the floor below the broken mailbox. Nothing with the curious yellow envelope. The tossed mail was addressed to Bill McDonald, Post Office Box 38, Parlin Fork, CA.

The yellow letter in my hand came from Bill McDonald, as did the torn fragment of an envelope in my back pocket.

An older woman with a little hunch in her back came from the back room with a broom and wastebasket.

"Let me give you a hand with that, Miss Tapson," I said.

She was wheezing from the effort and didn't push back against my offer to help. She held out the broom and parked her eighty-year-old frame on a wooden stool from the auto parts side of the building.

"What happened here, Miss Tapson?"

I swept up the discarded mail in a pile. Based on the multiple overdue notices from the local utility company, Bill hadn't checked the box in quite some time.

"Came in and found it this way. Probably them damn kids with their Pokémon searches."

While the Pokémon fad had hit town a few years ago, it never involved prying open someone's mailbox.

"Sheriff McCauley tell you about the broken box?"

She wrinkled her brow. "The sheriff? I haven't seen him."

"He was bringing you Bill McDonald's mailbag."

"Why would he do such a thing? Bill drunk again?"

The way Miss Tapson was wheezing, I was reluctant to be the one to tell her what happened to Bill. I'd seen enough dead bodies today and didn't want to shock the old woman into an early grave.

"I thought the Sheriff found the bag and was bringing it back to you."

She shook her head. "Nope. Haven't seen him."

I leaned the broom against the wall and placed the trash can near her stool.

"I best be on my way, Miss Tapson. I'll ask the sheriff about your mailbag."

"Thank you, young man. Tell the Sheriff I'll be here till five."

I made the decision to keep the found envelope rather than turn it over to Miss Tapson just yet. There was something I needed to find out, and since the envelope didn't have a stamp on it, it really wasn't tampering with the mail, was it?

I trudged back to my bookstore and flipped the open sign over. I sorted my mail, taking note of one I'd have to take a look at later. I'd turned on the lights and parked at my desk when the bell attached to the front door chimed.

I glanced up and spotted Ruth Ann Willow entering. She made a straight line for me, not pretending to browse the bookshelves. I managed to slide the yellow envelope with her name under a returned copy of a French translation of *Fifty Shades of Grey* because, honestly, no one would ever look there.

"Had some excitement this morning, huh, Tim?" she said.

"Last thing I expected when I opened up this morning."

"You see what happened, or able to tell the sheriff anything about how Bill ended up at your front door?"

Ruth Ann pressed closer to the desk, her eyes drilled into mine, waiting for an answer while the letter hidden between us smoldered invisibly.

I held my hands up. "I have no idea, and I couldn't tell the sheriff anything."

I saw Ruth Ann's shoulders relax. Relieved, perhaps.

"Anyways, I wanted to come over and say I'm sorry for the way I snapped at you this morning. I don't know what came over me. With what happened to Bill, I got wrapped up in it, I suppose."

"Don't worry about it. Say, what do you hear about Bill blackmailing folks here in town?"

Her shoulders tensed again. With a glare that made me glad I was behind a desk, she leaned closer and said, "Why? What have you heard?"

I felt the tension rolling off Ruth Ann. Whatever Bill McDonald had on her must have been worth killing for.

"Nothing, really." I didn't lie. I didn't know what secrets hid in the yellow envelope. "Just rumors, is all."

"Well, rumors got Bill McDonald killed. Just you remember that."

Without waiting for a response, Ruth Ann turned on her heel and marched out of the bookstore.

Once she left, I slid the yellow envelope out from its hiding place. I rubbed my finger over the surface, imagining Polaroid photos capturing Ruth Ann in an incriminating misadventure. But the envelope felt flimsy, not rigid enough for photographic evidence of any sort.

Normally, curiosity doesn't get the better of me. I don't skip ahead to the last chapter of my books, and I don't skip television show episodes so I can find out what happens next. So why was this envelope pulling me to open it and discover its secrets?

I couldn't go to the sheriff because he stuffed a similar envelope in his pocket and he'd kept the mailbag, probably to see who else got a yellow letter like his.

The hell with it. The thing wasn't really mail without a stamp, was it? I'd found it on my property, hadn't I? I used a pair of scissors to slice open the flap. A single folded sheet of paper slid out when I shook it over my desk.

Unfolding the paper, I expected the smoking gun, telling me who killed Bill McDonald. Instead, it was a single sentence: "I know what you did, and now you need to pay."

Dammit. Pay for what? To Whom?

I shoved the letter back into the envelope and tucked it back under the French *Fifty Shades*.

I tried to straighten up the shelves while thinking if the vague threat from Bill McDonald was enough for Ruth Ann to take him out. I shot straight up. She was the one who said he was killed. How did she know he didn't just take a drunken fall and hit his head? But the untorn envelope meant she hadn't gotten his extortion demand yet.

What did he hit his head on? My front door didn't cave in the back of his head. He might have landed there, but the injury to his head happened somewhere else.

I strolled outside, and sure enough, there was a drop of blood on the sidewalk. And another at the corner of the building. I remembered the fallen mailbag, and it made sense that Bill was attacked there and dropped his satchel before he staggered off to die on my doorstep.

Why I didn't spot it before, I couldn't say. Probably shock from finding Bill's body. There was a dark slick area a dozen feet from where the mailbag fell. As I drew closer, I recognized it for what it was, blood starting to congeal. The flies buzzing around the stain confirmed as much.

A stack of empty wooden pallets leaned against the wall of the hardware store next door. One lay over on its side and blocked half of the narrow walkway between the two buildings. I hefted it back into position when I noticed one of the heavy wooden rails was missing from the fallen pallet.

I pulled a splinter from my finger. The pallet was rough-hewn and stabbed me with a wooden spike in my fingertip. There was something else on my finger—a speck of fine dust.

The damn splinter made my finger bleed, and I started back to the bookstore to grab my first aid kit. But, you know how when something's out of place, it makes you stop and take notice? That's what happened when I spotted a length of wood, looking like it came from the pallet resting near the recycle bin. At first, I mistook it for a hunk of wood that had fallen from the bin. The bright red bloodstain on the end of the two-foot-long length of wood told me otherwise.

I wasn't about to touch what I knew was the murder weapon. It proved Bill McDonald didn't suddenly collapse and die. He was murdered.

I started to call the sheriff and hung up. He was already involved in covering up the crime by making off with the mailbag and being quick to dismiss the notion that Bill's death was anything but the result of an inebriated mishap.

Rather than call 911 and have Connie bring the entire town together again, I found Deputy Sheila's number and tapped it in. I explained what I'd found and urged her to come and see for herself.

I waited on the corner until Sheila's patrol car pulled to the curb. My knees buckled when I noticed she wasn't alone. Sheriff McCauley got out of the passenger door, and the tight set jaw forecast the reception I was about to receive.

"Now what, Barnes? You find 'ol Bill's ghost?" McCauley said with a smirk.

"You need to see this, Sheriff. It could be the murder weapon. Bloodstains and all," I said. I wanted to sound a little more under control, but it came blurting out.

"Listen to you. Murder weapon. Someone's been watching too many episodes of Law & Order."

"Where is it, Tim?" Shelia asked. She'd stepped in between the Sheriff and me, defusing McCauley's prodding.

I pointed it out to her and stayed in my spot. I wasn't sure what Sheriff McCauley was going to do once word got out that Bill hadn't stumbled and knocked his head on something. More like someone did the knocking with that wooden club.

Sheila knelt near the bloodstained scrap of wood. "Sheriff, you should see this."

The sheriff's eyes cut from me to Sheila and back again. "You stay put," he said as he joined Sheila.

"Well, dammit," he said. "I missed this when I grabbed Bill's mailbag. Shoot some photos of it and bag it up, would you?"

"On it, boss," Sheila said.

"Sheila, be careful of that wood it's—" I said.

"Ouch,"

"Got splinters," I finished.

A rough splinter stuck through her rubber glove.

"How'd you know that?" the sheriff asked.

I explained about finding the broken pallet and stabbing myself with a dry splinter shard.

"Whoever used that to club Bill McDonald to death will have a hand that looks like it lost a fight with a porcupine," the sheriff said.

"You believe someone here in Parlin Fork killed him?"

"I do. I always did. I just couldn't say it out loud and get the folks all riled up."

"It was because of his extortion, wasn't it?" I asked. My throat was about to close up after the words came out.

"That's my assumption. Bill's been at it for a while, and folks were getting fed up."

I whipped the yellow envelope from my pocket and held it in front of me. "How many people in town got one of these?"

Sheriff McCauley bit his lip and nodded. "Ten that I know of. Including me." The sheriff pulled a yellow envelope from his jacket pocket.

"Why would he try and blackmail everyone?"

The sheriff shrugged. "He'll take that to the grave, but knowing him, I'd bet it was simple greed. You've seen the letter, It was anonymous with a demand to send money to a post office box. It's not rocket science to figure out who the box belongs to."

The sheriff made my discovery of the owner of box 38 seem a little smaller. He'd also assumed the letter was addressed to me.

"I can't imagine anyone around here doing something so bad that Bill thought he could blackmail them for it," I said.

"Small towns don't have secrets, at least not for long. I've been seeing someone who's married. That's what Bill was trying to get me to pay for. It's really not that much of a secret."

"Ruth Ann?"

He grinned. "See, I told you."

I handed him the yellow letter addressed to Ruth Ann. "I didn't until now."

When he went to take the letter, I froze and held it tight for a moment before letting go.

"Sheriff, whoever killed Bill got a letter too."

"Yeah, I figure as much. So?"

"Not all of a letter. I found this on Bill this morning." I showed him the partial section of an envelope. "Whoever killed him grabbed their letter and tore it away."

Sheriff McCauley nodded. "Not bad. But I can't go door to door and ask everyone in Parlin Fork to show me an envelope."

"You might not have to." I felt a piece fall into place.

"Sheila, can I take a look at that piece of wood for a second?"

She looked to the sheriff, and after he nodded, she held the plastic evidence bag so I could see the bloody scrap of wood inside. The rough wood, the bloodstain, the light-colored dust, and the envelope told a story. And I think I knew the ending.

"Sheriff, I know who killed Bill McDonald."

"Wanna share with the class?" the sheriff said.

"Come with me."

I led the sheriff and deputy Sheila across the street to the Parlin Fork Bakery. Sandy Owens was behind the counter shoving a tray of freshly baked bear claws into the glass display case. The sweet aroma of coffee and hot donuts was a powerful distraction.

"Hiya, Sheriff, what can I get you?" Sandy said, wiping her clear plastic gloved hands on her apron.

Sheriff McCauley glanced at me. "It's your show, Barnes."

I cleared my throat. "Sandy, I notice you're wearing those gloves. You don't usually wear them; what's that about?"

She frowned, and her forehead creased. "I wear them from time to time. Why?"

"I see you have a couple of Band-Aids underneath. Cut yourself?"

"It happens. A common industry risk, I'm afraid. That's why I'm wearing the gloves."

"It wouldn't be from splinters, would it?"

Sandy's face went pale.

"I don't know what you're talking about."

"Sheriff, the light-colored dust on that piece of wood—it's flour. Flour from Sandy's hands when she bashed Bill's head."

"What? Sheriff, you can't be serious. I never...."

Shelia dug in the trash can by the door and retrieved a torn yellow envelope.

She held it up, and Sandy's knees buckled.

"Why, Sandy?" the sheriff said.

"That damn drunk was going to ruin me."

"What did he have on you, Sandy?" I asked.

She slumped on the glass case. "He was going to tell everyone that I've been buying my award-winning muffins from the big box store down in Eureka."

"You killed him for that?" the sheriff asked.

"It would have destroyed my business. Everything I've worked for, that damned drunk was going to take away. I couldn't let that secret out. I'd never be able to show myself in public again."

"That's not going to be a problem for you, Sandy," the sheriff said as he put Bill McDonald's killer in handcuffs.

"Not bad book-boy, not bad," Deputy Sheila said. "To think, Sandy threw it all away over a muffin. Crazy, huh?"

I nodded and left the bakery, wondering how many secrets were worth dying over in the Parlin Fork Letters. I'd found my own yellow letter in the mail Bill was going to deliver. I stuffed it deep down into my pocket. Some secrets are meant to be kept.

PILLAR OF THE COMMUNITY

By Sharon Love Cook

Margot Talbot entered the Che-Che Lady hair salon and headed for the reception desk. "I need a cut and set with Betty Ann," she announced.

The receptionist glanced down at her schedule. "Do you have an appointment, Mrs. Talbot?"

Margot shook her head. "I just wrapped up a closing and had no idea when I'd be through." She stepped past the receptionist's station to peer into the rear of the salon. "There's Betty Ann," she said, sounding triumphant, "and she's alone."

"Take a seat, please." The receptionist moved to the adjoining door where she called, "Betty Ann, can you take Mrs. Talbot now?"

The hairstylist rolled her eyes yet adopted a hearty tone: "Of course. Send her in."

Seconds later, Margot Talbot plopped herself into the chair.

"What can I do for you, Mrs. Talbot?" Betty Ann draped her client in a thin, plastic cape.

Margot ran her fingers through her dyed hair. "I need uplift. I need oomph. I need a new look for tonight's gala."

Betty Ann chuckled. "Big night with the hubby, huh?"

"Hardly," she sniffed. "Tonight the Business Women's League is presenting me with an award: Entrepreneur of the Year." She sighed. "They're expecting a speech."

Betty Ann shook her head. "Mrs. Talbot, it seems you're in the news every day for some award or another."

Margot closed her eyes as Betty Ann spritzed her hair with a spray bottle.

"Small town standards, Betty Ann. In the city, I'd be just another successful lady executive."

Betty Ann knew her client expected praise; she didn't disappoint. "I don't believe that. You're a go-getter, that's what you are. Didn't I read where you bought that old apartment building near the bridge? Going condo, I hear."

Margot smiled at herself in the mirror. "I'm thinking about it."

"It'll happen. Folks around her say, 'Whatever Margot wants, Margot gets.'"

Instead of preening, her client frowned and glanced around to see if anyone was listening. Satisfied they were alone, she leaned toward Betty Ann and said, "Are you familiar with Eleanor Pemberton?"

"The old lady who lives in the big house on Larkspur Lane?" When Margot nodded, she said, "She used to come in regularly for a perm. Haven't seen her for a while, come to think of it."

Margot slapped the chair's armrest. "Good! The less I see of Eleanor Pemberton, the better."

The fierce expression on Margot's face startled Betty Ann. "Well, I admit she's a little crabby, but— "

"Crabby? Eleanor Pemberton is a witch, a witch who delights in torment-ing me."

Betty Ann glanced warily at her client. "How can an old lady disturb a firecracker like you?"

Margot sank back in the chair with a sigh. "Okay, I'll give her the benefit of the doubt. The old witch is probably senile."

"What do you mean?"

"A month ago I heard the Pemberton house might go on the market. You may not realize that house was once my family's homestead. When I spotted Eleanor Pemberton at the bank, I asked her nicely if she'd let me know because I was interested. For once she was civilized, saying she'd do that. We shook hands and parted. Lately, due to her senility, I don't think she recognizes me."

"What makes you say that?"

Margot closed her eyes, a pained expression on her face. "That old lady knows me alright. You see, thirty years ago the Pembertons destroyed my family."

"How did they do that?" Betty Ann secured the top layers of her customer's hair.

"It's a long story," Margot said, watching herself in the mirror. "You see, my father was a brilliant inventor, way ahead of his time. In order to finance his latest invention he'd taken out a loan, using our house as collateral. I was in high school then, about to graduate." She turned to gaze out the shop window. "I'd planned a picnic for my classmates, a lunch to be served by the pond. Mother and I worked on the menu. The invitations had gone out and..."

"Yes?" Betty Ann prodded the woman, who seemed to have drifted away.

"And then one day I came home from school to find Mother crying. She told me that Father's project had encountered problems. Did I tell you he was ahead of his time? The ignorant officials of this town couldn't recognize his genius. When his financial backing didn't come through, the bank foreclosed on our house." Her voice broke. "We had to move out." She dabbed at her eyes.

Betty Ann, having finished clipping, set out plastic rollers. "That's a darn shame, Mrs. Talbot."

"Later we found out that Eleanor Pemberton and her husband had snatched up our house at the banks auction. Meanwhile, my family was forced to move into an apartment downtown. We were devastated, going from a fourteen-room house with a putting green to a downtown apartment building frequented by foreigners. You have no idea."

"A shame," Betty Ann said, rolling Margot's fine hair in curlers.

"Knowing how much the picnic meant to me, Mother swallowed her pride and visited Mrs. Pemberton. She pleaded with her to allow me to have the lunch at the house—just for one afternoon. Do you know what that evil woman said?"

"What?"

"She said it was out of the question. The landscapers would be working on the property. Poor Mother, President of the Ladies' Literary League, was humiliated."

"Doesn't Mrs. Pemberton's grandson live with her now?"

Margot's laugh was harsh. "That's her nephew, Dwayne. He lives in the boathouse with the spiders and mice. I'm sure he's paying the old bat a hefty rent."

"I heard he was a Vietnam veteran, hospitalized for a couple of years."

Margot tapped her head. "He was a little 'off' even before the war."

The hairdresser stepped back. "Come sit under the dryer, Mrs. Talbot. Bring a magazine if you want."

Before the hair dryer was lowered over her head, Margot raised her eyes to Betty Ann. "Believe me, this story is not over. As God is my witness, I intend to get my family home back."

"Oh, I'm sure you will, Mrs. Talbot," Betty Ann said, plunking the dryer down and turning up the heat. "I don't doubt that at all."

* * *

Later that afternoon, Margot Talbot stood impatiently in a long queue at the post office. What was holding up the line, she wondered. Craning her neck, she saw the cause of the delay. It was her nemesis, Mrs. Pemberton. Leaning over the counter, the old woman demanded in a shrill voice, "Why can't I send it fourth class?"

"Because fourth class is for books, DVDs, and periodicals," the exasperated clerk replied.

Margot stared daggers at the woman. The old bat, the richest woman in town, conniving to save a penny or two.

After finishing her business, Mrs. Pemberton headed for the exit, leaning heavily on a cane. When she was abreast of Margot, the younger woman impulsively reached out to grip her sleeve.

"Mrs. Pemberton? You remember me—Margot Talbot, real estate broker?

I spoke with you about your house." She flashed a dazzling smile and pressed a business card into the old woman's hand.

Mrs. Pemberton frowned, staring at the card. "No, I don't remember. Where did you get the idea I'm interested in selling?"

Margot felt her cheeks flush. "I heard it from another real-estate agent. In the meantime, should you decide—"

Mrs. Pemberton shoved the card back. "I've decided nothing, and if I did, you'd be the last person I'd call."

Someone behind Margot giggled; she turned to glare.

After concluding her business at the counter, Margot marched outside. In front of the post office, she spotted Mrs. Pemberton climbing into a dusty Mercedes station wagon pockmarked with rust. Dwayne Pemberton, a long gray pony tail hanging down his back, helped his aunt into the back seat. Before getting back inside, he flipped a cigarette butt onto the sidewalk. It rolled to rest at Margot's feet. As the car pulled out into traffic, it backfired, engulfing her in a black cloud of diesel exhaust. She coughed and shook her fist at the retreating pair.

"I'll get you, Mrs. Pemberton," she muttered.

Twenty-five years ago the woman had destroyed her life. Margot had been powerless then. Today she had the means to fight back, and she intended to do just that.

* * *

That evening after dinner, Margot and Arthur Talbot adjourned to their spacious living room. While Arthur read, Margot restlessly paced, puffing on a cigarette and stopping periodically to rearrange the magazines on the coffee table. Finally Arthur lowered his newspaper to ask his wife, "Is something wrong, dear? You seem agitated. I noticed you've started smoking again."

Margot crushed her cigarette in an ash tray. "You're a lawyer, Arthur. Let me ask you a legal question."

Arthur blinked. "By all means."

"Suppose someone promised you something, yet they never came through on that promise. Are they legally liable in some way?"

"Was the promise put in writing?"

"No, it was verbal."

"And were there witnesses to this promise?"

"No, but we shook hands."

"Then my dear, you don't have a case." He picked up his newspaper and resumed reading.

Margot glared at her husband. "Arthur!"

He sighed and lowered the paper. "Margot, we've been over this subject before. I will not discuss Mrs. Pemberton tonight."

"But you don't understand. It was a month ago when we had a civil conversation. I nicely asked if she ever decided to sell, she'd contact me first. It would be to her advantage, selling to me. An outside real-estate agent would take five percent of the selling price. Mrs. Pemberton, the tightwad, understood and said she'd let me know."

Arthur nodded. "So what is your problem?"

"My problem is the old crank's forgotten. She must have dementia. Meanwhile, it's obvious she's at the point where she can't take care of the place. She's probably in her late eighties, for God sake."

"Mrs. Pemberton has a right to live wherever she wants, Margot."

She jabbed a finger at him. "What about me, Arthur? I'm fifty years old. How much longer do I have to wait?"

"You'll wait until Mrs. Pemberton is ready to sell her house."

"Her house? That is my house, my family's heritage." She stood over her husband, who shrank back in his chair. "I won't rest until the Pembertons accept that fact."

She stomped out of the room, slamming the door on her way out. Arthur sat quietly until he heard the upstairs bedroom door slam. Then he sighed, picked up his newspaper and continued reading.

* * *

Late that night, Margot sat in her home office finishing up paperwork. After shutting down the computer, she glanced at the phone, a landline. She moved to the bookcase and found a worn copy of the local phone book. Her finger traveled down the column of names: Peckham, Pellegrini... Pemberton.

She punched in the number. After several rings, a querulous voice answered: "Hello? Who's this?"

Margot replaced the receiver. She turned off the desk lamp and sat in the dark for several moments, smiling to herself.

* * *

"Lean your head back into the sink, Mrs. Talbot."

Margot felt her neck and shoulders relax as Betty Ann's strong fingers massaged shampoo into her scalp. "You don't know how good this feels," she said.

"Nothing at all, Mrs. Talbot. How's work? Any more awards?"

Margot yawned. "There's a citation from the community college. I often employ their interns." She laughed. "Free labor, but all in all, it doesn't amount to much."

"It's an honor to be singled out."

"Honors don't pay and time is money."

The hairdresser, who stood on her feet eight hours a day, knew all about time and money, particularly its lack. She changed the subject. "Heard anything from Mrs. Pemberton lately?"

Horizontal lines immediately appeared on Margot's forehead. "I'm convinced that woman is playing games with me."

"Why is that?"

"She's pretending not to know me. She's being cute, hoping I'll make a big offer."

Betty Ann worked peach conditioner through Margot's hair. "Are you going to offer?"

"I'll offer what it's worth and not a penny more. Lord knows the place is falling apart. My parents would roll over in their graves to see how those people have destroyed our home."

"Have you been inside lately?"

"No. I see it from a distance when I happen to pass by that way."

Margot didn't mention that she passed by that way often, usually at night when she couldn't sleep. One night she'd had more wine than usual and had driven midway up the driveway. With the headlights off, she'd sat in her car and gazed at the old homestead. Another night she alighted from her car. Keeping her head down, she crept to a line of bordering shrubs and hid in the shadows. The house and adjacent boat house were in darkness. The only sound was the night breeze rustling the trees. She crawled closer, hiding behind an overgrown rhododendron. Reaching into the pocket of her black trench coat, she removed a paper-covered rock on which she'd written: *Get out now!*

She'd sent the rock flying. The sound of shattering glass in the still night was both terrifying and exhilarating.

Now Betty Ann said soothingly, "All things come to those who wait, Mrs. Talbot."

Margot didn't bother replying. If she had, she'd tell Betty Ann that waiting was for the dull and ordinary. Margot Talbot was far from ordinary.

* * *

Before going home, she swung into the parking lot of the Village Liquor Shoppe. Lately a drink or two before bedtime calmed her. It worked better than the sedatives her doctor had prescribed.

As she reached the entrance, the door burst open. A grinning Dwayne Pemberton, a case of beer carried on his shoulder, emerged. With his long gray hair and dirty sheepskin vest, he looked like a vagrant. Leering, he said, "Afternoon, Miz Talbot."

With a look of outrage, she scurried past him. His laughter followed her into the store. She shuddered. Not only did the man look like an animal, he smelled like one too!

That evening, over a candlelight dinner, Margot mentioned the encounter to Arthur. "A person like that shouldn't be allowed in a village like ours. Years ago he'd have been locked up."

"I feel sorry for Dwayne Pemberton," Arthur said. " It can't be easy living in that boat house: no heat, no electricity."

"It's more than he deserves. The first thing I'll do is tear it down and build a nice, modern cabana." She took a sip of Cabernet and waited for her husband's response. When he remained silent, she took another sip and said, "I know you think it's foolish, Arthur, my wanting the house after so many years."

"I admit I don't understand why you, an astute businesswoman, would want a house that's so neglected. Especially with so many attractive properties on the market."

"What can I say? Ever since the Pembertons forced my family out I've vowed to get our home back." She shrugged. "Call it family pride."

His smile was patient. "I beg to correct you, dear. The Pembertons didn't force your family out, the bank did. Your father had taken out a huge loan to finance his...invention. Then he couldn't meet his mortgage payments. It happens all the time."

"You must admit Daddy's idea was ingenious. It was the provincial New Englanders, clinging to the old ways that ruined him."

Arthur chose his words carefully. "Indeed, installing electric heating rods under a driveway *was* an innovative idea. It was also enormously expensive, something your father didn't take into account."

"Are you aware that people in Beverly Hills have movie theaters in their homes? They're considered mandatory."

"That's Beverly Hills, dear. This is New England, and back in nineteen seventy-four people either shoveled their driveways or paid a kid to do it. No one was willing to spend thousands to melt snow."

Margot stood and threw her napkin at the table. "Are you calling my father a fool? I'll have you know he was a brilliant man. Someday that patent will be worth millions. Then we'll see who has the last laugh."

She knocked her chair over while rushing from the table. Arthur sat quietly until he heard the bedroom door slam. Then he picked up the chair and reached for the Cabernet, pouring the remainder into his glass. No sense in wasting good wine.

Late that night, unable to sleep, Margot roamed the downstairs of her house. In the kitchen, she picked up the wall phone and dialed the now-familiar number. When she heard the reedy elderly voice, she said, in a low, guttural tone, "Get out now!"

* * *

On Thursday, Margot rapped loudly on the door of apartment number twelve. She wrinkled her nose at the cooking smells wafting from a nearby window. The Santoros, an older couple, were what she referred to as "ethnic."

When Mrs. Santoro opened the door and spotted the building's new owner-landlord, her eyes widened. "Mrs. Talbot, is something wrong? My husband mailed the rent two days ago at the post office."

Margot got right to the problem. "Ms. Santoro, do you own that clothesline?"

She smiled broadly. "My Carlo put it up behind the hedge so no one can see it from the front. "

"Perhaps you didn't notice the new rules I posted. Rule number ten is no clotheslines. We have coin dryers in the basement for that."

"I see, but I like to hang my husband's t-shirts in the sun. They smell so nice and fresh, you know?" She stepped back. "Will you come in for a coffee?"

Margot pointed at the offending clothesline. "Take it down or face the consequences."

* * *

Driving home, Margot's head pounded. She hadn't slept well. The night before she'd driven to a local convenience store with an outside pay phone. She needed to be cautious in case Mrs. Pemberton had a tracer on her line.

Since she'd begun the late night calls and visits, they'd taken on a life of their own. Now she couldn't stop if she wanted to. If she attempted to restrain herself, she remembered the Pembertons' past acts of cruelty. One in particular had influenced her whole life: instead of entering Wellesley, as planned, Margot had been forced to attend a state college. There was no end to the humiliation, thanks to the evil Pembertons.

* * *

That evening, Margot knocked on the door of her husband's study. Lately, Arthur had been spending a lot of time holed up inside. She opened the door and flashed a wide smile.

"Darling, I have a legal question for you."

He raised his eyebrows and looked at her.

"I need to know the laws regarding eviction proceedings."

"May I ask whom you're thinking of evicting?"

"An older couple at my new building. They're breaking the rules. You wouldn't believe the smell of garlic oozing from their place. I'll have to have the apartment fumigated once they're gone."

Arthur shook his head. "Tenants are entitled to cook in their own homes, Margot."

"It's more than that. They're primitive. They hang their underwear outside." She moved to stand over him, smoothing his hair back. "Seriously darling, they're lowering the property values. Don't you want my condo project to be successful?"

Arthur stared up at his wife. He noted the dark circles under her eyes that she'd tried concealing. He knew she went out at night on mysterious errands and suspected it had something to do with the Pembertons. Margot had always been 'high-strung,' but now he had a bad feeling about her actions.

"I can't help you with this one, Margot. It's just plain wrong."

She stepped away from him. "Then I'll hire a lawyer. Imagine, my own husband refusing to help me."

"Suit yourself, my dear. You always do."

* * *

At midnight, Margot sat in her darkened living room finishing her drink. She debated whether to go out. She needed a good night's sleep, yet the urge—nay, necessity—to visit her old homestead was strong. Not only that, she had a hunch the old lady was truly rattled and on the verge of moving. The victory she had dreamed about was close at hand.

She stood and pocketed her car keys.

* * *

Halfway up the Pembertons' driveway, she turned off the headlights and coasted to a spot under a row of spruce trees. A full moon illuminated the house. To Margot, it had never looked so beautiful. Silently she got out of the car and crept closer. At the same time she scanned the ground for a hefty rock. As she reached for one, loud, angry voices rang out.

She stopped to listen. The high, shrill voice sounded like Mrs. Pemberton's. The other, low and raspy, was Dwayne's. The exchange continued for over a minute and then stopped. Seconds later a high-pitched, drawn-out wail shattered the night. Silence followed.

Margot, poised to flee, listened intently. The house was as still as an abandoned church. Suddenly, a light appeared above the front door, setting her in motion. She ran, her breath coming in quick gasps. Upon reaching her car, she leaped inside and turned the ignition key with trembling hands. She roared away, zigzagging down the dirt road, and didn't slow down until she reached her house.

Later, lying in bed, Margot shivered, remembering the angry voices, the loud scream. What had happened at the Pemberton house?

* * *

She soon learned of the outcome. On Thursday morning she stopped at the Village Cuppa. After placing her order for a decaf, no sugar, with skim milk, she glanced down at a shelf of newspapers. On the front page of the *Granite Cove Gazette*, below the fold, were the words: *Prominent Citizen Dies in Fall*. She snatched the paper and hurried for the door.

Inside her car, she read the story. According to the newspaper account, Mrs. Pemberton, age eighty-five, had died of a broken neck after falling down the stairs at her home. She was discovered by her nephew, Dwayne Pemberton, who had heard a scream and found her. "My aunt would get confused and wander the house at night," the distraught nephew claimed. The account concluded with a brief history of the Pembertons' long ancestry, dating back to the Revolution.

Now Margot edged her car into traffic. Her mind in a whirl, she debated her next move. She briefly considered telling Arthur what she knew of Eleanor Pemberton's death, but rejected the idea. Arthur, a lawyer, would tell her to go to the police. They in turn would wonder what she was doing at the Pembertons' house in the middle of the night. It would not look good for her reputation.

In the meantime, it was best to lie low. She would put the matter out of her mind for now. After all, she hadn't actually seen anything....

* * *

A half-dozen cars were parked outside Callahan's Funeral Home the night of Eleanor Pemberton's wake. As Margot entered the reception area, she spotted Dwayne Pemberton sitting on a sofa and reading a newspaper. The few mourners stood in small groups, ignoring him. He'd left the dirty sheepskin vest at home in favor of a sports coat whose too-short sleeves exposed hairy wrists. Dwayne didn't bother standing when Margot approached. Instead, he leaned back and grinned. "Well now, if it ain't Miz Talbot come a-calling. I didn't know you were friends with my aunt."

Margot ignored the remarks. "Dwayne, I'm very sorry about your loss. I just want you to know that when you're ready to do something about the house, I can help." She handed him a card. "Please call. I think we can do business together."

He stuck the card in his breast pocket. "I'm sure we can, Miz Talbot. I'm sure we can."

* * *

Weeks passed. She heard nothing from Dwayne. One day, as she drove past the village liquor store, she spotted the rusted station wagon outside. On impulse, she drove in and parked. Soon Dwayne emerged, carrying two cases of beer. She noticed this time it was imported beer he'd purchased. She rolled down her window.

"Excuse me, Dwayne?"

He put the beer into the back of the wagon, slammed the door and approached. "Miz Talbot, looks like you and me are regular customers here."

She attempted a smile. "I was just wondering if you've had a chance to think about my offer regarding your house."

He rested a forearm on her window and looked inside. Feeling his eyes on her legs, she discreetly tugged at her skirt. "I've been meaning to call and let you know," he said. "Tell you the truth, I'm sick of this pokey town. Bunch of hypocrites. I got a buddy in South Dakota wants me to go in on a bar with him. I've been thinking about it."

"That's a good idea," she said. "Here's what you do: Before you sell, you'll want to get three estimates from three licensed real-estate agents. The selling price will be what they average out to."

He grinned. "Miz Talbot, people say you're a real dynamo. I believe it."

She nodded. "Thank you. I'm proud of my reputation."

Before turning away, he winked. "You'll hear from me."

* * *

The call came two weeks later as she was leaving her office for the day.

She recognized the raspy voice. "It's me, Miz Talbot. I'm ready to talk business."

"Good. Did you get the appraisals?"

"I'm all set."

"Fine. Would you like to come to my office tomorrow?"

"No, you come here, now."

"Now?" She laughed. "But I don't even know the price. We'll need to draw up documents—at the very least, an Intent to Purchase Agreement—"

He cut her off. "You better come now, Miz Talbot, if you want first dibs. Otherwise I got a couple real estate ladies who're interested."

"No, no, that's fine. I'll bring a couple of standard forms, and—"

She didn't get a chance to finish. Dwayne had hung up the phone.

* * *

This time Margot drove the entire length of the driveway and parked in front of the house. Dusk was settling over the grounds. Inside, lights glowed dully. She grabbed her briefcase and got out, pausing to look around. Now that ownership was at hand, she assessed the property with a critical eye. The widespread neglect was obvious, yet she was eager to begin restoration. A labor of love, she thought, breathing the sweet night air. Every coat of paint, every flower bed would be a tribute to her parents.

She moved toward the house, steeling herself for what lay ahead: the unpleasantness of dealing with Dwayne Pemberton.

As she knocked loudly on the door, she noted the scarred wood, the peeling trim. She was about to knock again when Dwayne appeared wearing a camouflage vest and holding a can of beer. He glanced at her briefcase. "Miz Talbot, you're a fast worker."

"No sense in wasting time," she said, following him through the foyer and into the living room. Her practiced glance took in the cracks on the walls and water stains blotting the ceiling. The rug under her feet was spotted with soot from the fireplace. For a moment she remembered cozy winter nights, sitting around the fireplace while her father read *The Night Before*

Christmas.

"Beer, Miz Talbot?"

"No, thanks." She sat gingerly on a stained chair cushion. "I have to drive."

He stretched out on a sagging couch, his beer can balanced on his chest. "Normally I'm not allowed in the big house. Auntie didn't trust me."

Margot cleared her throat. "I understand your father and Mrs. Pemberton's husband were brothers."

"That's right. Yet when my father was down and out, old Caleb wouldn't loan him a cent. Didn't approve of Dad, the black sheep of the family." He took a long drink from the can, watching her.

"And yet you ended up living here."

"If you could call it *living.* As she got older, Auntie was afraid to be alone out here in the sticks. So, I got to sleep in the boat house in exchange for doing chores. Now and then she threw in a couple bucks for gas and driving her around."

"I see." Margot leaned down to open her briefcase. "Shall we discuss the sale? Do you have the real-estate agents' estimates?"

Dwayne got to his feet. "Speaking of the boathouse, wanna see it? I fixed it up pretty good—put in insulation and a wood stove. C'mon, I'll show you."

Margot forced a smile. "Why not?"

She followed him out a back door off the pantry and shivered when something skittered past her foot in the overgrown wet grass. The boathouse door creaked when he opened it.

"Lemme turn on a light," he said, producing a book of matches from his pocket. He lit an oil lamp on a table next to a rumpled cot. Soon a weak light illuminated the shabby interior. "Over there's my wood stove. Comes in handy winter nights."

Margot glanced around. Cobwebs hung from the corners and the smell of mildew permeated the air. Seeing her wary glance, he said, "It looks much better in the daylight. A coat of paint and you'll have it looking like something in a magazine." He lowered himself onto the cot and reached underneath to drag out a six-pack of beer held together with plastic rings. Removing a can, he said, "Sure you don't want a beer, Miz Talbot?" He flipped open the tab. Warm beer ran over his hand.

"No, I don't. Let's go back to the house. I'd like to go over the documents."

He took a long swallow and looked around the room. "Like I was saying, the boathouse could look real nice. You could fix it up for a rental property. I says to myself, it's like getting two houses for one."

"What did the appraisers say?" she asked. "I need to see the estimates."

"There are no appraisers. I don't like strangers nosing around." He winked at her. "That's why I called you to do business."

"I don't understand—"

"It's easy, Miz Talbot. I want a million-five for the place. Simple as that."

She stared at him and laughed. "I assume you're joking, Dwayne, but if you're not, I've run out of patience. This house is falling apart. It should be razed. You'd be lucky to get four-hundred thousand."

He lit a cigarette and leaned back on the cot. "Well, I guess we won't be doing business together...a shame."

She turned to the door. "Let's discuss this tomorrow when you're sober."

He crumpled the beer can in his fist. "I'm sober now. I want my money, and guess what? You're gonna pay it."

"I don't have that kind of money."

"You've got that nice house out by the country club and that apartment building you're turning into condos. Mr. Talbot's got a fancy office downtown." He grinned at her. "I've done a little digging, Margot."

The thought of Dwayne Pemberton nosing into her affairs was infuriating."You're awfully bold for someone who's committed a murder."

His eyes narrowed. "Who are you calling a murderer?"

"All right, I didn't want to say anything, but you forced me to. I was here, outside your house the night your aunt died. I heard you two arguing and I heard her scream. You pushed her, didn't you, Dwayne?"

He merely shrugged at the accusation. "I overheard her talking to a lawyer. She was planning to leave this house to the historical society. Meanwhile, her next of kin who's been waiting on her hand and foot would get squat."

She put a finger to her lips. "This conversation will go no farther than this room. I can promise you that."

Now it was his turn to laugh. "Bet your sweet ass it won't." He moved from the cot to an old maple bureau. From the top drawer he removed a manila folder which he handed to her. "Speaking of your midnight visits..."

Inside were several eight by ten inch photos, all taken at night. In the first picture, she recognized herself crouching by the rhododendron bush, her face startlingly white against the shadows. In the second, she was running down the driveway to her BMW, visible in the background. Silently she flipped through the incriminating stack.

"I used a special nighttime lens," he said, looking over her shoulder. "In 'Nam I did reconnaissance work. Comes in handy." He reached into his pocket and withdrew a flat black cylinder. "Listen to this," he said, pressing the device.

Immediately her voice, deep and guttural, filled the room: "Get out! Get out now!"

He clicked it off. "The first few calls I traced to your house before you switched to a pay phone." He shook his head. "You make a lousy spy, Miz Talbot." Before she could comment, he added, "I also have plaster casts of your tire tracks, not to mention your fingerprints on the rock you threw. If that ain't enough, any handwriting expert could identify your writing."

Margot struggled to keep her voice steady. "Regardless of your so-called evidence, the police would never believe you. They'd laugh. I'm a pillar of this community while you're nothing but a crazy person."

He took the folder from her hand. "You might be right, Miz Talbot. But I know someone who'd be very interested in what I have to say. His name's Lenny Santoro and he's the editor of the city newspaper. Matter of fact, you know his parents. They're the ones you evicted from your fancy condo building."

"The Santoros? You mean...he's their son?"

"Check it out. Poor folks had to move in with Lenny 'cuz they had no place to go." He grinned at her. "Just imagine: Mrs. Margot Talbot, pillar of the community, kicks an old couple to the street. Then she scares an eighty-five year-old lady to death with phone calls, broken windows, and midnight visits." He threw his head back and laughed.

She took a step back. "You can't frighten me, Dwayne. *You* killed your aunt. No one would believe your stories."

He leaned against the bureau. "Maybe not, but something tells me you don't want to take that risk." When she didn't respond, he added, "Look at it this way: I take the money and leave for South Dakota. You get to keep your reputation, your business, and the house." His eyes moved over her body. "Don't look so worried, Margot. You're getting what you wanted." He crossed the room to clamp a hand on her shoulder. "Now quit stalling and write up that deed."

She nodded, shuddering as his hand massaged her shoulder.

"Write it up nice, Margot." His voice was husky in her ear. He pressed against her. "Mmm, your hair sure smells pretty...."

WHO POISONED IVY?

By Kari Wainwright

Lily, Larkspur, Laurel—all lethal. And so were the plants.

I discovered that after my parents moved to a new house in Denver where the next-door neighbor girls were named after poisonous flowers.

As a teen, I learned how toxic these little blonde girls were. If you weren't on their "friends" list, you'd better be prepared for the bitchiest bullies of your life. They demolished reputations as effortlessly as spring snows destroyed blossoms.

Eight years later, another daughter joined the McPherson family, and her parents broke their alliterative pattern. They called their afterthought baby, Ivy.

By then, I'd escaped the neighbors' clutches by attending college elsewhere. After helping my parents move to a retirement home, I no longer cared what went on in my old neighborhood.

Ironically, I'm also named after a flower—Rose—beautiful, but thorny. My barbed personality led me to police work.

And two divorces.

I'd spent the last seven years in homicide for the Denver Police Department, but nothing prepared me for the phone call I received that Monday morning.

"Homicide. Detective Carr."

"Help! I've been poisoned." Her voice shook.

"Ma'am," I answered. "You need to get to the nearest ER. I'll get an

79

ambulance for you. What's your address?"

She told me and I yelled at my partner, "Get an ambulance."

Sara Wilkins said, "Gotcha. Help is on the way."

I returned to the caller. "What's your name?"

"Ivy," she gasped.

"What makes you think you've been poisoned?"

"I can't—" Her voice faded to nothingness. The thud that followed echoed in my ears.

I took my gun, placed it in my shoulder holster, grabbed my black jacket. The hole in the lining grew bigger every day from friction with the gun. My weapon had murdered another jacket. "Sara, come on."

She pulled on her blue jacket, tightened her brunette bun, and being a foot shorter, strove to match my long stride

My short, siren-red hair should have been a warning to guys, but my natural curves still made some of them want to take an intimate road trip. Thank goodness I carried a badge so I could pull the faster ones over.

The older cops called us Cagney and Lacey, while the recruits had no idea who they were. Not having seen the TV show, I didn't know either.

We hustled to my black Dodge Charger. Lights and sirens announcing us, we wove our way through the mid-morning traffic rush, fueled with adrenalin and hope. Hope that the caller would get help in time.

I wondered why Ivy phoned me instead of calling 911. But since someone had possibly attempted homicide, I needed to respond.

We arrived in her neighborhood, one of Denver's older ones where the houses were brick from back in the day when wooden houses were outlawed due to fire danger.

Paramedics' vehicles formed a barrier around the front yard with yellow police tape adding another layer behind them. Neighbors, wearing their curiosity like cloaks, watched from their yards. The spectators might prove helpful.

Sara and I ducked under the tape, and after putting on our regulatory gloves and booties, we entered the house. Police work definitely wasn't about style.

A woman's body sprawled on the kitchen floor, was partially obscured by the medical team. Pale, slender legs stuck out from the bottom of an even paler nightgown. From the middle of the pack came a voice I recognized—the coroner, Tina. She pronounced the woman dead.

The uniforms surrounding the dead woman dispersed. One of them, a handsome young man, said as he passed me, "We tried to be careful with the evidence, ma'am."

I nodded and considered becoming a thirty-eight-year-old cougar. There's something devilishly sexy about well-developed biceps and triceps and deltoids and anything else that flexes.

Back to business. We moved closer to Ivy to realize she was probably in her early twenties. Gone too soon. Her brunette hair still wore its bedtime tangles. On her side, one arm was stretched out. "What do you think, Tina?"

She studied Ivy. "No sign of outward trauma. She's awfully young for a heart attack or stroke. The pathologist, Dr. Graham, should have more information after the autopsy."

That was one of the weird things about Colorado's crime fighters. An elected coroner pronounced the death at the scene but didn't perform the autopsy.

On the scuffed wooden table, a teacup rested on its side, a trail of light brown fluid creating a trail that dripped on the floor. Tea leaves stuck to the bottom of the cup, leaving me to wonder if I needed to hire a tea leaf reader.

Torn and wrinkled birthday paper surrounded three open packages. Ivy's gifts included an ornamental teapot, a package of exotic tea leaves, and a tin of scones along with a jar of English lemon curd. Too bad stealing evidence was a bad thing. I *love* lemon curd.

Sara and I worked Ivy's modest home with evidence markers and a camera. I lost track of time, only to notice a clock when a windowless white van appeared in the driveway. Ivy was on her way to a cold slab and a lonely morgue drawer.

The forensic team arrived next to collect, label, and store pertinent items. I explored a desk top full of mail: the usual utility bills, a food bank donation flyer, and a birthday card with a syrupy sweet floral motif on the front.

The card was for Ivy McPherson and signed by her older sisters: Lily, Lark, & Laurel.

The card singed my fingers and I released it as if it were on fire.

* * *

The envelope had Laurel Parker's address on it. I knew I could find her phone number, but this was one death notification I needed to make in person. I wanted to gauge her reaction. Plus, I couldn't quite get rid of the small sense of glee I felt about delivering bad news to her. I'm not always the best person in the world.

On the drive to Laurel's, I asked Sara to gather information on one of my former tormentors. She relayed the news that Laurel had one DUI, two bankruptcies—and three dead husbands.

Some people were unlucky in love. Then there was Laurel. She seemed to make her own luck.

Far from modest, her castle-like house dominated its surroundings with turrets, gabled dormer windows, and an imposing wooden front door full of studded nails. The manicured landscape contained no errant weeds. Dandelions knew not to enter the premises on penalty of death.

The large metal knocker resounded through the house. Since no one appeared, I thwacked it again.

The door slowly swung open, disappointing me when it didn't creak ominously. It also disappointed me when no bloodsucking vampire appeared. But the biggest disappointment of all was Laurel. *The woman looked damn good.*

She held a fingernail file in her hand. "What do you want? Can't you see I'm in the middle of something important here?"

Sara and I flashed our badges. Laurel didn't seem impressed.

"May we come in?" I asked. "We have important news."

She shrugged and stepped aside.

We entered the barren foyer, only to walk into the next room, a cold, wintry-white furnished living room.

"Ma'am, you might want to sit down," I suggested.

She busied herself filing a fingernail, then looked at my face. "Do I know you?"

I showed her my badge again and she squinted, actually reading it this time. "Ohmigod. You're that neighbor kid, Roly-Poly-Rosy." She eyed me up and down, her face full of scorn. "At least, you've trimmed down some of the weight."

Sara gave the blonde one of her starkest glares. "Ms. Parker. We're here to tell you that your sister, Ivy, is deceased."

Blast it, partner. You stole my thunder.

Laurel's file stopped mid-rasp. She sank onto the nearest couch. "She can't be. I just saw her yesterday. Hard to believe, but it was her twenty-first birthday. It was always strange to have such a young sister."

Sara and I sat on the other sofa, one at each end, like gargoyles with guns. "Who else was there?" I asked.

"Well, Lark and Lily, of course. You remember them, don't you, Roly—"

I interrupted. "That's Detective Carr to you. Anyone else?"

Laurel tapped her lip with her nail file. "Let's see. I don't remember their names, but some people from Ivy's cause came, some food bank or other. Rather scruffy."

I didn't know if scruffy referred to the people or the food bank, but I made a note to contact the organization listed on Ivy's pamphlet. How like Laurel to discount these volunteers as if they were nobodies.

Sara turned her attention from photographs on the mantelpiece to the thrice-widowed Laurel. "Ma'am, can you tell me how all your husbands died?"

Laurel bristled like a startled cat. She huffed. "What do the tragic deaths of my husbands have to do with poor Ivy?" She almost squeezed a tear out of one eye.

Sara continued, "We're not sure, Ms. Parker. But death does appear in your life more often those most people's."

"The accidents that took my dear husbands' lives were investigated by the police, I can assure you." She stood. "Now, I think it's time for you to leave. I'm sure you can find your way out."

I turned around when we reached the front door. Laurel stood at the other end of the foyer. "You haven't asked how your sister died. Aren't you curious? Or do you already know?"

Her fingers turned into talons. She shrieked. "Get out of my house."

* * *

Next stop: Larkspur McPherson's house. She'd reverted to her maiden name after her divorce. While her home wasn't imposing like her sister's mansion, her rambling ranch looked inviting.

That look didn't extend to the owner. Lark answered the doorbell wearing a summery yellow top, black shorts, and a glower. "I know why you're here, so you needn't come in." She slammed the door.

I rang the bell again. No response from her, so I yelled. "I'm sorry, ma'am, but we're detectives and we need to ask you some questions."

Lark and I had been in the same grade when we were neighbors. We almost had fun together once or twice.

"Lark, it's Rose from Jackson Middle School. I am so sorry about Ivy."

Still no response from her, but a couple of neighbors paused their everyday lives to pay attention to the loud cop on the block. Sara and I walked toward them, flashing our badges along with friendly smiles.

The man and woman seemed a bit nervous, but their golden retriever was all wagging tongue and tail. We introduced ourselves, including Bama, the dog, who stuck her nose in my crotch. At least the couple, Jack and Cindy, shook hands. They lived two doors down from Lark and didn't seem surprised that she was being visited by the police.

Cindy waxed enthusiastic as she related the tale of a feud that had gone on between Lark and her neighbor, Susan. Lark accused the other woman of training her messy tree to deliberately scatter its prickly pods on her lawn.

The feud went on and on. Trash dumped on the other's doorstep. Threats made over the fence rang through the block.

One night, high winds assaulted the area and the damaged tree toppled over with a thunderous crash. Next morning, Susan was found deceased beneath it.

Although that event raised a lot of questions, Sara's first was, "What kind of tree was it?"

Jack finally spoke. "A female ginkgo. Like many females, very attractive, but difficult to deal with."

That earned him a wifely elbow to his midsection and ended our conversation. They finished their afternoon dog walk with the kind of half-annoyed, half-jesting exchanges that only a long-married couple would have. Bama woofed her farewell and paraded alongside her people until they arrived home.

* * *

Our last visit of the day was to the youngest sister of the threesome—Lily, two years younger than me. I remembered her as being a delicate child, slender, with elfin features.

We shuffled our way through heavy traffic to her apartment complex—a maze of several buildings, each with its own weed-filled parking lot, a small green space, and token pine trees. We found her building, then made our way to the fifth floor.

The door opened at my first knock revealing a fleshy, heavy-set woman with a drink in her hand and a cigarette in her mouth. She wasn't necessarily unattractive, but rather well-used. The elf had disappeared, probably a long time ago. Lily flicked ashes from her cigarette. "Rose and friend?"

I nodded. "May we come in?"

"Sure, you betcha." She waved us into her living room overflowing with gossip, beauty, and travel magazines. "Just pitch stuff off the chairs."

She waved her cigarette around in a parody of an old Bette Davis movie. I wondered if we were in for a bumpy ride.

I sat on the edge of a deep chair, the Bermuda Triangle of furniture. It looked like it could easily disappear people. I didn't dare lean back. "I am Detective Carr and this is my partner, Detective Wilkins. You seem to remember me as a neighbor of yours when we were kids—Rose. Do you know why I'm here?"

She drank the last sip of her drink, then banged the glass on the nearest table. "Yeah, Larky and Laurie called. They said Ivy died, or somethin'. What happened to her?"

The first sister to actually ask about Ivy slurred her speech and worked to focus her blurred eyes.

"We don't know for sure, but before she died, she said she was poisoned. Any idea who would want to do that?"

Lily's head flopped back, and her gaze wandered to the ceiling. Was she waiting for answers from above? "Dunno," she mumbled before she slumped over in her chair in a stupor.

* * *

Back at the police station, I pulled up the records of Laurel's three husbands and Lark's dead neighbor.

Sara sunk onto her desk chair. "Are you really going to review all those cold cases tonight?"

I briefly glanced at her. She looked exhausted, but with two children at home, she'd hardly get any rest there. "Go home, partner. Tell the kids Aunt Rose says to be kind to you."

She laughed. "As if."

Sara gathered her things, then squeezed my shoulder as she passed. "Will it do any good to tell you to go home, be kind to yourself, and get some rest?"

My eyes focused back on my monitor, I said, "As if."

As she arrived at the elevators, I hollered, "Don't forget. Ivy's autopsy's scheduled for nine tomorrow."

I read until my eyes glazed over and my concentration was as dead as one of Laurel's studded doornails.

* * *

Coffee bean aroma wafted past my nose. I cracked one eye open to see a mug full of rich brown liquid. I sat up and then wished I hadn't. "So, this is what it feels like to be ninety years old?"

Sara handed me the coffee. She offered me an egg sandwich to go with it.

"Blast it, partner, where's a donut when you really need it?"

She laughed. "You wouldn't eat one now, anyway. This is for me. I know how you are about autopsies." She took a bite from the sandwich as we headed for the car.

On the way to the morgue, I told Sara what I'd learned last night. Summing things up as we parked, I said, "It looked to me like the investigators did their jobs as best they could. In Laurel's three cases, she was the main suspect, but they couldn't find any evidence to use against her. She must have had help getting rid of anything incriminating, because each time, there was no proof."

"Yeah, it's funny how juries like at least a little something in the proof department. Especially if the accused is blonde and beautiful." Sara continued, "What about the ginkgo tree killing?"

"There was evidence that the tree was poisoned, causing it to die, thus making it vulnerable in the storm."

"You're kidding. One of them *poisoned* a tree? That's outrageous."

"At least it wasn't a dog," I responded.

Sara made a face at me. "What did they do to the poor ginkgo?"

"Evidence pointed to some bark being pulled back, a hole drilled and filled with copper sulfate. Unfortunately, no one could prove who did it. The night the tree succumbed to the high winds, Lark had an alibi. A lover who swore she didn't leave the bedroom all night. Looks like a lot of my time is going to be spent delving further into these cases."

We entered the morgue, a building that never seemed to warm up, no matter the weather. Sara, the braver one in this atmosphere, approached the pathologist, Dr. Graham, and Ivy McPherson, laid out on a steel autopsy table. I followed more slowly.

Dr. Graham probably flourished her trademark smile under her mask, but I couldn't tell for sure. It looked like the doctor was almost through with her procedures. I glanced away.

"I got an early start," Dr. Graham said.

Studying the ceiling rather than my surroundings, I asked, "What have you learned about manner or cause of death?"

"Not a lot. Right now, manner of death is undetermined. No way I can tell if this is a homicide or a suicide. It could even be an accident."

"And cause?" I asked. "Did Ivy generally have good health before this event?"

"Now, that is interesting." The doctor pointed to the brain sitting on one of her trays. "If someone wanted Ivy dead, all they had to do was wait a few months. She had an inoperable tumor. Only pain and suffering in her future."

"Holy—!"

"My sentiments exactly," Dr. Graham said.

"Do we have to wait the standard four to six weeks for results from toxicology?" I asked.

"I have a friend at the lab. Maybe I can talk him into getting the results in three and a half weeks." Graham chuckled.

Like the professional law enforcement officer that I am, I stuck my tongue out at her.

* * *

Over our salad lunch, Sara and I munched and talked. There was a lot to digest, and I wasn't counting the food.

Sara asked, "What's next?"

"The food bank. I've made an appointment with the woman who runs it, Abby Freeman."

We drove to the Mary Hobbs Food Bank, named for a woman who worked for years feeding people who needed help. We drove past cars full of families, hunger, and desperation. Some of them seemed to think we were trying to sneak in line and honked at us.

After parking on the other side of the warehouse, Sara and I walked past people handing out sacks and boxes of vegetables, fruits, canned goods, hams, and little candy bars for the children. We heard so many "Thank yous" and "Bless yous" from the ones on the receiving end, that my eyes teared up.

"Gets to you, doesn't it?" Sara said.

"I've just got something in my eyes, is all."

After a few minutes, we found Abby directing the volunteers to their various positions in the loading lines.

"Thanks for seeing us," I said. "I know you're busy."

"Ya think?" she answered.

I laughed. I hadn't expected sass from someone doing such saintly work. We moved to the side, out of people's way.

"Are you here because of Ivy?" Abby asked.

I nodded.

Sara showed the brochure from Ivy's desk, now residing in a sealed evidence bag. "We heard some people who work here attended Ivy's birthday celebration this weekend. But we don't know their names and we need to ask them some questions. Can you help?"

Abby pointed to a group of young people, two women and a man. She waved them over to us and told them why we were there.

They announced their names, almost in unison: Debbie, Tamara, and Doug. They wore similar outfits: tank tops, shorts, and tattoos.

Tamara caught me staring at one of hers, a heart with a pink ribbon wrapped around it, and a woman's name. "My mom died of breast cancer last year."

"I'm so sorry," I said. "That's really hard."

"Yeah." She blinked back tears. "But you're here about Ivy?" Tears streamed freely down her face.

Debbie joined in the crying, then wiped her eyes while Doug sniffled.

He said, "We can't believe it. We just saw her."

Debbie stepped forward. "Have you checked out her sisters? They seemed like an awfully cold bunch."

"Did they talk to you?"

89

"Are you kidding?" Doug asked. "They just stared at our tattoos. acting as if they were contagious."

Tamara shook her head vigorously. "Can you tell us how Ivy died?"

"I'm sorry, we're still working on that."

"Oh." She seemed deflated.

Sara spoke up, asking about Ivy's relationship with them and others who volunteered there.

Debbie, eyes sad as a basset hound's, said. "Ivy was a driving force here. She helped Abby get food supplies and did several promotions for the cause. This community will never be the same without her."

Her two friends nodded their agreement.

Abby approached, saying she needed them to get back to the line.

"One more question before you go," I said. "Did any of the sisters say anything unusual or suspicious?"

They shook their heads, wrapped their arms around each other, and trudged to work. Tamara looked back over her shoulder, her eyes full of pleading. I thought she might have more to say, but she was silent.

* * *

Waiting for the toxicology results was one of my least favorite aspects of police work. While we were in limbo, Sara and I sorted through the evidence and pictures we had. We talked with Ivy's neighbors, who all seemed to like her. I went back to the food bank to see if I could learn any more. I wound up helping to box food before I left for home to grab a few hours' sleep.

During the day, I was Ivy's advocate, but at night I scoured Laurel's and Lark's case files.

Turns out Laurel's first husband's cause of death was listed as a heart attack. I would have loved to exhume his body but didn't have anything close to probable cause.

Second husband slipped in the shower, fell through the glass door, and conked his head hard on the tile floor.

The third one died in a hunting accident, supposedly mistaken for a deer.

I'd never seen a stag wear a bright orange vest, but then I wasn't a drunk hunter out for any trophy he could get.

I decided to investigate the last case, so I notified the detective, Bill Harper, who worked it. Once he learned I wasn't in the business of pointing fingers, Bill agreed.

We drove into the nearby mountains until we came to a field that stopped at the edge of the forest.

Bill surveyed the area from his car seat. "This is the first time I've seen this place without snow covering everything. Maybe now we can find evidence."

"Let's go," I said, bounding out of the car. Now that the accumulation of fall and winter snows had melted, surely we could find something.

Being heavyset, Bill was breathing hard by the time we got close to the trees. After he quit sounding like a wounded dragon, I asked about the line of fire for the bullet. Was that ever ascertained?

"It looked like it came from somewhere in this field, probably close to that barbwire fence."

Even though there were only two of us, we plotted our grid search, close to the fence. We'd been going at it for almost two hours when I pushed some dried growth out of the way. Metal glinted in the Rocky Mountain sun. I grabbed a glove and a bag from my pocket and picked it up. Somebody hadn't policed their brass. "Bill, I've found something."

I looked at him. He was doubled over and breathing hard. I figured I'd better get this guy out of here before I killed him.

The casing only told us the caliber of the bullet. I hoped there might be some evidence on the casing, like a fingerprint, because without the weapon that was used, I was up the creek with no paddles, no canoes, no life vests.

As we headed toward the car, we still looked for anything else that could help our case.

Another glint in the sunlight. Some strands of blonde hair caught in a fence post danced in the mountain breeze. Bill saw it first and announced its presence with what voice he could muster through his lack of oxygen.

I almost pranced the rest of the way. Now we had her. Even if there were no hair roots, there would still be mitochondrial DNA, which would show her mother's genetic side.

While waiting for the lab tests to be done, I turned my focus to the killer ginkgo tree. I read the autopsy report on Lark's neighbor, Susan. She had several scratches and blunt force trauma, including a fatal blow to the head. Studying the pictures of her body location compared with that of the tree, it seemed difficult to me to accept that the ginkgo was the culprit that killed her.

I checked the police report to learn the name of the man who spent the night with Lark. I also learned he moved to Florida a few weeks after the tree incident. At first, he didn't want to talk to me, but when I told him about Ivy's recent demise, he opened up.

It was a tale of an evil ex-girlfriend—one with no conscience or scruples. He knew of her plan to poison the tree but claimed he hadn't known that was part of a murder plot. It was after Susan was dead that he found out that Lark killed Susan, then got Laurel and Lily to help drag her body out of the house. The three sisters waited until the storm passed, then struggled to arrange Susan's body under her dead tree. Not an easy task.

I wasn't sure if his testimony alone would be enough to convince a jury of guilt. Especially when he was reluctant to be in the vicinity of the deadly McPherson sisters again, let alone testify.

Later that day, Ivy's toxicology report came back. Cause of death was the poison aconite, from a lethal plant. Someone had mixed aconite leaves with the special blend of tea she had received for her birthday. Manner of death was still undermined.

I had the three sisters picked up separately for questioning.

Laurel sashayed into the station as if she owned the place. According to her, she wasn't guilty of any crime other than bad luck. She accused me of bias against her because of our past. I assured her that my only bias was against murderous housewives. But without the evidence results, I couldn't hold her.

Lark, on the other hand, refused to say a word. Since she had no weapons with her, she tried to kill me with a homicidal glare.

The last sister we questioned was Lily. She chewed on her lip until it bled. I handed her a tissue and a proposal. Since it appeared that she hadn't actually committed murder, we could grant her leniency if she gave up her sisters. She cried, chewed her lip some more, and after more coaxing and sweet talk on Sara's and my part, answered our queries, and promised to testify.

Lily was allowed to go home, but I had the gratification of cuffing her sisters. They didn't go quietly, but that just pleased me more.

When the results came back on the casing found near Laurel's last husband, her fingerprint was on it. The hair strands turned out to have some roots still connected, so we had full DNA. I took great pleasure delivering the news to Laurel and her handsome attorney.

I was at my desk the next morning filling out paperwork when Tamara, Ivy's friend from the food bank, entered.

She handed a white envelope to me. "I wasn't sure if it was the right thing to do, but Ivy asked me to save this and give it to you only if you arrested any of her sisters." She turned and sped out of the homicide unit.

I put on a pair of gloves. A tremor ran through my hands. *What was I about to find out?*

Ivy started out by telling me I was her hero. The time I'd returned to the neighborhood to help my parents move, I'd pulled Ivy away from the danger of being run over by a speeding car. I'd saved her, but not the ball she was trying to retrieve. I'd forgotten all about the incident until now.

Since she learned I worked homicides, she wanted my attention. She believed her sisters were getting away with murder. When she'd tried talking to the different investigators, she had no proof of homicides, so they didn't seem to listen to her. But she thought I would.

When she'd discovered her terminal cancer, she decided now was the time to bring an end to her sisters' heinous actions.

The saddest part was when she admitted poisoning herself to get investigations started. I didn't usually cry over victims, but I recalled holding that shaking toddler after I rescued her, and tears trickled. Thinking of her dead on her kitchen floor, I wanted to take her hand and help her up off the cold tiles.

I went down to my car and drove to the old neighborhood. Looking at the McPherson house, the dam broke. Tears followed.

I hoped Ivy knew I'd listened to her.

THE FALL OF THE TECH TITAN

By Jennifer J. Chow

At the small private beach gathering, I watched Dr. Gil Yoshida step across the golden sand and up to the portable podium. He wore a starched dress shirt with tie, looking like he belonged on the cover of *Forbes*—in fact, he'd been profiled there last month and called "America's New Tech Titan." From the waist down, though, his pants were pure athleisure.

There were other cracks in his polished veneer. Dr. Yoshida got his Ph.D. as an honorary degree. He hadn't even gone to college. His expensive tailored shirt looked frayed, like he'd worn it too many times before. I knew it'd been hand-selected by his assistant, Deanna Park. She stood to the left of me, fiddling with her salt-and-pepper hair, her dark brown eyes glassy. How many of his speeches had she gone to over the last few decades? Was she getting tired of being an uncredited business partner?

"Friends and family," Dr. Yoshida said, "thank you for accepting my invitation to come."

I, for one, hadn't had a choice. I'd been pushed to attend the weekend getaway because it was a pure business arrangement. I was the newest hire and Dr. Yoshida's voice to the world on the buzzy social media app Sound Bitz.

Pulling out my phone, I made sure to record everything he said. I could often massage the quote nuggets, making him sound charming, intelligent, and approachable. His personal brand revolved around the tagline: "Stay Smart." I was tasked to capture that brainy aura from him, condensing his words to five-second sound bytes and blasting them to the internet. It was a cushy job, and I was lucky to have been picked, especially after the grueling three rounds of interviews. No doubt my college degree in marketing from Cornell University had upped my chances of getting in.

Dr. Yoshida motioned for me to come closer. I stepped forward, distancing myself from Deanna and the other three guests here at the intimate retreat.

He fiddled with the podium's microphone, angling it closer to his mouth before speaking again. His voice rang out clear in the balmy summer air. "I mean, welcome friends and *new* family." Dr. Yoshida aimed his gaze at Cydney Ito, a great-niece who'd recently discovered her connection to the tech titan only after conducting an unrelated DNA test.

He continued, "This weekend marks a celebration I nicknamed 'The Bold and The Gold.'"

Someone let out their breath from behind me. I bet it was Deanna. She'd thought up the celebration name. Or rather, she'd changed it from Dr. Yoshida's original title of "The Bold and the Old," which didn't have quite the same ring.

Dr. Yoshida retrieved a crystal plaque from inside the podium and said, "I'd like to award this honor to my faithful employee, Her—"

A song suddenly rang out. "We Will Rock You" by Queen. Dr. Yoshida's ringtone. It seemed to come from behind—and below—him.

"I wonder who that is." Dr. Yoshida put down the plaque and looked around him. He backed up a few feet, stooped down, and found his cell phone. Good thing it had a heavy-duty case on it. For a tech man, he always seemed to be misplacing or dropping his cell everywhere. It had something to do with having a slippery phone case, combined with his love of mesh sports pants.

"Huh-llo?" he said into the phone, splitting up the greeting into two syllables in his signature way.

We waited while he chatted. By the time Dr. Yoshida had finished, we'd all learned the finer details about his upcoming cataract surgery.

Dr. Yoshida had an irritating habit of dropping tasks whenever new things vied for his attention—like incoming phone calls, texts, and emails. I definitely wouldn't put any of his awkward comments about blurry eyesight on Sound Bitz.

He finally remembered the rest of us. "Okay, let's try this again." He lifted up the plaque. "Herbert Ames, I want to congratulate you on working with us for forty years."

Herbert ambled forward.

"Thank you for overseeing the financials of the company as CFO," Dr. Yoshida said, presenting the plaque.

Herbert took the award and stood next to Dr. Yoshida. Next to the tech titan, I noticed how the faithful employee's posture had a slight stoop to it. Probably from hunching over financial documents and peering at Excel spreadsheets over the years. I wondered if Dr. Yoshida would've been a tech titan without Herbert's help. Although Dr. Yoshida had registered multiple patents in his name, his riches were really from investing in the right tech companies at ideal times.

Deanna hurried forward and used a fancy camera, not her phone, to take a photo of a smiling Dr. Yoshida and Herbert. She snapped about a dozen pictures before stopping.

Herbert left the "stage," which was actually a man-made beach. The sandy area faced the modernized tiki huts we were staying in. The beach made for nice photos, with the backdrop of the "ocean" behind it—again, artificial, but with the best gentle waves that money could buy.

"Now, it's time for the bold," Dr. Yoshida said. He reached inside the podium and pulled out a certificate. Then he beckoned to the new intern, who'd been selected through an online application process.

Ace Bittinger might have been the company's newest intern, but he looked kind of old to have taken the unpaid position. He had to be at least thirty-five.

Dr. Yoshida handed the certificate to Ace. Then they both turned toward Deanna, who aimed her elaborate camera at them.

"Smile," she said.

Dr. Yoshida flashed his genial grin while Ace's mouth remained a flat line. I'd never seen the man smile, even when sitting in the massaging recliner at our comfy company office.

"You're part of our bold new ventures," Dr. Yoshida said, slapping the other man on the back. "Lead us forth to our next generation of inventions."

"Or acquisitions," a male voice mumbled from behind me. It had to be Herbert.

"A round of applause for the bold and the gold," Dr. Yoshida said.

We all clapped politely.

Dr. Yoshida loosened his tie. "Now that we've marked the occasion, I think a swim is in order. Why don't we go to our huts and meet back here in ten minutes?"

Everyone agreed and moved toward the tiki structures. They looked flimsy at first glance, but I think the straw had been glued on top of a more substantial foundation. Inside, they had plenty of room for modern conveniences and appliances. Plus, the huts were teched up with smartphone entry. Each individual home was connected to our personal phone, so we didn't need keys or even cards to swipe. A touch of the button on our phone would unlock and lock our doors. The ultimate in safety, Dr. Yoshida had assured each one of us.

The huts faced the fake beach and ocean in a small semi-circle formation. My hut lay farthest to the left while Dr. Yoshida got the prime central location.

I moved over to my vacation home and used my phone to enter it. Everything was luxurious in the hut, despite it basically being a studio with a small attached bathroom. It even had a private lanai, though I hadn't gone out to relax on the balcony yet. We'd only arrived an hour ago to this secluded spot.

It took me longer than ten minutes to change out of my clothes and into the new bikini I'd bought. The tying of its thin straps spent more time than I'd anticipated. When I came back out, nobody had entered the water yet. They all gathered in front of Dr. Yoshida's hut.

"What's taking him so long?" Deanna muttered. She wore a conservative one-piece black swimsuit with ruffled skirt.

"I don't know," Ace said. "Shouldn't take much to throw on swim trunks."

He had on baggy blue ones with a palm tree design.

Cydney moved to the door of the hut and knocked on it. "Great-uncle?" she said. "Are you almost ready?"

Silence.

"Maybe he needs more time to get ready," Herbert suggested. He himself wore a complete ensemble of SPF-protected shirt, sun hat, and shorts.

"I'll just text him," Deanna said, her fingers flying over her phone.

We stood and waited a few more minutes before Ace broke the silence.

"Maybe we can go in the ocean first," Ace said. "Dr. Yoshida can join us when he's good and ready."

"Nuh-uh." Herbert wagged his finger at Ace. "You're new here, but let me tell you, we don't do anything without Dr. Yoshida's say-so."

"I'm going to call him." Deanna dialed, and we heard the voicemail pick up.

"But he always answers his phone," I said. "Do you think he's okay?" I mean, sixty wasn't super old, but still...

Cydney banged on the door. "Great-uncle, is everything all right?"

"Isn't there some sort of keycode you can punch in?" Ace asked.

We all looked at the slick surface of the smartphone door lock.

"It's not one of those models," Deanna said, "but I think he might have given me permission to enter. Let me check."

She opened up an app, and after five minutes of tinkering, we heard a click from the door. Deanna pushed it open.

We found Dr. Yoshida lying curled up on the futon, near a side table, with his back to us. Was he taking a nap?

Deanna moved to stand next to him. "Do you still want to take that swim?" she asked.

He didn't answer.

She tapped him on the shoulder. He didn't appear to notice.

Deanna peered closer. "It can't be."

I stepped to the edge of the futon. At that angle, I noticed Dr. Yoshida gripping his phone. Why hadn't he put it away on the side table with the notepad and calculator if he'd wanted to rest?

Deanna made a strangled noise.

"Are you okay?" I asked. Her face had started turning green. Deanna clapped a hand over her mouth and rushed to the bathroom.

"Something might be wrong here," I said, but I remained frozen in fear along with the rest of the group.

Finally, Ace edged over to Dr. Yoshida. He checked the man's pulse but shook his head. "Hard to tell if it's just really faint," he said, shoving his hands deep into his pockets.

"Is Great-uncle all right?" Cydney asked in a small voice.

I wasn't sure. "Why don't you call 9-1-1 just in case?"

"Okay," she said, but before she could press the three digits on her phone, a loud roar sounded from outside. A spray of sand hit the window of the hut. Her eyes widened. "Is that an...earthquake?"

Poor girl from the Midwest. None of the rest of us even moved while she peered around the hut in a frenzy. "What can I dive under?"

The ground hadn't even trembled, so there had to be a different cause.

Herbert looked outside through the open door. "I think it came from the beach area."

"Are you sure it wasn't a quake?" Cydney asked.

Herbert and I volunteered to check out the situation. Once we got to the beach, we saw nothing beyond a pile of disturbed sand.

We sat down near it in the sunshine. It was truly a beautiful day, but I still shivered.

The paramedics came within twenty minutes, which was fast, given the secluded location of the resort. Once they showed up, the rest of the group wandered out of the hut in a daze.

Cydney approached us first and sat nearby, but kept her eyes firmly on the water. Ace came out next, and he stood behind the podium, leaning against it for support. Deanna showed up last, but she didn't make it far from the hut before she looked up at the sky, curled her hand into a fist, and shook it in the air.

Herbert called out to them and said, "Come join us over here. There's nothing more we can do for Dr. Yoshida. Let's leave it to the professionals."

His tone was strong and confident. They obeyed without protest, and we arranged ourselves in a small circle.

Cydney continued to keep her eyes on the water as she spoke. "I want to go home. First, Great-uncle gets knocked out. Then an earthquake hits."

I raised my eyebrows at Deanna. Did she want to tell Cydney the potentially awful truth? Deanna jerked her thumb back toward Dr. Yoshida's hut. Guess she'd let the paramedics break the sad news to the girl.

"Just so you know, it wasn't an earthquake," Herbert told Cydney, gesturing to the odd pile of sand.

"Weird," she said. With her sandaled feet, she pushed the sand around—and revealed an odd device half-hidden there.

"What is that?" Ace asked.

Cydney crouched next to it. "Huh. Looks like a pipe bomb."

"And how would you know?" Ace said.

"School prank," Cydney didn't bother to elaborate.

Five minutes later, the paramedics walked over to us with grim looks on their faces. "We couldn't revive him," they said.

Cydney gasped, and Deanna put an arm around her shoulder.

"What happens now?" I said.

"You all need to stay put until the police show up," one of the paramedics informed us.

Cydney's eyes grew wide. "Wait, we can't leave? I wanna go home."

"Sorry, everyone has to remain here until the cause of death is determined." The paramedic hesitated. "By the way, do you know if he touched anything strange before he died?"

We looked at one another in puzzlement.

"Never mind," the paramedic said. "Sit tight while I call this in."

After he left, Deanna said, "Why did he ask about Dr. Yoshida touching something?"

"The death. It must be suspicious," Herbert said as he rearranged the sun hat to shade his eyes better.

Cydney moaned.

"And why does he need to call it in?" I said. "Didn't you already tell the emergency operator the situation, Cydney?"

She stammered. "I said my great-uncle had collapsed and was unconscious. To send in the paramedics."

"Only the paramedics?" Deanna asked. She scooted away from Cydney's side.

"What do you mean? It was a medical emergency. That's who you're supposed to ask for," Cydney said.

I knew what Deanna was getting at, though. If something suspicious was going on, Cydney's call to request *only* the paramedics served to delay the police from getting involved. And the later they came, the more the killer could hide their evidence.

Our nerves showed up in different ways. Herbert fiddled with the brim of his sun hat. Cydney blinked fast, like she was holding back tears. Ace dug his toes in the sand, and Deanna turned her head away from us, to keep an eye on the paramedics.

I knew I was the new employee on the scene, but I didn't want to be at a company where a killer worked. Or be near a family that had a murderer in it—Cydney was on my list of suspects, along with everyone else here.

Waving my arm around to encompass the beach, I asked, "When did you all end up changed into your swim stuff and out here?"

Deanna pivoted my way. "I was second on the sand. Ace was here before me."

Cydney held up three fingers.

"I was fourth," Herbert said.

Deanna pointed at me. "You were the last to show up." I didn't like the tone of her voice.

"Had some trouble with my bikini," I said.

Ace gave a soft whistle. "Sure took your time getting here."

"This was not the vacation I was promised," Cydney said and stood up. "I'm going for a swim."

Once she left our group, everyone else scattered. Deanna moved closer to Dr. Yoshida's hut, Ace walked along the beach, and Herbert ambled toward a palm tree in the distance, the only shaded spot in the area.

I watched Cydney swim, her strokes firm and sure. What else had been promised her on this vacation from her dear great-uncle?

Striding over to Deanna, I said without preamble, "Now that Dr. Yoshida's gone, will Cydney inherit everything?"

She startled. "Of course not. That girl doesn't know anything about running a business."

"Who gets control then?" Dr. Yoshida didn't have a significant other.

In a weak voice, she said, "In case of his death, the company passes over to me."

Wow. From assistant to owner, all in the span of an afternoon. That must be some heady promotion—and a great motive for murder.

But Deanna had gotten sick when she'd found Dr. Yoshida's body. She must have cared about him. Unless her stomach had heaved out of guilt, remembering how she'd killed him.

Deanna stared at Dr. Yoshida's hut. "I'm not sure I can talk about this anymore."

"I understand," I said, giving her some privacy to grieve.

Next, I marched over to long-time employee, Herbert. He'd have the most insight on company dynamics and drama.

Herbert sat with his back to the palm tree.

I crouched beside him. "Don't want to be a bother, Herbert, but as you know, I'm new to the company. I need to pick your brain before you go off and retire."

"It's about time I did," Herbert said. "Forty years is a long time to be in one place, and there are things I want to cross off my bucket list."

"Were you one of the first employees?" I asked. "There before Deanna showed up?"

"For sure. I was one of the originals. Deanna got hired way after I came on board. Only when business was really booming."

"She got hired as an assistant from the get-go?"

"Indeed."

"And she never wanted anything more?" I asked as I stared at her profile.

"I always did think she had a crush on Dr. Yoshida," he said.

Interesting. "Actually, I meant her wanting to be an equal business partner."

He shifted his hat. "Maybe," he said, "but bamboo ceiling and all that. She couldn't go up. At least not in those days."

"What about you?" I said. "Did you get anything beyond a plaque for all those years you worked for Dr. Yoshida?"

"Raises now and then. But I also loved working with numbers and got along well with Gil. He was my brain buddy," Herbert said.

"How so?"

"Gil had a fine mind. 'Stay Smart' wasn't just a logo. He lived it out. Did tons of mental math, Sudoku puzzles, that sort of thing."

"Inspiring. I should do more of that."

Herbert started yawning. "Sorry, the afternoon sun often gets to me."

"I'll leave you to your quick cat nap then," I said.

Before I'd finished my sentence, he'd already dozed off.

I heard splashing and focused on the shoreline. Cydney emerged glistening from the ocean. I walked toward her as she squeezed the water out of her long, black hair.

"Ugh, I forgot my towel," she said.

"I'll walk you over to your hut to get it."

"Thanks," she said, picking up her phone, which she'd casually tossed in the sand.

As she moved toward the huts, I said, "Which of them is yours?"

"The one to the right of my great-uncle's."

"And you didn't hear anything while you were changing into your gorgeous swimsuit?" I figured a compliment would only help get her talking more.

She touched her tankini suit with gold accents. "Thanks."

I brought her back on topic. "No arguments or yelling from his hut?"

"Nothing like that. Well...he did get a call."

"He did?" I said.

"I heard him on the balcony. My screen door was open."

"Who was he talking to?"

104

She shook her head. "I don't know."

"How'd you know he was on the phone?"

She tugged her earlobe. "That loud ringtone. You know, the song with the stomping."

"'We Will Rock You,'" I said.

"Right. He picked up because he did his usual hello greeting. But he must've had bad reception."

We reached her hut, and she unlocked it with her phone. I stayed in the open doorway, watching her retrieve a beach towel.

"What makes you say that about the poor cell service?" I asked.

She wrapped the towel around her. "Because the call dropped. And the phone rang again. But farther away. He must've moved inside the hut by then."

After joining me at the front, she glanced next door. A tear slid down her cheek.

"I'm really sorry about your great-uncle," I said. "It must have been tough, just learning about him and then...."

She swiped at her cheek. "I've been fine without him for years. I'll be okay. But if you don't mind, I think I'll go sunbathe alone for a bit."

"Yes, of course." I let her go.

As she wandered back to the sandy beach and laid out her towel, I let my gaze travel along the shoreline. Ace remained out there, walking on the soft sand. I decided to question him as well.

"Hey there, new intern," I said once I reached him.

He paused in his ambling.

"What a way to get introduced to the company, huh?" I said.

"Yeah." He chuckled. "Especially after all the hard work to get in. The multiple rounds of interviews. Panels of judges."

"The tougher it is, the sweeter the reward," I said.

"You're probably right." He kicked at the sand near him. "Do you think my internship is still valid? Or will the company go under now?"

I looked in Deanna's direction. "I'm pretty sure it'll end up in capable hands."

"Good to know," he said.

"By the way, did you happen to hear anything from Dr. Yoshida's hut when you were changing?"

He shook his head. "Nope, but I was the first on the beach, remember? Besides, I'm on the other side of Deanna. She was the one right next to Dr. Yoshida."

"Yeah, thanks." I should talk to Deanna again.

I heard the faint cries of sirens right before I sidled up to Deanna. Must be the police coming. And I had almost figured out the culprit for them.

"Deanna," I said. "Can you walk me through where everybody was in the hut after we discovered Dr. Yoshida? Herbert and I had to leave to check on the explosion on the beach."

"Honestly," she said, "I was in the bathroom right up until the point Cydney came in to tell me the paramedics were on their way."

"Did you two talk long?"

She bit the inside of her cheek. "Can't tell. I was feeling so weak. Cydney actually had to support me out of the bathroom."

"That tells me everything I need to know," I said.

When the police arrived, I made sure to stand next to the podium as I greeted them.

After they'd checked Dr. Yoshida's body and secured the area, the officers questioned each of us in turn.

When they got to me, I said, "It wasn't an accidental death, and I know who did it. In fact, I have the evidence right here."

"What?" An officer raised her eyebrows at me.

"It's in this podium. But don't worry, I didn't touch a thing."

They looked inside and noticed what appeared to be a calculator in a sealed plastic bag.

"It belongs to Ace," I said.

I explained my findings to the police officers: As overheard by Cydney, there'd been a call to Dr. Yoshida from his lanai. Ace had already planted the phone there—the only place one could access that wasn't covered by the smartphone lock. The burner phone, disguised in a calculator case, was picked up by Dr. Yoshida using his usual greeting of "Huh-llo"—or maybe he'd been actually surprised to see a calculator on his balcony. I didn't know how blurry his sight had become with the cataracts. Whatever toxic substance he'd touched had been on that phone. Then a second call from Ace had come in on the real phone inside the hut. Dr. Yoshida had gone there, distracted like always, and placed the calculator on the side table.

Ace soon hurried over to us. "What are you all talking about?"

I felt confident at confronting him with the police by my side. "The calculator inside the podium. The one you hid."

He attempted an incredulous look. "A calculator? Can't be mine. Maybe it belongs to Herbert. Or Dr. Yoshida, who's always talking about staying smart."

"Nope. The two of them were brain buddies. No need for calculators."

A bead of sweat dotted Ace's brow.

"You almost got away with it," I said, "after planting that pipe bomb on the beach. An explosion meant to make us leave the hut so you could pick up the incriminating calculator." I pointed to his baggy swim trunks with pockets.

"Too bad not all of us left." I gestured at Dr. Yoshida's hut. "Deanna and Cydney stayed, although Deanna was pretty much out of your way. She was too busy being sick in the bathroom."

He wiped his brow. "It was a shock for her, finding Dr. Yoshida like that."

"How'd you get Cydney out of picture? By asking her to check on Deanna? That would give you the opportunity you needed."

Ace backed away from me and pleaded with the police officers. "You don't believe anything that woman is saying, right? She was the last one to get changed into her bikini. Giving her plenty of time to do away with Dr. Yoshida."

"Oh, please," I said. "Being first gave you the opening you needed to plant the pipe bomb in the sand. The only thing you didn't account for was Herbert asking us all to gather together and remain on the beach. Otherwise, you could've ditched the phone somewhere, maybe even dropped it in the ocean while swimming. Instead, you had to stick it in the podium."

Ace threw his hands up in the air. "Everything you're saying is ridiculous, the product of an overactive imagination."

"Is that right? But I bet your fingerprints on the bag with the calculator won't be so imaginary."

"What could possibly be my motive?" he said. "I'm just an intern and wouldn't want to jeopardize my role."

"Well, this isn't your first time dealing with the company. You told me you went through rounds of interviews before."

Ace started pacing before the podium in agitation.

I continued, "But the unpaid internship only requires a simple online application and screening. You must've been burned before by the company—"

"Not the company." Ace's face turned a startling shade of red. "Dr. Gil Yoshida. He had it against me and deserved to die. I applied so many times in the past and always got blocked by him."

I exchanged a look with the police officers.

Ace scowled. "I had to settle for working at a hardware store."

"Is that how you got a hold of the materials for a pipe bomb?"

"And knew which deadly chemicals to mix together."

As he got handcuffed, Ace said, "Dr. Yoshida didn't think I was smart enough for his company, but I showed him in the end. I was brilliant enough to apply for the unpaid internship under a fake name and exact my revenge."

After the police took Ace away, I still had one more post on Sound Bitz to put up. It would be in legacy of Dr. Yoshida and a pat on the back to myself at the same time. I broadcasted a line from his last speech, which I thought also embodied my recent sleuthing win: "It's time for the bold."

THIRTEEN SECONDS

By Lawrence Kelter

1971

Burton County, Ohio—4:00 a.m.

A few quick sips of Folgers wasn't nearly enough octane to clear Sam's cobwebs. His vision was blurry, the whites of his eyes streaked with red veins. Even so, he sensed that something was wrong the moment he opened the doors to the vast commercial chicken house. The raucous birds had their own unique cadence, one that had greeted him practically every morning for eleven years. The narrow building, four football fields long, was packed with an ocean of white birds pecking and hopping—thirty-five thousand herky-jerky heads all moving at the same time. Too tired to think, he pressed a steel thermos to his lips and guzzled pure black adrenaline until the vessel had been drained, then put his eye to the opening, hoping he had a swallow left. Up at 3:15, a quick shower before flying out the door—no one gets used to those hours. His foreman told him the schedule would get easier with time—after eleven years he was damn sure it never would.

The wakey juice finally kicked in. Focusing past floating feathers, he noticed that some of the birds were forming a perimeter on the floor, pushing the other birds back. A few pushy hens spilled over the widening barricade, but essentially the floor within the margin was emptying around a body, covered in blood.

* * *

The bureau chopper was available, but I'd never gotten used to those flying death traps, and with a belly full of fast-food tacos...well sir, I didn't want to lose my lunch. It was a leisurely drive from FBI headquarters in Cleveland to the crime scene in Burton County—long enough to sip a fountain soda and allow those belly bombs to go quiet on their own.

Elton Matts, my supervisor, stepped outside his strait-laced bureau persona to brief me on the case. "We've got a dead duck in a hen house."

There's nothing funny about a murder but the notion of it...after all the shit we'd lived through since the Kent State shootings a year back...I don't mean to make light of a serious situation but the image. "Ha!" I mean, hell, that's funny.

Ohio is the third biggest chicken-producing state in the union. You can't drive from one point to another without getting stuck behind a tractor-trailer snowing chicken feathers out the back.

Local homicide and the county coroner had been unable to determine the cause of death. There were no bullet or stab wounds, no shell casings, just one big, baffling wound. The bureau was asked to send out a firearms examiner. Now we're caught up.

There was nothing but ice left in the big soda cup as I pulled up to the poultry farm, where several police vehicles were parked outside. Taking it in, the building seemed endless. I'd seen commercial poultry structures from the road but didn't have a true close-up perspective of how immense these structures were. I took one last drag on the straw and swallowed a mouthful of iced water before getting out of the car. A local detective approached me before I could slip on my jacket.

"Leila Barnes," she said. "You Ringer?"

"SA Morris Ringer." I hauled out my flip wallet and flashed my credentials

"How was your ride down here from the big city?"

I laughed on the inside. Only a local Ohioan would call Cleveland the big city. For a boy from Brooklyn, Cleveland was a flea on an elephant's ass. But that elephant's ass had been my home ever since losing my wife, Kate. The familiarity of Brooklyn was something I needed to put in the rearview mirror, the streets we walked, the places we'd break bread. "Clear shot all the way down 422."

"You FBI boys holding your own without J. Edgar looking over your shoulders?"

"What makes you think he's not?"

"Pushing up daisies, last I heard."

"*And...?*"

"*Ha.* What about his replacement, Gray? What with all the heat Tricky Dick's taking over the war—sure was smart, him filling Hoover's chair with one of his flunkies. No wiggle room for Nixon while Hoover's finger was on the trigger."

"No comment," I said, pure deadpan. Where I was from, the neighbor-hood women would call Detective Barnes a yenta, the Yiddish word for a busybody. "I hear you've got a corpse for me to look at. What's the story?"

"Picture's worth a thousand words, isn't it?"

"So, they say."

"Well then. Let's go."

I'm not phobic, but the idea of a chicken-filled monolith set off my alarm bells. Thoughts of a chicken avalanche reignited the taco bombs I was hauling around in my gut. "Do we need any safety gear?"

"Not no more," she said as I followed her inside.

"Why's that?"

There wasn't a chicken in sight. Save for police personnel, there wasn't a warm-blooded creature in sight.

"Not knowing the cause of death, FSIS got their panties in a bunch—con-demned every last hen in the damn building—the whole lot has got to be put down—Department of Agriculture rules—more than thirty thousand birds, don't you know."

"That's a shame."

"Gonna be some empty bellies around these parts."

My guts tightened into a knot as I made my way to the body. There was a gaping hole in his chest. What was left of a man was covered in blood. Most of the internal organs were missing or severely damaged. The ribs were gone except for a few fractured stumps. The spinal column had been ripped out in the lumbar region. What had once been a man was now a head, arms, and legs held together by shreds of flesh. Standing over the body, I could see right through the chest cavity down to the floor. "I'm glad you called us for assistance."

"The chief made me do it. Against my advice, I might add. I've got an exemplary case close record—damn proud of it, too." I had to hand it to her, she wasn't a kiss-ass.

"Okay, Miss Marple, show me what you've got."

"Say *what?*"

"What happened here, detective?"

She gave me the stink. "Something you want to say, Barnes?" I had a thick skin that had grown tougher after God took Kate, and I realized that a lifetime of living in earnest hadn't earned me any brownie points with the Almighty.

She backed down. "He wasn't murdered here. Killed off-site, dumped here. Should've been blood spatter every which way."

"What took out this guy's midsection?"

Her shoulders rose and fell. "Ain't that what *you're* supposed to tell *me?* You're the ballistics expert." She pushed a stick of gum into her mouth. I watched her chew, softening the gum between her molars, her jaw muscles bulging. "I don't know, artillery of some sort, maybe a rocket launcher. Isn't that what you're thinking?"

I didn't know what to think. "A projectile of some sort pierced the upper body—went clean through. I saw a fatality somewhat like this in the war."

"You served? Which war?"

"The big war, the war to end all wars. I saw a soldier smother a grenade to save his men. Brave guy. The blast tore a hole right through him. Most terrifying thing I ever saw. Have we IDd the victim yet?"

"No personal property on him. He's John Doe for now."

Tragic—a man loses his life and leaves the world without the dignity of his name. "You've got a team working on it, right?"

She nodded, then turned away and spit out her gum. "My daddy fought in the big one. He was a bombardier—miracle he came home in one piece with the Nazis taking potshots at him through the canopy of a B-17."

"Scary shit, Barnes. Your father is a hero."

"You betcha he is."

"How soon can we get the body to the morgue? I want it tested for trace metals left behind by the projectile. It's as good a starting point as any."

"We were waiting on you, boss. Just say the word."

* * *

The local hotel was an artifact. The floorboards creaked, and the lights flickered. The window-mounted air conditioner rumbled like a cement mixer. The mattress had a trench in the center, and it aggravated the bejesus out of my bum shoulder. A doc was trying to talk me into surgery, but I wasn't having it. I didn't like surgeons. One said he could save my wife.

I fixed a cup of tea before checking out of the Bates Motel. It was blacker than coffee and twice as bitter by the time I arrived at the ME's office.

Confession: I like coroners. Unlike Hollier than thou surgeons, they spare you all the bullshit about how they're the only ones who can save your life. By the time the ME puts his hands on you, it's game over. Nothing to crow about.

The doc was weighing the remnants of an organ. It looked like something you'd use to make a meatloaf. "Dr. Mule?" I asked. He looked up when I walked in, a bald head with two black caterpillars across his forehead. They rose above his wire-rim eyeglasses, looking like they were trying to make a break for it.

"Ah, Agent Ringer, I presume. You're early."

I winced and rolled a kink out of my neck. "Bad mattress."

"Hotel over on 59?"

I nodded.

His cheekbones rose. "Gets 'em every time. It's clean, though, and I'll take a mediocre night's sleep over bedbugs every time. I'll give you the name of a better place—just remodeled, cheaper too." His eyes settled on the cadaver, then shook his head. "Twenty years, and I've never seen anything like this."

"Spectrographic analysis of the residual tissue?"

"Samples went over to the state crime lab last night. They're kind of slow, but I called in a favor, and they're gonna bump Mr. Doe to the head of the line."

"The sooner, the better because I've got no idea what made this giant hole."

"It wasn't traditional ordnance, I can tell you that," Mule said. "There's no indication of char—no traces of ballistite or nitrocellulose high explosive, so we can rule out a bazooka or a rocket launcher. No gunpowder or cordite. The lab is looking for possible cross-contamination from hair, fiber, and such."

The phone rang. Mule picked it up on the first ring, "Morgue." The buzz of the fluorescent lights filled silence while he listened. "Yes, he's here. Just a minute."

He held out the phone, and I walked around the autopsy table to grab it. "This is Ringer."

"Ringer, I've got some good news and a shit load of bad. Can I assume you want to hear the good news first?"

"I'll take it any way it comes."

"John Doe's got a name," she said. "Abagail Maynard filed a missing person's report late last night. Her husband Leroy didn't come home after work Monday and ain't been seen since he clocked out. She came by the station with a wallet-size wedding photo. A call came in about a car sunk in Lake Milton. Sounds like it might be Leroy's Chevy. Pending Abagail making positive ID, I'd say Leroy Maynard is the man we found with the picture window in his chest."

"That a *hell* of a lot of bad news."

"Oh, darlin', that's not nearly the *bad* news."

Hairs rose on the back of my neck. "What?"

"Leroy Maynard was discharged from the Ohio National Guard."

"Discharged?" I asked timidly.

"Yessir, discharged—end of last year. Don't *that* just make your day?"

* * *

I was back in Cleveland two hours later, tapping my toes while I waited to be seen by Neil Viscer, the special agent in charge. He was known as "Mr. Big" around the office, not because of his rank but his stature. He was gargantuan with hands like an ape and a neck as thick as a steampipe. Tailored suits couldn't mask his hulking appearance. One and all knew he'd made his bones cracking heads in back alleys.

"He's off the phone. Go on in," his secretary said.

Oh, joy. One transfer to Anchorage, please.

Viscer held a Bob Feller autographed baseball in his hand. If Feller's hands had been as big as Viscer's, he would've thrown double his career twenty-six hundred strikeouts.

"That was Director Gray on the phone," he said. Gray, Hoover's replacement, was not only one of Nixon's closest cronies but his largest bleeding hemorrhoid. He tossed the baseball in the air and caught it before turning to me. "Ten days, Ringer."

It took a moment for the tumblers to fall into place—the first anniversary of the Kent State shootings was less than two weeks away. The blight had never been cured. It had merely gone to the ground, waiting for the worst possible time to resurface. What had transpired that day in 1970 should never have happened—M1 rifles fired into a crowd of student protestors. It was an act of unspeakable cowardice.

My Kate, she didn't like cowards.

The National Guard was still being tried in the courts. Americans were still pitted against Americans, people were bitter, the country was divided. One hundred fifty thousand troops were still deployed and fighting a war no one wanted. Nixon was less popular than the clap.

"T-minus ten and a Kent State national guardsman turns up dead in a hen house. *Goddamn.*"

Talk about having egg on your face. I bit my tongue.

"Nixon might as well pop on a red nose and take pies in the face. Do you have any idea what the papers will do with this?" He tossed the ball and snatched it out of the air once more. "Gray wants this squashed."

"Squashed? How exactly am I supposed to do that? I'm investigating a homicide."

"Take the case over from the locals. Control the flow of information. Keep it on the damn down-low."

"Sir, I can't just—"

"Find a loophole, Ringer. *Make* it a federal matter—whatever it takes." He squeezed the ball in his hairy monkey hand. Filled with carbon, he would've compressed it into a diamond. "Do you understand what I'm saying, Agent? Investigate. Put someone behind bars. Shut it down. Kill it. Bury it. That's what I want. Can you do that? Because if you can't..."

If I can't, what? Christ, the way he was glaring at me and digging his fingers into that ball—It felt like my hat was on too tight.

* * *

Mule's motel was better than the hay-stuffed mattress motel I'd slept at the day before. I hung a do-not-disturb sign on the doorknob, but it didn't stop Detective Barnes from pounding on my door thirty minutes after I'd settled in for the night. I half-expected it. Viscer was leaving nothing to chance.

"Just got a call from my CO. Why the hell am I off the case?" she asked, her face red, her eyes feral. I've never been pulled off an active investigation before, so tell me what the hell happened before I put my steel-toed boot up your ass."

The parking lot was empty except for a linen delivery truck. "Stop causing a scene," I said. Taking her by the wrist, I yanked her into my room. "Just calm down."

Part of me wished I could tell her, but Viscer's dictum was on a need-to-know basis, and Barnes didn't need to know shit.

"You get this invested in all your cases?" I asked. "You and Maynard blood relations or something?"

"Just doing my job the best I know how."

"Look, Barnes, I drove to Cleveland and back, checked in, and put my feet up. I've got no idea why you were pulled off the case."

"Horse shit?"

"Look, the Kent State disaster is just coming up on its first anniversary. Maynard was National Guard and had been on campus...well, draw your own conclusions." There was a thin line between outright spilling the beans and assuaging the truth. I figured I'd walked the tightrope the best I could.

Barnes rolled out a desk chair and plopped down. "My CO said the FBI is classifying the matter a hate crime and, as such, is a federal matter." She went quiet, averting her eyes. She slowly pulled her gaze off the carpet. "Any chance you'd speak to my CO, shove FBI cooperation down his throat? I'd like to stay close to the case if I could. I mean, seeing Leroy Maynard with his guts blown all to hell...makes one hell of an impression."

"No doubt." I got back on the tightwire. "Look, having a local onboard makes my job somewhat easier—as long as you're willing to play ball. You're not the gabby type, are you, the kind who blabs to reporters?"

"No, sir. I'd sooner smack one upside the head."

"I'll see what I can do."

"I'd appreciate it."

I filled a glass with tap water. "Tell me what I missed."

Her jaws must've swelled from all the venom pumping through her system because she spoke begrudgingly. "We pulled that Chevy out of the lake."

"And...?"

"It's his. Found his lunchbox on the backseat, and the VIN number matched DMV records."

"Any visible evidence?"

"Nah. Washed clean. No signs of blood. I figure they stun-gunned him or something before he got in."

"Canvassing for eyewitnesses?"

"Not so far." She turned away, embarrassed for her lack of results. "We're talking to everyone with a pulse."

I tried snapping off a yawn, but it was already out. "I'm exhausted, Barnes. Just give me the broad strokes?"

"Leroy Maynard wasn't a great guy—bad-tempered...kind of a prick."

"Bad-tempered enough for someone to blow a hole in his midsection? Does he owe money? Diddling someone's missus?"

"That's what I've got so far. You want *War and Peace*? It's gonna take a minute."

"Just hoping Maynard's execution had nothing to do with the campus shootings."

"Yeah," she said, rising from her chair. "No shit."

* * *

I slept like a log in the new motel and would've slept longer, but the phone rang before my alarm went off. It was my boss, Matts. "Ringer, *you* just getting out of bed?"

"I slept in a ravine the night before last night. Just trying to triage my shoulder back into shape."

"I guess you're not interested in catching the worm."

I turned my head so as not to yawn into the receiver. "Not strictly speaking, no. What's up?"

"Got my hands on Leroy Maynard's military jacket."

"Was the son of a bitch at Kent State?"

"Yes, unfortunately—M1 in hand. He wasn't one of the shooters, but he was part of the National Guard unit on Blanket Hill where it all went down."

"Guilty by association. He was there, and he had a gun—motive enough for a fanatic to take a life in these crazy times."

"That's what I'm thinking as well."

"Local PD says he wasn't exactly Mr. Rodgers. Makes him the perfect anniversary target for someone wanting to piss on Nixon's fire pump."

"Suspects?"

"Not yet, sir."

"How about narrowing down the murder weapon?"

"Give me a minute—I'll unpack my OUIJA Board."

"Tisk, tisk, tisk," he sighed. "Well, as long as you're slacking, I need you to head over to Wright-Patterson Air Force Base this afternoon. We received intel that war protestors are headed over there. The base is running tests on fighter planes, and with the Kent State anniversary on the horizon..."

My God, not this again—Nixon wants a muzzle on everyone. The Kent State volcano was about to blow—I could feel it. "Can't the locals handle it? I'm kind of busy over here."

"I know you are, but 'Mr. Big' wants bureau eyes on the demonstration, and you're the closest man we've got."

"Gee, don't I feel special." The line went dead.

* * *

I met Leila Barnes for breakfast at the local greasy spoon, a sty called Hog Hollow. She was in a booth next to a window with her face in a mug of joe.

I slid along the Naugahyde bench seat that was spiderwebbed with cracks. "Good morning. You might like to know that my day has already gone to shit—have to babysit a demonstration at the airbase instead of working the case."

"Airbase?" she asked as she chewed her food. "Not Wright-Patterson?" It looked as if something was stuck in her throat. She hacked a piece of bacon into her napkin and lubed her throat with coffee.

"Everything all right?"

"Bad piece of bacon."

"Never heard of such a thing."

"My husband works at the base. I passed him on the way in. He had the Hog Hollow Special before heading off to work."

"Sorry I missed him. What does Mr. Barnes do?"

"Aviation compliance," she muttered. "You could've glommed a ride off him if you weren't so fond of your beauty sleep." She snickered. "Say, want some company on the ride? Wright Patterson is pretty gosh darn big, and I know it like the back of my hand. Might get you back here sooner."

"I appreciate it, but you're needed here, working the case. What's this Hog Hollow Special you speak of anyway?"

"Enough chow to clog an aorta." She called the waitress. "Darla, one special for the gent. How you take your eggs, Ringer?"

"Over easy."

"Over easy—you heard him, sweetheart?"

Darla fashioned an A-Okay with her fingers before handing the order ticket to the cook. She struck me as diner-chic, tall with a narrow waist and a salon hairdo—she added a little class to the place, but it was like painting lipstick on a pig.

"She's a talker," Barnes said. "The beauty parlor gals know everyone's business. I'll chat her up at the end of her shift."

"You do that. I won't be back until evening. Any developments—you ring me up at the base and have someone drag me to the phone. We good?"

I could see the wheels in her head grind to a halt. Maybe those gears had run out of grease, or maybe kowtowing to a fed rubbed her the wrong way. Either way, she wasn't happy.

* * *

Darla's knees buckling on the way to the table should've been a dead giveaway. Driving to the base, that Hog Hollow Special felt like a medicine ball sitting in my gut.

The protestors carried picket signs and shouted through bullhorns, doing their utmost to be seen and heard, but outside the perimeter fence, they were harmless. Typical of the times—they were anti-war, anti-establishment, and, most notably, anti-Nixon. They called us pigs, warmongers, and fascists. Nothing I haven't heard before.

The installation commander sat back and let them spew for a while, then addressed them in person, listening to them attentively before serving milk and cookie rations. The gesture struck me as condescending, but the crowd soon dispersed. Not the man's first time at the rodeo, I guess.

I called Matts from a vacant office and left a salty message. "Done babysitting. Headed back for some honest work."

Mule tracked me down right after and reported that little of consequence was discovered on the spectrographic analysis of Maynard's tissues, no ferrous compounds, no trace of propellants, no lead. Microscopic bits of poultry flesh were embedded in the tissues surrounding the gaping hole in Maynard's chest. Not the news I was hoping for.

No need to top off the tank with mess hall chow before heading back. The Hog Hollow Special was still lying in my stomach during the long walk back to the parking field. I was on my way when I heard a blast coming from an open hangar, then men roaring within. It was an odd-sounding boom, very different from ordnance discharge. Another blast, air-charged, like some manner of giant paintball gun. Riotous laughter. The commotion drew me like a moth to a flame. Stopping dead in my tracks, lightning crackled across every brain synapse. It took moments for the electrostatic storm to subside and my mind to clear; behind it was the epiphany I'd been praying for since the moment I saw the gaping hole in Leroy Maynard's chest. Hot-footing it back to the office, I picked up the phone and barked at Matts's secretary, "Find him wherever he is and drag his ass to the phone."

* * *

Days later

FBI Director Gray placed his greasy hand on my shoulder at the press conference. I've no doubt his name is listed in the thesaurus as a synonym for chicanery, duplicity, and fraud. He was the kind of bureaucrat my Kate would've hated. I shrugged off his hand. He, nonetheless, remained alongside me with his smug, shit-eating grin for every press photo. He didn't say much, other than meaningless prattle. "You've done your country proud," and "You're a rising star." I was pushing fifty—prehistoric by bureau standards. Smart money was on the Goodbye and Good Luck Award.

Leila Barnes and her husband, Emerson, had been arrested and charged with Maynard's murder. That morning at the Hog Hollow, it was bacon that was stuck in her craw.

Their son, Gary, wasn't injured or killed by National Guardsmen at Kent State, but he was collateral damage all the same. Kent State shockwaves buried Gary Barnes in an avalanche of murdered students, angst, and hysteria. When therapy failed, he took a catastrophic turn for the worse. Succumbing to the lure of street drugs, his parents were bedside when the ER physician called the time of death.

His body was barely cold when Leroy Maynard was targeted and murdered. Witnesses testified that Maynard was responsible for fanning the flames of hysteria, inciting fellow guardsmen, and making them fear for their lives. Whipped into a frenzy, they fired into the crowd for thirteen devastating seconds, an act of utter spinelessness.

What I witnessed in the hangar at Wright-Patterson crystalized the murderer's MO. Aircraft with terrain-following radar used in the Vietnam War flew at high speeds no more than a few hundred feet off the ground. Pilots were encountering thousands of bird strikes each year, resulting in untold crashes and loss of life. The Air Force assigned the Aeronautical Systems Division at Wright-Patterson to address the bird impact hazard, where an engineer named Emerson Barnes developed the idea for (I kid you not) a chicken gun.

I now understood why Leila Barnes soft-pedaled her husband's position at the base, mumbling aviation compliance. Aviation compliance, my ass. He was the chief FAA liaison officer, a damn colonel.

What I witnessed at the airbase was a bunch of engineers preparing to conduct a routine test on the structural integrity of an F-111 fighter jet in which a compressed air cannon was loaded with a dead four-pound chicken and fired at a speed approximating four hundred miles per hour. I'd come across the test crew horsing around, firing chickens at the jet, hysterical at the sight of the birds streaking through the hangar and bouncing off the canopy.

Bureau forensics proved my theory by firing a four-pound supermarket chicken into a cadaver secured to a steel frame. For all practical purposes, the hole in the cadaver matched the hole in Leroy Maynard's chest. He was murdered with a compressed air chicken canon. No lead, gunpowder, or explosives were used, nothing more than a chicken and air.

We swept the hangar and found traces of Maynard's blood and bits of organ tissue on the hangar's concrete floor. Emerson Barnes's electronic access pass showed that he alone was in the hangar after hours at Maynard's approximate time of death. He was alive when that bird blew a hole through him, drawing breath until the moment of impact.

The idea of killing a man with a chicken gun was diabolical. Dumping the corpse in an immense chicken house...genius.

Director Gray reveled in his success during the press conference and throughout the catered luncheon that followed. Tying Leila and Emerson Barnes to the gruesome murder of a national guardsman gave Nixon's spin doctors all the ammunition they could possibly ask for. The story Washington once wanted buried was now being fed to every news agency on the planet.

A part of me wishes I hadn't seen those men horsing around with the chicken canon and that Leroy Maynard's homicide investigation had concluded in an entirely different manner. It took another three years, but Nixon finally got what was coming to him. The press called it Watergate but more than that, it was his Waterloo. I was retired when the story hit the papers. I have to say Tricky Dick's resignation eased my conscience more than a little.

And while the irony of a coward murdered by a chicken may elude some, it's one investigation this put-out-to-pasture agent will never forget.

* * *

NOTE

The poultry test is now part of a series of stress tests required by the FAA before a new jet engine design can be certified, Snopes.com reports. The test takes place in a concrete building, where the engine goes at full speed, and the cannon uses compressed air to shoot chicken carcasses into the turbine.

DARBY O'MALLEY AND THE BODY IN THE PINOT BLOCK

By Anne Louise Bannon

I sat overlooking the vineyard, the noon sun turning the leaves of the vines bright green, and I couldn't help thinking how good my life was. Then I saw the buzzards circling.

They looked like they were hovering above the block of pinot noir vines, so I got my Gator UTV going and headed that way. I wasn't too concerned. After all it wouldn't have been the first time some coyote or deer had gotten into the vineyard and given up the ghost. If I rushed it was because I knew my seventeen-year-old daughter, Betty Mae, was somewhere out in the vineyard. Stiffs, even a bird or a mouse, really freak her out and, of late, it's one of those rare occasions when her dear old father (*aka* me) is wanted.

My vineyard manager, Etian, and his assistant, Alonso, were also out there somewhere. I wondered if they'd seen the buzzards.

As I stopped at the end of a row in the middle of the block, I saw a brightly colored bit of fabric among the tan remains of that spring's weeds. I picked it up. It was one of Etian's face masks. Etian Valenzuela insisted on wearing wild prints instead of one of the Sonata Winery and Vineyards masks we'd made early in the pandemic.

The funny thing was, the mask smelled moldy, and Etian was allergic to molds. He was fond of saying that he could tell when we had powdery mildew on the vines without looking at them because his chronic congestion got even worse. Of course, his chronic congestion probably had more to do with the over-the-counter nasal spray he constantly used. He was hooked on it, never mind that he used it so often it didn't work like it should have. But he did also get congested around molds and mildew.

I looked down the row just in time to see a buzzard land next to a blue and tan dress shirt. I jammed the mask into my jeans back pocket and rushed down the row, shooing the bird away before it could do anything. Sure enough, Etian had fallen on his front. I rolled him over. His face was flushed, but there was no pulse, and his eyes were open and unseeing. I gagged.

Shaking, I ran back to the Gator and got on the radio. Mobile phone reception was practically nil out where we were on the northern edge of the Santa Ynez Valley. So, if we were anywhere that didn't have a landline, we needed the radio. Patricia Lopez, the tasting room manager, answered the radio and called 911.

"Where's Betty Mae?" I asked when Patricia got back on the radio. Frantically, I looked through the vines. "She's out here somewhere."

"On the vineyard perimeter doing laps. At least, that's what she said when she left an hour or so ago." Patricia's voice trembled. "Are you sure Etian is dead?"

"As sure as I can be." I gagged again as I glanced back down the row.

Patricia muttered something in Spanish, I wasn't sure what. My wife, Alicia, is Mexican. We'd been married nineteen years and were together for eight years before that, so you'd think I'd have picked up more Spanish.

I wondered again where Alonso Rubio was. He, Etian, and I were supposed to have a meeting in the vineyard that day. It was the usual debate—okay, fight—over canopy management, as in how we were going to deal with the leaves on the vines that year. Some leaves must be pulled so that the grapes can ripen, but if too many leaves are pulled, the grapes will burn in the California sun. Etian and Alonso seldom agreed on anything, let alone how to handle the canopy of leaves over the grapes. Worse, Etian had the annoying attitude that he was right and the rest of us were idiots.

I heard wheels rolling up the hill from the chardonnay block, about thirty rows down from where I was. Diane Freeling pulled up in the small electric van we use for carting people around. Diane's official title was winery associate, but we usually referred to her as the cellar rat. It's a generic term for someone who helps out doing whatever is needed. Diane had signed on the previous fall after her father's winery had gone out of business, thanks to buying a batch of smoke-tainted wine. He was hardly the only one to go under that year and we'd been close enough, ourselves.

"Where's Betty Mae?" I called as Diane pulled up.

"Right here, *Papí*." Betty Mae trotted up from the opposite direction. She has my tall and lanky build and near-sighted vision with her mother's black hair and rich brown eyes. Betty Mae wears contacts. I prefer glasses.

It was hot that day. Betty Mae had on neon-green bike shorts and a matching cropped exercise top, and her running shoes. Diane, a slender young woman, was wearing shorts, a tank top, and a Sonata baseball cap with her thick brown hair pulled through the back in a ponytail. We'd been in the high 90s the day before, and I was pretty sure we were already warmer than that. I was sweating and sucking down water as fast as I could. Betty Mae poured water over her head from the metal bottle she carried.

"Darby, what's going on?" Diane asked, stopping the little open-air vehicle.

"Looks like Etian died out here." I reached over to Betty Mae, who suddenly went ash-colored.

"Oh, my God!" Diane jumped out of the van.

As she took off running down the row, I got Betty Mae into my Gator and held her. We both trembled and sniffed.

"Oh, my God!" Diane gasped as she came back up the row.

She pulled her hands from her pockets and bit her thumb. The radio crackled with Patricia's voice. Help was on the way.

"Thanks, Patricia." I took a deep breath and tried to unknot my stomach. "Diane, take my Gator and Betty Mae. You need to get down to the main building as fast as you can so you can bring the emergency vehicles in. Betty Mae, you stay down there or go to the house."

"Yes, *Papí*." It was a testament to how rattled she was that she didn't complain. And I was too rattled to appreciate it.

The last thing I wanted to do was wait out there with Etian's mortal remains. Still, someone had to keep the buzzards away. I watched Diane driving the Gator off with Betty Mae next to her and thought I would never tease Betty Mae about her phobia again.

I put on some more sunscreen. I'm a redhead and fair and prone to sunburn. Let me tell you, putting on a shirt, tie, and tux jacket on top of a sunburnt neck, then ripping through the solo part of a Vivaldi concerto is quite the experience in pain.

* * *

My name is Darby O'Malley, and if you're a classical music geek, you may have heard of me. I'm a concert violinist. If you're a fan of classical music, you've probably heard of my wife, pianist Alicia Mendoza, known for her incredible interpretations of Rachmaninoff. Playing classical music professionally is how we keep the lights on at the house. We also own Sonata Winery and Vineyards, in northern Santa Barbara County, or as Alicia refers to it, the Hobby That Ate Our Lives. I'm the winemaker, and, yeah, it started out as a hobby. Alicia runs the business part of the venture. It was part of the deal we made with each other. As long as the winery pays for itself, we can keep making and selling wine.

The pandemic made 2020 a massive challenge for us. Admittedly, we've always assumed we could have a bad year and have built up reserves both on the music and winery side, which helped us through. But Alicia and I lost all our concert income because nobody was going to concerts. (It was also very strange being in the same place all the time. Normally, we're out of town every other week.) The winery took almost as big a hit financially. Between the tasting room being closed and restaurants not buying wine because they weren't selling any, we lost a lot of sales. Our wine club (people who have agreed to buy and have shipped a certain number of bottles a year) saved our backsides, and even grew a little. On the music side, album sales helped, especially when Alicia's recording with the L.A. Philharmonic of

Rachmaninoff, Piano Concerto No. 3 in D Minor, Opus 30, was released in November to lots of critical acclaim. It is some of her best work.

Late that spring of 2021, things were finally opening up. We had some concert dates scheduled for later that year. The winery business was still shaky because in 2018, we'd lost almost all the pinot noir from the block where Etian had been found. There had been a brush fire in the hills next to the block right before harvest and some of the grapes had picked up what's called smoke taint. It hadn't shown up until a year after we'd harvested it, and it had tainted everything from the block. Losing a whole year of our flagship wine, not to mention replacing all those barrels it had been in, was not going to make 2021 any easier. Losing Etian and finding his body was horrible enough. That it was such a critical time for the vineyards only added to the trauma.

* * *

The next few days after Etian died were awkward. Everyone at the winery was shook. I must confess, most of us didn't particularly like Etian, even though he was one of the best viticulturists in the business. He'd annoyed all of us with his superior attitude far too often. His death left us all with that sad shock that's normal when someone dies suddenly and an uncomfortable guilt that we weren't more grieved. We all tried to stay focused on the winery business, but our shock and guilt only made things feel worse.

"I feel really bad for him," Patricia told me that Thursday morning as we got ready to open the outside tasting room. "But I have to say, I'm kind of glad he's gone."

"Really?" I didn't want to say that I was glad, too.

I uncorked a bottle of 2017 pinot noir, hoping we'd get enough customers in to empty it.

"I wasn't going to say anything, but..." Patricia was in her mid-thirties, with dark hair cut short and a spectacular collection of body art. "He was getting creepy. Kept staring at me."

"You, too?" Alicia asked, coming out from the offices.

In addition to being an incredibly passionate and versatile pianist, my wife is smart as a whip. Her long, straight, black hair was just getting threads of gray, and she'd added some padding to her figure since we first made a splash as classical music's hot, young couple just over twenty years ago. People are sometimes surprised to see that she's actually of average height, but that's because she looks shorter when we're photographed together.

"Casey was saying the same thing," Alicia continued. Casey Wold is the events manager and publicist for the winery. "She wasn't sure what to do about it because it wasn't really anything actionable."

"Thanks be for that," I grumbled, picking at the callous on my left forefinger.

Betty Mae sauntered into the outside tasting room, a shaded deck with tables and chairs spread out for social distancing, and the bar where we were.

"Are you talking about Etian?" she asked.

"What else?" her mother asked.

She sighed. "It's sad that he's gone, and I learned a lot from him." Betty Mae has a bent toward growing things that Alicia and I do not have, which is why I needed the best viticulturist I could find. She made a face. "But…"

My gut squeezed. "What did he do, *mija?*"

"Nothing, *Papí.*" Her face scrunched up again. "He just stared at me."

"Darby?" Alonso Rubio wandered up from the chardonnay block off the deck. The short, dark-haired man in his early fifties had graying temples and piercing black eyes. He doubled as assistant winemaker and assistant vineyard manager, but it was no secret that he'd wanted Etian's job. "We need to talk about leaf pulling."

"I know." I grimaced, wishing we could have taken off a month or so to get over Etian's death.

But we needed sales and customers. I opened a 2018 cabernet sauvignon, then the two premium blends and glanced at the clock under the bar.

"Betty Mae, time for you to take off," I told my daughter.

"What? We're not open yet."

"We will be in a minute," Alicia said. "And we do not want to risk our license because you're underage and we're serving."

"Like I've never drunk wine," she grumbled.

"Don't you have a math test or something to work on?" I asked her.

Betty Mae has been going to school virtually, like everyone else, even though her school in Los Angeles had partially re-opened the month before. Before the pandemic, she lived during the week with my aunt and uncle in L.A. and went to school there. I'd done the same when I was a teen, as had my sibs. Mom swears that's how she survived our adolescences. When the pandemic closed everything down, Betty Mae came home, and it had been, um, interesting.

Once again, Betty Mae's eyes rolled like the reels on a slot machine. "Dad! We're done for the summer. Remember?"

Odd how I was *Papí* except when she was annoyed with me. Which was often. Then I was Dad.

She huffed as she left, but she did leave. Alicia grabbed Patricia and Alonso to help with the current wine club shipment. I went to the front of the tasting room to put out the sign directing customers around to the back deck. Diane pulled up in the little van. She'd been out opening the gate to the main road and hanging out the open sign there.

"Hey, Diane." I adjusted another sign pointing to the deck. "Why don't you go help Alicia with the wine club shipment?"

"Sure."

As she went to the back offices and warehouse, I pulled up my face mask and hurried back to the deck, hoping the heat wouldn't keep people away.

I don't know if it was the heat or that it was Thursday, but we did not do a lot of business that morning. The second group to come in was just finishing up when Sheriff's Investigators Doug Lombard and Francisco Esposito wandered across the deck, their black masks in place.

"Hey, guys," I said happily to them with a wave, then turned to the two women and one man who were pushing their glasses away. "Can I get you folks anything else?"

They shook their heads, and I quickly rang up their tasting fees.

Alicia came out to the bar from the offices wearing her green Sonata mask.

That Francisco and Doug were dressed in suits and in the tasting room just after 12:30 in the afternoon wasn't so remarkable. We were friends, after all, and being Sheriff's Department Investigators, they were prone to working odd hours. They'd sometimes drop by for a glass of wine and lunch after ending an early shift. But that day, they had a stern cast to their eyes that told Alicia and me that they were still on duty. Francisco was a tall man with graying temples, otherwise dark hair, and a long face. Doug was shorter and younger than Francisco, with brown hair and eyes.

"What's up?" I asked, fidgeting with my mask again.

They glanced at each other.

"Uh, we need to talk to the two of you separately," Francisco said. He nodded me to the back edge of the deck while Doug stayed at the bar with Alicia.

"What do you know about Etian Valenzuela's heart condition?" Francisco asked as we sat down at the far table.

"I didn't know he had one." I looked at Francisco, not sure what to make of his question. "All I knew about was his mold allergy. The guy snorted nasal spray like he was an addict. But I guess he did have something wrong with his heart." I tried to puzzle it out. "It was a heart attack, wasn't it?"

"Not really." Francisco sighed. "Do you know where his spray went? It wasn't on him or in the vineyard."

"Huh. He was never without it, and he had the squeeze bottles every-where." Something stirred in my memory. I'd found one mask, but it wasn't necessarily the one he'd been wearing. "Did you find his mask?"

"Not that, either."

"Well, if the coroner's not sure what killed him, I've got something that may help." I got up, still certain that Etian's death had been from a natural cause.

"Hold on, Darby." Francisco sighed. "We know what killed Etian and we have reason to believe that he was murdered."

"What? How?" My eyes widened. "You're asking about the nasal spray. There was something in it, wasn't there?"

Francisco glared briefly at me. "What do you know about forty barrels of bad pinot noir that Etian sold?"

I thought about it. "Forty? That doesn't sound good."

Francisco watched me carefully. "Why not?"

"We lost forty barrels of smoke-tainted pinot last year. I told Etian and Alonso to pour it out and told Etian to send the barrels to Delia Pinchot. You know how she likes making furniture out of them."

Delia not only made gorgeous furniture, she donated a hefty chunk of the proceeds to various charities in the area.

"Did you see them do it?"

"No." I shook my head and tried to remember back the year before. "I think that was the afternoon Alicia and I did the four Beethoven sonatas for violin and piano on Zoom. It was the first one we were able to sell tickets for." I swallowed. "Are you saying that Etian sold it instead? Damn. I trusted him."

I had to. Up until the pandemic, Alicia and I were only home every other week or so. I slid my glasses off my face and kept polishing them.

Francisco shook his head and wrote something down. "What about him getting fresh with your kid?"

I squinted at him. "Yeah, she told us about that this morning, only she said he just looked at her."

Francisco sighed. "Are you sure about that?"

"Betty Mae?" I snorted and put my glasses back on. "If he'd tried anything else, she'd have taken him down."

Not only do we tend toward strong women in my family, all of us, male and female, have good self-defense skills.

"True." Francisco laughed softly.

"Francisco, what's going on? If Etian was murdered, and you're asking about his nasal spray and a heart condition, does this mean someone put something in the spray? Maybe nitroglycerin?"

Francisco cleared his throat and looked at me.

I gaped. "You mean, I was right?"

"That doesn't make you look too good, Darby."

"Oh, for crying out loud." I shook my head. "I was guessing. My cousin's a chemist and our grandfather used the nitro spray the last few years he was alive. You know I didn't kill Etian. I have no reason to."

"He was ogling your daughter and he sold a bunch of bad wine out from under you."

"Both of which I could have simply fired him for. And I still needed him for canopy management on the vines. Trust me, we can't afford any more losses around here." I got up. "Besides, I've got something you really, really need to see. Come on."

Alicia stayed in the outside tasting room, although Doug was already in the warehouse, presumably questioning the others. I took Francisco back to my office and shut the door. I hadn't realized it until the day after Etian died, but I'd left the mask I'd found in my jeans pocket. Somehow, it had landed on my cluttered desk.

"Here." I handed it to Francisco. "I found it at the end of the row where I found Etian."

"You removed it from the crime scene." Francisco shook his head.

"I didn't know it was a crime scene until you told me Etian was murdered. Smell it."

He sniffed, then pulled his mask off his nose and sniffed again. "That smells like mold."

"Etian's allergy. He was always complaining about it. When you first asked about the mask, I thought he might have had anaphylactic shock. But if somebody wanted him to use a tainted bottle of nasal spray, putting mold in his mask would make sure he did."

Francisco shot me a glare. "It would." He swore under his breath.

"And I think I know some people who might have a motive." I looked at the closed door. "They're in the warehouse now."

"So, who do I question?"

I thought about it. "I'm not one-hundred-percent sure and I don't want to get anybody in trouble. Can we talk to them all at once?"

Francisco shrugged. "It's not exactly procedure, but I suppose we could. I think Doug already is."

We left the office and went into the warehouse. As Francisco and I had thought, Doug had everyone gathered in a ring near the door to the deck. Alicia hung in the doorway, keeping an eye out for customers.

"All I heard about was the tainted wine that he'd sold," Diane was saying. "But none of us had any idea about the grapes."

Patricia winced nervously. "I mean, I'd sometimes wonder when someone who wasn't on the contract list would show up during harvest, asking for their grapes. But Etian would just say that he'd forgotten to put that contract on the list."

I frowned. "How often did that happen?"

"Last three harvests, about two or three times." Patricia shrugged. "Then there were the two contracts that we had to turn down because of the fire next to the pinot block. We barely had enough grapes for ourselves."

I looked over at Doug. "What happened?"

"Etian was underselling your grapes," Doug said. "His girlfriend told us when she said that Etian didn't have a heart condition and wouldn't have been using nitroglycerin spray. Then he'd sell the rest of them, himself, and cut you out of it."

"What?" I yelped. I looked over at Alicia. "I trusted him."

All of the wine we make and sell comes from grapes that we grow. But we grow a lot more fruit than we can use, so we sell it to other small producers, and sometimes some big ones who need extra.

Alicia shrugged. She'd had no idea what Etian had been up to, either. I looked over at Alonso.

He fidgeted then looked away. "I didn't know."

"Did you help him pour out those forty barrels of tainted pinot?" I asked, swallowing back against the ice in my gut.

Alonso's eyes grew wide. "He said he'd take care of it and he did. At least, I thought he did."

I looked at him, wondering.

"Looks like you've got a motive," Diane said, her arms folded across her chest.

"Maybe. Patricia." I turned to her. "Why didn't you say anything about the contracts?"

135

Patricia gulped. "Um. I should have. Um." She shuddered. "Okay. Etian threatened me. He'd caught me not checking some IDs in the tasting room and was going to tell you if I didn't keep the contracts to myself. Then he got mean, and I was afraid."

Francisco and Doug looked at each other, apparently not sure what to make of what they were seeing and hearing.

Alonso cursed under his breath. I looked at him, then Diane.

"But the thing is," I said slowly. "Etian's nasal spray was missing when he was found. There were four people that I know were in the vineyard that day."

"I was in the tasting room doing inventory," Patricia said.

"I know," I said. "You called 911. You couldn't have done that if you were in the vineyard. But I was one of those four people. Betty Mae was there, and Diane was. She came by in the van just after I radioed Patricia. And Alonso was out there. Right, Diane?"

She gulped. "Yeah. I'd taken him over to the cab sauv block."

The block of cabernet sauvignon vines is right next to the block of pinot noir, and well within walking distance.

"Which means, Alonso, you could have been right there to take the nasal spray," I said. "All you had to do was walk the rows, wait for Etian to keel over, take the bottle and hurry away before I got there."

"But I didn't!" Alonso gasped. "Besides, I had no reason to kill Etian."

"Are you sure he wasn't forcing you to cover for him?" I asked.

"Are you kidding?" Alonso snorted as he fidgeted. "He didn't want me anywhere near his shady deals."

"But you knew about them," I said. "And you lied just now when you said you didn't."

"I didn't know." Alonso shook his head. "Not for certain. I was just trying to get some proof before telling you, so you'd fire his backside."

"Which is why I don't have a motive for killing Etian," I said. "I could have ruined Etian by telling everyone what he was up to." I paused. "Once I knew about it." I looked at the little group surrounding me. "But there is one other person who had good reason to hate Etian and who was with the body right before she left to lead the emergency team to the pinot block."

"I didn't do anything!" Diane yelped.

"You went running down the row the second I told you about Etian," I said. "And when you came back up the row, you were pulling your hands out of your pockets."

"So?" Diane swallowed. "I didn't have any reason to kill Etian. I didn't like him, but I didn't have a reason to kill him."

"Except that you knew that he'd been selling tainted wine and even Alonso didn't know about it." I walked up to her. "Your father's winery went out of business last year, too. I'd heard that he'd gotten nailed by some smoke-tainted wine."

She gasped when she saw Francisco and Doug moving toward her, then bolted toward the back of the warehouse. We ran after her, but she'd disappeared into the barrel room.

"Any back exits?" Francisco asked.

"No," I gasped, then looked up. "But there is one top exit."

At the far end of the darkened, cool room, just above the twelve rows of barrels, there was a ladder on the wall that led to the roof. The hatch let blistering sunlight inside. Francisco and Doug scrambled outside, while I ran to the front of the inside tasting room. I saw Diane heading for the parking lot as I left the doorway. Fortunately, Doug saw her, too, and caught her in a flying tackle before she got to her car.

Francisco later told me that she'd called her father's pharmacist to get a couple extra bottles of nitroglycerin spray, claiming that her father had lost the ones he'd had. Then the search warrant pulled up several Google searches on her home laptop on the effects of nitroglycerin overdose. As part of the plea bargain, she confessed to trying to hurt Etian, not necessarily kill him. It's hard to say whether that was true, but she's doing time now, so I suppose it doesn't matter.

* * *

A week after the arrest, I watched as Betty Mae and Alonso argued about the long-range weather forecasts and whether they should pull more or fewer leaves. I'd made Alonso the vineyard manager, but I think he got that it's only going to be for the next five or so years, assuming Betty Mae follows through on going to U.C. Davis for viticulture. The odds are pretty good, if I know my kid.

Yes, the pandemic was a pretty bad shadow in my life. So was finding out that a trusted employee had been cheating me blind. Life is full of shadows, but Alicia and I have survived. As I watched my daughter and Alonso start pulling leaves from the pinot noir vines, and saw the full, green clusters of berries underneath, I was grateful. I have a good life. Even when the buzzards are circling.

ANY TIME THE HUNTER

By Zara Altair

Grass Roots

Detective Jane Sharpe leaned over the coagulated blood on the victim's throat. She pushed back a strand of dark hair escaping from her ponytail. The early morning September sun hit the back of her neck full force. Bits of dry grass stuck to the victim's neck, and a wasp's delicate legs picked through the clots. She heard a worker up in the vineyard singing in Spanish.

The dead man was short, maybe 5'7" and rotund. Early forties. Brown hair trimmed short, high-priced running shoes, jeans, t-shirt. No jewelry. No distinguishing marks she could see. A Mr. Ordinary. Except most ordinary people weren't lying dead in the grass in a vineyard on a mountainside. She'd have to wait for the Coroner's report for more details.

She stood up and looked around, adjusting the Sonoma County Sheriff windbreaker she'd grabbed for the early morning call. Above the body, the hill went up to rows of grapes. But here, only dry grass under the oak trees, a large warehouse building with six sliding doors, and the old farmhouse divided into rental units. She saw one up and two down in back and had seen the front with the lawn and stone wall in front when she entered. Behind her, the road. Beyond that, the creek and dense riparian woods. Up the road, more structures, oak trees, and a path up the mountain. A miniature paradise. All of that, but nothing that showed her where the man had died. The body was like a big cat's kill that was dropped when the animal was startled.

"You called the coroner?" she asked a deputy.

"Yes, coming," he answered. "You got here first."

"Okay." She pulled her phone out and requested assistance from two more deputies. "We need witness interviews," she said into the phone.

Then she turned to the deputy. "Who found the body?"

The deputy pointed to a man in his thirties, plaid shirt, blue jeans, standing just behind the crime scene tape. The hilltop vineyard served as a backdrop to the old house, neighboring oak trees, and the gathering group of hill dwellers. "William Hunter," the deputy said.

Jane nodded. "Move the crime scene out. Extend the tape beyond that warehouse." Then she turned to Hunter.

He was big, had an outdoorsy look. The plaid shirt and jeans weren't just an affectation. In his mid-thirties, he looked fit and imposing. Up close, he towered over Jane's 5'8" frame.

"Detective Jane Sharpe," she said, pressing record on her voice recorder and taking out her notebook.

He said, "Bill Hunter."

"Tell me how you found him."

"I was taking out my target," he said, pointing to a foam buck archery target resting on its antlers, feet up in the air, by the house. "I come out in the morning to practice."

Workers on the hill whistled back and forth—some kind of signal.

"You live in that bottom unit?"

"Yep, that's me. Been here seven years."

"You knew the deceased?"

"Jim. Yeah. He's been here longer than I have."

"Jim?"

"Yeah, Jim Norton, Private Investigator."

Jane wrote PI in her notebook. Can of worms.

"He lived in the front. Got his office set up in there. Mostly it was online stuff, you know. Background, finding people. He helped me many times."

"What do you do, Mr. Hunter?"

"Bill. Call me Bill."

"Okay, Bill. What do you do? Why did you need a private investigator 'many times'?"

"I'm The Hunter. Look me up online. Bounty stuff, you know. Finding people and bringing them in. Mostly bail skips."

God help her, a private investigator and a bounty hunter. This was going to be one for the books. In her six years in Violent Crimes, this was a first.

"Know anyone who'd want to hurt him?"

"I didn't know his business, you know. Just used him. No idea who his other clients were."

"Were you buddies? Go drinking together? Poker games? Anything like that?"

"Nope. Strictly business. Most people here," he waved an arm to encompass the hill, the buildings, the road, "keep to themselves. That's why we live here. People either come for a couple of months, hate it here, and leave, or they stay a long time. We take care of each other but don't hang out together."

"Take care of each other?"

"You know, share food, keep out the trespassers. Jim was good at that, seeing as he lived in front."

"I saw the No Trespassing signs."

"Yeah, well, those blond environmentalists, they sneak through the gate, bring their dogs...."

"I saw the No Dogs sign, too."

"Yep, quiet and calm here. Private. Anyway, Jim said he visualized a copy of the Constitution and a shotgun as he approached and then asked them if they spoke English."

"Spoke English. I don't get it."

"Yep, tripped up those trespassers, too. They'd answer yes, and then Jim would ask them what part of No Trespassing they didn't understand."

"So Jim wasn't afraid of a confrontation?"

"With those wishy-washy, self-important yuppies? You've got to be kidding. If they didn't leave then, he asked them if it would be okay for him to come picnic in their front yard. That was usually the end of it."

"But no big confrontations?"

"Nope. Not that I ever saw. He was usually glued to that computer. He worked for Josh Overbrook. You know him?"

"We've met in court." The county's famous or infamous criminal attorney described Josh Overbrook, depending on who was talking.

"Notice anything different with Jim lately?"

Hunter thought for a moment. "Nope...but he said he was working on a big case."

"Anything about that case?"

"No. Jim didn't talk about his cases. Didn't I say that already?"

"You did."

It was Jane's turn to sweep her arm in a circle. "Everyone here like him? Anyone here that had a beef?"

"Nah. Jim was a quiet guy. Like I said, he was glued to that computer."

"Any buddies? Friends that came over?"

"Well, his girlfriend."

"Know her name?"

"Cindy...Kandy...Kendra. That's it. Kendra. Don't know her last name. Sweet gal, from what I could tell."

"You've been a big help. If you think of anything else." She handed him her card.

Jane heard a motor burble, and then the iron gates between the big stone pillars hummed open. Then a deputy was shouting, and someone shouted back. A Harley Pan America special purred up to the crime scene tape.

The rider hopped off and removed his helmet. Buzzcut towhead blond, not too tall, forty-ish, and a swagger. "You the detective?"

"Detective Jane Sharpe," Jane said. She didn't say asshole out loud. But Hunter did as he scooped up his archery buck and went inside. She was certain she was about to meet the worm in paradise.

"You can't block off the road. I have a business to run here."

Jane walked over as he started unzipping his jacket. It was red, white, and blue with black protection areas and an amazing number of zippers. A deputy held up the tape, and she ducked under.

Cologne. He was smothered in cologne underneath that flashy jacket. He wore a long-sleeved navy shirt with a small white pattern. When she looked closely, they were Daleks. A shirt sprinkled with Daleks, tailored to skim his body.

"Detective Jane Sharpe," she said.

"I'm Kyle Woods. I own this property. This is my vineyard, and these are my rental units." He tilted his head, pursing his lips somewhere between disapproval and a sneer.

"Mr. Woods, this is a suspicious death. We need to secure the area. There will be a lot of people here soon."

As if on cue, the coroner's van and the crime techs arrived at the same time.

Woods looked at the deputy extending the tape around the warehouse.

"Wait. Stop. You can't block that off. I have my equipment in there."

"Mr. Woods, this is a crime scene. You'll have to wait. Your tenant, Jim Norton, had his throat cut. Taking care of that incident is the first priority here."

"Jim Norton," Woods said. "He's dead?"

"Yes, he is. We'll be searching his premises, but more importantly, this entire area. Let us do our job."

She waited for him to acquiesce, then asked.

"How well did you know Norton?"

"I didn't. I mean, I said hello. He paid his rent. Never a problem. We didn't socialize."

She pulled out a card and handed it to him. "It's best if you leave and let us do our work. If you think of anything, anything at all about Mr. Norton, get in touch."

Woods made a production about getting his cycling jacket back on, zipping in all the appropriate places. Then he rode back down through the big gate, his jacket flashing red, white, and blue under the trees.

The coroner carried his bag toward the body.

"Jane," he said, raising an eyebrow.

"I didn't touch, just looked."

* * *

Knife Skills

Kendra Sansome talked while she peeled lemons in her kitchen. "Jim was quiet, but he was fun." She used her knife to cut thin strips of lemon peel. The kitchen was clean, filled with pots and pans and tools Jane didn't recognize. Kendra was a private chef. She'd told Jane she had a dinner party that night.

"He liked learning new things," Kendra said. "He was always showing me some new discovery he'd made. Neuroscience or breeding orchids. It didn't matter. He loved information."

"That was fun?"

"He always had some wry comment about whatever it was he'd discovered. Once he'd cooled down from the new enthusiasm, he wanted to be outside. I don't mean hiking rugged mountains or camping. Just being outdoors. Walking in nature. Just *being* there. He knew all the birds wherever we went."

She put down the knife, gathered up the strips of lemon peel, and placed them in a plastic bag.

Jane's morning had been filled with tasks. Writing the search warrant. Getting the judge to sign. Going back to the mountain and supervising the techs as they searched Jim Norton's two-bedroom apartment. It hadn't taken long for the tech to find Kendra Sansome's contact details on Norton's computer and on his phone once they had them back at the substation.

Kendra lived on the valley floor. She wasn't next-of-kin, so Jane had to deliver the news herself. Kendra was silent, burst into tears, sobbed for a few minutes, and then said she would help however she could. She was mid-thirties, efficient. Her blond hair was pulled up in a knot on top of her head, and freckles dotted her nose.

Kendra started working on a yellow pepper, pulling out the seeds, scraping the inside clean, then cutting thin strips. She looked at the clock. "My assistants will be here in thirty minutes. What do you need to know?"

"Whatever you can tell me about Jim, especially anyone that might hold a grudge or want to harm him."

"Jim and I...it wasn't love. We were friends. We both liked jazz and went to live events, sometimes at wineries, sometimes at clubs. He liked to help me with the garden. I was up at his place a few times. It's peaceful up there. I met his neighbors. That hunter guy, what a piece of work. The Indian. Oops, I mean Native American. He had nothing good to say about North Dakota. That girl, Bonnie, the one who does tile work."

Jane hadn't met those last two. Another detective had interviewed them.

"Did Jim get along with them?"

"Everyone up there...they were private. No group parties or anything like that. People were friendly but kept to themselves. There wasn't enough social interaction to create friction. He never mentioned any problems. Even though they lived close together, it was as if each one had a nest and defended it from intruders."

"What about his work?"

Kendra scooped up the yellow pepper strips and put them in a plastic bag.

"He didn't talk about his work except in vague terms. A big case. Too busy to spend time together. An annoying client. But details? No. The thing about his work is that most people he was investigating had no idea he was snooping around in their lives. It was all records. Financial transactions. Stuff like that. It was nothing like TV. You know, those flashy private investigators." She stopped chopping a red pepper and looked at Jane. "I'm sure you have the same response in your job. Am I right?"

"Nothing like."

"Yeah, so there was no following people down dark allies or car chases. Jim was a nerd. A nice nerd, but a nerd. He actually hired other people for that watching stuff. What do you call it?"

"Surveillance."

"Yeah, surveillance. Sometimes when he worked for attorneys, he needed to know who someone spent time with. What do you call that?"

"Known associates?"

"Yes, that's it. But details, who people were, his clients, I didn't know names. But nobody knew. How could they be angry enough to kill? It doesn't make sense." She put down her knife. "It doesn't make sense at all. Jim was kind. Genuinely kind. He actually helped old people across the street. Complete strangers. If he saw someone who needed help, he helped."

Jane saw tears welling.

"Kendra, I'm sorry. I think that's enough for now." She handed over her card. Kendra stuffed it in an apron pocket.

* * *

Back at her desk in Santa Rosa, Jane went into catchup mode, organizing information. She read witness interviews from other residents on the property. She filled in the Crime Report, logging victim information, witness information, a summary of witness statements, and a synopsis of the crime. She logged the search warrant for Norton's home and the structures near the location of the body.

She was still waiting for forensic results of the crime scene and the coroner's report.

All this was putting together information, but she still had no suspects.

Her phone beeped. The dispatch operator.

"This call was for Blakesley, but he's out on a gang fight investigation. You're in charge, so I'm connecting him to you."

She waited for the click.

"Detective Jane Sharpe."

"You're searching in the wrong place," a male voice said.

"Who is calling?"

"Dave Longview. I live up at the Woods vineyard. I talked to a detective yesterday. I found something."

* * *

146

Lion's Trail

By the time she was back on the hill, the vineyard workers were gone, and the crime scene techs were packing up for the day.

Longview was waiting for her just inside the big iron gate. He was forty or so, with black hair, dressed in the standard t-shirt, jeans, and dark cowboy boots, and a hunting knife strapped to his belt. People up here had nothing in common with the upscale bedroom community in the valley.

Jane parked and got out of the car. "Detective Jane Sharpe. Are you Dave Longview?"

He nodded his head, then gestured up the hill. "Up there," he said, glancing at her boots. They weren't her regulation Magnums but lightweight boots coming up over her ankles, good for hiking the rough hills.

"Tell me," Jane said as they hiked up the hill between rows of grapevines.

"I come up to the top to watch the sunrise some mornings. Jim did that, too. Sometimes I'd see him up here. We didn't talk much, just watched the sun come up over the next ridge."

"You said you found something?"

"Yes, this morning. It's quiet up here before the vineyard workers get here. After the sun came up, I was walking back down the side over there," he gestured to a tall wire fence separating the property from a hillside estate. "And I noticed scuff marks in the dirt. I'll show you."

They trod up the hill in silence until they reached the top. She looked out over a valley toward another ridge. Below her, hillside estates dotted the slopes underneath the trees. Grapevine rows surrounded them.

"Over here," Longview said, gesturing toward the fence separating the vineyard from a neighboring estate.

They walked a row between the vines toward the property edge. Little puffs of dust flew up from their feet as they went. Jane felt the heat of the day rising from the earth. They reached the end of the vineyard row. Along the fence line, a trail of bare earth led down the hill back toward the entrance gate.

"I grew up tracking," Longview said. "That's why I noticed."

"What did you notice?"

"Two things. First, come over here." He led her to a spot in the trail. "See the footprints? They make a pattern that isn't uniform. So that caught my attention. And then, here," he stepped closer to the fence where shrubbery from the estate poked branches through the fence. He squatted down.

The dust clumped together in dark patches. "That's blood."

Longview stood up. "And see this."

Jane struggled to see where he was pointing. Dirt, dust.

"Drag marks."

Jane started to move closer.

"Don't," Longview advised. "Leave it for your crime team. This is where Jim was killed. Then someone tried to drag him down the hill."

Jane pulled out her phone and called the crime scene unit. "We've been looking in the wrong place," she said. She gave directions.

"Thank you," Jane said to Longview.

"There's more."

"What?"

"There's a reason Jim's body was left down there. Come over here."

He led her up the side trail a little way.

"See that?"

Jane did see it. A big paw print in the dust.

"Mountain lion." He waved toward the next hill. The side was covered with vineyard rows, but up above, California native scrubland persisted. "Usually, it's up on that hill. There's a rock outcropping. That's his home. But he patrols. He's been here since before the vineyard." He sighed. After a moment, he said, "This place was very beautiful before Woods decided he needed to join all the others growing grapes. He cleared everything."

He paused for a moment, lost in thought. Jane couldn't read his face. She looked down at the paw print. Further down the trail, she saw the coagulated dirt under the bushes.

Longview broke out of his reverie. "I'll show you the lion's trail. See there?" He pointed a few feet away. Jane looked where he pointed. She couldn't see anything except dirt.

She shook her head. "I don't see it."

"Just one toe print. The rest of the paw print is covered in dust. But you can follow the lion's trail down the hill."

And they did. Longview pointed out each paw print as they went down the hill.

"The lion went parallel to the drag trail. I think he was curious. You can see from the prints he wasn't in a hurry, didn't get ready to pounce. He just wanted to see what was going on."

Jane couldn't see all that from the faint marks in the dirt, but she listened.

They followed the trail of prints until they were about forty feet from where Norton's body was found.

"The lion stops here," Longview said. He pointed down at the ground.

Jane couldn't tell the difference, except the paw prints seemed closer together.

"I'll bet you that's when whoever killed Jim saw the lion. He dropped the body and left. Lions are unpredictable."

"We need to change the crime scene parameters," Jane said.

"Don't move," Longview said and grabbed her shoulders.

Jane heard the dry sound and looked down. Three feet away, a rattlesnake was curling into a spiral. Before she could think, the snake extended with speed she could hardly see and struck at her ankle, hitting the top of her boot.

"Move like hell," Longview said.

They were down the hill before Jane could look at her ankle. There, in the padding at the top of her boot, two small punctures dented the smooth leather. Her heart raced. No, it was pounding. Her hands shook.

"You were lucky," Longview said.

Jane nodded, unable to speak. All her life in California, this was her first encounter with a rattlesnake. It had missed her skin by millimeters.

"People think it's idyllic up here," he continued, "but life is real. The snakes like the lingering warmth in the evening." He looked at her trembling hands. "Your killer probably had the same reaction when he saw the mountain lion."

Her heart was slowing down. She took in a deep breath, let it out, and had a thought. How did the killer get past the iron gate?

* * *

Hornet's Nest

Evidence is data, and Jane collected it all. For the next two days, Jane filled the murder book with bits that came in. The crime scene team had scoured the hillside where Longview had led her to the murder scene. The blood in the earth belonged to Norton. Deep in a clump of poison oak, they found the murder weapon, a curved knife for harvesting grapes. She was waiting for fingerprint analysis.

Her phone buzzed.

"Detective Sharpe, it's Mike in Forensic IT. I have something for you to see."

Down the hall, the IT room was silent, glowing with computer screens. An enormous redhead who looked like he practiced the caber toss on weekends rose from behind a bank of screens.

"Over here," he said, reaching behind to roll over a chair so Jane could sit next to him.

"Your victim was organized. His files are organized around clients, and under those, separate cases. And they are arranged by year." He pointed to the screen. "Here are all the cases for Josh Overbrook." He clicked on a file. "You can see how he could retrieve information quickly." He clicked back. "And all these other cases, some of them are repeats for others. But this is what I wanted to show you." He moved the cursor to a file. "It isn't tied to a client. Norton was conducting an independent investigation, and we need to turn it over to major crimes. It's human trafficking."

"Do you think he had a client for this?" Jane asked.

"No. Seems it was his own research. There's a note file." He clicked open a file folder. "Slavery. Young people bought in from South America *and* Southeast Asia and then transported here to work. Involuntary servitude.

Field workers, housemaids, janitors, food prep, etc. I did some of my own digging on the dark web." Mike shook his head. "It's good that he found the ring, but I don't understand why he didn't get us involved."

"Was he following anyone in particular? Trying to narrow down the source?"

"Possibly. The name in his notes is Kyle Woods."

* * *

Kyle Woods shook his head. He did that thing with his lips between disapproval and a sneer. His clothes were rumpled, his face wan, but after several hours of the interview, he remained obstinate.

Silence filled the interview room. Jane moved her chair closer to Woods so they faced each other only a couple of feet apart. On the other side of the table to her side, the area's most expensive attorney, Josh Overbrook, sat in hip sartorial elegance.

Jane's stomach tightened, but she kept to her professional interview training. The fingerprints on the pruning knife belonged to Woods. She'd gone with her backup team to Wood's home in the valley nestled among fields of roses. He was guilty. She wanted a confession.

Jane picked up a thick folder that lay on the table beside her. She opened it a thumbed through papers. Then she looked up at Woods.

"I don't want you to be nervous about what I'm going to say. You have a long road ahead, Kyle. This is only the beginning. When we're done, you'll be meeting with the FBI about other matters. Let's finish this. We know you killed Jim Norton. The boot prints at the crime scene match your shoes. Your fingerprints are on the pruning knife. I know you did this, and will not allow you to put yourself in the awkward position of lying to me."

Woods leaned back as if trying to escape her eye. Overbrook glanced at her, knowing what was coming next. He had his methods in the courtroom, and she had hers in the interrogation room.

"If you are not willing to be completely honest with me, then I advise you to say absolutely nothing."

Woods crossed his arms. But Jane saw his fingers drum against his upper arms and waited. He glanced at Overbrook, who may or may not have nodded slightly. Jane waited.

Woods leaned forward, looking at the floor. Jane fought holding her breath. He put his head in his hands. Silence. A long silence.

"He told me he was going to tell the FBI," Woods mumbled to the floor. "He was up there waiting for the sunrise."

Jane waited. Overbrook did not move.

"The little weasel. Snooping around behind people's backs. What kind of life is that? I hit him."

"You hit him, and then what?"

"I hit him again. The weasel actually fought back. He said I was despicable. Despicable. I am the one who has property. Who built a vineyard from scratch. He was just my tenant."

Jane brought him back to the scene. "You hit him."

"Yeah. He was punching me. I had the grape knife. That's it. I used the grape knife and stopped that little worm."

"You used the grape knife?"

Woods looked up from the floor, his eyes asking for understanding.

"Yeah. I scraped it across his neck. That was it. He started bleeding and fell to the ground. I wanted to get him away to my truck. Everything would have worked out except for that cougar."

More silence.

"I ran. I didn't want to get mauled."

"So you dropped Jim's body and left."

"Yeah." Woods looked at Overbrook. No help there.

"You killed Jim Norton and attempted to hide his body, but left because of the mountain lion."

Woods looked at the walls and then the ceiling.

"He had no right, snooping around in my life. I did. I sliced his neck."

The interview was over. Jane started to get up.

"Wait," Woods said. "What's going to happen to me?"

"Mr. Overbrook will explain the next steps."

Jim Norton's hunt for truth had led to a hornet's nest of deceit, servitude, and to his death. Jane pushed the lever on the binder that opened the rings to the murder book. She added the transcription of the interview and interrogation of Kyle Woods. She rubbed her ankle where the rattlesnake had hit. Just a little pressure, no puncture. The smallest remembrance of her probe into a hornet's nest. Soon it would dissipate, and memories of this investigation would be all that remained. She snapped closed the binder rings.

Her phone buzzed. "You're up. A body over by the Russian River."

HERE COMES SANTA CLAUS

By M. M. Chouinard

All my life I've wanted a normal Christmas, but when you're raised by a latter-day hippie atheist and a lapsed Catholic, the struggle for 'normal' is real. And last year's Christmas was objectively the strangest yet, because while the definition of a 'normal' Christmas is relative, I'm gonna go out on a limb that killing Santa Claus is never a part of it.

It didn't help that my relationship with Santa has been rocky since I was a little girl. My mother took me to see him several times, or so I've been told. In the only picture I have to support this claim, I'm leaning as far away from Santa as I can, screaming, with tears pouring down my face. I never believed in Santa, although I did send him a letter once to test out the whole deal; I asked for a Cabbage Patch Kid, and of course didn't get it. Even back then I was big on gathering evidence—a fortuitous characteristic for a future investigative true-crime podcaster—and despite what my mother says, I maintain to this day that asking for the pinnacle of unobtainable childhood excess was the best way to prove the whole thing a hoax.

So it probably wasn't surprising when, as my brother and I arrived at the ritzy Christmas party his San Francisco CPA firm held at the Morgana Excelsior Ballroom, I was deeply uncomfortable to discover we were expected to take a prom-style picture with Santa before we entered.

"Seriously, who forces adults to take pictures with Santa Claus?" I whispered to Leo.

He shot me a sideways glance above his pasted-on work smile. "It's supposed to be fun, Capri. Just go with the flow."

I kept my bah-humbug to myself. These were his work colleagues after all, and since he'd just transferred back to the Bay Area after a heartbreaking divorce, I wasn't going to be the girl whose bad behavior became the office joke. So, I pasted on a matching smile, tried not to be annoyed that Santa was nose-deep in his cell phone, and turned to the too-perky photographer wearing an elf dress and light-up reindeer antlers.

"Scooch in over there." She waved her red-and-green lacquered claws toward jolly Saint Nick.

Who, it turned out, was a little *too* jolly. As the photo elf encouraged me to *hug right up next to him*, I caught a distinct whiff of Jack Daniels emanating from his wonky beard. As I forced myself not to shudder when he put his arm around me, his hand stroked the length of my arm down to my wrist, then diverted to my tush.

If it hadn't been Leo's work function, I would have slugged the guy right there. Instead I settled for whispering a quick seasonal message in Father Christmas's ear about how I'd snap his favorite candy cane if he didn't move his hand *toot sweet.*

Once the picture was taken and I'd grabbed a medicinal flute of champagne off the sleek silver beaux-art bar, I pulled Leo aside and told him what had happened.

He glanced back. "You want me to rough him up? But you never know, he might have a squad of back-up elves with brass knuckles behind the bar."

I narrowed my eyes at him. "You're lucky you're my favorite brother. Let's go find our table."

* * *

We grabbed goody bags as we made our way through the bar area to the ballroom proper. When we entered, I had to swallow my gasp. The intricately carved octagonal pattern in the dark-wood ceiling echoed the pattern of the carpet, while floor-to-ceiling taupe curtains hung between mahogany columns on the walls. Each round table was set with cut glass and china so expensive I was afraid to touch it, all illuminated by white-glass puffball-chrysanthemum chandeliers. This was how CPAs partied? For the first time I was glad I'd worn the full-length red mermaid dress my best friend Heather insisted I borrow for the event.

Two other couples had already made it to our assigned table, and Leo introduced me as we settled in. Two seats to my right sat Sean Buffen, a late-forties-something white man who looked so uncomfortable in his rented tux and yellow polka-dot tie that he made *me* squirm. Between us his wife, Sandra, a petite blonde twenty-something, wore a coral gown that brought out the peaches in her cream complexion.

"Sean oversees our non-profit division," Leo told me.

"How you've managed to slog through that morass of thankless do-gooders for twenty-plus years I'll never know," the woman two seats down from Leo said while raising her martini glass.

Sean flushed red. "We don't all have a brother-in-law in the company."

The woman's smile managed to acknowledge the truth of the jab and dismiss it at the same time. Leo cleared his throat and introduced her as Roberta Chafe, who ran the company's second largest account, Epstein and Sons. She was a tall white brunette in her early forties, and wore an elegant black gown with an intricate pattern of ruby rhinestones across her bosom. Her husband, Oscar, was a fifty-something Latino with the sort of snow at his temples that made women swoon, and he appeared to know it. He was a neurosurgeon, according to Leo. He was also the sort of brash manspreader who was pushing us right out of our place settings.

Some people hate the type of chitchat a table of strangers forces on you. For me, the opportunity to ask increasingly invasive questions while observing group dynamics is like a buffet of gourmet delights—another fortunate character trait for my investigative toolkit. Within fifteen minutes, I'd uncovered that Roberta's passion for accounting was exceeded only by her passion for designer purses and shoes, Sean's resentment at being stuck with the company's poorest accounts was exceeded only by his resentment at an empty wine glass, and Oscar's admiration of his own good looks was exceeded only by his admiration of Sandra Buffen's. That last bit of information came less from my investigative abilities and more from Oscar's stockinged toes accidentally gliding up my ankle in the mistaken belief it was Sandra's—until I speared his foot with my stiletto. Because, seriously, first a perverted Santa Claus and then a wannabe corporate Lothario? There was only so much I was willing to take in one evening.

After Oscar yelped like the stuck pig he was, I excused myself to the little girl's room and asked if anyone wanted anything from the bar. That apparently broke the it's-not-polite-to-leave-your-table seal, because my movement triggered a mass exodus. When I looked back over my shoulder, everyone, including Leo, had scattered to hobnob with the other tables or refresh their drinks.

* * *

I wasn't surprised to find a line outside the restroom that stretched well past the T-intersection of the exterior halls. These venues always had limited facilities, especially when you factored in ladies having to wrestle themselves in and out of fancy dresses. I berated myself for leaving my cell phone on the table and settled for my favorite analog pass-the-time game, deducing information about the other women in line. The one in front of me wore a dress that was simultaneously too tight and too loose in exactly the wrong places; like me, she must have borrowed hers, and if so, she wasn't one of the well-paid account executives. The woman in front of her had diamonds dangling from her ears that would have made Elizabeth Taylor jealous; either she or her partner was higher up in the hierarchy.

By the time the line dropped down to just three people in front of me, I was bored with my guessing game and shifted into full-on snooping. As I tilted forward in a surreptitious attempt to read Borrowed Dress's text conversation, someone grabbed me from behind, nearly knocking me over.

I whipped around to find my North Pole Nemesis, even drunker than he'd been earlier, pawing at me like a bear raiding a garbage can. I shoved him away, and he stumbled back a step. But even as he tried to regain his balance, he came forward at me again. So I did what any sensible woman in my position would do—sent a pointed jab directly at his jingle bells.

This time he didn't stumble. He sank slowly to his knees, then collapsed back with a squishy thud onto the gorgeous carpet. Face-up, eyes wide open, mouth gaping like he'd just caught Mrs. Claus diddling an elf.

"He's out cold," Borrowed Dress said, her voice tinged with awe.

"No way," I said. Because while I'm no slouch with my fists, Santa was over six feet and at least two-hundred-something pounds. One hit from me—especially while in a gown that corseted me like a sausage casing—couldn't possibly lay him out like a three-day-old fish. "You're not fooling anybody, Kris. If this is your way of getting out of a harassment charge, it's not gonna work."

But he didn't move. He didn't even twitch.

"You killed him," White Diamonds said helpfully.

My mouth popped open and closed. Was that even possible? "He's just passed out drunk." I dropped to the floor next to him, or rather, I awkwardly lowered myself as fast as my uber-restrictive gown permitted, then thrust two fingers on his carotid artery.

No pulse.

I stuck my head down in front of his gaping mouth to check for breath, but no air came out. And, oddly, while the scent of alcohol wafted off of him, his mouth smelled minty fresh. I blew into his open eyes—he didn't flicker or flinch.

Panic flared through my chest, and I gaped up at my two bathroom-line compatriots, now surrounded by a growing crowd of gawkers. "You guys saw—I didn't even hit him that hard. Right?"

They took a step back from me.

I pointed to Borrowed Dress's phone. "Call nine-one-one, fast. He needs help."

She didn't react at first, but when I repeated my request in a high-pitched screech, she jolted awake and put the call through. Unfortunately, my screech also drew one of the building's rent-a-cops, who pushed his way through the onlookers and zeroed in on me.

"What happened?" he asked, pulling his radio off his belt.

"He's unconscious," I understated, figuring this was no time to make assumptions that reflected poorly on me.

He told his radio to call the paramedics, then asked, "Has anyone left the building in the last few minutes?"

"Nobody's left in the last hour," a voice crackled over the line.

"Lock it down, then. Nobody out, and nobody in but emergency services."

I briefly considered telling him I was the culprit, but decided there was really no reason to add to the situation's confusion. Besides, the ballroom was on the top floor of the Excelsior Financial building, accessible only via direct elevator and an emergency staircase. Locking it down really didn't involve much effort on anyone's part.

"Everyone stand back," he said to the crowd, now large enough to block all three hallways leading away from us. "The paramedics need space to get through. And Santa needs air."

I nodded vigorous agreement—even though I was pretty sure he didn't.

* * *

During the brief time it took the paramedics to arrive, I scooted back against the wall and took a series of deep breaths. Leo's head bobbed up and down over the crowd—when he caught sight of me, he visibly paled. By the time he made his way over, I'd regained the power of mostly logical thought, and my profession kicked back in.

"Give me your phone," I said.

Much to his credit, he didn't second guess. Once he unlocked it, I snapped several pictures from as many different angles as I could manage.

"Hey." The security guard reached out to stop me. But the paramedics appeared, and the crowd parted like a broken zipper to let them through.

"What happened here?" the short, white, woman paramedic asked the security guard.

"Ask her," he gestured to me.

My throat constricted as I tried to answer. "I—he— Look. He grabbed me, and I pushed him off. He didn't take the hint, so I hit him, and he fell.

But I didn't hit him *hard*, I swear."

The other paramedic, a tall Asian male, finished checking Santa's vitals. As the woman knelt down to perform some test, he snapped open Santa's jacket to start chest compressions, and tossed aside the lumpy pillow stuffing Santa's costume.

It hit the carpet with a clinking thud—something costume padding rarely does.

After a quick glance around me, I took advantage of everyone's distracted state to discreetly reach over and lift the pillowcase. A slew of goodies poured out.

"Hey! That's my bracelet!" called a sixty-something platinum blonde with nearly translucent skin and eye makeup a raccoon would envy. I spread out the pile, revealing several watches, a half dozen sterling-silver star ornaments like the one I'd glimpsed in my goody bag, an assortment of credit cards and cash, and yes, several bracelets. Including one that looked suspiciously like—

I grabbed my wrist. Sure enough, my ruby bracelet, the one piece of jewelry my grandmother Philomena had left to me, was gone. Santa hadn't been copping a feel during the picture—he'd been distracting me from his pickpocketing.

As I decided whether to risk tampering with evidence by snatching up grandma's bracelet or risk abandoning it to the eternal purgatory of an evidence bin, two uniformed police officers arrived. The short, dark-haired white officer's nameplate read *Stankle,* and the tall, lean black officer's called her *Walker.* They secured the scene by directing the security guard to corral everyone back into the main ballroom—except me. They wanted to keep an eye on me, they said, and plunked me down in a chair pulled from the kitchen area.

The paramedics determined PDQ that there wasn't anything they could do for Santa. Once they officially called it, Stankle searched his pockets looking for ID, and found a wallet.

"Artie Malloy," he announced. "Nothing that indicates any next of kin."

After handing the wallet to Walker so she could double-check it, Stankle finished going through Santa's pockets, but found nothing else. Something about that bothered me, but I couldn't put my finger on what.

He turned to me. "You're the one who was with him. What's your name?"

"Capri Sanzio."

His eyes snapped up from his notebook and scanned my face. "The podcaster?"

I died a little inside, because I knew exactly how much most police don't like dealing with true-crime podcasters. "Um. Yes. That's me."

Sure enough, his eyes narrowed. "I see. And what brings you to a Christmas party for an accounting firm?"

I explained, then told him what happened to Santa.

"You assaulted him?" Stankle asked.

I bristled. "He assaulted *me*. *I* defended myself."

"He's the one who ended up dead."

The woman paramedic cleared her throat. "Ms. Sanzio didn't kill him. The ME will have to say officially, but there's a contusion on the back of the skull." She knelt and pointed to it. "Under here, and there's a distinct indentation that reaches over to the side. He couldn't have gotten it falling on any floor, let alone a carpeted one. He was already dying when she hit him."

My mind flew back to our encounter. He'd been stumbling, and had an odd expression on his face. I'd assumed both were because he was drunk, but a serious blow to the head explained it just as well. He wasn't trying to grope me—he was probably trying to get help. And that fit far better with his minty-fresh breath, and how only his beard smelled like alcohol—he probably sprinkled it on himself to encourage suckers like me to assume he was being inappropriate rather than felonious.

"But why was he still conscious, then?" I asked.

"That's exactly why head injuries are so dangerous. You can be hemorrhaging internally despite walking around like everything's fine," she said. "Your punch may have dropped him to his knees, but you didn't kill him."

"Oh, thank God." I squeezed my eyes shut for a short prayer—then my true-crime mode kicked back in. "But who did, then? Could it have been an accident?"

The paramedic's expression turned wary. "The ME will have to determine that."

Stankle pointed with his head down the short hall behind us. "He came at you from that direction?"

I nodded. "But the only thing down there is the coat room."

Stankle strode toward the room and opened the door. "Nobody in there now."

"Did you see anybody else come out of there?" Walker asked.

"I didn't, but I was focused on Santa and the whole scene turned kinda chaotic after I punched him. People came from all different directions to see what was happening."

"Christmas seems like a really messed-up time to assault Santa," the male paramedic said.

I considered pointing out that Christmas was really the *only* time you could assault Santa, but decided it was wiser to point out the bag of valuables on the floor. "What's really messed up is when Santa turns out to be a pickpocket."

The officers turned to examine the mound, and clarified with the paramedics where it came from.

"That bracelet with the rubies is mine." I recounted my earlier experience. "I thought he was just getting fresh when we took our picture with him, but turns out he was distracting me from his sleight of hand."

"So possibly someone noticed something missing and figured out what happened, then tried to recover it," Walker said.

"And got nasty when Santa wouldn't hand it over," Stankle said.

That struck me as odd—why smash him over the head when you could just call the security guard, or pull out your phone and call nine-one-one?

I gasped as I realized what was bothering me about the scene. "Where's his phone?"

The officers turned to me. "He doesn't have one."

"Right," I said. "But he had one earlier. It annoyed me because his nose was buried in it while we set up for the picture."

The officers searched him again, but found nothing.

Stankle strode toward the coat-check room. "Maybe that's what he was doing in there, putting his phone into his jacket, and someone confronted him."

"Uh..." Walker peered back toward the hall entrance. "Shouldn't we leave this for the detectives?"

Stankle hesitated.

Words could not express how much I wanted to get inside that room, and there was no way that was gonna happen once the detectives showed up—especially if it was one of the ones I knew personally. So I said, as innocently as I could manage, "Or, how cool would it be to have everything all figured out and ready to hand over when they get here? They aren't the only ones smart enough to figure this out."

Stankle glared at me, and for a moment I thought I'd overplayed my nonchalant double-dog dare. Then I figured, in for a penny, in for a pound. "And they'll be here really soon."

Stankle strode into the room.

Walker followed him, and I tiptoed along. After all, my DNA was already on Sticky Fingers Santa thanks to my KO, so what did it matter? But I figured it was best not to push my luck, so I hung back near the door in hopes they wouldn't really notice. Stankle put his hands on his hips and surveyed the room, probably wondering how to go about searching the four-hundred-plus coats hanging from the racks when he didn't know what Santa's phone looked like. At least, that's what *I* was wondering as I scanned the room—until I spotted a red-velvet sack peeping out from the edge of the back-most rack, half-hidden under a coat.

"Officers?" I called, and pointed to the bag.

Walker reached the sack first and took pictures while Stankle snapped on a pair of nitrile gloves from his jacket pocket. When he carefully lifted the bag and turned it over, more jewelry and bills poured out, along with at least ten more of the silver star ornaments.

"Someone must have caught him in the act," Stankle said.

"Then wouldn't the person who caught him be the one who ended up bashed and dead?" Walker asked, snaking the words right out of my mouth.

Stankle shrugged. "Maybe he had a partner, and they had a dispute."

"Why would they have a dispute *here*, while the event is still going on? Wouldn't they divide everything up later, once they were free and clear?" I noticed their expressions seemed on the verge of remembering I had no right to be there, so I hurried to distract them. "He does have a partner, though. The woman dressed like an elf, the one taking the pictures. And I'm still not seeing a phone."

Stankle double-checked the Santa sack, then searched the coat. "Someone must have taken it."

"And the only reason for someone to take it is if there's something important on it," Walker said.

Stankle stood back up and gestured to me with his head. "Come with us, please."

We crossed through the corridors to the entry vestibule. The elven photographer, eyes closed and earbuds plugged in, leaned back in her chair next to a sign that read 'Santa's off feeding his reindeer.' I rolled my eyes so hard they almost got stuck in my brain.

When the officers told her what had happened to Santa, the blood drained from her face and she went silent. When they told her about the pilfered goods, her eyes widened to the size of plum puddings, and she couldn't talk fast enough.

"I barely know Artie, I swear. The agency sends us on, like, *tons* of jobs and this is only my second Santa gig. My first with this guy." She tapped at her phone. "My boss'll tell you, I never even talked to Artie before he called yesterday to confirm."

"You talked to him by phone? So you have his number?" I asked.

She flinched like I'd smacked her. "That doesn't mean anything, I totally talk to everyone before I meet up with them—"

I held up my hand. "I just mean if you have his number, can you call his phone?"

"Duh. Of course I can." She looked at me like I was crazy, but didn't move.

Officer Walker's jaw tensed like she was trying hard not to lose her temper.

"Then please call it."

Clarity whacked Elven Barbie between the eyes, and her brows popped up. "Oh, right. Sorry. Yeah." She scrambled to find his number, then called it.

"Let it ring," Walker led us back to the coat room, then held up a hand for quiet. We listened carefully, but still couldn't hear anything.

I waved toward the doors. "You sent everyone into the ballroom. If someone took the phone, good bet it's in there."

Stankle pushed through the bar and the ballroom doors with the three of us still in tow. He called for attention and quieted everyone. Then, leading with his ears, he marched down the center of the room, winding his way between tables crowded with confused and alarmed faces. Walker gestured for me to accompany her around the perimeter. As we neared the entrance to the kitchen, a tinny song reached my ears. I followed it over to the sideboard that ran along the wall, and the song got clearer: *Grandma Got Run Over By a Reindeer.*

I peeked over and around and spotted a light coming from behind the sideboard. I called to Walker; she wiggled her gloved hand behind the back and pulled it out. After declining the call from 'Hot Elf,' she swiped and tapped.

"It's locked." With a wave to Stankle, she turned on her heel and strode out of the ballroom. I chased after them as best I could in my mermaid dress, feeling like Morticia Addams in a five-hundred-meter dash. I was still several yards behind when Walker stooped down, stuck Santa's thumb on the phone pad, and smiled victoriously. "Thank goodness it has the right kind of biometrics. We're in."

As I caught up, she swiped and tapped again. "No recent calls or texts."

"Try his pictures," Stankle and I said in unison.

She scrolled and tapped some more. "Well looky here. A video, taped about forty minutes ago."

We watched over her shoulder as she hit play. After a few seconds, the mostly black screen shifted and a sliver of light split it in two; we were peering out from between two coats, behind a coat rack. But all we could see was a pair of black high heels under shapely legs, and a pair of dress shoes under not-so-shapely trousers.

"I don't appreciate being threatened," the woman said. She was trying for haughty, but fear tinged her sass.

"Cut the crap. You're not the one calling the shots here and we both know it," a male voice responded.

I squeezed my eyes tight for a moment against the painfully bad thug talk. Whatever was happening here, it didn't involve professionals.

"I don't know what you think those documents mean—"

"See? You have zero respect for me. I'm not stupid. They mean you've been embezzling, plain and simple. But, hey, if the docs are really so innocent, I suppose I can just send them to Hewitt and he can take it from there."

The male feet took a step away, but the woman must have grabbed him, because he stepped back into frame.

"What do you want?" Her voice was now wheedling and desperate.

"Twenty percent of that two hundred thousand, and twenty percent from here on out."

I stared up and registered excitement in the two officers' faces—not only were they gonna solve a murder, they'd stumbled on both embezzlement and blackmail, too. Like some sort of law-enforcement hat trick, *if* they could figure out who the people in the video were. I widened my eyes fiercely at the phone and willed Santa to adjust the camera so we could see some faces.

Santa must have had the same thought, because that's exactly what he did. The camera moved forward, then slowly pivoted upward toward the couple's heads.

Or it would have, if Santa hadn't dropped the phone.

Both officers and I winced at the sound of the phone clanking against the metal coat rack, then stared into a row of hems.

"Hey! Who's there?" the man's voice called out.

"He's taping us!" the woman called.

A jumble of footsteps ensued, along with the screech of metal wheels on the antique floor. Someone grunted and metal chinged against metal, followed by a sickening crunch and a man's grunt of pain.

But another cry followed, this one from a different voice. Footsteps retreated and a door opened.

"He punched me in the—" The man's voice was now far higher, and I felt less guilty knowing Santa himself had believed in using that particular maneuver for self-defense.

"Grab the phone," the woman said.

The footsteps grew louder. The picture shook, and then the recording stopped.

Stankle swore. "Completely useless. He didn't get their faces."

"He didn't have to." I smiled a big Grinchy smile. "When he scrolled up, I recognized the bead work on Roberta Chafe's dress, and Sean Buffen's tacky yellow polka-dot tie."

* * *

By the time the homicide detectives arrived, Officers Stankle and Walker had Roberta and Sean cuffed in two separate rooms. As soon as the pair realized the jig was up, they were all too eager to drop a dime on each other. They both admitted they'd caught Santa in the act of recording them, most likely so he could blackmail them himself. However, each claimed the other had been the one to smash Artie in the head with one of the hefty wooden coat hangers. Unfortunately for Sean, while he was smart enough to wipe his prints off the coat hanger, that didn't get rid of the touch DNA he left on it. Not that it mattered: they were both headed to jail regardless, Roberta for embezzlement and Sean for blackmail. But Sean's resentment over being stuck with crappy accounts while clients treated Roberta to fancy dinners dug him a hole that ultimately added twenty years for murder on top of everything else.

I convinced Officers Stankle and Walker that, in the spirit of the season, there was no reason not to return Artie Claus's pilfered items to their rightful owners—the theft wasn't relevant to what got him killed, and the only judge he'd face now was Saint Peter. So while the detectives were off interviewing Sean and Roberta, we set up a discreet little production line: Stankle photographed each object, Walker documented who claimed it, and Leo and I handed each item back.

As I watched the relieved happiness light up each person's face when I handed them their belongings while Roberta and Sean were being were led out to the elevators in handcuffs, I understood fully for the first time why Santa Claus is a thing. The warmth that spread through me with each smiling face? It was the same feeling I got when I helped solve a crime and got justice for someone's child or parent or spouse, with an extra dash of holiday happy. And while it may not have been a *normal* Christmas by anyone's standards, I'm pretty sure *that* feeling is what Santa's spirit is really all about.

A GOOD JUDGE OF CHARACTER

By Tina deBellegarde

June put the cat carrier on the floor by the counter. She was relieved because Samson just kept gaining weight and June was not getting any younger. Samson meowed, begging to be released.

"Ever since I picked him up from here this morning, he's been so skittish."

The girl pulled the earphone out of her right ear to answer. "It's to be expected that a cat will be skittish at the vet." The girl spoke as if it were a great effort on her part, then she snuck a peek at her phone when it buzzed.

June wondered if the young girl behind the counter was being difficult or if she really didn't hear a word she was saying. Kids these days, they barely listen to a word anyone says anymore. If they don't hear it on their phones, they're not listening.

"I don't mean he's been skittish here, I mean he's been skittish since he came home from his procedure. I was so nervous leaving him here overnight. I was afraid something like this would happen."

The girl came around the counter and knelt down next to the cat and started to make cute little noises. She opened the case to let Samson out, but he retreated deeper into the carrier.

"Come on big boy. You can do it. Let's see how handsome you are."

She reached into the carrier and gently pulled the big orange tabby into her arms, but not for long. Samson untangled himself and jumped to the ground. He scooted to the back of the room and hid under a chair, leaving little damp paw prints along the way.

"And that's another thing. He's been leaving paw prints everywhere." June pointed to the ground.

"Where?"

"Oh, for goodness sake. Right there."

The girl squinted, tilted her head. Then got closer to the floor. "Oh, yeah, I see them now. Well, that's common also. Cats sweat through their paws. It's summertime, and let's face it, he's at the vet, he's going to be nervous."

June rolled her eyes. This girl wasn't listening. "Can I just see Dr. Roberts, please?"

Snapping her gum, the girl looked up his schedule on the computer. "He isn't free for another hour. Would you like to come back?"

"No, I'll wait right here." And June did just that.

When she finally got to see Dr. Roberts, she explained the whole thing again and Samson was no friendlier than he had been earlier. June was able to scoop him up, but as they approached the examination table, Samson leapt from her arms and back to the corner leaving a fresh trail of wet paw prints.

Doctor Roberts watched Samson cowering under the chair and then looked back up at June. "Yes. I see what you mean, but cats are naturally high-strung. They are always on alert. Being nervous is their nature. I'm sure Samson's unhappy to see the vet's office again. He just had his procedure yesterday and is in no rush to repeat it. Sometimes spending the night away from home upsets them, too."

"I suppose you're right." June grudgingly had to admit that the doctor was no more helpful than the ditzy girl at the reception desk. "I don't know why he would be that way at home. I wanted to make sure it wasn't a side effect of the anesthesia or the procedure. As long as he's fine, we'll run along. Now, if I could just get him into the carrier."

After several unsuccessful attempts, Dr. Roberts left her to the task on her own. He had another patient waiting.

Once they finally made it home, June brewed a pot of coffee as she waited for Hazel to arrive for their afternoon cup together.

Hazel rushed in, all flustered. She slammed the newspaper down on the countertop and looked expectantly at June. "Have you heard? I can't believe it."

June would have none of it. "What are you yammering on about?"

Hazel had been June's best friend for seventy years, but she still thought the woman was a drama queen.

"I'll tell you what I'm yammering on about. Walt VanPatten's body's been found in the gazebo. Tonight's performers were setting up their equipment about to do a sound check and, lo and behold, they found him. Dead. Right there."

"Dead? Now, why would he go and die there?"

"I don't think he planned it that way, June."

"Walt was in fine health. I don't understand. What happened?"

"He's dead is what happened. He had a big gash on the back of his head. Sheriff thinks he was murdered."

"Murdered? Well, if that isn't the most exciting thing that's happened to this town in the last fifty years."

"June, really. Sometimes I wonder if you have a heart."

"Are you telling me you liked him? Nobody liked Walt. Does it mean I think he should've been killed? No, but I'm not going to lose any sleep over it, either."

"You're right about that. Walt wasn't a nice guy. I heard even his wife didn't like him. In fact, rumor has it she's having an affair."

"Honest, Hazel, don't spread rumors about the dead."

"I'm not. His wife is very much alive." Hazel was very pleased with herself.

"Still, it's unbecoming."

"I suppose you're right." Contrite, Hazel concentrated on adding cream to her cup.

After their coffee, they moved from the kitchen to the front porch to prepare for their weekly dinner party. Every Thursday night of the summer, a different band performed in the gazebo for the pleasure of the community and to take their minds off the heat. Since June's house was right on the town square, she had front row seats. Her large front porch could accommodate all of her friends and everyone brought a dish for the pot luck.

Jerry and Barbara arrived first. Barbara was all a buzz with the news of Walt's death.

"I know no one liked him, but without his money, most of the businesses on Main Street wouldn't exist. Even Jerry's accounting office is half owned by Walt."

Jerry nodded his assent. "He was a necessary evil."

Phil and Theresa, who were on their way up the steps, overheard them. Phil said, "I wonder how this will affect all these businesses."

Theresa, who worked at VanPatten's office, had the inside scoop. "I heard that in many cases he had partnership agreements with rights of survivorship. That could mean good things for the businesses on Main Street."

Everyone sipped their lemonades and considered what Teresa had just said when Samson stuck his nose out the front door and ventured on to the porch to greet the guests. One by one he sniffed. Once he was satisfied, he moved on to the next guest.

"What a sweetheart Samson is." Barbara bent down to pet the chunky tabby.

"I have to say I'm happy to see him so relaxed. He hasn't been himself all day. He spent the night at the vet's and came back a nervous wreck." June bent down and gave him a scratch behind his ear. She was relieved to see that Samson's wet paw prints were nowhere to be seen. She had her baby back.

Samson transitioned from sniffs to encircling each leg, finishing off each victim with a good leg rub before moving onto the next person.

"Samson, stop that. You're leaving hair on Jerry's pants."

"Oh, that's alright. I don't mind," Jerry said. He was a true animal lover and wouldn't let a few cat hairs ruin his night or his clothes.

"That reminds me," Barbara said. "I heard from Nancy, who heard from her sister who works at the sheriff's office, that when they found Walt's body, the back of his suit jacket had a lot of animal hairs on it."

"Well that's easy to explain. There must be squirrels all over the gazebo,"

Phil said.

Barbara kept going. "Not really. Sheriff says that they found no hairs in the gazebo. You know that Walt was one impeccable dresser. Not a thing out of place. Sheriff thinks he was killed somewhere else and then moved to the gazebo."

"Wait a minute. Doesn't Walt have a dog?" Theresa asked.

"No, his wife has a dog. He's known to hate Vivian's poodle and would have nothing to do with it," Jerry said.

"Well, I wouldn't be too happy with my wife or her dog if she were having an affair," Phil said.

June made the rounds with the lemonade pitcher. "That's just a rumor."

"I don't think so." Hazel looked over her shoulder. "I heard that Kevin Roberts was seen leaving that new French restaurant up Route 26 with Vivian last weekend."

"Kevin? As in Kevin Roberts? Our friend? My vet?" June was shocked.

"Shhhh—"

Kevin Roberts made his way up the steps, waving to his friends as he reached for a glass of lemonade.

Out of the corner of her eye June saw a flash as Samson ran off the porch like a bat out of hell. All that remained were his wet paw prints on the porch floor.

BAGPIPES, HAGGIS, AND BURNS

By Abigail Leigh Reed

A Bavaria Schnitzel Mystery

Bavaria "Varia" Schnitzel pinned a tartan tam-o'-shanter to her sister's head and gave it a tilt as her mother shoved through Varia's front door.

"Ouch. Watch the pins," Nicha said. "I have a scalp under that tammie."

"The price of looking Scottish, dear," Mother said. "Quite a cold snap we're having, even for January twenty-fifth." Hannelore Trostenberg faked a shiver. "Thank goodness Isla loaned us wool kilts and sweaters for her traditional Burns Night supper."

"Isla wants everything to go well her first time hosting the haggis celebration, especially with her brother back in town," Varia said. "She's been a worrywart trying to equal her mother's perfect-hostess skills."

Hannelore crossed her hands over her heart. "Davina MacTavish, may you rest in peace."

"Anyway, Isla wants some friendly faces with low expectations at the supper for support." Varia smoothed her sash as her daughter, Chloe, strolled into the living room, carrying a bowl of freshly popped popcorn. Trotting behind her, Wetzel, a black and tan Dachshund, waggled his tail in hopes of spillage.

"Plaid, plaid, and more plaid," Chloe said with round eyes and a silly grin.

"Tartan, Chloe," Varia said. "Plaid is any crisscross pattern of two or more colors, but tartans are plaids named for a particular Scottish clan or community."

"You're not Scottish, Mom," Chloe said.

"I'm well aware, but we're masquerading as part of the Wood clan tonight."

"Ha!" Nicha guffawed. "Just call us Wood nymphs."

All four of them giggled.

Celebrating fanciful holidays and events—and, apparently, famous people's birthdays— was an amusing perk of living in Schoneburg, California. The uniquely international village, harboring more tourists than residents, allowed people to experience various cultures and traditions.

"And we'll have a wee bit o' fun with our Scottish friends tonight." Varia did her best to mimic a Scottish burr.

"I'm almost thirteen," Chloe said. "Too bad I can't go."

"Don't be *too* jealous, niecey-pooh," Nicha said. "We have to eat haggis."

Chloe scrunched her face. "What's that?"

"A giant sausage made from animal parts we don't usually eat," Nicha said.

Chloe blurted a teasing laugh.

Hannelore pulled her phone from her purse. "Bavaria, you and Municha stand together in front of the fireplace and let me take a picture."

"*Oma,* hand me your phone." Chloe set the popcorn on the coffee table. "You need to be in this picture too. Dad would've wanted you three in kilts for his Wall of Funny."

Chloe and her father had been kindred spirits, and Varia cherished this snatch of her husband's personality in their daughter, especially after losing him two years ago. "You should carry on his tradition," Varia said. "We'll frame it, and you can hang it with his collection of fun-loving family photos."

"Excellent idea." Hannelore jumped in between her daughters.

"Say 'Haggis!'" Chloe said.

After the photo, Varia hugged her daughter. "Don't forget to lock the door and feed Wetzel. I have my cell phone, and I left Isla's number by the phone in the kitchen."

"Mom, go already. I'll be fine."

Varia picked up the mixed floral bouquet—a hostess gift for Isla—kissed Chloe's cheek and stepped out the door with her mother and sister.

The air was indeed nippy, and the stars shone brightly in the clear sky. The women began walking the three blocks to Isla's house, pulling their tartan shawls close. Bagpipes droned faintly in the night air, growing louder with each step.

They rounded the corner to the final block and crossed paths with Fritz. He carried a pastry box from his bakery, located across the street from The Grimm Gnome, Varia's German gift shop.

Sizing up his appearance—Varia could never help herself—she admired how the dark green and blue tartan trousers hugged Fritz's hamstrings. "No kilt tonight?"

"Lederhosen in the bakery and Biergarten is one thing." Fritz smirked as he fell into step with them. "A kilt's a little too free for me."

"But you could wear a *Sgian-dubh*," Varia said.

"A what?"

"The knife Scots wear in their sock." She waved a hand. "Probably best you stick to lederhosen. My life won't be in danger when Wetzel wins the Dachshund races."

"Pretzel wins her fair share." He scowled.

"Now, children..." Hannelore teased.

"You're right, Mother," Varia said. "This is Isla's night. Truce?"

Fritz met Varia's sideways glance. "For tonight."

A lone piper, in full Scottish Highland regalia, stood piping inside Isla's picket gate. Paper lanterns lined the path through the garden to her home. On the front door hung a grapevine wreath decorated with thistle, miniature bagpipes, and a burnt-edge card with "Burns Night" calligraphed alongside Robert Burns's image. They knocked, and a man Varia didn't recognize answered.

Hannelore stuck out her hand to greet the burly man with red hair and a close-cropped beard. "You must be Davina's son." She grabbed his hand and gave it a vigorous shake. "These are my daughters, Bavaria and

Municha, and our friend, Fritz. Isla invited us."

"Welcome, welcome," he said with an authentic Scottish burr. "I'm Isla's brother, David."

"I recognize you from a photograph your mother carried." Hannelore dipped her head. "Sorry for your loss."

David nodded and sighed. "Don't stand on ceremony. My sister's in the kitchen. You can put your belongings in the den, first door on the left."

As Fritz entered the foyer, he gave David an uncomfortable grin.

"You work at the bakery on German Street," David said.

"I *own* the Black Forest Bakery." Fritz slid his free hand into his pocket and glanced at Varia. "Let's find Isla."

Hannelore bustled through the foyer to her friend, Vivian Keltner. After they hugged, Vivian jerked her head toward her husband. Mayor Keltner engaged in an on-the-verge-of-heated discussion with a man whose body language reminded Varia of an old-timey, door-to-door salesman who stuck his foot in the threshold. Vivian frowned.

"And the quarrel continues," Fritz said. "Those two, Doorman David, and a handful of others, argued at the bakery this morning. I had to ask them to keep it civil."

"Explains your hand-in-your-pocket entrance. Who's the guy with the mayor?"

"Jim Jackson," Fritz said. "He and Isla's brother are business partners, trying to organize an event at the amphitheater."

Varia and Fritz made their way to the kitchen.

Isla stood at the stove. Her cheeks pinked as they proffered their gifts. "Stargazer lilies and daisies, how lovely. And you know I can't resist your jam tarts, Fritz." She turned the gas lower to keep the haggis from boiling and retrieved a vase for the flowers.

"You pruned your roses in the front garden," Varia said. "I plan to hack mine back next weekend."

"Bare sticks jutting from the ground look so sad," Isla said, "but they'll be beautiful come spring. The fairy garden I created among the rose bushes is adorable. You can never have too much good luck, and it cheers the thorny stalks."

"Later, when you're not so busy, show me how you used the gnomes and fairy houses from my store," Varia said.

A chorus of odd-sounding, duck-like calls to the rat-a-tat-tat of drums came from the backyard. "The rest of the band is warming up." Isla pointed out the kitchen window to the three men standing in the lamplight from left to right, Clive—a wiry blond, Graham—sporting a mustache and glasses, and Keith—an auburn-haired could-be-movie-star. "Hamish, the bandleader, piped in your arrival."

"We heard the bagpipes droning from blocks away," Fritz said.

Isla laughed. "That's probably why the upright pipes are called drones."

"How do you know the band?" Varia asked.

"The Scottish community is small," Isla said. "The pipe and drum band is a close-knit group, great friends. They've been together for years."

Isla placed the vase of flowers on the kitchen island. "We're almost ready for our Burns Night supper."

Isla gathered the two dozen guests into the great room around the long dining table Frankensteined together with three separate pieces. The men, staggered at every other chair, drew slips from a bowl for their cross-table companion. Hamish used his excellent bagpiper's lung capacity to string out the pronunciation of the name he plucked. "Neeeeshhhaaa?"

"Nick with an A, NICK-uh." Varia's sister smiled and moved to the chair opposite Hamish, whose eyes brightened.

Once everyone had a seating placement, Isla clinked one of the tabletop whiskey carafes with a spoon. "Burns Night. A time to celebrate Scotland and everything we Scottish love, from bagpipes, haggis, and Rabbie Burns, to thistle and whiskey, family, and friends. Let the festivities begin with the Scots' national poet's "Selkirk Grace."

> "Some hae meat and canna eat,
> And some wad eat that want it,
> But we hae meat and we can eat,
> And sae the Lord be thankit."

After the first course, a traditional cock-a-leekie soup, Isla and the guests required for the main course service took their leave. Graham and Clive knocked shoulders, tussling for passage through the doorway.

Hannelore fingered the embroidered thistles on the tablecloth and napkins. "Such fine needlework."

"Davina was an absolute artist with thread," Vivian said.

Isla and David returned, both with two large bowls. "Neeps and tatties." They placed them on each end of the table. "Turnips and potatoes," she explained to her non-Scottish friends with a wink. David took his seat. The bagpipes skirled. "That's my cue." Isla rushed to the kitchen.

Two pipers led the procession, and two drummers followed Isla, who carried the haggis on a silver salver. The musicians played the dinner call—humming vibrations of "Brose and Butter"—band pins on their sashes gleaming, and the red and blue drone cord tassels swinging. They circled the table and back to the head, where Isla placed the feast prize and invited her brother to perform a rousing rendition of Robert Burns's poem "Address to a Haggis."

> *"Fair fa' your honest, sonsie face,*
> *Great Chieftain o' the Puddin-race!...*
> *...His knife see Rustic-labour dight,*
> *An' cut ye up wi' ready slight..."*

David picked up a knife. He cut the haggis casing along its length, spilling its tasty guts, and continued the verse until near the end. Hefting the haggis over his head, he recited the last line.

> *"...But, if ye wish her gratefu' prayer,*
> *Gie her a Haggis!"*

He lowered the salver to the table to a round of applause. David doused the haggis with a splash of whiskey and lifted his tumbler. "Raise your glass and shout 'The Haggis!' "

As dinner began, Varia picked at the haggis on her plate, and Nicha did the same. Their eyes met, and they nodded with resolve. They each forked a helping of the crumbly sausage and took their bites together. Memories of their childhood teamwork to force down brussels sprouts flashed.

"A little peppery," Varia said. "Works well with the tatties." She sipped her dram of whiskey.

After dinner, guests performed songs and poems penned by Burns in the great room. Hamish set down his bagpipe and pulled a blushing Nicha from the sofa to dance with him while Keith, Graham, and Clive continued to play. In a corner, Hannelore and Vivian chatted with a group of women.

Varia snuck away to check her phone on the off chance she'd missed a call from Chloe. Fritz, tight-lipped and shoulders tensed, stood in the foyer cornered by David and Jim. She slid past the abruptly hushed men.

Jim gave Varia a steely stare as she hurried into the den. She skirted around the duffle-style bagpipe cases and drum gear to her purse. Chloe hadn't called her, but she couldn't resist a quick check-in.

Chloe answered. "Mom, aren't you at the party?"

"Just checking in on you and Wetzel."

"We're fine."

Varia imagined the eye roll she knew accompanied Chloe's heavy sigh.

"If that's all you wanted, I'm at a good part in my movie."

"I'll let you go. Enjoy." Varia tucked her phone back into her purse. *Teenage years loom.* Not wanting an uncomfortable repeat with the men on her return, she slipped out the front door to make her way around the house to the back entrance.

Varia followed a pathway strung with twinkle lights from the front flower garden to the backyard. A hedgerow lined the property, and a picket fence separated the tree-dotted lawn from the vegetable garden filled with ruffly lettuces, radishes, and carrots.

Voices drifted from behind an oak tree. Varia stopped, unsure if moving forward would interrupt. *I can't catch a break.*

"Listen to me," one Scottish man said. "Money, loads of it, is at stake. My cousin's trying to find a picture."

"Your cousin, Evan?" a deeper voice asked. "He's probably drunk, and you're paranoid." Graham emerged from behind the tree, adjusting his glasses, and strode toward the house.

Clive followed. "But, Graham, he's gonna text me—"

"Snivel to Hamish or Keith."

The drummers strode through the French doors to the great room, so Varia entered the kitchen to the aroma of warm honey.

Isla was prepping dessert. She whipped heavy cream and gently folded in whiskey, honey, toasted oats, and fork-smashed raspberries. Varia helped dish the traditional cranachan, layering whole raspberries with the cream mixture, topped with a couple more berries, a smattering of toasted oats, and a honey drizzle. They placed the dessert glasses on the kitchen island with a tray of shortbread cookies so people could help themselves.

"The cranachan is ready," Isla called out to her guests.

Hamish topped two cranachans with shortbread and handed one to Nicha. Clive's phone chimed. He pulled it from his pocket and stepped away from the island.

People mingled about the house, some taking their dessert to the back patio to sit around the fire pit. At one point, David took the chance to pitch his latest venture to those lingering inside.

"A win-win for everyone," he said. "Jim and I handle booking the talent, tickets, stage sets, sound, and manage advertising and sponsorship opportunities for the local businesses. All the town's responsible for is the promotion."

"Our amphitheater stays mostly booked," Mayor Keltner said. "The nearby university hosts our main draw, the summer theater season."

"One hundred percent booked would be better," David said. "We're already talking with the pipe and drum band and several other local groups. You don't want to be the mayor who let the big bucks slip through his fingers."

Mayor Keltner bristled.

"David, please," Isla interrupted. "It's Burns Night. Leave business matters for another time."

Salvaging the party atmosphere, Keith picked up his bagpipe and played a sprightly tune.

Varia approached Isla. "Now may be a good time to show me your fairy garden."

Isla grinned and led the way to the front door. As they passed the den,

Isla's shoulders slumped. "You'd think the pipers would be more careful with their equipment."

Varia stepped to the den door. Tartan towels, pipe brushes, corks, and spools of string exploded from the unzipped bagpipe cases. "They weren't a mess a while ago."

"I'll talk with Hamish when we come back in the house," Isla said.

Once outside, Varia asked, "Is the tension between you and David getting any better?"

"I'm trying." Isla shook her head. "David couldn't be bothered to come home and visit Mom before she passed. Not even for her funeral. But seven weeks later, he swooped down from Oregon, banking on an inheritance." She sighed. "I didn't want him turning our Burns Night supper into a business opportunity."

"Feel better?" Varia asked.

"You're a wonderful friend." Isla smiled. "Let's go to the fairy garden."

They followed the same route Varia had taken before, but instead of turning toward the backyard, they veered left until they reached a stone patio on the right. There, surrounded by Isla's dozen pruned rose bushes, a kilted, male body sprawled facedown amid the magical fairy garden's miniature houses.

Varia grabbed Isla's arm and struggled for a stuttered scream. "Who is it?"

The women shuffled closer. Straggly blond hair fanned around the man's head, and a yellow tasseled cord cinched his neck.

"Oh, gawd." Isla raised trembling hands to her face. "Clive."

Varia knelt beside him. Her heart raced, thumping like a drum in her ears. She checked his wrist for a pulse and stared at Isla. "He's dead. Go call the police."

"No, no, no." Isla stood frozen.

"Isla! Call 9-1-1."

A sobbing Isla ran.

* * *

Deputy Bruce Langley stepped from the sheriff's department's SUV as two other police cruisers pulled to the curb of Isla's home. He conferred with his fellow officers before coming through the picket gate.

Varia and Isla huddled on the front step, and David stood by the door.

The deputy frowned as he eyed Varia. "You didn't touch anything, right?"

"Only his wrist to check—" Varia choked up.

David stepped forward. "I'll show you where he lies." He gestured to the garden path.

"You ladies go inside," Deputy Langley said. "I'll be with you soon."

Waiting just inside the door, Hannelore and Nicha were ready to offer hugs. Hannelore wrapped her arms around her daughter, and the floodgate of Varia's tears released.

Isla melted into Nicha before collecting herself.

Varia pulled away from her mother's hug, sniffled, and wiped her eyes.

"You both must be freezing," Hannelore said. "Let's go to the kitchen and get you girls warm. Vivian put the kettle on for tea."

Varia and Isla sat on chairs at the kitchen island. Across from them, a sole serving of cranachan remained.

Isla pinched the bridge of her nose, but tears streamed anyway. "Clive didn't have his dessert." She sighed. "He'd been so excited because it reminded him of home. His mother's cranachan was his favorite."

Nicha patted Isla's back.

Hannelore pulled teacups from the cupboard, and Vivian warmed the bone china teapot with hot water.

"Sorry to intrude." Jim entered the kitchen with a faint scrape against the tile. "I wanted to take some whiskey to the band. They're pretty cut up, and I know David's busy outside."

Isla pointed to a bottle behind Jim on the counter. "How thoughtful. You can find glasses in the great room's hutch."

The teakettle whistled.

Jim turned back around. "Ladies, let me get that for you." He reached for the kettle and hollered when he missed the handle, burning his right hand.

Hannelore flipped the faucet from hot to cold. "Hold your hand under the water."

Jumping forward, Vivian asked, "Isla, do you have antibacterial ointment and gauze?"

"In the guest bathroom medicine cabinet, we have ointment and adhesive bandages, but I don't think there's any gauze." Isla started to stand.

"You sit. I'll go." Nicha ran to the bathroom.

"Plastic cling wrap will do," Hannelore said to Isla.

"Top drawer." Isla stayed put. "Below the coffee pot."

Varia's mind whirled, replaying snippets of the evening in slow motion. How did this perfectly orchestrated party turn so foul?

Returning, Nicha handed the medication to her mother.

After Vivian patted Jim's hand dry, Hannelore squeezed the ointment onto his burns and cling-wrapped his hand. She swiped lint from the arm of his gray sweater, crumpled the paper towels, and threw away the trash.

Varia stood. "I'll take the band a finger of whiskey, but the bottle should wait until after everyone talks with the police."

"Someone else will need to do that." Deputy Langley strode into the kitchen. "And the bottle can definitely wait. The forensic team will arrive shortly. I want to interview Varia first. Someplace private?"

"I'll take the drinks to the band," Nicha said.

Isla showed Varia and Deputy Langley to the office she and David had shared the past three weeks. Two desks lined the walls—Isla's overlooking the vegetable garden, and David's sparse space viewed a corkboard pinned with a Colton Hills Music Festival poster and pricing structures.

Varia took Isla's desk chair while Deputy Langley sat in David's seat. The deputy dug right into his investigation. Varia explained how she and Isla had discovered Clive, the mess in the den, and the conversation she overheard between Clive and Graham.

"Someone strangled him with the yellow cord," Varia said.

"Appears so," the deputy agreed. "How well did you know Clive?"

"I'd bumped into him, small town and all. But we were acquaintances, not friends."

Deputy Langley stood. "I may need to speak to you again. And, Varia, you will let me know immediately if anything else comes to mind."

They walked back to the great room.

The deputy questioned Isla and David. Then he led the remaining band members, one at a time, to the den before heading to the office for their interviews.

The spirit in the great room had lost its vibrancy. Varia blamed not only Clive's demise but the evil-eyed officer standing guard dog over the party. Officer number three paced in the front garden while the forensic team worked.

After the kitchen was spotless, Hannelore and Vivian had no busy work left to keep their minds off murder. Instead, they revisited their friend Davina's needlework—wall hangings, throw pillows, doilies, and a closer examination of the thistle tablecloth and napkins.

"You know our mother," Nicha said to her sister. "She wallows in *pretty* when things go bad. How are you doing?"

Varia plunked onto the chair next to Nicha at the table. "I'm confused. What about you? You and Hamish have been hard to separate tonight."

"We haven't spent the whole evening together. Hamish has his band. But he asked me out for Saturday night." Her eyes twinkled. "And I said yes."

Hamish returned to the great room, and Nicha went straight to him.

Varia's stomach knotted. *A moth to a flame.* She'd need to keep an eye on her sister. Hamish had to be a murder suspect, as did Graham and Keith. Any of them could overpower wiry Clive, who stretched to five-foot-nine if he wore heels and stood on a molehill.

The disheveled bagpipe cases intrigued Varia. They had been in a neat cluster when she'd checked her phone. *Tassels.* Red and blue tassels swayed from the bagpipes during the haggis procession. She squeezed her eyes closed at the memory of Clive in the garden. The yellow braided rope around his neck—a tasseled cord like those tied to bagpipe drones.

Deputy Langley continued to interview his way through the guest list.

Varia rewound the conversation from behind the old oak tree. Graham hadn't been receptive to Clive's concerns, but the phone chime must have been the expected text from his cousin. Where was Clive's phone now?

Jim returned from his interview, cradling his injured hand. "Bakery Man, the deputy wants you next."

Fritz walked across the room—to Varia's untimely delight. When she'd gone to the den, David and Jim had trapped Fritz in the foyer. *Did he see anything?*

A snap decision led Varia to the guest bathroom across the hall from the office. She pretended to be occupied and waited for Fritz. When he stepped out, she ambushed him. "I'll be fast because I'm sure you're supposed to send in the next hot-seat sitter."

"Yes, your mother."

"My mother..." Varia's heart sank. She and Fritz meandered toward the great room.

"Deputy Langley has to speak with everyone," Fritz said.

"Of course, you're right. I have a quick question. While you talked with David and Jim in the foyer, did anyone enter the den after I'd left?"

"Thank God for Hamish and his bagpipes." Fritz scoffed. "He went by and into the den, and Keith followed. I took the opportunity to make my getaway. David and Jim are relentless. They want the bakery as a sponsor for their next music festival." He sneered and slipped away into the great room. "Hannelore, it's your turn."

Hannelore stood, walked to Varia, and squeezed her daughter's hands.

"You'll be fine, Mother."

Hannelore took a deep breath and headed down the hall.

After their interview, Deputy Langley trailed Hannelore to the kitchen for a glass of water. Varia asked to speak with him again, and they returned to the office.

"Did you find Clive's phone?"

Deputy Langley steepled his fingers. "Why do you ask?"

"Clive was waiting for a text, a photo. I think the message came through while he stood in line for dessert. His phone chimed, and he left the room. Maybe the killer's picture is in that text."

"Interesting theory. Have a password for me?"

"No, but I could ask the band members. Maybe they'll have a good guess."

Deputy Langley raised one eyebrow, implying she'd better not butt in.

"Hamish and Keith were in the den after I checked my phone, but before Isla and I found Clive."

"How do you know?"

"I asked Fritz. I passed him, David, and Jim in the foyer on my way to the den."

"Go join the others." Deputy Langley groaned. "I need to check on a few things."

The deputy went to the front garden, and Varia returned to the great room. Hamish and Nicha sat close on the sofa, and Hannelore on the adjacent love seat. The other guests sat scattered about the room and kitchen. Varia wanted a quieter place to think and chose a chair by the French doors. Away from the crowd and overlooking the backyard, she reviewed the evening in her head. The puzzle was coming together, but she needed one crucial piece to connect it all.

Deputy Langley returned with two evidence bags in hand. He stood in front of the bagpipers and raised the first, containing a yellow tasseled rope. "Hamish, is this your drone cord?"

"Aye, it is. The new one Keith picked up for me."

"I gave him the cord tonight," Keith said.

The deputy held up the other bag. "The band wears a special pin on your sashes. But all we found of Clive's pin was the backing. Did you argue and throw him out of the band?"

"What? No." Hamish shook his head. "Clive was a great friend and band member. You can't think—"

"Hamish Findlay, I'm detaining you under suspicion of murder."

The bagpiper sucked in his breath and clutched his sash, his pin catching the light. "I didn't kill Clive."

A band pin. The piece that eluded Varia finally fit. She rushed to the trash can in the kitchen and dug out the paper towel wad her mother had thrown away. "Wait," Varia yelled.

"For what?" the deputy asked. "I have my murder suspect."

"I don't think you do." She walked toward Deputy Langley as she opened the paper towels to reveal soft, buttery-colored lint and two yellow threads.

Hannelore gasped.

Varia turned to stare at the man sitting in the wingback chair near the fireplace. "Jim Jackson is your killer."

"I...I..." Hannelore stuttered. "I wiped those threads from his sleeve when I bandaged his hand."

"I hardly knew Clive." Jim crossed his arms. "I had no reason to kill him."

"True enough," Varia said. "You didn't know Clive well, but his cousin knew you." She turned to the pipers. "Who can call Clive's cousin and have him resend the photo?"

"Which cousin?" Keith asked.

Graham pulled his mustache. "Evan in Colton Hills, Oregon."

"I have Evan's number." Keith rose to go and make the difficult call.

"While we wait for the photo," Varia said, "check the bottom of Jim's shoes."

Deputy Langley pointed at the sullen officer. "I'll check the shoe, and you help Keith with the call."

The deputy knelt at Jim's chair.

Jim struggled but failed. Stuck in the sole of his shoe was a scratched band pin.

"How did you know?" Deputy Langley asked Varia.

"I heard the pin scraping against the kitchen tile," she said. "I didn't know what it was at the time, but between the pin backing and Hamish's glinting pin on his sash, it all made sense. Jim must have seen Keith give Hamish the drone cord and Hamish placing it in his bagpipe case."

"He was in the foyer." Hamish's eyes were wide. "Pipers always keep extra supplies in their cases."

"And I bet," Varia said, "if you have medical professionals examine Jim's hand, you'll find rope burns beneath the kettle burn. A painful ruse to cover up evidence."

Keith returned. His red-rimmed eyes glared. He held up his phone and showed a picture of Jim Jackson. "Jim swindled a boatload of money from Colton Hills. He had sold tickets, sponsorships, and program advertisements, and Colton Hills promoted a fake music festival. Evan warned Clive so Schoneburg could avoid the scam. The town has proof. They just didn't know where to find Jim."

"Jim, what is he talking about?" David asked. "The festival was set and ready when you sent me to our next event."

"I plead the fifth." Jim's beady eyes squinted.

"Jim Jackson, you're under arrest for the murder of Clive Buchannan."

* * *

Isla wiped her tears as an officer placed David in the cruiser and drove away, following the car with Jim. "David's always moved from one get-rich-quick scheme to the next, but I don't believe he'd intentionally scam anyone. My brother has a good heart. He just loses track of it sometimes."

Varia hugged her friend. "He'll be back. The police need David to answer questions and help nail Jim for swindling."

The coroner's hearse pulled up. Detective Langley helped ready Clive's body for transport. Holding back tears, Hamish, Keith, and Graham stood guard and played "Amazing Grace" as the coroner carried Clive away.

"Auld Lang Syne is the traditional end to a Burns Night." Isla drew a ragged breath. "But the hymn is a fitting tribute."

"We'll let you get some rest, Isla," Varia said. "I'll call you in the morning."

Hannelore squeezed Isla's shoulders. "Your mother would've been proud of your Burns Night supper."

Nicha touched Hamish's arm as she walked past him.

"Come on, ladies," Fritz said. "I'll walk you home."

The drone of bagpipes faded into the night.

FOUL BALL

By Maurice Givens

I hate hospitals. They are cold, impersonal, and smell of disinfectants. The aroma hit me the instant I opened the hospital door. The stark white walls didn't help the impersonal feel. A girl behind the desk, about sixteen, had one of those teenage hairdos: every strand for itself. Roosevelt Phips, one of the best catchers in Major League Baseball, had dropped dead behind the plate during a game against the Pelicans. H was at the hospital, and so was I. I'm homicide detective Palmer Simms with the Chicago Police Department, Area 2.

I showed my badge. "I''m supposed to meet Mr. George Richards from the coroner''s office." It's amazing how a Black person gains respect when a badge is displayed.

"Yes, sir. He's downstairs in room sixteen."

Richards was standing in front of an examination table when I greeted him. He looked up as I approached. I said, "What do we have? All I know is this guy died suddenly."

Richards turned and spoke to a man standing next to him. "Dr. James, this is Sergeant Simms from homicide. Palmer, Dr. James is one of the team trainers."

"Why homicide?" asked James. "Nobody killed him. He was hit in the head with a baseball."

"It's routine," I said. "With a sudden, and possibly violent, death, the corner calls someone from homicide. What can you tell me?"

"I was in the dugout when Bill Hooks, that's the manager, said Roosevelt got hit in the face mask with a foul ball and fell over."

"Do you have an opinion as to what happened?" I asked. "Was it the blow to his head that killed him? Did he have any other medical conditions that could explain this?"

Dr. James said, "I suppose the ball hitting his mask could have done it, but catchers are hit like that every game. They don't fall over dead from it. The masks are pretty good protection. I know of no other conditions he had, medical or otherwise. He didn't complain of anything, and his last physical didn't show any problems."

I asked, "Who was the attending physician from the hospital?"

"That was Dr. Washington," James said. "He said to page him if he was needed."

"He's needed."

Dr. James picked up the phone, "Would you page Dr. Washington, please?"

I moved closer to the examining table to get a better look at the corpse. "Tell me, Dr. James, did you notice anything unusual when you reached him on the field?"

"No, he just wasn't breathing. I started CPR and rushed him to the ambulance to come here. I tried the automatic external defibrillator, but couldn't get him back."

I was interrupted before I could continue. "Excuse me, I'm Dr. Washington. Did someone page me?"

"Yes, I'm looking into the death of Roosevelt Phips."

Dr. Washington folded his arms across his chest. "Yes, this is a strange one."

I get very attentive when someone says a death is strange. "In what way?"

Dr. Washington pointed to a small bruise on Phips' forehead. "Well, this didn't seem like enough to cause a fatal injury."

Richards put his hand on my shoulder, "Palmer, we'll know more after we do a post-mortem. Right now, all I've got is questions."

I'm more attentive when the coroner says he has questions. I suspected this could end up being a homicide. "Doctor James, I need to get Phips' equipment from the ballpark."

"The grounds people should be at the ballpark for a while longer."

"Please have them stay until the evidence technicians get there. I'll get in touch with you or Doctor Washington if I need anything else."

I called back to the station to have evidence technicians get all of Phips' equipment and uniforms from the ballpark.

When I returned to the squad room, Captain Woodson grabbed me. "How does it look, Simms? Is it going to be a quick accident determination?"

Nothing like putting on a little pressure. "I don't know, Captain. Dr. Dixon, the ME, just got the body, but the hospital doctor didn't think the foul ball was enough to tag him. Richards says the ME is going to take a good look to see if it might be something else, maybe some drug or something. The team trainer said all the players would have left the ballpark by now, so I plan to go there tomorrow and talk to the umpires and players to see if any of them noticed anything out of the ordinary."

The captain walked me to my desk. "Keep me informed. A big-league ball player dropping dead on the ball field doesn't look good."

* * *

I had to pause and look when I reached the ballpark the next morning. The Sun rising over the right-field wall bathed the third-base dugout in an orange glow. The bats neatly stacked in their racks reflected the sunlight, giving an almost surreal look. Rhinos manager Bill Hooks had met me at the ballpark entrance. "I'm glad you could get here early," he said. "I was hoping we could talk." he had taken me across the field through the dugout to his office on the side of the team's locker room. "If you're still asking questions, does that mean it wasn't the foul ball that killed Phips?"

"The medical examiner hasn't made a report yet, so I can't say what killed him, because I don't know. I want to find out what you saw, and I want to talk to yesterday's plate umpire to see what he saw."

"I don't know what more I can add. The foul ball hit him in the mask and

192

stunned him a bit. The ump gave him time to recover, then Phips fell over. I, the trainer, and the doctor rushed out."

"Did the bat hit him?"

"No, only the ball."

So far, all the stories were the same. "What time do the umpires generally get here?"

"They should be getting in about now. I'll take you to their locker room."

In the locker room, Hooks walked up to one of the umpires. "Frank, this is Sergeant Simms. He's looking into Roosevelt's death."

The umpire extended his hand, "Morning, Sergeant. What can I do for you?"

"Tell me what happened yesterday."

"Josh Logan was batting. He hit a couple foul tips. One to Phips' chest protector, and the last one to his mask. Phips staggered and fell to his knees from the force of the ball. I called time to let him recover. He went to stand up, but fell back to his knees. He knelt for a few seconds, then fell over on his side. The manager, trainer, and team doctor rushed out of the dugout, but when the doctor looked at him, he wasn't breathing. The trainer started CPR while the team doctor examined him. The manager called for a stretcher cart. Roosevelt's teammates rushed from the dugout and gathered by the on-deck circle looking on. The Pelican's bench stood in front of their dugout. That's about it."

"Did he get hit by the bat?"

"No, just the ball."

This didn't make sense. A perfectly healthy man dies from a foul ball that barely left a bruise?

"Did you see anything unusual?" I asked. "Could something have been thrown from the stands?"

"What is this? Do you think something else killed Phips?" asked the umpire.

"No, I don't. At the moment, I'm collecting facts surrounding the incident."

"No, there was nothing unusual and nothing thrown from the stands."

I got pretty much the same answer from the players; nobody saw anything except the baseball hitting Phips' facemask. I left the locker room and the ballpark as puzzled as I was when I entered. I had gotten nothing to shed light on Phips' death.

When I got to my car, I was assaulted by my phone.

"Palmer, this is Paul Dixon. Can you come over to the morgue? I think I found something."

"Can't you give it to me over the phone, Doc?"

"I think you need to see it." Dr. Dixon had that teasing tone again.

"Okay, I'll be over. I'm leaving the ballpark now." I called to fill the captain in.

"Captain, I'm going to the morgue. Dixon thinks he may have found something."

"Let me know if he found anything important."

* * *

I liked visiting the morgue less than I liked visiting hospitals. They're not just impersonal; they seem to exude an impersonal finality. When I walked in, Dr. Dixon waved me over to the table where Phips was lying.

"Here's what I wanted to show you." Dixon pointed to Phips' chest.

I examined the body as closely as I knew how. The way he was acting, I knew he had something up his sleeve. "I don't see anything."

"I didn't either, at first. I kept telling myself that a foul ball couldn't have killed him. I went back over the body, looking for something else, anything else. Look closely right here," Dixon pointed to a small purple stain on Phips' chest. "There is a tiny puncture wound there."

I bent over the body and looked again. Then I saw it. It was so small, there was no wonder I missed it. "Oh yeah, I see it now. What is it? Why is it purple?"

"The purple is where I did a toxicity test. The stain means some kind of toxin is in the wound."

I wondered how this case could get more confusing. It now was an apparent homicide. But what I saw here and what Dixon said was implausible. "You make it sound like somebody stabbed him with a needle full of poison. You know that can't be, because he was playing baseball."

Dixon leaned against the examining table. "Palmer, all I can tell you is this is a puncture wound that has poison in it. And on top of that, the wound is in an area that was covered by his chest protector."

"What? So now you're saying somebody took off his chest protector, stabbed him with a poisoned needle, put his chest protector back on, and no one in the ballpark saw it being done."

Dixon held his hands out, palms up. "I can only tell you what I found. I'm calling this a homicide."

"Great, just what I need. Can I use your phone?"

"Sure, it's back in the office."

I walked to the office, trying to piece this case together. I called the evidence techs to tell them to be careful with Phips' gear, that the stuff could have poison on or in it. I then called the captain.

"Captain, the Phips case just turned into a homicide."

"Any other good news?"

"The ME says it looks like he may have been killed with a poisoned needle." I waited for the captain to tell me he was calling the men in white coats.

"The next thing you're going to say is the needle came from a blowgun."

"I was thinking about it."

"Very funny. What next?"

"I'm going over to the ballpark to talk to the manager again. The game should be over about the time I get there."

"Keep me in the loop, Simms."

* * *

The game had ended half an hour before I arrived. One of the park workers took me to the manager's office to wait until the post-game activities were over. I didn't have to wait long. "Sergeant Simms," Hooks said as he entered and moved to his desk. "I didn't think I'd see you again."

"The medical examiner's office is classifying Phips' death as a homicide."

"What? How can that be?"

I ignored his question. "Is there anybody on the team he didn't get along with?"

"You can't possibly think one of the players had anything to do with this."

I said nothing and waited.

"No, I don't know of anyone who had a problem with Roosevelt."

"I'll need to talk to your players again. How's your team schedule?"

"This series is the start of a home stand. We have an afternoon game tomorrow and then a day off before Baltimore comes in."

"Good. I'd like to start talking to them now and finish after your game tomorrow."

Hooks walked with me to the park gate after interviewing the players. The players were beginning to leave, and they all looked at me as I passed. One player stopped me. He was slight, maybe five feet ten inches, and looked skinny for an athlete. His cornrows ended a little below his shoulders. With his honey-colored skin tone, he looked to be no more than nineteen. I played ball in school, and this guy was a bit on the small side.

The player reached out to shake my hand. "If you need anything from me, just ask." When the player gripped my hand, he passed me a note. I put the note in my shirt pocket and waited until I was in my car before reading it. "Tonight, Trianon Lounge, 10 o'clock."

* * *

I'd never been to the Trianon Lounge. It's a relic of the 1950s and 60s. Once a thriving, elegant ballroom, the Trianon was now an elite watering hole with occasional bands. I spotted the ball player sitting at the end of a long bar and sat next to him.

He spoke without looking at me. "Why were you still hanging around the field?" he asked. "You don't think Roosevelt's death was an accident, do you?"

This was the first player to show interest. It struck me as weird that none of the others had asked me about Phips' death. "Why do you care?"

"I don't. The man was an ass. He won't get any sympathy from me."

Was this a motive? Was he the killer trying to find out how much I knew? "Why was he an ass?"

"The son-of-a-bitch was pushing PEDs."

"PEDs?"

"Yeah, performance-enhancement drugs. Steroids. He tried to talk me into taking them. I told him I didn't need that crap. 'You have to bulk up,' he said. 'I can show you how to do it without drawing attention to yourself,' he said. I told him where to put his steroids.

"I want to be like Larry Doby. How can I do that, taking steroids? I ask you, how? It would be an insult to Doby's memory. No, I'm not sad he's gone. His type is bad for the game. But I'm thinking the only reason you're still at the park is because it wasn't an accident. I may not have liked the guy, but nobody deserves to be killed. I don't know if the steroid thing was a factor, but thought you should know about it."

My motive for this center fielder was fading, but a new one was emerging. Was Phips pushing drugs? Did he get on the wrong side of his supplier?

"Do you know who he was giving steroids to?"

"No. Look at old and current team pictures, and compare them. Look at who got muscles, and got them quickly. That would be your first clue."

"How much do you weigh?"

"One fifty, why?"

"For what it's worth, is it possible he wasn't trying to talk you into cheating? Could he have wanted you to put on some weight? If you want to be like Larry Doby, you need to gain about 30 or 40 pounds. Thanks for the tip." I left with him watching me.

I spent a restless night trying to figure this mess out. Why would pushing steroids get Phips killed when a bunch of players were taking them? The puncture wound in Phips' chest was so small it had to be a needle of some kind. The nagging question was how did he get stuck with a needle under his chest protector, during the middle of a ball game, in a full ballpark, and nobody saw it?

* * *

The next morning, while I was reviewing my notes and scratching my head, my phone rang.

It was Evans, one of the evidence techs. "I've got something to show you."

"I'm on my way." When Evans said he had something, I jumped.

I walked into his lab but didn't see him. "Over here, Sarge. It was ingenious. We almost got caught by it ourselves. Thanks for telling us to be careful with this stuff. Here's your culprit." Evans handed me a clear hard plastic case with a small, thin needle inside. "That needle was in the chest protector, pointed at the catcher's chest." I started to open the case. "Careful," he said, "it still has something on it. I sent a sample out for tox screening. I'll know what it is when it comes back.

"It's really something," he said. "Think about it, the wearer won't get the poison until something or somebody hits the front of the protector. You go to a crime scene, and you look at the people there as possible suspects. Not in this case. This thing is random. Who knows when a ball will hit the protector? Or when they will bump chests celebrating a win? Totally random. The killer could have been anywhere when Phips was poisoned. Almost a perfect murder."

This didn't sound logical to me. "Wouldn't he feel the needle?"

"Nah, a baseball comes off the bat at over 100 miles per hour. The force of the ball hitting him would mask any needle prick. He wouldn't have noticed it. You need to look for someone who had access to his chest protector."

"Right." I thought for a minute. "I think I know who to talk to."

* * *

I went back to the ballpark. This time to talk to someone who would be considered completely innocent. Bill Hooks greeted me when I entered his office. "A few more trips here, and I'll put you on the roster."

"I wish my visits were under better circumstances. Who's your equipment manager?"

"Jerry Scott. Why?"

"Where can I find him?"

"What's going on, Sergeant?"

"I want to talk to him."

"About what?"

"Where can I find him, Mr. Hooks?"

"He's probably in the equipment room, back of the locker room."

Hooks followed me to the equipment room. Scott was standing by a table, lacing up a player's glove. Everything about him was average. Five-foot-eleven, brown hair, about 190 pounds, casual khaki pants, and a yellow polo shirt. He was the man nobody could describe.

"Mr. Scott, you and I need to talk. We found the needle."

"What needle?" Hooks asked. "Do you know what he's talking about, Jerry?"

"Mr. Hooks, I need you to move out of the way and keep quiet." I got closer to Scott. "Well, Mr. Scott, you want to tell me about the needle?"

Faster than I could react, Scott pushed me over a bench, with me ending up on my ass on the floor. By the time I was able to get to my feet, he was through the locker room and dugout and running across the field toward the center-field wall and an exit to 36th Street. Running after him, I pushed the talk button on my radio.

"4672 Boy, in foot pursuit!"

I was trying to run and talk at the same time. "Suspect...is leaving...the center-field door...at Rhinos ballpark...now on 36th Street...heading to Wentworth."

"4672 Boy, what is your location?" dispatch asked.

"On Wentworth...heading south...from 36th Street. He's...now going west...on 37th."

"212 is on the scene. We're at 37th and Wells. Where is he now, Sarge?"

"He's...headed right...to you."

"212, is everything okay there?" dispatch asked.

Scott offered no resistance.

"10-4, the suspect is in custody."

* * *

I walked into the interrogation room to try to break Scott down.

"What do you do at the ballpark, Jerry?"

"When we travel on road games, I pack and unpack the players' equipment. You know, things like bats and uniforms. I make sure the equipment is in good shape and repair it when it's not."

"Did Phips' gear need fixing?"

"His chest protector was unraveling a bit, and I sewed it up."

"Okay Jerry, we found the needle in the chest protector." I placed the evidence case with the needle on the table. "You're the only one who could have put it there. You going down for this by yourself?"

Jerry said nothing.

One of the lawyers from the state's attorney's office came into the interrogation room. "Did you read him his rights?"

"Yes, I did."

"Good. The needle in the chest protector is prima facie for premeditation, we're going for murder one. Let's keep everything by the book. I don't won't to lose this on a technicality."

I gave Scott a stern look. "So, Jerry, you heard the state's attorney. You gonna burn alone? We know you didn't think up the needle scheme. We know you're dealing steroids. Why would you kill someone over steroids? What else are you dealing? Who's the supplier? Who's giving you the stuff?"

Jerry said nothing.

"Suit yourself. Murder one is life, no parole. You talk to us, and we'll let the state's attorney know."

Jerry said nothing.

"Hope you enjoy spending the rest of your life in prison." I left the interrogation room.

Captain Woodson met me outside the room, "You know we have nothing to hold him on. We have nothing linking him to the needle. Everybody in the locker room had access to that equipment."

"Yes, I know. But I think he did it. I don't know why he did it. If I can figure that out, I could probably make a case."

"I was hoping the state's attorney coming in the room would put a scare into him. I'm releasing him in an hour."

* * *

The next day, Captain Woodson stuck his head outside his office door. "Palmer, you got a sec?"

"Sure, Captain. What's up?"

"Close the door. They brought Jerry Scott in this morning," he said.

"I thought we didn't have enough to hold him."

"We don't. He's in the morgue."

"What? Do we know what happened?"

"Not yet. I've asked the ME to expedite the autopsy."

"Damn. He was my only lead. I'm going to the morgue to see what Dixon has."

* * *

The ME was vague about Scott. "I don't know what to tell you, Palmer. There was a residue of sleeping pills in his stomach, but not enough to hurt him, and he had a prescription for them. He shouldn't be dead."

My best suspect was gone, and I needed answers. "Let's take a different approach," I said. "What could kill him and not be detectable?"

"That rules out poisons. No physical trauma. The only thing I can think of is heart attack. But I examined his heart, and it was healthy."

I was clutching at straws, "All right, what can cause a heart attack and not leave a trace?"

"Offhand, maybe arterial air embolism."

"Bring it down to my level, Doc."

"If you put an air bubble in an artery, it will look like a heart attack, and not be detectable. That would take someone with medical knowledge. There was a small needle mark on the inside of his elbow that might support that theory."

"Why would someone let that be done to them?" I asked.

"They wouldn't. If somebody tried to do that to me, I would fight like hell."

I was wondering how someone can get stuck with a needle and not fight. Then I had a thought. "What if you give him sleeping pills so he doesn't fight while you put the needle in?"

"That's a possibility."

"You said it takes someone with medical knowledge?"

"Yes, that's right."

"You may have just solved my case."

"Simms," the doctor said, "keep in mind that an embolism isn't detectable. You have nothing you can use in court."

"Then I'll need to find something I can use. Do you know what pharmacy filled the sleeping pill prescription?"

"Here's the pill bottle."

I looked at the pharmacy name on the bottle. "Can I use your phone?"

"You know where it is."

The captain answered my call. "What ya got, Palmer?"

"Captain, can you send a couple of uniforms to bring in the Rhinos' team doctor?"

"You got something?"

"I think so." I told the captain what I was thinking.

"Sounds good to me, but why would the team doctor do this? What possible motive would he have?"

"One of the players said steroids were being used. I think the doctor is providing the prescriptions."

"Okay, I'll have him brought in."

"Thanks, Captain. Can you transfer me to Sally?"

"Hold on."

I think Sally is the smartest computer person in the department. I wanted her on this case.

"Hello, Sergeant Simms," Sally answered the phone. "What can I do for you?"

"I'd like you to look at the Rhinos' team doctor, Alfred Larson. I want to know his background, any problems he has or had, you know what I'm looking for."

"I should have it by the time you get back."

* * *

I called Sally when I returned to Area 2. "Palmer, your doctor was a bad boy. He was sued for malpractice in California. Not once, but three times. He had his medical license suspended for a year."

"What were the suits about?"

"Wrong diagnosis that twice led to unnecessary surgery. He moved here five years ago, got an Illinois license, and started working for the Rhinos."

I asked, "Why would Illinois give him a license with that kind of record?"

"A lot of times, there's no database for this stuff."

"Your suspect is in interrogation room two," Woodson said when he passed my desk. "I want to be in on the questioning."

"Let's go see what he has to say," I said.

We entered the interrogation room and sat opposite Dr. Larson. "You have an interesting history, Doctor," I said. "Three lawsuits, loss of license, very interesting. Anything you want to talk about?"

The doctor was silent.

"How about supplying steroids to the players? I'm guessing you're not the main supplier. Then I'm thinking, with the history you have, why would you risk supplying steroids?"

The doctor remained silent.

"Who are you writing prescriptions for?" Woodson asked.

"I'm not pushing steroids," Doctor Larson said.

"C'mon, Doc, help me out here," I said. "Why are you risking your license pushing steroids?"

"I said I'm not pushing steroids."

I said, "I have a player that says drugs are being given to some on the team, and Phips was doing it."

"I know nothing about that," Larson said.

"Then why," Woodson asked, "did you kill Phips and Jerry Scott?"

"What?"

"You heard me, Doctor."

"Prove it," the doctor said.

"Doctor," Woodson said, "we have evidence that Scott was killed by an embolism."

"There's no such thing as evidence of embolism," Larson said.

Woodson lied, "That used to be true, there is now."

"And most people," I said, "don't realize that we can get fingerprints off a body."

Woodson pulled a photograph from a file folder and slid it in front of Larson.

"What's this?" the doctor asked.

"That," Woodson said, "is a photograph of the puncture wound on Scott's arm."

Dr. Larson looked between me and Woodson. "I have nothing to say."

I pulled the bottle of sleeping pills from an evidence bag. "Here's your problem, Doctor. These pills were found in Scott's apartment. Your prints are on the bottle. So, your prints on the prescription bottle and your prints on Scott's body. Sounds pretty good to me."

Larson looked at the photographs.

"Tell us about the steroids, Doctor," Woodson said.

"And why you had to kill Phips and Scott," I added.

"It wasn't steroids," Larson said.

"What was it?" I asked.

The doctor lowered his head.

"It's a gambling cartel out of Vegas," he said. "They told me to get the team to throw the playoff games, or they would tell the team owner about my past in California. I like being with the Rhinos. I didn't want to lose that or my Illinois license. Phips was the team leader, so I went to him. When I told him how much the cartel was going to pay the players to lose, he got mad and said if I talked to any others on the team, he was going to the manager. I couldn't risk that. I had to get rid of him. Then you started questioning Jerry. He had to be shut up. I couldn't let him say I was the one who gave him the needle."

I asked, "Why would Scott put the needle in Phips' chest protector? What did you have on him?"

"I told him it was a prank," Larson said. "I told him Phips would feel something like a mosquito sting. It would be funny to see him try to figure it out."

"Who is your contact, Doctor?"

"I don't know. He never gave me his name. He would show up when he needed something."

"Doctor," I said, "when we talked to the Rhinos' owner, he already knew about your past. He said everyone deserves a second chance."

The doctor was taken to a holding cell. Later, Captain Woodson stopped by my desk. "Good work, Palmer. I can't imagine a mind that would think up a murder plan like that."

"A brilliantly sick one, Captain."

THE TIME THIEF

By Michael Allan Mallory

December was a special month at Moose Ridge Lodge. The Swiss chalet-style hotel was decked out with all the trimmings: living potted Christmas trees, strings of pine boughs, Douglas fir wreaths, red ribbons, and, naturally, red poinsettias. The luscious deep greens and bright reds showed off against the blond timber frame. Viewing the decorations from behind the lobby desk, Charlotte Joubert inhaled the fresh pine scent and felt at peace. The lodge looked so festive; it was her favorite time of year.

She turned and noticed the plush moose doll on the shelf behind her had tipped over. Charlotte sat it up again. Stuffed cloth moose legs dangled over the shelf, arms out wide, ready to hug, its loveably goofy face smiling. She returned the smile. After a long dry spell, the lodge was profitable again, an added boon being that her former employer, Cruikshank Dynamics, had rented out the entire thirty-room facility for the weekend for a private event.

The good times were not to last.

Mindy returned from her break to take over the front desk. Charlotte had just slipped into her adjacent office when she was interrupted.

"Charlotte."

She looked up. Standing in her doorway was a distinguished sixty-something man with a full head of flowing gray hair and a stylish Van Dyke beard. Gordon Cruikshank gave off a prosperous Dutch burgomaster vibe that would have made him at home in a Rembrandt painting. Something was off, though. For all the years she had worked for him, she'd never known him to look this discombobulated.

"Is there a problem, Gordon?" she said with a pang of dread. It was he who had rented the lodge for the weekend work seminar, and the hotelier wanted a happy customer.

His face was solemn. "I have a situation. I need your help."

"Please, sit down." Her stomach tightened. This wasn't good, she thought and hoped she could ameliorate whatever the issue was.

He settled into the chair opposite her. Sporting a white turtleneck under a gray full zip fleece sweater, he pushed up the sleeves to display bare forearms. "My watch was stolen."

A watch? She exhaled, relieved the issue was nothing more serious. Outwardly, her face maintained the appropriate gravitas. A theft was still a theft.

Gordon hastened to add, "It may not seem like much, but the watch is a Rolex Submariner."

She returned a blank look.

"It's worth thirty-five thousand dollars."

Her eyes grew large. "Gordon, what are you doing with a thirty-five thousand dollar wristwatch?"

"It was my brother's. I got it after he died."

"Oh, I'm sorry." That explained why she hadn't remembered it. Three years had passed since Charlotte had left her job as Director of Human Resources. She tried not being judgmental; however, as a small business owner, she suspected it might be difficult to persuade her staff not to be wasteful if she were flaunting a high buck timepiece under their noses. But Gordon was Gordon. And how could she be critical of him when it was due to his generosity that the lodge was fully booked?

"We do have a lost and found," she thought it prudent to mention. "Perhaps someone turned in the watch."

He shook his head. "Already checked with the front desk clerk."

"I guess that would've been too easy. Where did you last see it?"

"The business center."

Like most hotels, Moose Ridge Lodge had a room off the lobby with computers and a printer for the convenience of guests.

He shrugged. "One minute, the watch was there, the next, it was gone. Someone stole it."

Stole was a dangerous word in her vocabulary. "It's not that I don't believe you. We just need to be careful before making accusations. You're positive the watch was taken and not mislaid?"

"There's no doubt."

"You want us to do a search?"

"I wish it were that simple. I'm convinced the thief has to be one of two people."

"I see. Want me to call the sheriff?"

He waved off the idea. "God, no. The situation is delicate enough without dragging in the police. That's why I want your help."

"I don't understand. What are you asking?"

"I want you to investigate."

"Whoa!" She blinked back, incredulous. "This is grand theft. You need a cop. I'm not a cop."

The bearded face appealed to her. "You and I worked together a long time. Charlotte, you're one of the sharpest, most perceptive people I know. As HR director, you prescreened a ton of job applicants. You often asked more perceptive questions than the hiring managers."

Charlotte shook her head. "That's not the same thing!"

"Close enough for me."

"Oh, come on, Gordon. Who do you think I am, Columbo?"

The sardonic mouth tugged back the Van Dyke whiskers. "Actually, you look more like a mature, Midwestern Clarice Starling."

She shot him a side-eye. Well, there'd be no silence from this lamb if she went along with this crazy scheme.

In an attempt to mollify her, he said, "I know it's an imposition. The thing is, you know these people. You worked with them." His shoulders hitched beneath his fleece sweater. "Give it a try."

She slumped in her chair. How could she refuse? Gordon had been a great boss; she'd loved working for him. When, four years earlier, she'd expressed her desire to resign and purchase and run a lodge in northern Minnesota, he'd given her his blessing to make a graceful exit from Cruikshank Dynamics on her terms. She owed him for that.

With a reluctant sigh, she caved. "I'll talk to them."

"Thank you!"

"Which two do you suspect?"

"Wade Torres and Dustin Schumacher."

She nodded. She did know these two. Not well, though well enough to understand the personalities she'd be dealing with. Both men were respected, highly-paid employees. Why on earth would either risk his job by doing something as dumb as stealing the boss's wristwatch? It made no sense. Charlotte's eyes flicked to the wall clock. Forty-five minutes until she needed to check in with the kitchen staff about dinner. With hands folded on her desk, she leveled receptive silver-gray eyes at him. "So tell me what happened."

He visibly relaxed. "The afternoon training session was on break. Most folks stayed in the dining hall. Me, I hustled to the business center to take a call on my cell. Took a water bottle with me. Klutz that I am, I knocked over the bottle when the call ended. Water splashed everywhere, on the desk and carpet. My wrist got soaked. Removed my watch and set it aside while I zipped out around the corner to the men's room to grab some paper towels for the mess. Got back, and the watch was gone."

"How long were you away?"

"Twenty-five seconds. Thirty tops."

Charlotte visualized it. The door to the business center was made from one long sheet of tempered glass. Anyone walking by could easily see inside, couldn't have missed a fancy watch lying unguarded on the empty narrow desk.

"First thing I did was search the room," he continued. "Didn't take long. It's small and pretty bare, so I bolted out in case the thief was still around. I saw Wade on his cell by the lobby hallway. In the opposite direction, Dustin was just stepping into the dining hall."

"The dining hall is a hundred and fifty feet the other way. You saw Dustin from the back. Sure it was him?"

"Hard to miss. He's wearing a green striped rugby shirt."

"Right," she smiled. "Anything else?"

"Yeah, while I'm standing in the hall, the women's restroom door opened, and Lola Orso came out."

Charlotte pressed her lips together. "Could Lola have taken the watch? The lobby restrooms are steps away from the business center."

"Not Lola. I'd never believe her capable of that." It seemed unimaginable to him.

That she could believe. From her interactions with Lola, Charlotte remembered her as professional and ethical. "I take it you spoke with her."

"You bet. She said no one else was in the women's restroom. Just her. The hall was empty when she walked in. That was it, so I asked your desk clerk—Mindy?—if she'd seen anything. She hadn't. Nobody else came by the lobby. And nobody turned in a watch." Gordon held Charlotte's gaze. "Who else could it have been? Has to be either Wade or Dustin."

"So it would seem."

"I spoke with them individually. Both said they didn't do it. Didn't see anything or anyone."

"Of course."

"After that, I went to the dining hall. The next session was just starting. I told the crowd my watch was missing and asked if anyone had seen it. No one had."

She felt compelled to add, "In case there's any doubt, I can vouch for my staff."

"Oh, I'm not suggesting your people had anything to do with it. I know you vouch for them. That's what made you a great HR director. Nobody was better at vetting interviewees than you."

Charlotte returned a self-effacing smile.

Gordon leaned forward and spoke from the heart. "Which is why I'm asking for your help. You understand people."

She made a face. "One problem is that your public announcement's given the thief warning and time to toss the watch."

"Maybe not."

She cocked an eyebrow.

He sat up, looking pleased with himself. "I isolated Wade and Dustin. Took them to the fireplace lounge to talk in private."

"How'd that go?"

"Not well."

"Duh, no surprise."

"I offered amnesty if the watch was returned."

"And it wasn't."

"No."

"Did you have them empty their pockets?"

"I didn't. It seemed too intrusive."

She sighed. "That was a missed opportunity. I mean, you went as far as accusing one of them of being a thief." She stopped at a new thought. "Did either of them volunteer to empty their pockets?"

Gordon was taken aback. "Come to think of it, no."

She looked at him pointedly.

He squirmed. "I see what you mean. There's still a chance. They're still in the room being watched by Victor Patel."

"Good." She nodded approvingly. Patel was the take-no-crap chief of operations at Cruikshank Dynamics, Gordon's bulldog. He wouldn't let Wade or Dustin pull anything while under his watch. That painted the situation differently. Standing up, she smoothed out her cowl neck sweater and took in a preparatory breath. "Well, time's awastin'. I'll talk to our friends. You'd better let me do this alone, Gordon. They might clam up with you there."

"Right."

"Just to be thorough, ask Lola to join us."

"You don't suspect her?"

"She's a witness. Was close to the business center. Maybe there's a memory we can jog loose."

"I'll round her up."

"Good." Charlotte shot him a warning look. "And no promises. This may be a wasted effort."

"Understood.

* * *

The fireplace lounge was a retreat within a retreat. Spacious yet cozy with a fieldstone fireplace, clothbound padded chairs, reading nooks, built-in bookcases, and a six-foot fully decorated spruce tree by the corner window. Pine garland draped from the open rafters, and rows of potted poinsettias lined the bottom bookcase shelves.

Charlotte gave a chin jut to the straight-backed man with deep-set eyes in the archway who stood as imperturbable as a Buckingham Palace grenadier. Victor Patel acknowledged her with a sly wink and moved into the hall with his smartphone. She swallowed a deep breath, steeled herself for action, and entered the lounge.

Wade Torres was admiring ornaments on the Christmas tree while, on the other side of the room, Dustin Schumacher inspected book titles. Both men looked bored to the bone and were doing anything to pass the time. At her approach, they swung about.

Wade—lanky, square-jawed, with chiseled good looks and an easy manner—blinked with surprise. "Charlotte? Hello." He flashed a friendly display of white teeth.

His rugby-shirted companion was more circumspect. "Why are you here, Charlotte?" Dustin Schumacher adjusted his spectacles, looking behind her. "Where's Gordon?"

She could feel the tension roll off them. Nobody, including her, wanted to be there. "This is awkward for all of us. Gordon asked me to speak with you. Be a fresh pair of eyes."

Wade snorted. "Do his dirty work, you mean."

Her face clouded. "I hope neither of you feel that's what this is. I'm trying to help resolve a problem. This won't take long. Please." She gestured toward the chairs in front of the gas-fed fireplace.

Wade took the moment in stride, easing his lanky frame into a padded armchair and made himself comfortable. A little too comfortable, she thought, for someone under suspicion of theft. A little too devil-may-care.

Dustin planted himself in the adjoining chair, sitting stiffly, rubbing the back of his hand. His feet shuffled against the carpet like a kid sent to the principal's office.

Just then, the clack-clack of hard heels on wood caught their attention. Through the archway strode a fortyish woman with flowing dark hair and a figure that dangerously filled out a belted magenta sweater dress. Her gait slowed as she stepped onto the carpet and saw the others. "Oh, sorry. Didn't mean to interrupt. Gordon asked me to come here." Lola Orso's sultry eyes looked back with uncertainty.

"Been expecting you. Please join us." Charlotte pulled out another chair to form a rough semi-circle by the fireplace. After everyone was seated, she offered a smile of reassurance to three unreceptive faces. In a cordial, non-threatening voice, she began. "I'm not here to judge. We're just reviewing what happened with Gordon's watch. You three were the closest to the business center when his watch disappeared—"

"Hold on," Lola cut her off, looking aggrieved. "You can't think I had anything to do with it."

Charlotte felt the other's apprehension more than heard it. "I'm not saying you did. What I was about to say was that you might have seen or heard something helpful. Just give me a few minutes, and we'll be finished."

The reassurance seemed to blunt Lola's anxiety. The tension melted from her shoulders.

Dustin was not so easily placated. "For the record, I'm here under protest. I don't like being called a thief."

"Same here," Wade piped in. "This whole thing sucks."

"It does suck," Charlotte agreed. "I've got better things to do myself. I'm just trying to help resolve the situation before it...escalates." *Gets ugly* was the phrase she wanted to use but decided against it. Too dicey. Long ago, she'd been told that one of her talents was making people feel at ease and getting them to open up about themselves. She hoped putting on her old human resources hat would work some magic.

After studying her for a few seconds, Dustin exhaled noisily. "Fine, let's get this over with."

He was unusually testy. She remembered him as a good-humored, sometimes brash thirty-five-year-old, the top salesman at Cruikshank Dynamics, a people pleaser with big ambitions. Great with customers. She understood his irritation. Anyone would feel that way. Dustin eventually settled down, pushing up the bridge of his glasses. "Well, not much to tell. I'd popped outside for a quick smoke. Came back later to the dining hall. Not much later, Gordon came in and tells everyone his watch is missing. Then he pulls me and Wade aside for a *private chat*." The acrimony in those last words hung in the air.

Charlotte acknowledged his feelings with a nod. "And the two of you have been in this room since?"

"Right."

"Let's go back to earlier. Did you see anyone else in the hallway?"

"Did I see anyone? No."

"You had to walk by the business center on your way to the dining hall. Did you notice if the watch was there?"

"See the watch? Nope. Wasn't paying attention."

"Did you hear footsteps or people talking?"

"Not from the hallway." Dustin massaged the back of his hand. Inhaled deeply. "There was a bunch of voices from the dining hall." He made a gesture of finality that he had nothing further to add.

She turned toward his colleague. "How about you, Wade? Can you run through what you did?"

Cruikshank's new vice president of sales cracked a smile, having reclaimed his previous good humor. Yes, she thought, the man could slip on the charm with the ease of a silk jacket.

"I had some calls to return," Wade said. "Gordon was in the business center, so I went to the alcove bench by the lobby. And before you ask, no, I didn't see or hear anything or anyone else—except the front desk clerk."

"Did you see Gordon exit the business center?"

"No. I was looking the other way. Great view of Lake Superior from the lobby. Didn't notice anything else. Was busy on a call."

"So you wouldn't have heard anyone behind you?"

"Not likely. I get tunnel vision on the phone. It wasn't until Gordon came up to me that I realized he was even there."

Charlotte frowned thoughtfully. "You wouldn't have seen Lola when she and Gordon talked outside the restrooms?"

"No. They were some forty feet behind me."

"That's not that far away."

"It is when you're focused on listening to the guy on the other end of the phone."

"Of course. Thanks." Charlotte sat back a little, folding her hands in her lap. Looked to the woman next to her whose lustrous dark hair draped across her shoulders, a thick strand of which she coiled lazily around her finger. "Your turn, Lola."

"What do you want to know?" the soft voice purred.

"Gordon said you also didn't see anyone in the hallway when you entered the restroom. That right?"

Lola gave a quick nod. "Yeah. Nobody else was around. Though I didn't look behind me," she added as an afterthought.

"You didn't hear footsteps or other sounds?"

"No."

"You were alone in the restroom?"

"Yup."

"Hear any outside sounds while you were in there?"

"Couldn't. The hand dryer was loud."

"You then exited the restroom and—what?"

"I saw Gordon walk out of the business center. He looked upset."

"What did he do?"

Lola squinted as she dredged up the memory. "He kinda spun around like he was looking for something. He glanced up and down the hallway. Saw me and made a beeline over. Asked if I'd seen anyone. I told him what I told you." Her sleek eyebrows lifted apologetically. "Sorry I can't be more helpful."

"No worries," Charlotte said in a distant voice, her gaze lost on the hearth's flames as she pictured the events as described. She was starting to agree with Gordon. One of these people must be the thief. But which one?

"Charlotte?"

It took a moment for her to realize someone was calling her name. Dustin's spectacled moon face stared at her.

"I'm sorry," she said, snapping out of her mental fog.

Dustin said, "I asked if there was anything else?"

She'd spaced out for a moment. The others looked at her with the same fidgety expectation. They wanted to be done with her and this place. She had no reason to detain them. "Sorry, a thought crossed my mind. Um, no, that's all. Thanks for your time, and I apologize for the inconvenience."

The three rose to go. Charlotte remained seated. Wade paused, turned, and looked at her with a curious expression. His words even more curious. "I trust you, Char," he said. "You're fair. I know you won't make a rash judgment."

As he left, she frowned at the hole he'd made in the air. "What an odd thing to say," she muttered.

She put away the chairs and nearly exited the room successfully. Two steps out, she felt something was out of place and was pulled back into the lounge. She saw it in a second. At the nearest bookcase, she reached over the poinsettia to the shelf above to straighten the dangling legs of the plush moose doll, the brother of the one in the lobby. The moose smiled at her, and she smiled back with a revelation.

"Ohhh, that's right."

In her office later, Charlotte racked her brain, trying to work out why Wade's parting comment had made her skin tingle. In need of a mental boost, she pulled a mini peppermint stick out of her candy cane jar. It didn't take long to realize that one wouldn't do. This was going to be a three-cane problem.

* * *

Twenty minutes later, Gordon was summoned to Charlotte's office. He was not alone. His dispirited companion was instructed to take the seat opposite her. After closing the door, Gordon lowered himself in the other chair, a glimmer of anticipation in his eyes.

She did not disappoint. The hotelier reached into her desk drawer and withdrew a Rolex watch which she presented to him.

"Fantastic! *Thank you.*" His relief was replaced by curiosity. "Where'd you find it?"

Her gaze shifted to the man next to him. "Just where Dustin put it."

The bespectacled face hardened. "You got it wrong. Wasn't me."

"Oh, Dustin, don't go there," Charlotte softly admonished. "Admit the truth."

He stared back in silence as he worked his jaw muscles.

Gordon slipped on the watch and leaned in toward her. "I told you you were good."

She allowed herself a little swell of pride. "As you said, I didn't work all those years in HR for nothing. You learn a lot about how people behave under the pressure of a job interview. I've seen it all. For example, Dustin is your top salesman. He's great in his element. Clients love him. Out of his element, though, he's not as nimble. He's a terrible liar away from his comfort zone. When I spoke with him in the fireplace lounge, he showed several signs of prevarication."

Dustin glared. "Prevari-what?"

"Not being truthful. You fidgeted too much."

"Says you."

"And there was your hand."

"What about it?"

"You kept rubbing or scratching it. Was it itchy?"

Gordon's eyes narrowed. "I don't follow."

Charlotte gestured for him to be patient. "I'm getting there. So after you spilled the water and left the business center for paper towels, Dustin walked by and saw your unattended Rolex. For some reason, he snatched it, turned round, and went back to the dining hall. I have no idea why he took the watch. It must've been on impulse, a bad one, which he realized later when you hustled him and Wade into the fireplace lounge. By then, it was clear you suspected one of them was the thief. Problem was he couldn't get rid of the watch because you had Victor Patel keeping an eye on them."

Gordon nodded. "Which was the whole point."

"Right. Dustin expected you to return. Maybe with the police. He had to dump the watch yet couldn't leave the room."

Dawn broke on Gordon's face. "It was in the fireplace lounge? That was a risk. He could've been seen."

"A risk, yet one he had to take. One thing in his favor was after a while, neither Wade nor Victor were paying much attention to him. They were just trying to pass the time. Dustin was clever. Across the room from Wade, away from the entryway, he paused in front of a bookcase where it took him less than two seconds to get rid of the watch."

"Where?" Gordon pressed. "Where'd he stash it? Behind a book?"

She shook her head. "He stuffed it in one of the poinsettia pots. Angling his body to mask the action."

"A poinsettia pot? They're all over the lodge. At least a dozen in that room alone. How did you figure that out?"

Charlotte leaned in. "Did you know that the sap from a poinsettia makes some people break out in a rash? When Dustin jammed his hand in the pot he must've broken a stem and got sap on his skin. Made it itchy. He kept scratching the back of his hand when I talked to him. I didn't make the allergic connection right away. Something Wade said that put me onto it."

"What was that?"

"He made a comment about me not making a rash judgment. *Rash.* The word stuck in my head until I remembered the sap connection. It made me wonder why Dustin's hand was that close to a poinsettia."

A quietly stewing Dustin shook his head. "That's bogus! Like Gordon said, those plants are all over the lodge. That's not proof." He jabbed his index finger at her.

Instead of being intimidated by the gesture, Charlotte grabbed his hand and turned it over. "Oh, look, is that a rash? Pretty fresh, I'd say. Sorry,

this is one thing you can't deny. You've been literally caught red-handed."
It took extra willpower for her not to smirk at that. "And, oh, that looks like
dirt under your fingernails."

Dustin jerked back his hand.

Clearing her throat meaningfully, she spun round her flat-screen LCD.
"There's also this." On the screen was a paused video image of the fireplace
lounge. The angle was skewed, yet Wade Torres could be seen admiring
the Christmas tree, while on the other side, Dustin stood by a bookcase, his
hand poised above a shelf."

She pressed a keyboard key, and the image advanced, showing his hand
movement. "Down and up." She paused the image. "His body's in the way,
yet you can see it looks like something's in his hand. When his hand comes
back up, it's empty. I checked the plants there and found the Rolex."

Gordon grunted approval "I'd call that proof."

A crestfallen Dustin slouched in his chair.

Gordon stared at him. "Why? Why did you do it?"

The other's eyes flared. "*Why?* Because you promoted Wade to VP of Sales.
That should've been my job! I'm your best salesman."

"Dustin, you *are* my best salesman," Gordon said in a pained voice.
"You're awesome at motivating yourself. The thing is, the Vice President of
Sales has to be good at motivating *others*. That's not you. That's Wade."

An uncomfortable silence followed.

After a minute, a forlorn Dustin sighed. "I suppose this means I'm fired."

Gordon confronted him. "Are you sorry?"

"Hell, yeah! I screwed up. I know it. I saw the watch. Wanted to lash out
at you. Stupid thing to do. I can't believe I did it. Saying sorry isn't enough."
He hung his head like a puppy being scolded for wetting the carpet.

"I think I believe you. No, Dustin, you're not fired. It's the holidays, a
time for goodwill."

An incredulous Dustin sat up. "For real?"

"Yes, for real. But don't screw up again."

"Roger that."

"If you can get past your feelings on Wade's promotion, I can overlook this incident. However, if you can't put this behind you, you're always free to resign."

Dustin swallowed hard. "Message understood, boss. What'll you tell the others about the watch?"

"Oh," Gordon laughed, "I'll just say I found it on the floor behind a planter. They'll think I'm getting absent-minded in my old age. Now go back to the dining hall, and don't ever give me reason to distrust you again."

A chastened Dustin stood up. "I won't let you down again." He shuffled out of the office.

"That was generous," Charlotte said.

"I meant what I said. I believe in second chances."

"Still very generous of you."

He shrugged it off, his brow furrowing at a new thought. "Wait, that image you showed us. You have cameras?"

"Installed last month. So new, I forgot about them. The idea is to let me keep an eye on things if I'm in my office. I'm testing them out in a few rooms. One's in the lobby, another's in the dining hall—"

"And one in the fireplace lounge."

"Yessir."

"Funny, I don't remember seeing any cameras."

Charlotte winked. "I don't want guests to feel like they're being watched, so I installed spy cams." She reached behind her, pulling up a plush moose doll, and set it on her desk. "The cameras are inside."

"You're sneaky."

"Why, thank you, Gordon. I try."

POETIC JUSTICE

By Nancy Cole Silverman

Old lady Fogel was dead. Of that, there was no doubt. She had been dead and cremated for better than five years. And her urn—an iridescent blue turquoise and brass affair—remained at the Desert City Crematorium. Unclaimed.

No one at the Sunset Assisted Living Center where Mildred Fogel had once been awarded the prize for the home's Oldest Living Resident was surprised when she passed. It's what old people do. They expire. Both the coroner and sheriff agreed that the most likely cause of Mildred's death was an accident; she was searching for something, fell, and hit her head. The case, if indeed there really was one, had long since grown cold, and was for all practical purposes, closed. Mildred had simply died as she had lived her last years, alone in her small apartment, attended to solely by those who brought her meds and her meals and stopped by to open and shut the blinds.

But Desert City Crematorium's newest Girl Friday, Angie Durst, was on a mission. Her boss, Mr. Ladd, had instructed her to do a little spring cleaning, which included finding a final resting place for Mildred's ashes. And Angie was determined to find someone who could help her locate a more appropriate spot for the old woman's urn than the inside of the crematorium's janitorial closet where Ms. Fogel's urn had recently been moved.

A card attached to Mildred's urn listed her as: Age: ninety-six. Occupation: schoolteacher. Last known residence: The Sunset Assisted Living

Center. Next of Kin: none.

Unwilling to see the old woman's ashes added to those other lost souls in the potter's field north of the city, Angie began her search at the Sunset Assisted Living Center. She hoped to find someone who knew something of the old spinster or that the facility itself might have some final memorial site where Angie might respectfully place Ms. Fogel's ashes.

Sitting at the reception desk that morning were two young women, Sally and Kathy, identifiable by their white collared shirts with Sunset's bright sunny logo above their name tags. They were similar in appearance and age—long dark hair, mid-twenties, lots of eye makeup—and together were totally absorbed in a fashion magazine on the desk in front of them.

"Excuse me." Angie leaned over the counter. "I'm here about one of your former residents. Mildred Fogel? I'd like to speak with someone who might remember her."

Sally, whose dark hair was pulled to the side with a fancy butterfly barrette, looked up—her brows pinched. "I'm sorry, Mildred Fogel?" Who cared about some old lady who had passed years ago. "I really can't help you. We're not supposed to talk about former residents, and our general manager, Mr. Blundt, he isn't here right now."

"Oh, don't be such a hard ass, Sally. Maybe somebody outside knew her." Kathy pointed toward sliding glass doors.

"Fine," Sally huffed. "You can check the courtyard if you like. One of our residents might remember her."

"Ask for Ruby," Kathy added. "She's the one with the red hair. If anyone remembers her, it'd be Ruby Ullman. She's been here the longest."

"Yeah, but watch out." Sally shook a finger, "She's a feisty old gal. Full of crazy stories. And if she doesn't like you, she'll wallop you with her cane—it's her weapon. And watch your bag. She's a bit of a kleptomaniac, that one."

"Aren't they all?" Kathy giggled.

Angie thanked the girls for their help and headed for the courtyard, where six wheelchaired residents were bundled with lap blankets despite the mid-morning desert sun. Spotting Ruby's graying-red hair, Angie stopped in front of the old woman's chair.

"Excuse me, Ruby? My name's Angie. I was hoping you might be able to help me. I'm curious about a former resident. Mildred Fogel—"

"Mildred!" Ruby gripped her cane and adjusted her blanket on her lap. "Oh, Good Lord, finally. 'Bout time. You here because of the break-ins?"

"Break-ins? I'm sorry, I don't know anything about any break-ins. Was there a robbery?"

"Oh, please, it wasn't a robbery. It was a murder...but you can't tell them that. They dismissed me as though I was crazy. They didn't want to waste time on some old spinster school teacher."

"They?"

"The police, girl. What's wrong with you? You daft? You're going to have to do a much better job if you're here to investigate."

"I'm sorry, I'm not—"

"Let me tell you. It wasn't the first time Mildred and I told them someone was breaking in and leaving things, but they didn't believe us. Not any more than I believe Mildred hit herself on the head and died. Woman and I taught school together for better than thirty years. She was in better shape than I was. No siree. Mildred didn't fall. Someone murdered her." Ruby held her cane up and shook it. "And I know who did."

"Who?" Angie dodged Ruby's cane.

"Bobby Downs! The handyman, that's who. Boy always was a problem, and still is."

"Ruby, calm down." Sally came running from behind the glass doors and, ducking Ruby's cane, suggested she had had too much excitement for the morning. "Let's get you back to your room, okay?" Then pushing the old woman past Angie, she added, "You'll have to excuse Ms. Ullman. When she gets like this, she doesn't make a lot of sense."

* * *

"Murdered." That was the term Angie used to describe Mildred's death as she sat in front of Mr. Ladd and informed him why she didn't think she could let go of Mildred's ashes...at least not yet. "Not until we know what happened. I mean, what if she really was murdered?"

"And you think holding on to an urn full of ashes is going to help you prove that?"

"Well, no. Not really, but what else is there?"

"Angie, let me remind you, you are not a detective. And finding out how Ms. Fogel died is not part of your job description. The only thing that concerns you is—"

"I know...it's finding a better location for her ashes than the inside of the janitorial closet. But—"

"Look, Angie, if you're really so concerned, go ahead, call the police. Tell them exactly what you told me. But whatever you do, those ashes don't come back here."

* * *

Convinced Ruby might have known something the police didn't and inspired by Mr. Ladd's suggestion, Angie called the local sheriff and was directed to Detective Marks, head of the cold case unit. Marks was, if nothing else, accommodating.

"I investigated that case, and I remember Ruby. She was beside herself. Screaming and yelling that some maintenance guy named Bobby had murdered Mildred. She kept saying he had hidden drugs in Mildred's apartment, but we couldn't find anything. Bobby did have a record, but Mr. Blundt, the general manager, stood by the boy. Said he was an exemplary employee and thought Ruby was confused. Bobby had gotten himself into some trouble in high school when Ruby knew him, but no more. Blundt was certain of it. But, if it will make you feel any better, I'll review the case and get back to you."

* * *

The next day, Angie returned to the Sunset Assisted Living Center with Ms.

Fogel's ashes. Perhaps Ruby might like them.

This time, Mr. Blundt met Angie as she entered the facility, and upon learning she wanted to speak with Ms. Ullman, directed Angie to Ruby's room.

As Angie approached Ruby's apartment, the door opened, and out came Sally.

"Oh, it's you," Sally said, "You're back."

"I am, and Mr. Blundt told me it was fine for me to see Ms. Ullman."

"Whatever," Sally snapped. "Just don't disturb her. She's easily rattled, and it takes forever to calm her down."

"I'll try my best." Angie slipped in front of Sally and closed the door behind her. "Ruby?" The old woman sat in her wheelchair and stared out the window. "It's Angie. We met the other day. You have a moment?"

Ruby whipped her chair around, a surprisingly spry move for the old woman. "It seems I have a few left. What is it you want? Have you something to report about Mildred's murder?"

"Actually, no. And I'm sorry if you're confused." Angie dropped her bag on the end of the bed and sat next to it. "I'm not here about the break-ins. I'm here because I work for the crematorium, and I thought since you and Mildred were friends and taught school together, you might like her ashes. So I brought along her urn." Angie reached into her bag and took out the urn.

"Mildred's ashes?" Ruby rolled her chair closer to the bed and poked the urn with the end of her cane. "Oh, good God, girl. That's not Mildred's ashes. I already have Mildred's ashes. They're under my bed. They're in a blue and brass urn exactly like the one there. Go ahead, take a look."

Angie got down on her knees and looked under the mattress. Sure enough, an urn matching the one Angie had brought with her lay sideways beneath the bed. She pulled it out and placed it on the bed next to Ms. Fogel's urn. "So, this is Ms. Fogel's urn?"

"You think I'd have anyone else's ashes beneath my bed?"

"Then whose ashes are these?" Angie pointed to the jar on the bed.

"The question, my dear, is not whose...but what?"

"What? W...w...what do you mean, what?" Angie winced.

"Cocaine, my dear!"

"C—co—cocaine?" Angie stepped away from the bed.

"You have to understand. Mildred and I had an agreement."

"An agreement?"

"Actually, it was a very simple arrangement. A few years ago, before Mildred was murdered, we attended a cremation seminar. We decided right then and there that was the way to go...pay now and go later. Laugh if you like, but it all seemed very efficient. After either of us passed, the cremation society would pick up the body and take care of all the particulars like filing death notices and such. All we had to do was pick out an urn, and when the time came, they would take care of everything. So we bought a couple of matching urns and agreed that whoever went first would keep the other's urn along with a set of final instructions."

"Like what?"

"Neither of us ever had anyone. No family. No living relatives. It didn't really matter much where we ended up. We were both just a couple of old spinster school teachers. Taught English together at Desert City High. The highlight of our time back then was the Friday Night football games. So each of us wrote out some final instructions, and since I survived Mildred, I filed hers along with my own and put them in my dresser drawer. You can have a look if you like." Ruby pointed with her cane to the dresser.

Angie opened the drawer. Sure enough, there was an envelope marked Last Will and Testament.

"Oh, and I sent a copy off to Stephanie Sachs."

"Who's Stephanie Sachs?" Angie looked around Ruby's sparsely furnished room. Unfortunately, there wasn't much of anything to will.

"Stephanie was a former student. Nice girl, always wanted to do the right thing. Started working for Coach Webber in the athletic office during her senior year and stayed on. Could have made much more of herself, but I think there was some boy in the picture, and she didn't want to leave Desert City."

"So you sent her a copy?" Angie held the envelope up.

"Along with instructions that it not be opened until we had both passed."

"And she agreed?"

"Of course. Stephanie was always an A student. Told us both she'd put the envelope in the file cabinet and follow whatever our last wishes were to the letter."

"And just what is it you wanted Stephanie to do?"

"Nothing very difficult. Once we had both passed, she was to come by here, pick up our urns, and toss our ashes in with the chalk in the field striper."

Angie's jaw dropped. "The field striper?"

"Oh, for God's sakes, girl. Certainly, you know what a field striper is. It's the chalk machine the coaches use to stripe the football field."

"You wanted your final resting place to be the football field?"

"Why not? We loved football, but when Bobby played, we had to forgo our Friday nights in protest."

"Bobby?"

"Bobby Downs. Our handyman. Oh, dear, I do hope this won't be too difficult for you to understand. I told you about him before. We knew Bobby back from when he was Desert City High's star quarterback. Coach used to call him Bobby Touch Down. But believe me, that kid was scoring more than touchdowns. He was nothing but trouble. Particularly in the classroom. Didn't know his Dickens from his Balzac and didn't give a damn. We never would have passed him, but Coach Webber wasn't about to lose a game—and he didn't want to lose Bobby. The school didn't have a chance, and every time we tried to bench Bobby for his grades, Webber overruled us. Bobby was trouble then and still is now. I'd forgotten all about him until we moved in and realized he was working here. We figured out right away he was the one breaking in and leaving things."

"Leaving things? Excuse me, but isn't the idea that when someone breaks in, they steal something?" Angie figured Ruby was confused and had mixed up her facts.

"You going to listen to my story or not?" Ruby shook her cane.

Angie backed up. "Go on."

"Bobby used our rooms to stash his drugs. Figured no one, least of all the police, would think to look here. But here they were. It was Mildred that figured it out. Found a bunch of Oxycontin in her dresser drawer. It's not unusual for seniors to have a few pain pills in their possession, but a cache of it? Hardly. And then later, she found a bag of cocaine hidden in her closet. Together it looked like a damn pharmacy, pain killers, and all kinds of meds we figured Bobby had stolen from the residents, a few pills at a time."

"And you reported it?"

"Of course we did. We notified Mr. Blundt, and he came in with his management team and swept our rooms. But when he couldn't find anything, he thought we were nuts. So we figured Bobby had moved his stash and hid it in some other resident's room. But the damage was done. Everyone here thought we were nothing but a couple of wacky old school teachers with a grudge against one of our former students. Then later, we found Bobby's stash again in Mildred's room and decided we'd catch him ourselves."

"What did you do?"

"We hid the drugs in Milly's urn, and then Milly hid the urn. We were going to show it to Mr. Blundt, but he was off that day. And then that night, Bobby came looking for his stash. When he couldn't find the drugs, he went crazy. He ransacked Mildred's apartment—tore through everything. I guess he didn't find the urn or didn't want to look inside. I started to hear noises coming from across the hall, but by the time I was able to open my door and wheel myself to Milly's, she was dead. Lying there on the floor, and Bobby was gone."

"And you're sure it was Bobby?"

"Of course, it was Bobby. Who else would it be? He's the handyman. He has a key to all the apartments. He could come and go as he pleased, any time of day."

"And after you found Mildred, who called the police?"

"I did. And they came right away, and the coroner, too. The detectives said it looked like Mildred was searching for something. That she must have tripped and hit her head. I told them I didn't believe it. That I thought

Mildred had been attacked."

"And did you tell them you suspected Bobby?"

"By the time the police got there, Bobby was in the room, and I was afraid to say anything. Bobby told the sheriff he had been out back replacing a security light. When he saw the lights from the ambulance arrive, he came inside to investigate. Neither the detective nor the coroner agreed with me that there had been any foul play. They thought I was just babbling. And when Mr. Blundt arrived, he said I was understandably upset and offered to get me something to calm my nerves, but I didn't want anything. I wanted my friend, and she was dead."

"I'm sorry. That must have been very upsetting."

"Yes, but that's not the end of the story. If it was, you wouldn't have that urn full of cocaine. After the coroner left, Mr. Blundt called the cremation society and arranged for them to picked up Mildred's body. I looked around for Mildred's urn—you know, the one we bought together—but couldn't find where she hid it. So when the cremation people came, I gave them my urn instead. A couple of weeks later, I get the urn with Mildred's ashes back in the mail. Meanwhile, the center here had cleared out her apartment, and I found the other urn with the cocaine in a box in the hallway they were about to send off to Goodwill. At first, I didn't know what to do. If Bobby found it, he'd think I hid it. So I toyed around with selling it on eBay. I'd seen where a man bought Veronica Lake's ashes on eBay and kept them on his dresser next to his mother's urn. At least that way, I would know where they were. But then I had a better idea. I'd return them. So I called an Uber and took the urn back to the cremation office. I told them they had sent me Mildred's ashes by mistake. That I didn't want them and handed them the jar with the cocaine inside. Mildred's ashes I kept and put under the bed."

"So, the crematorium had the urn with the cocaine all this time?" Angie realized that Mr. Ladd could have had no knowledge of the exchange as both she and Mr. Ladd had started working at the crematorium just the month before—hence Mr. Ladd's big push for spring cleaning.

"Exactly," Ruby said.

"And Bobby never knew?"

"He was convinced I had hidden his stash, and to this day, he keeps harassing me. Last time I beat him with my cane. Told him I didn't want him coming into my room and to get out. But now that you're here with the urn, I think we might be able to put an end to it."

"We?" Angie looked over her shoulder. Ruby couldn't possibly mean her. "You want me to help you finish what you and Mildred were trying to do and set up Bobby?"

"Why not?"

"You know I work for the crematorium, right? That I'm not a detective?"

"Well, looks to me like you've done more than the detective did. Besides, if you were to succeed, there might be an attractive reward in it for you."

Angie picked up the urn of cocaine and considered the risk. She could walk away. Take the urn filled with cocaine to potter's field, bury it, and be done with it. But, that would leave Ruby with Bobby, who would forever make Ruby's life difficult. And a reward was something Angie could use. Still, her skills were far from that of law enforcement. And despite Ruby wanting to resume whatever sting operation she and Mildred had previously tried to mount, Angie doubted, with Ruby in a wheelchair and Angie, barely five-foot-two, that they'd be any match for Desert City High's former star quarterback.

"You mind if I think about it?"

"I'm not going anywhere. But it'd be a great help to me if you would. I'd sleep better knowing Bobby's not around to threaten me anymore."

* * *

It didn't take long for Angie to make up her mind. In fact, she got no farther than the parking lot when she realized she had no choice in the matter.

A broad-shouldered young man, dressed in a white-uniformed shirt sporting the Center's logo on the back, was crouched in front of the driver's door of her car with his back to her.

"May I help you?" Angie clutched the key fob. Whoever he was, he was poking something beneath the car's front wheel with a long stick.

"This your car?"

"Why?" Angie asked.

"Because, lucky for you, I came along before you did."The man turned and faced her. In his hand, he held a long stick with the writing body of a snake looped across the end of it. "Found this deadly critter coiled up beneath the front wheel of your car. Ready to strike."

"Ugh!" Angie jumped backward.

The man tossed the viper into a trash barrel next to the car and covered it. "Don't worry. We get snakes out here all the time. Desert's their home. But this one won't bother you again. Long as you're careful, that is. You here visiting Ruby?"

"Yes. How did you know?" Angie clutched her bag to her shoulder.

"Seen you here before. Name's Bobby Downs. Ruby and I are old friends. She used to be one of my English teachers in high school. You?"

"Yes, she was my teacher, too." Angie was thinking on her feet, which was hard to do considering the shock of seeing the writing snake beneath the front wheel of her car, as well as Bobby Downs, Ruby's nemesis and Mildred's murderer, standing directly in front of her. "But it was a long time ago." Then clicking the key fob to unlock her car's door, she explained she needed to go. "If you'll excuse me, I'm late for a dental appointment. But thanks for the help."

* * *

Once back in the car and safely out of the lot, Angie picked up her cell phone and called Detective Marks. Perhaps by now, he had reviewed Mildred's death and found something he'd missed. But no such luck. Marks said he was about to call Angie and tell her he hadn't seen anything to indicate foul play and officially close the case when—

Angie blurted, "Cocaine!"

"What?"

"Mildred Fogel's ashes. They're not Mildred's ashes at all... It's...it's cocaine. At least that's what Ruby told me. Mildred's ashes were under

Ruby's bed the whole time. Bobby was using Mildred's apartment to stash his drugs, and when Mildred found them, she and Ruby hid them in the urn. And then—

"Slow down. You found cocaine?"

"Yeah—"

"Bring it in. We need to talk."

* * *

Ordinarily, the sheriff might not have been so willing to participate in a sting operation with an old lady like Ruby or Angie with no experience in law enforcement. But once the detective confirmed the white powder inside the urn was cocaine, they decided on a plan.

Angie agreed to wear a wire so that Detective Marks and his undercover operatives could listen in as she questioned Bobby. The idea was that Ruby would set up a meet in the lobby with Bobby. But rather than Ruby and Bobby meeting alone, Angie would be there, and she would tell Bobby exactly what Ruby had told her about her suspicions of Bobby using Mildred's apartment to hide his drugs. The detective had told her to stick close to the truth. To let Bobby think Angie had found his stash and was ready to make a trade if Bobby would agree to leave the old lady alone. Then, once Bobby had the urn in his possession, the agents would swarm in and arrest Bobby, and Ruby would be free of the man who haunted her the last several years of her life.

Only it didn't work that way.

By the time Angie got to the Sunset Assisted Living Center, Ruby was in the lobby. But she wasn't alone. She was arguing with Kathy, the receptionist, and the two were wrestling with a small bottle of pills.

"It's mine. You've no right to take it." Ruby clutched the pill bottle in her hand.

"Give it back," Kathy demanded. "It's not yours."

"Sally!" Ruby screamed for the other young receptionist. "Where are you? Stop her. I need your help."

"What's going on?" Angie rushed to Ruby's aid.

Kathy let go of Ruby's arm. "She's taken one of the resident's pills. She thinks they're hers, but—"

"They're not. Are they, Ruby?" Bobby stepped in front of Ruby's chair. "You stole them, didn't you? You're up to your old tricks again, aren't you?"

"I don't know what you're talking about." Ruby clutched the bottle in her hand, then spotting Sally, her accomplice, tossed Sally the bottle.

But not before Bobby, Desert City High's former star quarterback, backed up, intercepted the bottle, then turned and grabbed Sally before the young girl could escape.

Angie looked at Ruby. "It was you! You killed Mildred. The drugs were yours, not Bobby's."

"What are you talking about?" Ruby grabbed her cane and swung it wildly above her head, her cheeks red as her hair.

"Not so fast." Detective Marks, who had been idly standing by the reception counter dressed like a delivery driver, had heard it all and grabbed Ruby's cane. In another second, the old woman would have landed a severe blow on Angie's head. "I think you have some explaining to do, ma'am."

"Sally!" Ruby screamed.

"Don't you dare try to pin this on me." Sally struggled to release Bobby's grip on her arm.

"Sorry, Sally, you wouldn't be the first partner Ruby's left hanging." Bobby released his grip on Sally and stood behind. No way the young girl could run.

"Oh, please." Ruby said, "You think anyone will believe your story?"

"I might," Detective Marks cuffed Sally and told her to sit down. "But why don't you tell us what really happened the night Mildred died, Ruby."

"I'm not going to tell you anything." Ruby put her hands on the wheels of her chair, but Angie held the back of the chair steady. "You already know I think Bobby killed her—"

"I didn't murder Mildred," Bobby said.

"Because you didn't have any reason to." Angie took the urn from her bag. "You had no idea that Ruby had put the drugs inside this urn or that

Mildred had hidden the urn from Ruby."

Bobby stared at the urn. "You're right. I had no idea about an urn. The only thing I knew was that once Ruby moved in, she wanted me to work for her again. Just like I did in high school. Ruby needed a runner—that was me back in high school. Now it's Sally. Back then, I was flunking her class, and Ruby tried to get me benched. But the coach refused, and she protested. Even though she loved football, she wouldn't go to any of the games as long as I played. And when I got hurt and couldn't play, she said it was poetic justice. Some justice. When the docs wouldn't prescribe any more painkillers, Ruby stepped up. Said she could help me if I helped her. She'd get me the drugs I needed if I agreed to sell what I didn't use to my teammates. I guess she needed the money and was selling me some of her own prescription drugs. We agreed. Ruby hid my stash, and I expanded the business. Started selling coke and amphetamines. And when I was caught, I paid the price. Nobody ever suspected her. I kept my mouth shut, and because I was underage, my record was sealed. After high school, I cleaned my act up and got a job. But when Ruby moved in, I was on to her, and she knew it. Then Mildred died, and Ruby tried to blame me. I knew it was only a matter of time before I either caught her or she set me up. And now, here we are."

"Well, what did you expect?" Ruby sneered at Angie. "I knew the minute you showed up with the urn, I was finished. I'd have to convince you I'd hidden the urn from Bobby. Better to lose it than risk getting busted. I had to start over, and now you've ruined everything. I can't afford this place. Mildred inherited money, but me? I had to get creative. So I dealt drugs. But I never killed Mildred. She had an accident, exactly like the coroner said."

Detective Marks started to read Ruby and Sally their rights. "You have the right—"

"Oh, shut up," Ruby snarled. "I know my rights...you don't have to read me anything."

* * *

Three months later, Ruby died while still in residence at the Sunset Assisted Living Center. The D.A. thought it more humanitarian than waiting out a trial date in a jail cell. Meanwhile, Sally was convicted and sent to serve six years at the state penitentiary. Upon receiving word of Ruby's passing, Angie went to the nursing home and collected Mildred's urn from beneath Ruby's bed. She then took both Ruby and Mildred's ashes to Desert City High and met with Stephanie. It was Homecoming weekend, and Stephanie called Bobby, her fiancé. She asked if he would like to stripe the field for old time's sake. Bobby never said a word to Stephanie about his high school experiences with Ruby. But Stephanie had shared with Bobby that Mildred and Ruby's ashes would be mixed in the chalk striper. Bobby thought it odd. Mildred and Ruby had wanted to ensure Bobby would never be back on the field again, and yet, here he was, back on the field, distributing their ashes. Poetic Justice.

TRASH RACCOON

By Gabriel Valjan

The heat and summer stock were in high swelter in Prospect Bay. A stage production of *The Man Who Came to Dinner* was planned for the season. Phil Specter, the town's landscaper and gravedigger, was working the hedges in Courthouse Square with a trimmer that looked like your grandmother's electric knife when his wolfdog Cerberus decided to bolt towards the alley next to the Simon Playhouse. Phil had considered it nothing more than a dog's quest for some shade until he glanced over his shoulder and saw Cerberus on the sidewalk staring at him. The massive dog then turned tail and disappeared into Mamet Lane.

Orphaned after someone had shot his mother, Mabel, Cerberus seldom barked, howled, or whined. Everything he wished to convey, he did with a character actor's look and subtle gesture. Phil decided to follow his dog and held up his hand to stop the lone car on the street that early morning. The driver was one of Mr. Drucker's delivery boys on his way back to the grocery store.

Phil ventured into the alley. He ignored the sulfurous stench of trash that polluted the air. Cerberus saw it before Phil could say, "What is it, C?"

Swung open, the gate to the dumpster revealed a glimpse of a single Oxford shoe, black with a gloss high and bright as an eastern rat snake. The sole was smooth and tan because it was new. That shoe led to another; a sock to feet in silk, and the legs and body inside a tailored blue suit. Phil Specter reached for his cell phone. Cerberus turned his head as if to say,

"Not yet."

Phil Specter soon understood why.

On the corpse stood an armed trash raccoon. On his hind legs, he held a plastic knife in one paw, the remnant of a fluffernutter sandwich in the other. Phil looked down at the console and thumbed the number to Police Chief Shelby on his cell. Prospect Bay's sole man in law enforcement answered on the second ring.

"Morning, Phil. What can I do for you?"

"I need you at Mamet Lane, and bring Doc Perkins with you. We've got a body here."

Phil heard Shelby stand up because the office chair had rolled away and banged into the empty deputy's desk behind him. Shelby's wife had purchased him one of those special ergonomic chairs, the kind that came with a remote and lumbar support. Phil promised Shelby that he wouldn't touch anything, though he offered to take pictures of the crime scene with his phone.

"Leave the photography to Doc. Tell me what you see and, more importantly, who."

"That's the catch. I can't see the man's face."

"Oh, it's covered then."

"In a manner of speaking," Phil said. "Have you seen *Guardians of the Galaxy*?"

"The movie?" A note of surprise in the sheriff's voice. "I've seen it, yeah, but what's that got to do with anything?"

"Remember Rocket?"

"The talking raccoon?"

"I've got Rocket here, and he isn't talking."

"What is he doing then?"

"Eating a peanut butter and marshmallow crème sandwich, and he's wielding a knife. Don't worry, it's plastic. What should I do?"

"Let him finish his sammich."

* * *

Doctor Perkins exited the cruiser with Chief Shelby. Doc wasn't a people person, in that he wasn't a physician for humans. He was a veterinarian. Prospect Bay had no proper Medical Examiner, and Budd Perkins filled the gap until the county sheriff was notified.

Neither chief nor vet, or even the gravedigger, enjoyed surrendering a case to Sheriff Cox, who'd been Shelby's rival for both varsity letters and the gal who would become Shelby's wife. Cox the jock would attend college on scholarship, move to the next town over, and use his connections to secure a cushy job and pension. Shelby stayed local, married, and happy.

Doc Perkins was the first to ask Phil the question. "Did Rocket finish his fluffernutter?"

"He did, and he's fled the scene, but he left his weapon behind."

"I doubt the knife or a raccoon killed our man here."

Chief Shelby asked Phil, "Get a better look at the deceased after Rocket bailed?"

Phil shrugged. "I did, but I still don't know who he is."

Chief Shelby held Phil's shoulder. "There's time still, since you might be the one burying him." The lawman turned his attention to Perkins. "Any idea who our victim is?"

"Dirk Massey, and cause of death is for the County ME to decide. All I can do is take pictures, give you my opinion, and an approximate time of death. Protocol and procedure, remember?"

"No need to remind me, Doc."

While Perkins explored the crime scene and took the liver temp, the gravedigger and chief talked. Phil explained that he'd been shaping the hedges after he'd mown the lawn in front of the courthouse when Cerberus discovered the body.

Shelby looked towards the dead man, the actor Dirk Massey. "Familiar with his work?"

"No, but Ellen was a big fan."

It was always the same with celebrity deaths. People talked about them as if they were family members, their companion through all the milestones in life. The late Ellen Specter was no exception.

"What did she think of him?"

"Great actor. Terrible human being."

"One of them Broadway stage divas, then?"

"He did some Hollywood work, too," Phil said. "By the way, technically, it's divo." The chief winced. He expected an explanation, and Phil provided it. "Divo is the male equivalent of diva. Ellen made it a point to remind me of the distinction."

"Gender politics?"

"No, a crossword puzzle clue."

Perkins returned. "Preliminary guess is blunt trauma to the head, and our thespian here is recent."

"How recent?"

"Less than three hours. Body is still warm."

Phil and Shelby leaned back to look around the veterinarian. They noticed the small trickle of dried blood down the side of his face.

The chief's eyebrows lifted. "Think he fell?"

"Nope. Something or someone hit him hard and good on the top of his head."

"I don't see a weapon anywhere," Shelby said.

Perkins turned around and held his arms like Moses parting the Red Sea. "Gentlemen, welcome to the dumpster dive. May your quest be most fruitful and the least fragrant. I'm off to call County."

Perkins walked away, leaving Cerberus with his human and the sheriff.

"A divo, huh?" the chief said. "I take it our guy wasn't well-liked."

"On neither left nor right coast, according to Ellen."

"How disliked?"

"The gossip rags would create choice words that rhymed with his first and last name."

"That would cast a wide net, but lucky for us, Prospect Bay is a small town," the chief said. "We'll need to backtrack and establish a timeline for our great American actor."

"We?" Cerberus did nothing while Phil reacted. "I landscape and dig graves."

"You and your boy caught the case. Don't you want to solve it?"

* * *

Phil conceded and accompanied Chief Shelby because he knew the man lacked a deputy. Also, Shelby had been a constant friend during his wife's illness, and had encouraged the town council to hire him as Prospect Bay's official gravedigger, so Phil felt he owed the man. Chief Shelby, however, had a less obvious but crucial motive: Phil and the wolfdog were excellent sleuths.

The team of man and dog had proved instrumental in solving the murder of Harold 'Handsome Harry' Munster, the town's self-appointed agony uncle, art and food critic, and muckraker at *Prospect Bay Today*. Harry's journalistic venom had generated a long list of suspects, enough so that the newspaper had become known as *Painful Butt Today*.

And if what Ellen had said about the late actor was true, the entire cast and crew of the Kaufman and Hart play from 1939 (and later made into a movie with Bette Davis, Ann Sheridan, Monty Woolley, including a cameo by Jimmy Durante) were suspects. The chief would need all the help he could get interviewing the company.

First, Shelby and Phil drove to the Franklin house. They cornered the stage manager there. Barney, a lifelong aficionado of theatre, was eating breakfast at his mother's table when the trio arrived. Cerberus insisted on coming into the house. He refused to sit outside.

The dog frightened Barney, which made Shelby's job easy and his request easier. "I want to see the entire cast and crew at the Simon. Pronto."

"Now? This is summer stock. People have day jobs."

Cerberus lumbered up to Barney and placed his massive head on the man's thigh. Barney's eyes glanced down. Shelby asked Mrs. Franklin to bring over the phone. She owned one of those ancient heavy pieces of artillery from the last century. Black bulky body, heavy enough to dent a man's skull, it did offer the user one luxury and that was push-button dialing. Ma Franklin walked Ma Bell over. "So much for breakfast," she said.

The chief pointed at the relic and instructed Barney to start dialing. The manager hesitated. Cerberus started panting and Barney's face contorted. "The dog is drooling on me."

Phil answered, "There'll be less of a mess the sooner you start making the calls,"

"What will I tell them if they ask why the urgency?"

"Say it's official town business, and don't forget to come along, too."

Phil said that he had a question. He asked Barney, "Does Mr. Massey have anyone with him, like an agent, a secretary, or a publicist?"

"All the above in one person, and his name is Mr. Cutler."

"That sounds like a lot of work for one man."

"Ever hear the phrase 'one of the last big spenders'?"

"I think so. Why?"

"Dirk Massey isn't one of them. I'll make sure Bruce is there. Fortunate for you, he's staying with Mr. Massey at the Pemaquid Hotel."

"Will that be all?" Mrs. Franklin asked, hands on her hips.

The chief eyed the long and wide slab of fresh bacon in the dish on the table. She picked it up, about to hand it to Shelby when her hand changed direction, and she dropped it into Cerberus's mouth.

* * *

In the car ride over to the theater, Phil asked Shelby whether he considered Barney a suspect. The chief shook his head and said he doubted it. Barney Franklin was a chronic case of momma's boy, and he lacked the strength to swat and kill a fly. Dirk Massey was built like a leading man from the studio factory of yesteryear. It was hard for Phil to disagree with Shelby, because even lying on the fetid pavement, the man was six feet of attitude, wrapped in an ego, inside an expensive suit.

"If I recall the film version, there are more men than women in the cast."

"What are you saying, Chief?"

"Stands to reason, if Massey was murdered, it'd be a man, right?"

Cerberus barked and Phil's phone trilled. He answered it, mumbled a few words, and listened for a long minute. When he holstered his cell, Shelby asked, "Was that Doc?"

"He used that word preliminary again."

"I can picture his hands and the air quotes around the word. What did he say?"

"Definitely homicide."

"Anything else?"

"He wants it public that you made him do the dumpster dive."

Shelby shot Phil a look. "We had to work the case." He returned his attention to the road. "Anyway, did he find anything?"

"Just a whole lotta peanut butter and fluff inside the dumpster. Several bottles worth."

Chief Shelby cut the wheel and parked his car. "That must've been one happy raccoon."

* * *

The cast and crew sitting in the first few rows of the renovated Neil Simon Theatre had not shed a tear or expressed surprise when the chief announced Dirk Massey's death. If there was a reaction, it was heads turned to Barney Franklin and the murmur amongst them as to who would play the cantankerous and obnoxious Sheridan Whiteside. The late actor had stipulated in his contract that he would not tolerate an understudy.

While the audience discussed efforts to rescue the play, Chief Shelby evaluated the assembly for potential suspects. The men were a mixed bunch of midlife crises, and it'd take hours to interview them. The youngest and most able-bodied in the herd were the actresses who played Lorraine Sheldon, June Stanley, and ax-murderer sister Harriet Stanley. Of course, it was not lost on the chief that Prospect Bay's reigning beauty, the town's Venus on a half shell, would play the Bette Davis role of Maggie Cutler. The character's name compelled the chief to ask for Massey's beleaguered triple threat, Mr. Bruce Cutler.

"He must've slept in late. Massey works the man like a dog," someone said. He realized that Cerberus was on stage because he said, "No offense."

The wolfdog hunkered down and rested his head on his front paws. Cerberus seemed resigned to a long afternoon of Q and A. The chief stepped away to call the hotel and ask someone there to bring Mr. Cutler over, but not tell him that it was police business. He insisted that someone accompany Cutler.

Phil asked the man who played Jimmy Durante's character Banjo, "How does Mr. Massey treat Mr. Cutler?"

"Like a side of roast beef" was the answer.

"Roast beef?" Phil said.

"More like a roast boor," another voice said.

"Roast boar?"

"No, b-o-o-r." This illumination came from the young man who played Bert Jefferson, the love interest of Maggie Cutler. He looked built to do damage. Tall and rugged, he could use Ma Franklin's heavyweight phone as a lasso.

"May I ask where you were earlier this morning?" Phil asked Bert.

"Same place as everyone else, at the Pemaquid having breakfast."

"Everyone else?" Chief Shelby said.

"We all eat breakfast together. Builds team spirit."

Several heads bobbed in agreement. Cerberus raised his head at the sound of the commotion and then lowered it again.

Shelby asked, "All of you have breakfast together?"

"Every day," Mr. Mitchell, who played Ernest Stanley, said. "We meet every morning before we head off to work, those of us who aren't retired; in fact, we all meet after rehearsals for a drink before we call it a night."

Someone touched Mitchell's leg. "You're fessing to drinking and driving, idiot."

The chief's hands patted the air. "It's okay, folks. Don't worry about that. I know you're all responsible. Am I right to say that your two rituals occur at the Pemaquid Hotel?"

Heads nodded. Shelby turned to Phil. "Well, there's one massive alibi."

"Still no sign of Cutler. Do you believe he was asleep when Massey checked out?"

"Speak of the devil."

Cutler walked fast down the center aisle. He saw the cast and crew immediately and asked the chief from several feet away, "What's the meaning of this, Officer?"

"It's Chief Shelby, and this is my assistant, Phil Specter, and his companion Cerberus."

"The three-headed guardian of Hell?"

Cerberus opened an eye and closed it, the least interested in the assistant.

"Wolfdog," Phil said.

Cutler reviewed the faces in the row. "Where's Dirk?"

"He's dead."

"Dead?" The expression on Cutler's face seemed genuine enough, but both the chief and gravedigger understood they were in the company of actors, folks whose livelihood depended on illusion and deception. While they knew nothing about Cutler, the man had to have picked up some tricks of the trade from his employer and the company he kept.

Cutler appeared more frayed than nervous. Thin and gangly as Ichabod Crane, he moved as if he lived on caffeine and fumes from the coffee maker. The chief asked him to step aside and join him, Phil, and Cerberus for a private conversation. Stage left.

The chief had read somewhere, probably in a psychology magazine, that stage right received more attention from the audience, a carryover from the habit of reading from left to right. Stage left would remove Cutler from scrutiny.

"Can you tell me where you were this morning, Mr. Cutler?"

"In my bed at the hotel. I woke up moments ago."

"You don't join the cast for morning breakfast?" Phil asked.

"I'd love to, but Dirk is never-ending with tasks."

"About those tasks," the chief said in a calm voice. "Please elaborate."

"What isn't there to do?" Cutler said. His eyes looked to the ceiling, and he counted items on his hand. "There's his dry cleaning, his calendar and emails, the occasional snack because the hotel kitchen was closed, and fielding phone calls for him in three time zones. Shall I go on?"

"Three time zones?" Phil asked.

"New York. Broadway. LA. Obviously. London. Theatre."

"Obviously," Phil said.

"Must the hellhound stare at me?"

Cerberus understood Cutler because he ambled over in front of the man's feet, sat down, and stared up at him. While Cutler talked, Shelby observed the man's hands, face, and what he could see of his body under the clothes from Primark. No bruises. Nothing.

"Has Mr. Massey argued with anyone recently?" Shelby asked.

"You mean, who hasn't he argued with?" Cutler laughed that nervous laugh.

"He likes to get a rise out of people, then?"

"As if it were the reason for his existence. Oh, that's tacky, really a tacky thing to say."

"You're staying at the Pemaquid with Mr. Massey," Phil asked.

"Yes."

"No extracurricular errands?"

"What do you mean?"

"A call girl, drugs, anything of that sort?" Shelby asked.

"Boys, while I appreciate the tag-team interview here, and I understand you have a job to do, you can't be serious. In Prospect Bay? I'd cut and snort Sweet-n-Low with an AARP card and land the Early Bird Special before I ever scored an escort and ecstasy. Who has to count sheep when this little hamlet puts the Z in cozy?"

"Share the same room?" Shelby asked.

"Dirk and me? You've got to be kidding me."

Cerberus hit Cutler's foot.

"What's his problem?"

Phil said, "He wants you to answer the question."

"He had his own room, the best in the hotel. The man reminded me that I stole the air around him. I wasn't an actor, you know. Anything else, because I haven't had breakfast, and I'm starving."

"One last question," the chief said.

"Shoot."

"You mentioned snacks because the hotel kitchen was closed."

"Yeah, I did. So what?"

"What's with Massey and fluffernutter sandwiches?"

* * *

Mr. Drucker was a third-generation grocer who owned a spread that'd rival the national chains. His multiple-lane emporium was air-conditioned and stocked with the usual foodstuffs, but he'd expanded to include fine wines from every worthwhile appellation and vineyard, spirits from distilleries, and the latest microbrews from hipster entrepreneurs.

Sam Drucker was a hands-on man. He greeted customers by name, and his memory was sharp as that of a judge who could remember every man he sent to prison. He approached Shelby and Phil, one hand out, ready for a handshake, while he held his other hand out with a treat for Cerberus.

While the dog munched and crunched his delight, the chief asked about recent orders for fluffernutters sent to the Pemaquid Hotel. Drucker resisted at first, saying that a customer's account was kept in strictest confidence. The chief informed the store owner that a man, a valued customer of his, was dead.

"I suppose that terminates confidentiality."

"I would say it does," the chief answered.

"He did run a tab. I have it in my office. I hate to speak ill of the dead, but Mr. Massey was what our cousins in England would call cheap as chips."

"He was stingy then?" Phil asked.

"Cheap enough that he wouldn't spend the money to buy the vowel. Get it?"

"Yeah, I get the joke," Phil said, faking a smile. "Vowels a-e-i-o-u and sometimes y. The man was cheap as brass."

"Except brass kills," the chief said. "Brass, as in ammunition."

"Dirk Massey was shot?"

246

"No, and it was a bad joke," the chief said. "Why did you say the man was cheap?"

"My store offers premade sandwiches. Affordable, too. Any kind of sandwich you want, but this guy buys the ingredients and makes them himself."

"Did he buy in bulk?" Phil asked.

"Yeah, he did. You'd think he was a squirrel and burying nuts for the winter."

"You have someone bring his supplies over?" the chief asked.

"Sure, Teddy handles all my deliveries."

No sooner had Shelby asked whether Teddy was around, they saw him several feet behind his employer. Teddy made two critical mistakes. Mistake one was that he turned and ran, which was an admission of guilt. He knew Phil had seen him earlier that morning when he crossed the street. Mistake two was he thought he could outrun Cerberus.

He couldn't, and he didn't.

* * *

Teddy Dorsey swore up and down he was innocent and that it was an accident.

While he gave his statement at the station, Cerberus at his feet, he explained he always wanted to be an actor and that he'd ask the famous actor whether he could be his understudy. At first, Massey tried to be polite and said Teddy was too young to play Sheridan Whiteside. Teddy agreed but pivoted, asking Dirk Massey whether he could give him any pointers, any worthwhile advice on how to be a good actor. Massey told him to watch as many films as he could.

"How many fluffernutter deliveries did you make?" Chief Shelby asked.

"The cast has been practicing six days a week for the last six weeks. There are twenty-four slices of bread in a loaf of bread, so that'd last him close to a week. I'd say I see him twice a week because he'd run out of either peanut butter or fluff first."

247

"He loved fluffernutters that much?"

"That's not why he ate them."

"If he didn't love them, then why would he eat so many of them?"

"Because he was cheap, Chief. He refused to spend money at the hotel. He assumed the town's committee for the arts would give him a stipend for food and drink, but they didn't and he blamed that assistant of his for not doing his due diligence."

"Bruce Cutler," Shelby said.

"That's the guy."

"But you killed Massey," Phil said.

"I said it was an accident, I swear."

"I don't think so," the chief said. "I think you killed him because he wouldn't give you the time of day. No advice as an actor. He wouldn't open doors for you, is that it?"

"No," Teddy said. "It was an accident, I tell you."

Phil leaned forward, inches away from Teddy's face. "I saw you at the scene. The man's body was warm, left in an alleyway, like he was garbage."

"I can explain."

The chief joined in, trying to break Teddy. "Then you ran away from us at Drucker's. That doesn't make you look good, Teddy. Know how it makes you look? Guilty. Why? Because only a guilty person runs from the police."

"And flees the scene of an accident or a crime," Phil added.

"I can explain."

"Then explain," the chief said.

"We're all ears," Phil said and then apologized to his dog. "Bad joke, C."

Cerberus returned to his snooze. Teddy did explain. Dirk Massey had called him on his cell. He had bypassed Drucker and asked Teddy to use his employee discount for his week's fix of fluffernutter supplies. The man was that much of a tight-wad. He'd asked Teddy more than once to deliver the goods to him at Mamet Lane.

"Why Mamet Lane?" Shelby asked. "Did he need privacy?"

"No, he hated David Mamet, said he was overrated, and he thought buying his score there was giving the playwright the bird."

"Nice guy, I'll give you that, but I want to hear how all of this was an accident."

"I'll get there. I parked across the street, and I was walking toward him. He didn't see me, but I saw him. He's sitting there on the back steps to the theatre, near the dumpster. The gate was open."

"What was he doing?" Phil asked.

"Eating a fluffernutter, of course. What else?"

"And the bit about the accident."

"He's sipping soda or something. I'm sure there's a can by those steps." Teddy's face brightened because the detail was something he'd forgotten. "He puts his drink down, and some fluff must've dripped on him, because he's looking around for something to wipe his hands with, and that was when he put the sandwich down, and that's when it happened."

"What happened?" chief Shelby asked.

"A raccoon stole his sandwich and ran away. Massey chased it around the dumpster, round and round, but the raccoon was too fast for him. Massey was bent over, obsessed like a maniac."

"Rocket," Shelby said.

Teddy seemed confused. "What?"

"The raccoon. You were saying."

"When he came around that last time, he was out of breath, and he stood up too fast and smashed his head on the bolt arm, the thing the garbage trucks use to lift and empty the dumpster."

"Man hits his head, and he's bleeding, and you didn't think to call anybody?"

"I didn't see blood. I saw him holding his head. I saw a raccoon. Besides, I'd left my phone at Drucker's. I panicked, all right."

"Anything else?"

"Yeah, that raccoon sure enjoyed his fluffernutter sandwich."

TAMSIN & THE CHURCH LADIES

By Susan Daly

From the start, I suspected Mrs. Eudora Corby of having a secret set of Commandments especially for me.

Thou shalt wear a hat in church.

Thou shalt not wear Birkenstocks at the ACW meeting.

Thou shalt not encourage the Minister (thy husband) to deliver light-hearted sermons by snickering at his jokes in church.

So when the body of the People's Warden was found floating in the November River near the rectory dock, she might well have added, *Thou shalt not investigate murder.*

* * *

A single minister in charge of an Anglican parish must be in want of a wife.

An unmarried incumbent is a mixed blessing. While he provides the ladies of the congregation with endless opportunities to advise him and feed him, it's also their unspoken mission to find him a wife. Preferably from within.

Which is why the Excellent Women of St. Mary's by the River, November Falls, Ontario, took it as a personal affront when, after five years as their rector, the Reverend Michael Stewart, at 33, chose to marry without their advice, assistance, or approval.

He went outside the parish. Outside the faith. Even worse, outside the church's tacitly understood socio-political spectrum in the unsettling third quarter of the twentieth century.

He married a card-carrying feminist.

We met in a class at Mistawis College where Mike was taking extension courses, working on a master's in theology. It never crossed his mind that *Women in the Bible* would or could be approached from a feminist point of view. Granted, in 1973, Women's Studies as a discipline was so new the paint was still wet on the department head's door.

Mike was one of two men in the class, the oldest student and the only clergyman. I was the teacher, commuting from Toronto once a week to help set up the program. By the end of the course, he'd opened his eyes to a new (to him) world view and earned an A.

The church ladies weren't the only ones with their knickers in a twist over our whirlwind romance. My sisters at the collective were appalled. So were my various agnostic family members. Nonetheless, on the first Saturday in May, they all travelled north to the church wedding (despite its patriarchal roots) and mixed politely with the people of St. Mary's. I traded the fleshpots of Toronto for November Falls, a flourishing mid-sized town that offered three-season outdoors attractions among the rivers, lakes, and forests of near-north Ontario.

Over the next few months, I settled into the comforts of the rectory, mercifully *not* the rambling 1890s structure next door to St. Mary's. That had been off-loaded some ten years ago, and the parish had bought a low-maintenance, charming 1930s bungalow. It had the added advantage of being a good block away, making it more challenging for parishioners to treat our home as an extension of the church at all hours.

I had a room of my own, where I could work in peace on my doctoral thesis, *Women as Victims of Theology*, surrounded by books—mine and Mike's. I also had an office at Mistawis, where, come June, I was starting as a full-time assistant professor.

Settling into parish life wasn't quite so easy. Mainly due to the double threat of Eudora Corby, president of the Anglican Church Women (ACW), and Ron Tressider, the People's Warden.

Generally, the various members of the parish treated me as well as any minister's helpmeet might expect, with a mixture of welcome, friendship, cordiality, disapproval, and suspicion. It was a time when the Old Order was changing, and plenty of people, old and young, were open to new ideas. Others, both young and old, were not.

I found a new friend in Sharon Corby, Eudora's daughter, who worked five mornings a week as the Church Secretary. We hit it off soon after my arrival, when I showed up at the vestry office to take Mike to lunch. He'd been called away, so Sharon and I walked up to the Duke of York on River Street for a bit of bonding over fish and chips and beer.

She talked about her job. When she'd taken it on a few years ago, some parishioners were aghast she expected to be paid.

"Seriously? You mean, they think it's volunteer work?"

"Well, old Mrs. Wellcome did the job gratis for forty years. When Mike arrived, he was appalled, and tried to put her on the payroll, but she was so offended he had to back off."

"But somehow you got the job? With pay."

Sharon smiled. "Surprisingly, no one stepped up to do it for free. So Mr. Tressider had to give in."

"Oh, him. The People's Warden." A dyed-in-the-wool sexist.

"You've met him, eh?"

I nodded. "He knows all the misogynist bits in the scriptures—and they are legion—and he enjoys interpreting them against me."

He'd also informed me he'd been against the church getting rid of the oversized, falling-down, work-demanding rectory. Of course.

"Yeah, well, he's got his supporters, but he's been making himself unpopular. I don't believe he'll be People's Warden much longer."

"Oh?"

"He keeps finding more and more things to disapprove of."

"Me, for example?"

"He's pretty much in the minority. Most people are happy to have someone new and interesting like you, and really, it's not the way it was say, thirty years ago, when people's lives were defined first and last by their church affiliations. They have other lives now."

"I don't know. There seems to be this resistance group." I thought about the coterie of hard-core parishioners, who worshipped at the same altar as Eudora Corby and Ron Tressider. "They don't like my clothes, my politics, or even my name."

"Face it, Tamsin, they don't *know* your name."

"Yeah, that name tag your mom had made for me... *Mrs. Michael Stewart*." Three words. Three mistakes.

Sharon laughed. "I'll order you a new one. 'Ms. Tamsin Engler,' right?

"Thanks. Not that Ron will pay the slightest attention. Except to take the chance to stare at my boobs."

Sharon was quiet for a moment, then said, "I suppose you figure my mom's against you?"

"Uh, well...." I sipped my beer, trying to appear blasé.

"Don't take it personally. Thing is, she spent the last five years with one aim. To get Mike to marry me."

When I finished choking on my beer, Sharon said, "Don't worry. Mike and I understand each other. In fact...." She paused, then leaned forward and whispered, "He knows I'm a dyke."

Right. I rearranged my ideas. "And your mother...?"

"Not a clue. Nor anyone else in the parish. Hardly anyone in November Falls, even. That's why it's a relief to take a chance on telling you."

"I'm sorry it's so hard for you. But you know, Sharon, the times *are* a-changin'."

"So I hear. But not fast enough. Not in November Falls. Certainly not in the Anglican Church."

* * *

I mostly tried to avoid the People's Warden since nothing good ever came of my conversations with him. But one Saturday morning some five months after my arrival, I was enjoying the mid-September weather, washing our cars in the shady front driveway.

Along came Ron the Warden, walking Sophie the Schnauzer.

He paused in the driveway, ostensibly to pass the time of day, though more likely to assess my cut-off jeans and admittedly wet t-shirt. Sophie bounded towards me with a cheerful barky greeting, straining at her leash.

"Hey, Sophie... Good morning, Ron. Nice day." I keep my conversation uninspired with people like Ron.

"Good morning, Mrs. Stewart. Washing the car, I see." Equally uninspired, but I didn't miss his challenge.

"Oh, call me Tamsin, Ron. Since you can't seem to remember my last name is Engler."

"Hmmm, yes. Oh by the way, Mrs. Tressider and Mrs. Corby said they missed you at their ACW meeting Tuesday morning. I thought I'd mention it, since they specifically invited you."

"And I politely declined. I reminded them that since classes have started, I'm busy weekdays." I'd also hinted they might get younger members to attend if they switched their meetings to evenings, as many organizations were doing lately.

He gamely kept on. "Indeed. Well, Mrs.— Tamsin, as church warden, I'm in a position to know precisely what your husband is paid, and I know he can well afford to support a wife, without letting her work."

I didn't dare respond; there were too many points to tackle. It was also a challenge to avoid aiming the hose in his direction. I didn't want to get Sophie wet.

Finally, I said, "It's called 'earning a living,' Ron. Many people do it without having to justify it."

He reddened. "'Wives, submit yourselves unto your husbands.'" *So there*, his tone stated.

I rolled my eyes. "Yeah, Ephesians 5:22. It's such a hit with some men. I'll mention it to Mike. But he doesn't like to subject me to his will. Still, if Mrs. Tressider enjoys it, that's her choice."

The redness on his face increased. "How dare you! Mrs. Tressider is a good Christian woman and what she does is none of your business."

"And my marriage and professional life are none of yours, *Mister* Tressider." I turned my back and focused on rinsing off Mike's red Camaro (another point of disapproval). If I said anything more, someone would regret it, and I had to consider Mike.

At last I heard Ron dragging Sophie off down the road.

* * *

Just after sunrise on the last Monday in October, I dove from the rectory dock into the chilly water of the November River. I surfaced some distance out. That's when I caught sight of something ominously human-shaped floating among the lily pads near the shore, downstream from the dock.

I reached it in a dozen strokes. Yes. Human. And dead.

My cries for help pulled Mike out of bed in record time, white-faced and tousled. He didn't hesitate to dive in. We turned the body over, just in case. It was no good.

"Oh, my God..." Mike said. His face turned from white to gray when he saw it was the People's Warden.

I left Mike holding the body to go call police and ambulance.

The next few minutes—hours?—went about as crazily as one might expect. We stood on the shore answering questions, me shivering in my bathing suit, Mike dripping wet in his tartan pyjama pants and Grateful Dead t-shirt. (We made an interesting front page shot in the November News the next day.)

"Look, do you mind?" I finally told the police sergeant in charge. "My husband is about to catch pneumonia, and I'm not far off myself. We'll answer anything you like, but we're getting dressed first."

"Okay, ma'am. My men will be here for a while, but I've got to go break the news to Mrs. Tressider."

"Wait right here while I get dressed," Mike said. "I'm going with you."

* * *

The next few days were pretty much hell.

Parishioners were full of questions and theories and shock.

A steady stream of Excellent Women, having first dropped off casseroles chez Tressider, showed up at the rectory. ("I was just over at Brenda's, dear, and thought I'd pop by to see how you're holding up.") Fair enough. I *had* found the body.

We scored a few casseroles ourselves.

The police weren't saying much, except it looked like Ron had drowned some hours before his body washed up by our dock, and that he'd been unconscious when he hit the water, based on the blow to the back of his skull. He may have struck his head on a rock when he slipped and fell. Or not.

They spent days crawling over the rocky river bank, working out where he'd gone in. It could have been anywhere from the River Street Bridge, in the center of town, to our dock. That could mean St. Mary's itself, the Tressiders', the Corbys', or a few others. Or even the rectory.

The basic scenario was, according to Brenda Tressider, Ron had an appointment at the church that night.

Who with? Ron hadn't said.

Hadn't she noticed he didn't come in? No, she went to bed early Sundays, and was usually asleep when he came home. He was always meeting someone about church business on Sunday nights. So she hadn't known anything until Mike and the police arrived at her door at 7:30 a.m., and Sophie started demanding a walk.

No one admitted to having met with Ron.

After cancelling my classes the first day, I was able to escape back to the college, leaving Mike up to his ears in funeral arrangements and fielding questions from all over, including the Bishop.

By Wednesday evening, Mike looked like death warmed over. I slid my arms around him, and we held each other for a long time.

"It must be hell for you," I said, "when he's someone you've worked so close with at the church." I hadn't told him about Ron's charming little attacks. If Ron had complained to Mike about me, I never heard about it. "And a friend," I added, trying to be charitable.

"A friend?" He offered a hollow laugh. "Oh jeez, Tamsin, I loathed the guy. And he despised me. He never stopped making trouble. For me, and for a lot of other people, too. I swear my blood pressure took a hit whenever he showed up, saying, 'Michael? A word with you?'"

"Okay, I can relate." We settled onto the couch together and I revealed all.

Mike was equal parts disgusted and vindicated. "I was looking forward to having him voted out at the next vestry meeting. But now—completely unchristian of me—I can't help feeling relieved."

* * *

By Thursday, the day of the funeral service, rumors abounded, not only in the parish but the town of November Falls at large, that it might not be an accident. The police stopped short of calling it suspicious. At least, officially. No one was actually saying "murder" out loud.

Until finally, someone did.

There was no dearth of attendees, pallbearers, or clergy. Past incumbents, past wardens, even old Mrs. Wellcome, delivered from the retirement home by her daughter. Ron and Brenda had been members of the congregation for nearly 30 years, when they'd arrived in Canada from England just after the war as a young married couple. As an accountant, he had plenty of community and professional connections as well.

The church was packed.

Mike delivered a brilliantly worded eulogy, saying the right things about his nemesis without giving his feelings away, but without perjuring himself either. Much. He lauded Ron's devotion to his loving wife, his dedication to the parish, his tireless work in the community; even Sophie got a mention.

Ron's friends and supporters and colleagues all had wonderful things to say about him. If I didn't know better, I'd have thought he was up for sainthood.

Informal testimonials continued in the church hall downstairs, where the Excellent Women had laid on a feast of plain and fancy sandwiches, tarts, date squares, etc., all no doubt featured in *Our Favourite Recipes* church cookbook, plus coffee, tea, and lemonade. Again, the place was jammed and I hovered in the kitchen earning a few Minister's Wife Brownie Points by tackling dishwashing duty and replenishing the platters.

It wasn't till nearly 5 o'clock, when the crowd had thinned down to the home team and the general clean-up started, that the wind began to shift.

Who was still there? Barely a dozen. A handful of the committee, carrying empty platters into the kitchen. Mike was helping Ed, the sexton, stack the chairs. Sharon and I were collecting cups and saucers from the oddest places. Eudora had left earlier with a fierce headache.

Brenda Tressider, all in black, looked worn out. One of the Excellent Women offered her a cup of tea, and another directed her towards a chair. She ignored both.

"Look at you all," she called out, her voice sharp and clear in the nearly empty hall. We all stopped what we were doing.

"You've done your duty, haven't you? Buried my husband and provided the funeral meats and entertained the mourners. And now, you're going to clean it all up and go home. And where does that leave me?"

Her friend Elsie reached out a hand to her, but Brenda slapped it away.

Mike approached her, but she was having none of him, either.

"Don't you come near me, Mr. Stewart."

He stopped, awaiting events.

"You were trying to get rid of him, weren't you? You were planning to coerce the vestry to appoint someone else next month. After all he's done for the church, years before you came along. You turned everyone against him."

Everyone seemed afraid to move or speak. Except Mike.

"Brenda, I think—"

"No, you don't. You let your women's lib wife do your thinking for you. And she's got you convinced Ron had to be voted out. Just because he wasn't afraid to stand up for Traditional Values."

Mike's tight jaw told me he was working on a response that wouldn't turn the air blue. Sharon, standing close by, stepped in.

"Mrs. Tressider, we'll just get someone to—"

"To what? Walk me home? Shut me up?"

"Well..."

"There you go again, Sharon. Always trotting to the aid of the minister, eager to be his little helper. Even though that ship has sailed."

"What...?"

"Oh, come on. We've all seen you chasing after the rector. Such a joke, considering you've never had a man in your life. Even after he's picked up his new piece of fluff, you're still—"

"Brenda, hold it right there." Mike stepped up to her and put a hand on her shoulder. Gripped it, in fact.

"How dare you?" she demanded.

"I dare because you've crossed the line by slamming Sharon—who's been nothing but good to you—and Tamsin, who, as my wife and a newcomer, is in no position to fight back."

"Well, aren't you the little gentleman? And how do you feel about that, *Mzzz* Tasmin? I thought all you libbers wanted to fight your own battles?"

"Mike's right," I said. "I'm at a disadvantage, and you know it. The rector's wife must hold her tongue."

The others in the room were simply holding back, watching the show.

"Oh, lah-di-dah. Very well, I'll *go* home." She grabbed Elsie's waiting arm. Her friend was clearly relieved to do something useful. Another friend came forward with Brenda's coat and purse. I held my breath as they headed for the exit. But at the door, Brenda turned and issued her parting shot.

"You're not fooling anyone, Reverend. I know *you* were the one my husband met that night. And I know you killed him."

* * *

Some points of etiquette aren't covered in church manuals. Elsie & Co. hustled Brenda out the door and everyone else retrieved their dropped jaws and looked uncomfortable.

Mike was in a tough spot. He clearly had to stay in charge, but just as clearly he had a lot of skin in the game.

259

The Rector's Warden, Jim Lafferty (appointed by the incumbent, as opposed to elected by the people) stepped up and said, "Mike, why don't you and Tamsin and Sharon get lost and the rest of us will finish clearing up here."

"Thanks Jim. But first..." Mike addressed the room.

"We can't pretend we didn't hear what Brenda said. And you all heard what I said to her. She's in a hard place right now, no question. I know you are all smart enough and kind enough to take her words for what they meant. Reaction and fear and looking for answers."

Nods and murmurs of agreement went around the room.

"I will talk to Brenda when she's ready. Meanwhile, she has friends with her. And she needs your friendship, too."

He hesitated, then added, diffidently, "If anyone wants to go to the police with her accusation, I can't stop you."

"Great, Mike," Jim said. "Now, get outta here. All the gossips are dying to say something, and they can't until you leave."

I love Jim. His job includes saying things the rector sometimes can't. And of course, his words effectively shut everyone up.

* * *

Back in the rectory, Mike pulled out a bottle of excellent rye. Thank goodness.

"I'll kill that bitch." Sharon's voice was calm. I like how she doesn't apologise for using colorful language in front of Mike.

"I'll help you," I said.

Mike ignored our plotting.

"Like I said, she's in a bad place. But, no matter what she may think, I have no say in who the people appoint. And as for Sharon being after me—uh..." He broke off.

"It's okay. Tamsin knows you're not my type."

He grinned at us with relief.

"There's no logic, anyway," I said. "If she thinks Mike *was* able to keep

Ron from being warden, then why would he kill him?"

"And since I wasn't hauled into meeting with Ron on Sunday night, who *was* he meeting?"

"Someone must have got fed up with him," I said. "Though I gather he wasn't likely to get reappointed."

Mike nodded, looking glum.

"I've been getting complaints about him. Almost as many as I've been getting *from* him about other people. The choir director for letting a recovering alcoholic sing the solo at Easter. A couple who are secretly living common-law because one of them can't get a divorce."

"The Altar Guild president," Sharon added. "She allowed flowers in memory of someone's granddaughter who died after a botched abortion."

Mike poured us all another round.

"How did he even find these things out?" I asked.

Mike and Sharon had no idea.

I looked into my rye on the rocks for inspiration. "Did *anyone* still want him for warden?"

"Just my mother," Sharon said. I looked at her. "Yeah, she and Ron were twin souls."

* * *

Matters were edgy that evening and the next day. Lots of phone calls all over the parish, but surprisingly, none from the police. Mike made several attempts to talk with Brenda, but she refused to see him.

Friday afternoon, I had no classes. Though playing detective is definitely a *thou shalt not*, I bought a bottle of sparkling wine (having done my homework), put a pair of wine glasses in my shoulder bag, and went and knocked on Brenda's door.

Her friend Elsie let me in. I suggested to Brenda that we have a talk on the patio. She baulked, but I pointed out she'd said horrible things about me and Sharon, not to mention accusing my husband of murder in public. She owed me.

I showed her my chilled offering.

"Oh, Baby Duck! I love it. Ron wouldn't buy it. He called it fizzy pop."

Fortunately, she didn't suggest it was disloyal to drink it, and in the shady back yard, I got down to business. I poured her a generous glassful.

"Brenda, I know you have every right to be heartbroken and distressed. But why would you think Mike had anything to do with Ron's death?"

"Because Michael was the last person Ron saw before he turned up dead."

"And you know this...how?"

"Well, that's who Ron met Sunday night. As warden, he often had important meetings with the rector. It's part of his job." She took a biggish gulp of the wine. "Although, not so often, lately..."

Because in the last six months, Mike had been staying home most Sunday nights.

"And he said he was meeting Mike? Specifically?"

"Well, no... But he certainly implied it."

Oh shit. Was he using his known habit of buttonholing Mike to slip out with someone on the sly? No way would I suggest that. But I wasn't letting Mike get sacrificed.

I topped off her glass.

"Mike was home with me, like he is every Sunday night. We made pizza, opened a bottle of red, and..." I let the rest drift.

"*All* night?" she demanded.

"Yes. All night." Damn it, she was asking for it. "We went to bed and made hot newlywed love until well after midnight." And again, in the morning before I got up for my swim.

"Oh!" Her eyes opened wide. "Then he *was* meeting someone else." She drained the second glass and put it down with a bang. "That slut Sharon! After Michael rejected her, she cast her net for someone else. Anything in trousers." She reached for the bottle, but I slipped it out of her reach. It had already done its job.

"Brenda, it wasn't Sharon. Can you think of any other person? He needed support to get re-elected, right?"

"Oh, I don't know..." She looked confused. "Everyone seemed to be against him lately. He said you poisoned Michael's mind, and Michael was turning them all against him."

"Brenda...please. Just think. Maybe it wasn't someone out to get him. Maybe it was someone who still supported him. What if they were putting together a strategy?"

"Well..." Brenda gave it some thought, "That doesn't make sense, Tasmin. That would mean he was meeting a supporter. Not someone out to kill him."

"Yes. Unless they changed their mind."

"Well, you know, the only person left who seems to have stuck with him through thick and thick is Eudora Corby. I can't see her bashing him with a rock—oh! Wait. Do you think *they* were having an affair?"

Eudora Corby?

"No. I don't." I got up and grabbed my bag. "Well, it's been good connecting with you, Brenda. I'm glad we've cleared the air about Mike. Thanks for leveling with me."

"Did I? Have we?" She looked a bit lost again. "Oh, do you have to leave?"

"I'll be back," I promised. I'd bring Mike. "Enjoy the wine. Maybe Elsie would like to share the rest with you."

That thought seemed to perk her up, and I left through the side gate.

* * *

"Good evening, Eudora. Doris. Alice."

I'd entered the church by the side door close to the tiny flower room. On Friday evening, the Altar Guild team would be there to set up the Altar for Sunday's Eucharist service. Arranging flowers, filling the wine decanters, and counting the Host. Sharon had told me it was her mother's week on.

Of course they'd all heard Everything, but they greeted me warmly.

"Eudora, I wonder if I could kidnap you for a minute? I know it's awful of me to interrupt you when you're working. Just a walk round the back garden?"

Eudora looked rightly annoyed, but the ladies assured her they'd be fine. We went out onto the river side of the church property, down a stretch of lawn perfect for summer receptions and the like. The drop-off at the river was shored up by a haphazard bank of stones of all sizes, on the outside of a wide curve. The river below us ran fast and deep.

I wasn't sure how to start, but Eudora spoke first.

"I've heard what Brenda said about Sharon and Mike at the funeral."

"Oh. Well, she was upset..."

Eudora gave a little sigh. "They're such good friends, you know. I admit I *did* have hopes that she and Mike might..."

"Oh, of course. Any mother might hope that. Mike's a decent guy."

Eudora gave me a sweet smile. "He is."

"Actually, I wanted to ask you about Ron."

"Ron?" The smile vanished.

"Were you still planning to back him for warden next month?"

"No."

"Really? I thought—"

"He asked me if he could count on me to support him for warden. I said no." Eudora gazed out over the flowing water. "He knows things about people. Things he has no business knowing."

"I've heard that. Sharon and Mike said the same thing."

She nodded. "And he makes things up, too."

Oh shit.

"The terrible thing he said to me about Sharon." She was getting worked up. "Despicable lies... He said unless I supported him, he would make it all public."

Double shit. "I'm sorry. When was this?"

"Just before he died." She turned from the river and looked at me. Somewhere deep in her eyes, I could see endless pain. "He asked me to meet him here. I guess he told Brenda he was meeting Mike at the church."

"Sort of."

"There was nothing else I could do, was there? I had to protect Sharon from his lies. People are so cruel, aren't they?"

"Yes. They can be."

"I can't tell you how angry he made me, using my Sharon for his own selfish ends." Her voice was calm again, almost sad. "I just started pounding him on the chest. He tried to dodge me, but he slipped and lost his footing. He fell back onto the rocky embankment."

She shivered. "I swear I heard his skull crack."

I took her hand and squeezed it. "So it was an accident...."

"I know I should have gone for help. I climbed down the rocks—it was dark and slippery—I checked his breathing. He was unconscious. I managed to roll him into the water. Face down. I didn't care how far he went, or if anyone ever found him."

"You did it for Sharon," I whispered, unsure why I was saying anything at all.

"Like you said, Tamsin, it's what any mother might do. As you will find out yourself, if you have a daughter."

"Yes." What could I say? "Mike and I hope to."

God—or social change—willing, it would be in a more accepting world than the one that drove Eudora to such extremes to protect her daughter.

KILLING IT IN THE CATSKILLS

By Lori Robbins

I'm in the business of staging apartments. Dressing windows, not people, is my area of expertise. But when my grandmother wanted a shopping companion, I was happy to accompany her. At Nana's insistence, we met at Bloomingdale's.

"I bought my prom dress here," she told me, for the tenth time that day. I knew this story well. At that seminal event, circa sixty-plus years ago, she met Grandpa. The rest, as they say, is history.

I fingered a black lace cocktail dress. "You'll need something fancy for the evening. Try this on."

She frowned. "I don't want to look as if my next stop is my own funeral." And with that, she scooped up a scarlet dress with a scalloped hem and a hot pink number in shimmery silk.

I checked the price tag on the black dress and replaced it on the hanger. My fledging business was finally supporting me, instead of the other way around. That state of affairs would not continue if I started buying clothes that cost more than my monthly grocery bill.

Fifteen dresses, three more trips to the dressing room, and an intense consultation with a delighted saleswoman later, and Nana was ready for her weekend in the Catskills. Schlesinger's was the only resort hotel to survive the hipster-ification of what used to be known as the Borscht Belt, and Nana was thrilled with the prospect of reliving her glory days. She was going with Minnie Moskowitz. The two had been frenemies since their days at Brooklyn's Lincoln High School, where she and Minnie competed relentlessly for top billing in the school musical.

I escorted Nana back to her apartment, where she practiced her song in preparation for Amateur Night. Tossing the end of a feather boa behind her, she belted out "Give My Regards to Broadway" with her usual enthusiasm. I clapped, and she curtseyed, much pleased with her own performance. It was one of her favorite songs.

I helped her put away her new clothes. "What's going on besides Amateur Night?"

She smoothed the boa, which had lost an unfortunate number of feathers. "The package deal includes an unlimited buffet at every meal and twenty dollars' worth of chips for Las Vegas Night. There's live entertainment every evening."

"Don't get thrown out," I cautioned her. "If they suspect you're counting cards, they'll send you packing."

She laughed. "Give me some credit. By the time they realize what's going on, I'll be back at Port Authority with my whole trip paid for."

* * *

I spent the following afternoon trying to persuade a couple of empty nesters that their kids' collection of soccer trophies was not a major selling point of their cramped apartment. After fifteen minutes of admiring these same kids' school pictures (nursery school through college graduation), I tried to get them to understand a buyer's point of view.

"Mrs. Sender, I understand how you feel. But you have to trust me. All these mementoes are distracting. A blank canvas allows buyers to picture themselves here. Your photographs get in the way of that."

Mrs. Sender was not pleased. "I don't agree with your sense of style. These little touches make the place look homey. Lived in."

I was sympathetic. "These little touches make the place *your* home. So unless you've got some doppelganger out there who wants to take over your life, you'll get rid of this stuff in time for me to stage the place."

Mr. Sender put a consoling arm around his wife, and she burst into tears.

"Fine!" she sobbed. "Whatever you want. I don't even know why we're selling. We've been here for thirty-two years."

Mr. Sender and I exited the bedroom and walked down a brown-carpeted hallway, which had faded yellow walls and a series of disturbing clown pictures. While Mrs. Sender composed herself in the avocado-tiled bathroom, we sat in the living room. It was filled with more tchotchkes than a flea market.

"Don't worry," he said. "She'll come around. This is very hard for her."

I couldn't afford to lose this job. "No problem! Let me know when you're ready, and I'll have a team in and out in less than a day."

* * *

My mother, who has a knack for calling when I'm already feeling stressed, rang as soon as I got home. I kicked off my shoes and settled in.

"Julie, you need to make an appointment with my astrologer. I saw her today, and she sees a difficult time ahead for you. Something about a man in your life. I'm worried Matt will leave you, like all your other boyfriends. You'll die alone and unloved."

I poured a glass of wine. "Thanks for the vote of confidence, Mom. I'll let Matt know our days together are numbered." Thinking of my mother's previous three relationships, I said, "Are you sure your astrologer got it right? Your last boyfriend, if I remember correctly, wasn't exactly a keeper. Why didn't your astrologer warn you about him?"

Tania's tone became considerably less warm. "He was handsome, intelligent, and very in tune with his spiritual side. As for my astrologer, she did say he had a complicated past."

I tried to be diplomatic. "I agree that James was good-looking. I believe he was also married."

She huffed into the phone. "He's getting a divorce."

As had been the case since my parents' separation, I was the only person, besides Nana, who cared enough about Tania to be truthful. "Listen, Mom.

268

They're always getting a divorce. Problem is, they never do. Or, if they do, they end up marrying someone else."

She was relentless. "Will you let me make the appointment for you?"

"I would rather talk about your chakras than make an appointment with an astrologer. Especially if it's about my relationship with Matt."

Tania, who usually spoke a hazy, pot-inflected drawl, was sharp in her response. "Don't blame me if everything goes south. I warned you."

"Thanks, Mom, But I've got Nana on the line. I'll call you back."

Nana was sobbing. In a choked voice, she said, "Elvis is dead."

* * *

Less than twelve hours later, I was on my way to Schlesinger's Hotel. Bill, the driver of the hotel shuttle, picked me up at the Winesap Falls station.

I clutched both armrests as he navigated the narrow hill. "Did you know the guy who died?"

Bill kept his eyes on the road. There wasn't much traffic, and the few cars that passed us did so with insulting speed. "Oh yeah. Known him for years."

"What was his name?"

He looked puzzled. "Elvis. Didn't you know? It was Elvis Presley who died."

I checked his face, nervous he wasn't quite as sharp as he needed to be in order to safely handle the steep, hairpin turns. As gently as I could, I broke the news to him. "Elvis Presley died years ago. What was this guy's real name?"

Bill was patient. "That was his real name. If he ever had another, he changed it long ago. He was a regular at Schlesinger's, back in the day. Mr. Schlesinger brought him out of retirement for Las Vegas Week. But you got nothing to worry about. They took Henny Youngman in for questioning."

I wasn't familiar with Henny. After googling the name, I said, "The real Henny Youngman died over twenty years ago. Are you telling me a Henny Youngman impersonator killed an Elvis Presley impersonator?"

Distracted, he briefly wandered into the opposite lane. "Yep. Hard to believe, but true."

I felt a rush of sadness for the victim, a man I'd never met. "My grandmother always had such a crush on Elvis."

At the last minute, he swerved off the highway and onto an exit ramp. "I know. All the ladies did."

* * *

Bill drove the bus up and around a huge, circular driveway and parked in front of the imposing double doors of Schlesinger's Hotel. He rose, somewhat stiffly, from his seat.

"Arthritis," he muttered. Still, for a guy who probably cast his first vote for either Dwight D. Eisenhower or Adlai Stevenson, he looked pretty healthy.

The lobby, with its soaring, sky-blue ceiling and glittering chandeliers, retained vestiges of the hotel's former opulence. Closer to the ground, worn patches on the rugs, tarnish on the brass fixtures, and shabby lampshades told the sad story of Schlesinger's decline. I noticed none of that until later, because the most beautiful thing in the room, perched on a sofa that dwarfed her tiny body, was Nana.

She rose lightly to her feet as soon as she saw me. Despite her frequent disclaimers about being no spring chicken, she was one hell of a spry old bird.

"Julie! My darling! I knew you'd come."

I embraced her. "Don't worry. I'll bring you back to Brooklyn. Have you packed your stuff?"

She pushed me away. "Don't be ridiculous. I brought you here to help me solve the murder. I got you a room. My treat. What with the murder and all, I got a great discount." She looked earnestly at me. "Poor Mr. Schlesinger. He was already on the verge of going under. If word gets out that the equipment was faulty, he won't recover. And he's such a nice man. More important, if it really was murder, I don't believe for a minute that Henny Youngman was the killer."

It isn't easy to win an argument with a woman who, if she'd decided to put her formidable powers of argumentation to the legal profession, would have been a terror in the courtroom. But I had to try.

"Nana. Be reasonable. Investigating crimes is the job of the police."

She drew my arm into hers as she tested her first line of defense against my objections. "Let's eat. I'm starving. We can talk about it over a nice cup of coffee and some very tasty blintzes. When was the last time you ate blintzes?"

I refused to cave that easily. I have my pride. "The last time I ate blintzes, you made them for me and cautioned me to never eat them in a restaurant."

She shrugged. "I was young and foolish then."

"It was last month."

She laughed, and then clapped her hand over her mouth, in deference to the recent death of Elvis. "Indulge your old granny. At least give me a chance."

I sighed and followed her into the dining room. She gestured to the chafing dishes and raised her eyebrows at me. "They may not be the best blintzes you'll ever eat, but they are all you can eat."

* * *

We choose a corner table, as far from the other diners as we could get. After the waitress filled our cups from Schlesinger's Bottomless Coffee Pot, she began her tale. "The first night we were here, Henny Youngman performed. It was hilarious. But he made a lot of jokes about Elvis, which I'm sure he now regrets." She paused to clarify matters for me. "Not the real Henny Youngman. He died years ago."

"Yes, Nana, I know that. Please keep going."

She pinched my cheek. "Don't be so impatient." She glanced right and left to ensure no one was listening before resuming her tale. "Then the gambling started." She nodded sagely. "They wait until you've got a few whiskey sours in you. That didn't make a bit of difference to me. I still made a bundle."

She pressed her mouth into a prim line. "Poor Minnie. She lost forty-seven bucks. But what can you expect? She never had a head for numbers. Not like me. I never forget a card."

I sat back and folded my arms. "Nana. Get to the murder."

She blinked at me. "This is background information, dear. Haven't you seen any detective shows? You have to set the scene."

I didn't bother telling her that Minnie's losses at poker weren't relevant. She knew that, but the competition between the two women had survived more than fifty years. Murder notwithstanding, Nana was not about to forget Minnie making moves against Grandpa.

She put down her fork. Her hands were shaking. "Last night Elvis performed. We danced to "Jailhouse Rock" and had the time of our lives. He sang for about an hour, and the place was jumping. And then, Elvis came to our table. He invited me to the stage and sang "Love Me Tender" and "It's Now or Never" to me. You should have seen Minnie. She was beside herself with jealousy."

"Nana. Keep going."

She leaned forward. "The curtain came down at the end of the first set. Minnie went back to her room, but I stayed for the second set. Elvis walked onstage. He grabbed the mike. And there was a loud scary sound, a crack of electricity, and the terrible smell of smoke." She grabbed my arm. "He died. Electrocuted. And now, it's up to us to figure out what happened."

I was gentle. "It sounds like a faulty wire. Nana, look at this place. It's held together with chewing gum."

Nana's tone was urgent. "I think he was killed. And Henny is the prime suspect. Don't you see how important it is that we investigate?"

I held her hand. "You don't know Henny, other than how he presents himself onstage. Trust the police to figure out what happened. There's nothing we can do."

She regarded me with a good deal of affection mixed with some exasperation. "Of course, there's something we can do. We can find the real murderer. Julie, this is Elvis we're talking about. And he sang to me. I have an obligation." She stopped talking and gazed into her coffee cup. Lost, perhaps, in memories of days gone by.

After several minutes of silence, she looked up from her cup and hummed a few bars of "If I Were a Rich Man" from *Fiddler on the Roof.* Nana is devoted to musical theater and claims she does her best thinking while listening to Broadway songs. She segued with a few bars of "Sunrise, Sunset" and checked to see if I was following her line of thought.

"I get it, Nana. Money and love. The two best motives for murder."

She pinched my cheek again and steered me out of the dining room. "Let's go, my darling. We have work to do."

* * *

Forty minutes later, we lined up with Minnie Moskowitz and a dozen other hotel guests eager to escape the grim atmosphere inside the hotel. Nana had arranged a shopping trip to downtown Winesap Falls.

Mr. Schlesinger joined us. With an apologetic expression, he said, "Bill's having a little mechanical trouble with the bus. But no worries. He's kept it running for many years."

After a short wait, the bus arrived. Mr. Schlesinger sat in the back, perhaps because he wanted to keep an eye on his guests. Minnie sat next to Nana and me. She was a sweet-faced woman with platinum blonde hair and wide blue eyes. "Julie, your grandmother does nothing but sing your praises. And she's right. You're a real *shayneh maidela.*"

"Thanks, Mrs. Moskowitz. So are you."

She took out a compact and inspected her face. "Yes, I was quite a beauty when I was younger. Oy, but that was a long time ago." She grinned. "Did you know I used to date your grandfather?"

Nana was sharp. "Yes. I told her all about it."

Minnie responded in a stage whisper loud enough for everyone from the Catskills to Canarsie to hear. "Your grandmother is still jealous." She laughed. "Who could blame her?"

Nana spoke in a cool tone. "I never went after Murray. I'm not the kind of person to run after other people's husbands."

Minnie patted her hair. "It would have done you no good, my dear. My Murray was very devoted." Leaning over, she said to Nana, "Do you realize what a close call you had last night? What if Elvis called you to the mike for the second set? You could have been the one to die."

Before Nana could answer, the bus pulled into a parking lot off Main St. Bill announced, "Ladies and gentlemen, this bus leaves at 4:30. If you're late, you'll have to hitchhike home."

Everyone except for Nana dutifully laughed. When we exited the bus, she told Minnie, "Why don't you get started without us? Julie and I have a few errands to run."

Minnie was cheerful. "You bet. See you later." She entered a store called Totally Useless Stuff. It was filled with items branded with inscriptions that read *Greetings from the Catskills,* and *The Catskills are for Lovers.*

Nana sniffed. "Poor Minnie. She won't know it's supposed to be ironic."

I laughed. "Do you disapprove?"

She shrugged. "I'm happy the town has survived, even if it's lost its original charm. And speaking of charm, let's talk to Bill."

We re-entered the bus. Bill had a newspaper spread across the wide steering wheel. He and Mr. Schlesinger were deep in discussion, but both were quite willing to talk to us.

Bill said, "Elvis and Henny hated each other. Elvis was always making up to Henny's wife, which drove him crazy. The last time they performed together, and I'm going back many years, Elvis took a poke at Henny. Didn't hurt him too bad, but Henny was hopping mad."

Mr. Schlesinger looked worried. "I know all about those rumors. But Henny and Elvis didn't really hate each other. After they were both widowed, they became friends. They kept up the pretense of being enemies, because they thought if they gave up their fight, people would think they'd gotten old. Lost their edge."

Bill shook his head. "Hard to believe after what I heard them say last night."

With a start, Nana asked, "Did they argue last night?"

Bill eased the collar of his shirt. "I don't like to say."

Nana was brisk. "You already have. Tell us every word."

He looked at Nana, and his voice trembled. In the midst of his distress, some deep instinct must have told him he didn't stand a chance against the Clarence Darrow of Brighton Beach.

Bill spoke with obvious reluctance. "They were arguing about money. Then Henny told Elvis he was a washed-up has-been. If I didn't step in, they would have come to blows." He stopped. "You're not going to tell anyone, are you? I'd sure hate to be the one to get Henny arrested."

Nana thanked him and assured him we wouldn't say a word.

* * *

Mr. Schlesinger refused Nana's offer to walk to the center of town and instead entered the souvenir store. Peering through the window, I saw him join Mrs. Moskowitz. Nana and I did some window shopping and ended up on a bench facing the village green.

She withdrew a notebook from her capacious handbag. "Time to solve the murder. What do we know? And what do we think we know that might not be true?"

I thought through all that Bill and Mr. Schlesinger had told us. "The way I see it, we have two stories that contradict each other. Someone is wrong. Or someone is lying. The question is, who?"

Nana hummed a few bars from the song "Popular" from Wicked.

I was stunned. "You don't think?"

She looked miserable. "I do. And if I'm right, maybe Elvis wasn't the intended victim."

We entered the Municipal Building, which housed the police department. Speaking with as much confidence as if she were a member of the force, she asked for Detective Carren. The woman at the front desk was kind but firm. She agreed to give him a message but declined to say whether or not the detective was in the building.

Nana wasn't pleased, but she had no choice. "Tell Detective Carren I know who killed Elvis. He should meet me at Schlesinger's Hotel. And tell him to hurry. Before anyone else gets hurt."

* * *

No one spoke much on the bus ride home other than Mr. Schlesinger and Mrs. Moskowitz, who appeared to have bonded during the shopping trip. I was not yet convinced my grandmother was correct in her deductions.

I followed her to her room. "You don't have any evidence."

She was exhausted. "I have motive and opportunity. That will have to be enough. The police can figure out the rest."

I was still skeptical. "Mrs. Moskowitz is your friend. You've known her for more than fifty years. And how in the world could she have tampered with the mike? What does she know about electrical systems?"

Nana stretched out on the bed and spoke to the ceiling. "She was conveniently absent for Elvis's second set. I have only her word for it that she went back to her room. That checks off opportunity. Did you know she and her husband founded Murray's Electrical Supply Stores? She was the brains behind the business, even though he was the one whose name was on the storefront. So she had means. Maybe her motive was jealousy. She was furious when Elvis picked me instead of her. It all fits. And I'm sick about it."

We were interrupted by a call from Tania. "Julie. This is your mother."

I steeled myself for more news from her astrologer. "Yes, I know. Is everything okay?"

Her voice was as stern as it ever gets, given the amount of time she spends on an astral plane. "No. Things are not okay. I know about the murder. You'll have to admit now that my astrologer was right."

"Your astrologer said I was the one in danger. Not Nana. She's the one who was here when it happened."

Tania said, "But you're with her now. It's all connected. Everything in the universe is connected."

"Yes, Mom. But I'm in the Catskills. Not in outer space."

Her voice grew warmer. "I love you. Be careful and take care of your grandmother."

I looked at Nana. "I will, Mom. Thanks."

* * *

Nana told the receptionist to contact her if Detective Carren arrived. We then went to the dining room, where the atmosphere was subdued. Amateur Night had been cancelled, partly out of respect for Elvis's death and partly because no one wanted to touch a live mike. Minnie wasn't there. She told Nana she was tired and was going to order from room service.

I inherited my grandmother's hearty appetite, along with her petite frame and dark eyes. But neither of us could eat much. Nana tossed her napkin on the table. "I'm going to my room. Call me if the police arrive."

I wanted to go with her, but she brushed me off. "Finish your dinner."

The waitress came by. She cocked her head at me. "Not hungry?"

I pushed my plate away. "I guess not."

I wandered over to the dessert table and piled some cookies on a large plate. I figured my grandmother might be tempted. Among the many things we have in common is a love of all things sweet, although I'm not as hardcore as she is. She subsists mostly on candy and the occasional bagel. Her apartment is never without licorice sticks, boxes of chocolates, and a wide selection of hard candy. For Nana, peanut M&Ms counted as protein.

I knocked on her door, but there was no answer. I opened it with the spare key she'd given me, but the room was empty. I called and texted, but she didn't respond.

Heart pounding, I went to the reception area. No one had seen her. I had the kid at the front desk ring Minnie's room. No one picked up there, either. It was possible a crazed Mrs. Moskowitz was holding Nana hostage. But I couldn't believe that the plump, good-natured woman who'd bought seven Catskills-themed potholders was a killer. On the other hand, I'd only met her that afternoon. For all I knew, she'd also offed her husband prior to taking over Murray's Electrical Supply Store and getting the credit she deserved.

I called the police. They weren't terribly interested in a report about a grandmother who'd been missing for all of thirty minutes.

I went back to my room. Armed with a miniature canister of mace that Nana had bought me, I set out to save her.

* * *

I pressed an ear against Minnie's door but could hear nothing. I pounded on it, but the only response came from her neighbor in room 511, who was none too pleased when I charged into her room. Ignoring her protests, I picked up the hotel phone and told the receptionist Mrs. Moskowitz was sick, and they needed to use a pass key to get in.

Mr. Schlesinger arrived and with shaky fingers, opened the door to Mrs. Moskowitz's room. There was no one inside. He was fearfully pale. "You have to find Minnie. I don't know what I would do if anything happened to her."

I felt sick. "Where's Henny?"

He sat down and held his head in his hands. "I don't know. The police released him this afternoon, and he checked out."

With little to guide me, I sought clarity in Nana's favorite source of inspiration. Sixty years of Broadway musicals was a lot to process. And I didn't have a lot of time. The person who murdered Elvis was someone Minnie trusted enough to have allowed into her hotel room. Someone who shared her expertise in electronics. Someone with a grudge, someone who felt...the same way Max Bialystok did in *The Producers* when he sings the song "Betrayed."

Only one person had that kind of passion. And I suspected it wasn't Henny.

* * *

I raced across the dark parking lot as I considered my options. If I was right, and Bill was holding Nana hostage, I could capitalize on the element of surprise. Bill was old. Older than Nana. Maybe if I slammed open the door

278

and screamed at him, he'd have a heart attack. On the other hand, what if Mrs. Moskowitz was there and she was the one to keel over? Nana was less of a worry. She's tough. And she's one hell of a poker player. No one gets to her level of expertise without planning for the unexpected.

As it turned out, though, I was the one taken by surprise. The door slammed open, but not by me.

Bill was holding a rifle. Pointing to Nana and Mrs. Moskowitz, he told me to stand next to them.

Mrs. Moskowitz was crying. Nana was ashen but composed. She said, "Now, Bill. Julie means you no harm. Let her go, and we'll talk."

"No. It's too late. I thought we had something. Something special." He jerked the gun with an angry gesture. "I saw you smooching with Elvis. He was always the one people loved. Not me. Who was I? Just the bus driver."

Nana spoke with a soothing tone. "That's not true, Bill. We all liked and respected you. Please, put down the gun. You don't want to kill us, do you?"

He sobbed. "No. I don't. I wanted to kill Elvis."

She kept talking. "And you did. You won. Put the gun down and let Minnie and Julie leave. This is between the two of us. After all these years, we can be together."

He wavered. "You really mean it?"

No one could pull off a bluff like Nana. "Of course. If only I'd known how you felt. But that's in the past. Let them go." She kept her gaze on Bill but twitched her index finger at me. I knew what she was thinking.

When Bill loosened his grip on the gun, I was ready. I pulled the Mace out of my back pocket and blasted him in the face. Nana followed by conking him over the head with her heavy handbag. Because a lady never leaves the house without one.

* * *

The next morning, Mr. Schlesinger drove us to the bus station, and we headed back to the city.

Minnie tsked her disapproval. "How could you think I was guilty? I'm surprised at you."

Nana was apologetic. "I focused on the evidence. Not on what I wanted to be true. Same thing when I play poker. Count the cards and play the hand you're dealt. I will admit, though, you had no motive." With a mischievous smile, she added, "Unless you were jealous that Elvis picked me instead of you."

Minnie snorted. "If that were the case, I would have killed you, not him." She frowned. "Bill must have been delusional. You're not *that* good-looking, my dear."

Nana ignored her and poked me. "How did you figure it out?"

I thought back to my first conversation with Bill. "From the start, he tried to frame Henny. But Mr. Schlesinger had a totally different take on the situation. The only point they agreed on was that Bill was good with his hands, and Mr. Schlesinger wasn't. And the person who tampered with Elvis's mike had to have at least rudimentary knowledge of electrical systems. As for motive, Bill seemed very resentful of Elvis's popularity with women."

I hugged Nana. "I can't believe you didn't know how Bill felt about you."

Minnie rolled her eyes. "I wouldn't be proud of it."

Nana assured her, "Trust me. I'm not. But I am proud of Julie." She tapped her head. "She inherited her brains from me."

* * *

In the end, my mother's astrologer was right. I did have a man disappoint me, although it wasn't my boyfriend. Mr. Sender called and said his wife was so unhappy about leaving their apartment that they decided not to sell. But there was a silver lining. Minnie Moskowitz and Mr. Schlesinger hit it off, and she decided to relocate to the Catskills to help him manage Schlesinger's Mystery and Murder Nights. I began staging her apartment the next day. Which was filled, of course, with photographs of many generations of the Moskowitz clan, as well as several keepsakes from the Catskills. It was, after all, a memorable trip.

DEATH AT THE BOSTON VIGILANCE COMMITTEE

By Verena Rose

Saturday, July 7, 1860

Boston, Massachusetts

Horace Kingsley had arrived in Boston just in time to attend a meeting of the Boston Vigilance Committee. As he entered the hall where the meeting was being held, he immediately noticed a framed copy of a poster from April 24, 1851. It read:

CAUTION!!

COLORED PEOPLE

OF BOSTON, ONE & ALL

You re hereby respectfully CAUTIONED and

Advised, to avoid conversing with the

WATCHMEN AND POLICE OFFICERS

OF BOSTON

For since the recent ORDER OF THE MAYOR &

ALDERMEN, they are empowered to act as

KIDNAPPERS

And

SLAVE CATCHERS,
And they have already been actually employed in
KIDNAPPING, CATCHING, AND KEEPING
SLAVES. Therefore, if you value your LIBERTY,
And the Welfare of the Fugitives among you, Shun
Them in every possible manner, as so many HOUNDS
On the track of the most unfortunate of your race.
KEEP A SHARP LOOK OUT for
KIDNAPPERS, and have
TOP EYE open.

Two of his father's slaves were on the agenda for discussion, and unbeknownst to Cyrus, Horace was in Boston to help in their ultimate escape to freedom. Making his way to the front of the room, he approached a man he took to be a member of the Committee.

"Excuse me, sir, are you an officer of the Boston Vigilance Committee?"

"Yes, sir, my name is Edmund Jackson. I am a member of the Executive Committee. How can I help you?"

"I'm Horace Kingsley from Washington City. I've travelled to Boston in hopes of assisting with the release and relocation of two slaves currently in police custody. They escaped from my father's plantation on the Eastern Shore of Maryland, and I'd prefer they not be returned to servitude there."

As the two men talked, the room filled with men, both white and colored. Presently, a distinguished gentleman stepped up to the podium and banged a gavel calling the meeting to order.

"We'll speak further after the meeting," said Mr. Jackson.

After several items on the agenda had been discussed and dealt with, the chairman announced the next item was the recent incarceration of a slave couple who were arrested as runaways.

"Gentlemen, we have been asked to intercede for a couple who are currently languishing in jail awaiting transport back to Maryland. Their owner, Mr. Cyrus Kingsley, is demanding their immediate return."

"Excuse me, Mr. Chairman. My name is Horace Kingsley. The slaves you're speaking of belong to my father. I've come to Boston with the intention of helping them make their way to Canada. I was in hopes of arriving before they got snatched."

Numerous conversations erupted, and the chairman banged his gavel to bring the room to attention.

"Mr. Kingsley, do I understand you correctly? You want to help your father's slaves escape?"

"That is correct, Mr. Chairman. I attended medical school in Philadelphia, and while there, I became interested in the abolitionist movement. When I returned home, because of my belief that slavery is an evil, my father disowned me. I moved to Washington City along with my personal slave, whom I immediately freed, and became the city coroner. The escaped slaves are husband and wife. The husband is the brother of my assistant."

A young man rushed into the hall and yelled, "Everybody come quick! There's been a murder at the jail!"

Later that evening, in his hotel room, Horace Kingsley was still trying to come to terms with the events that had happened that day. He came to Boston expecting to help Nathan and Lily get to Canada. Instead, he had to figure out how to tell Noah that his brother was dead, and his sister-in-law was on her way to being sold down the river.

* * *

The next day

Standing on the platform, waiting for his train back to Washington City to arrive, Horace was approached by two of the members of the Boston Vigilance Committee.

"Mr. Kingsley, we are so very sorry for your loss. We've tried to get more information on the events that resulted in Nathan's death, but the police are not being very forthcoming. All we were able to find out is that the man your father sent to transport them back to Maryland showed up while we were having our meeting. The police claim that Nathan put up a fight, but we are not inclined to believe that."

"I do so appreciate all you've tried to do for them. I wish I had arrived sooner," said Horace shaking his head. "Now, I must get back to Washington as soon as I can. I think I know who came to pick them up and where Lily is being taken to be sold. My best friend is a constable there, and I'm sure he'll be happy to help me catch up with Nathan's murderer."

Shaking hands with Horace, the two men wished him good luck in his endeavor.

* * *

To find out who murdered Nathan and whether Lily is saved from being sold to a sugar plantation look for DEATH AT MILLER'S TAVERN, appearing in Malice Domestic 18: MYSTERY MOST INTERNATIONAL due out in April 2024 from Wildside Press.

AUTHOR'S NOTE

The Boston Vigilance Committee was originally founded in 1841, was reorganized in 1851, and continued its good work until it was disbanded in April 1861. The committee's goal was to protect escaped slaves from being kidnapped and returned to slavery in the South. Members of the committee worked with donors and Underground Railroad conductors to provide the escaped slaves with funds, shelter, medical attention, legal counsel, and transportation. They would also keep a lookout for slave catchers and would sound the alarm when any came to town. Some members also took an active part in rescue efforts.

THE SUSPENSION OF MICKEY HACKERSTEIN

By Arthur Vidro

My journalism and mystery-solving careers both began more than a generation ago when teenage me interned at a twice-weekly newspaper.

It was the strangest job interview I ever had.

James Carr said he liked my clippings but had been expecting a young man.

"You're really a Mickey?" he asked. We were in his private office, and he sat behind an oak roll-top desk.

I offered a smile. "My birth name is Michelle. My father wanted a son to name after Mickey Mantle but instead got me. He always called me Mickey. The nickname stuck. I like it."

"Fine by me. I remember seeing Mantle play. Even us Yankee-haters admired Mantle. Outstanding talent. How long have you been interested in journalism?"

"Since freshman year. After high school, I'd like to study journalism at State U., Mr. Carr."

"Hackerstein, do you have a driver's license and car? Some of the meetings you'll have to cover aren't near the bus line."

"Just earned my license, and my parents will let me use our old second car for all my newspaper work."

"How kind of them. Do you have any questions, Hackerstein? A good journalist always has questions."

He plucked a pipe from an ashtray. He added tobacco to the bowl, tamped it down, lit a match, took a puff.

"Is there SMOKING allowed?" That's probably not a smart question to screech at your prospective boss when he's puffing away while interviewing you. But I was caught off guard.

"Sure." He took another puff. An aroma of apple wafted overhead. "Why not? I don't just publish the *Nylsor Illustrated News*, I own the building. So I set the rules. Still interested in the internship?"

I learned long ago that the more important a situation I find myself in, the more I should think before speaking. I slowed down and chose my words carefully. "Your smoking does not dampen my desire to intern here. However, I have become accustomed to the school's new zero-tolerance policy and thus am surprised when—"

Jim Carr had whipped open a desk drawer and extracted a tumbler and a bottle of cherry brandy. I watched him pour and sip but held my tongue.

"Does your school's zero-tolerance policy apply to alcohol, too?" he asked.

"Yes, sir."

"At least you restrained yourself from shrieking. Just a little test I was giving you. A journalist should keep her wits and poise, no matter what." He produced a syringe, then opened a mini-fridge along the wall behind him and pulled out a tiny medicine bottle. "Zero tolerance per your school?"

"Yes," I said. The bottle wasn't of a type I had seen before. "No needles allowed. All medicines stay locked up in the nurse's office. But good luck bringing medicine to the nurse for safekeeping, because merely walking the corridors to her office with a drug on your person is a violation. Saying you were taking it to the nurse does not keep a student from getting suspended. Zero tolerance means no excuses whatsoever. Mitigating circumstances don't matter." I pointed to the bottle. "What's it for?"

"This," said Mr. Carr, "contains insulin. I can't go a day without it. In this building, medicines are fully tolerated, but illegal drugs are barred. Doesn't Hilltop High School make that distinction?"

"No, sir. Any drug, medically needed or not, is cause for suspension. Zero tolerance. We're not supposed to decide for ourselves whether a given exception makes sense." I shrugged apologetically. "I don't make the rules; I just obey them."

"Fine, Hackerstein, fine. But this summer you'll be here at the *Nylsor Illustrated News*, not at Hilltop High. We use common sense. Only a few prohibitions in this building—no lying, no illegal drugs, no plagiarism. I'll fire any employee who violates any of the rules. Even an intern."

I nodded."Zero tolerance in your own domain, eh, Mr. Carr?"

He smiled crookedly, displaying an underbite and the flash of a gold tooth next to an empty socket. "Hackerstein, I think you and I are going to get along just fine."

* * *

And we did. Jim Carr proved to be patient, smart, and a good teacher.

After I submitted typed copy to Mr. Carr, he edited it and then sent it to typesetting, a photoelectric process in which typists create galleys that get pasted down with hot wax onto page boards.

Mr. Carr relied on me a lot, because there were no other full-time reporters on staff. Except in the summer, he and some stringers did all the reporting. Plus, Mr. Carr edited the press releases sent in. And wrote the editorials. That's the advantage of publishing semi-weekly—one person can shoulder the load, if he works super-hard and stays healthy.

A dozen others worked there, too. The one closest to me in age was Jedediah Gilroy, the circulation manager. He brought the finished pages to the printer's shop, picked up the published issue from the printer, delivered them to the grocery stores, newsstands, and candy stores that sold our paper, refilled the coin-operated newspaper kiosks, and brought to the post office the issues for our subscribers, with mailing labels affixed and reams of detailed paperwork filled out properly. He maintained the subscription list, made additions and subtractions when warranted, and sent out reminders for folks to renew.

It took Jedediah Gilroy two weeks to speak to me. And even that was a muttered, barely audible "Hullo."

I looked up from the article I was typing about the city's decision to extend by a month the deadline for bids to remove residential trash. The current contract was close to expiring. Somehow, I couldn't make this exciting and was glad for a diversion. "Jedediah, isn't it?"

"Sort of. But everyone calls me Gilroy." His voice was soft but firm. "Glad you made it."

"Made what?"

"Made it to two weeks. Lot of people don't. That's why I don't waste words on them until the two-week mark. After two weeks, you can bet they'll probably stick around."

Gilroy was average height, thin, had long red hair, and just a few freckles. He spoke less than any of the other staffers, and about half his comments concerned how the Chicago Bears might fare in the upcoming season.

A telephone rang on Teri Nelluc's desk. She sold ads. She was about forty, looked fifty. To try to look twenty, she wore tons of bright lipstick, embedded her eyes in masses of mascara, and dressed like a teenager. She chain-smoked Virginia Slim cigarettes. Her ashtray was twice as large and heavy as anyone else's. I gave her credit for diligently emptying and cleaning the smelly tray every time she left the building; people knew not to deposit their own butts there. Now she gave a broad sweep of her hand to signal a desire for quiet.

I lowered my voice. "Why do people not last here?"

Gilroy waved an arm to encompass the huge but gloomy room. Metal desks and wooden captain chairs were scattered haphazardly throughout. Typewriters sat atop most of the desks; a few had nothing on top except an ashtray. The walls were gray cinder block. "We're all stuck in a basement. No windows. Fans instead of air-conditioning. No downstairs bathrooms. No health insurance. No paid vacations. No perks at all. The whole place is shabby, run-down. The sales team hates bringing clients down here. But the biggest reason people leave is the low pay. If you can get a job elsewhere, you'll get paid more."

I smiled. "You're all getting paid more than me."

"Yeah, you're the intern du jour. But in a way, we're all interns, building experience so we'll be ready when something better comes along."

I studied the young man. Probably close to twenty-five. Not a powerful specimen, but reasonably strong, reasonably intelligent, and from what I'd heard, thoroughly reliable. Any schooling he might have received wasn't needed on this job. Guess you could say the same about the salespeople. And the typesetters. And the receptionist. And the billing clerk. And the photographer. And the paste-up artist. And...

"And you?" I heard myself ask, realizing perhaps I shouldn't have. "Don't you mind the conditions?"

"Nah. It's Jimmy's company, so he can do what he wants. I don't make the conditions. I just live with them because I work here."

* * *

Each issue contained a Police Report submitted in person by Officer Calvey, a local cop about thirty who was built like a wrestler and towered over petite me by at least a foot. He worked hard on each report and insisted on receiving a byline though he didn't get paid.

Soon enough, Mr. Carr tasked me to go over the Police Report with Calvey each time he brought it in. I peppered Officer Calvey with questions to elicit more details and to clear up ambiguities. He used a matter-of-fact *Dragnet* style that I thought was fine for the newspaper, but he confided to me he had literary aspirations.

"I want to be like Joseph Wambaugh. You know," he explained, "the cop who turned crime novelist. Bestsellers."

I couldn't picture Calvey writing successful novels but didn't wish to discourage him. "How, er, ambitious of you."

"Promise me, Mickey, if you ever stumble onto a murder or some other juicy crime, you'll ask for Officer Calvey when you call the police."

I promised.

"Never know when a true crime can be turned into a fictional bestseller," he elaborated. "Any tips for me?"

Who was I—a mere teenage intern—to give tips to a veteran cop? Yet deep down we both knew I was the more advanced writer, so I tutored him as best I could.

"You might try giving the readers your name. Your byline is always 'P.O. Calvey,' which explains you're a Police Officer but doesn't state who you are. I don't even know your first name, Officer Calvey."

He chuckled. "You think 'P.O.'—" then he shook his head thoroughly, like an Etch-a-Sketch being erased."Please don't bother with my first name. If 'Officer Calvey' is too formal, then just call me 'Calvey.' Everyone at the department does."

Although I couldn't add much style to Calvey's sluggish prose, I sprinkled in some pizzazz as I covered village, school, and zoning board meetings. Mr. Carr edited my articles, teaching me what I should and should not do. My education was thorough. Richard, the paper's bohemian cigar-chomping production manager, taught me how to stat photos and let me watch (and provide headlines) as he dummied up the pages.

Sometimes I worked late, but I was never the last to leave. The last person out had to lock up, and management was selective in issuing keys.

One evening, when Gilroy and I were the last two at the office, he asked me to leave.

"Got to lock up," he explained, standing over me. "Don't want to lock you in."

I looked up just as my stomach rumbled. I blushed with embarrassment.

"If you're that hungry," he said, "we can grab a bite at the diner. I'm hungry, too."

I checked my purse to make sure I had enough for a veggie burger, then accepted. "I'll follow you there," I offered.

But my Chevy Citation had a flat tire. It was parked across the street from the news building—our tiny lot was filled when I had arrived, though now it contained only Gilroy's van, which slowly approached. He cranked down his window. "If you've got a spare, I can change your tire. But it'll take time. Let's eat first, then I'll bring you back here and fix you up. Okay?"

"Sure." I hopped into his van, and we headed for the diner.

* * *

I learned a lot during that meal.

"I was a punk," Gilroy confided, shaking his head. "No job, no school, no interests except hockey and football. Hung around with some bad dudes. One night we tossed a brick through the front window of the *Illustrated News*. Not to rob it. Just for kicks. That Calvey cop was nearby, chased us. The others got away. I didn't."

He paused, stirred a straw in his Coke, as if the story had ended.

"So, what happened next?" I prodded.

"Jimmy spoke to Calvey and me. Said I probably just needed a job, a purpose. Said if I came to work for him, he wouldn't press charges. So now I back Jimmy all the way."

When we drove back to my marooned vehicle, Gilroy hesitated, then pointed to the *Illustrated News* building. "Lights are on inside. I know I shut them off." He swerved into our parking lot, which was no longer empty. One sports car was there. Teri's.

"We'll just make sure everything's all right, then we'll fix your car," he said.

I had no choice but to follow.

The front door was not locked. We entered. "Everything okay?" I called out.

No response.

Upstairs, the vestibule light was on, and the reception area, water cooler area, and restrooms were all empty. The rear door was bolted from the inside.

Downstairs, a big basement with no place to hide, the overhead fluorescents gleamed. Sprawled on the floor, motionless, behind her desk was Teri Nelluc.

She looked asleep, but we couldn't wake her. I performed CPR. No use. She had breathed her last.

"Should we call for an ambulance?" I asked.

"Nah. That's for the living. Besides, when folks don't have health insurance, an ambulance ride could cost hundreds of bucks. I ain't paying."

Teri's chair, which had metal wheels, had rolled away from the desk, as if shoved by her falling body. Near her body was her ultra-big metal ashtray, now upended and more or less wiped clean; a large scattering of ashes; and a partially consumed lipstick-smeared Virginia Slim cigarette.

I felt more than a little queasy, never having stumbled upon a dead body before. Once when I was a little girl and our canary had died … but this was different. I summoned guidance from Mr. Carr and my school instructors. A journalist has to put her own feelings aside when there's a story at hand. A journalist learns by asking questions. I took a deep breath to compose myself.

"What do you think happened?" I asked, trying to mask my shakiness.

"Well…" Gilroy squatted for a closer look. "Maybe a heart attack? She came in to do some work, smoked one of those skinny cigarettes for broads, and while collapsing knocked over the ashtray. Sound cool to you?"

I got down on the floor. "Four problems with that theory, Gilroy. One, if she came here to work alone, wouldn't she have locked the upstairs door? Two, there are no papers on her desk she could have been working on. Three, there's a tiny trace of blood on one side of the ashtray. And four, there seems to be far more ash here than would be produced by that one Virginia Slim." I tried to peer under the desk but saw only darkness. "Is there a flashlight around?"

Gilroy fetched a light and shone it for me. I whistled.

"What is it?" he demanded, his insouciance faltering.

"Another cigarette."

"No big deal. She smoked a ton of them."

"Except," I added, "the cigarette that rolled beneath the desk is not a Virginia Slim."

"So how do you explain it, Mickey?"

"If she came here to work alone, she would have locked the front door as soon as she entered. I'm assuming she had a key?"

"Yeah," said Gilroy. "Jimmy gave keys to me and Rich and everyone in sales. Can't risk losing a sale..."

"Oh, here." I pointed on her desk at a large metal key ring; its hub was a miniature ashtray. "Here's her keys."

Gilroy brought out his own key ring, a twin of Teri's, and compared keys. "Yes, that double-edged key is for the office. Guess the others are for her car and house." He, too, touched nothing.

"Somebody else had to be here," I decided. "Either someone entered with her, or she left the door open so someone else could join her. That person was down here with her and then left, neither turning off the lights nor locking the door. Couldn't lock the door without a key, and if he or she used Teri's key to lock up, there'd be no way to get the key back inside."

"You sound like a shamus," said Gilroy.

"I read a lot. Especially Christie, Queen, Sayers, Gardner, Grafton, Lovesey—"

"Who are they?"

"Never mind. We need a look at that other cigarette." I used a ruler from my own desk to nudge the bashful cigarette out from under Teri's.

"No lipstick on this one," I observed.

Gilroy turned to the corpse. "Yeah. Teri used so much glop on her lips it was impossible for her to puff without leaving a colorful trail."

"This one is a Winston," I observed. "Someone else smoked it."

"Couldn't this Winston smoker have been here earlier? Anyone can use anyone else's ashtray."

I shook my head. "Teri always emptied her ashtray before leaving. It's a constant habit. I'm so used to it that if there were a cigarette in her ashtray when we left tonight, I would have noticed. You and I were the last ones here. That ashtray was empty when you locked up."

"Maybe this other cigarette has been under her desk for days?"

"Then why the extra ash around the ashtray? No, Gilroy, the Winston smoker entered after you locked up. The Winston smoker struck Teri with the ashtray. The Winston smoker left the building, not bothering to turn off the lights and not able to lock the front door."

293

"So where does that leave us?"

"Not sure. Wish I knew more about the victim."

"Old Gilroy can help you with that. Teri was divorced. Dated men constantly, juggling several at a time. Sometimes they'd pop in here to meet her. They were all six-footers, at least. Went through men like Kleenex. Her ex died about a year ago. Car accident. Teri was torn about whether to go to the funeral. Eventually she went, for their son's sake."

"There's a son?"

"Yeah, Chuck, early twenties, lives with Teri. I sometimes play against him in hockey games at the rink. He has a little gas station and car-repair shop."

"I wonder if he inherits. Might be a motive. This son was able to open his own station?"

"Nah. Teri told him he wouldn't get anywhere if he worked for others, so she put up the money for his business. I ought to call him. Maybe he'll know who was down here with Teri." He went to the far corner of the basement, where his own desk was, looked up the number, and placed a call.

I continued to study and ponder. Had to leave things the way they were for the police. I picked up my ruler and poked the Winston back into the gloom beneath the desk, wondering if it harbored fingerprints.

Gilroy returned. "Spoke to Chuck. He's laid up in bed. Chicken pox. Was supposed to go upstate today to visit cousins for a week. But now he can't. Said he hasn't left the house since seeing the doctor this morning."

"If that story proves true, he's not a suspect. Did you tell him—"

"No." Gilroy looked away. "Didn't have the guts to tell him about his Mom. Guess someone else will have to."

"Did he say anything useful?"

"Yeah. I said Jimmy had a question for Teri but we couldn't find her. Asked him where she was. Don't like to lie, but...in this case... Anyway, Chuck laughed, said he couldn't keep up with all her boyfriends, and that she keeps an appointment book in her work desk because it's too confusing even for her who she's seeing when. And just for weird pleasure, Chuck said, instead of calling the guys by names they like, she uses nicknames they object to."

I found my handkerchief and opened a desk drawer. No book. Next drawer, there it was. Still with the handkerchief, I opened the book to today's date. Teri had neatly scripted "Pietro Orenthro, 7 p.m., my house," then crossed out "house" and replaced it with "office." Last night she had seen Stinky at Lombardo's Restaurant at 8 p.m. Tomorrow evening called for a rendezvous with Tubby at Chez Marmite at 7:30.

"What do you deducify, Sherlock?" Gilroy asked.

"Looks like she was going to entertain Pietro at her house, but when she learned Chuck was going to be bedridden for a spell she changed the tryst to here. Do you know any cigarette smokers named Pietro?"

"I don't know anyone named Pietro, and I've never heard of a tryst," he grunted. "Do we call the police now?"

"Guess we have to." I called from my desk phone, not Teri's.

"Police department, Sergeant Selma Salem," I was told.

"I'd like to report—" Then I remembered my promise to Officer Calvey. "I'd like to make a report to P.O. Calvey. Is he around?"

"His shift tonight starts at 10. Can someone else help you?"

Then the idea struck me. "This is really an emergency," I admitted. "But I'd prefer to speak to Officer Calvey. Can you call him wherever he is and say Mickey Hackerstein of the *Nylsor Illustrated News* has a big crime story for him? I'm here at the paper."

"That's not protocol, but I know about Calvey's column and ambitions. I'll try to reach him, then call you back. Fair enough?"

"Sure." I asked Sergeant Salem two more questions, smiled in triumph at her answers, and hung up.

I was surprised at how well both Gilroy and I were handling ourselves in this basement of death. Nevertheless, we decided to get away from Teri's corpse and wait upstairs.

"How long do we wait?" Gilroy asked a half-hour later. "It's not as if we get paid overtime. Why not call some other cops if Calvey ain't around?"

"I'll wait up to another hour," I said. Murder at the newspaper seemed more important than my getting home in time to watch *Picket Fences*, my favorite show. "By the way, why do you and Teri have matching key rings?"

"Jimmy gave them to everyone last year as our Christmas bonus. Hey, I'm getting antsy. I'm not good at sitting and doing nothing."

"Then would you mind playing Good Samaritan?" I handed him my car keys and told him the spare tire was in the trunk.

"Yeah, I'll take care of that." Gilroy hustled out as the phone rang. Selma Salem had reached Calvey at the gym. He was on his way.

A few minutes later a large shadow blocked the doorway. It was Calvey. He tentatively entered and smiled at seeing me.

"Mickey! Working late, aren't you? Got a call you were looking for me. I hope it's important."

"Oh, it is." I spoke as earnestly as I could. "Remember that promise you elicited from me? If I stumbled upon a juicy crime like murder, I should call you?"

He nodded. "You mean—"

"Yes. There's a body downstairs. We think she's been murdered. But we need a pro like you to look at it."

He started to stride down the steps.

"Pietro Orenthro!" I called after him.

His head whipped around. "Yeah, what?" Then his face clouded. "Hey, how did you know—"

"It's enough that I know," I mused sadly.

He plodded downstairs, not knowing how much I knew. I phoned the police again. They arrived pronto.

* * *

The next forty or so minutes were a blur, as police arrived, Calvey was taken away without resistance, and technicians and detectives went downstairs to the crime scene.

Some other cops were still in the basement, preparing for and overseeing the removal of the corpse.

Mr. Carr had been summoned to the office and apprised of what had happened. He, Gilroy, and I were sipping instant Sanka, the only coffee the newspaper stocked. A beefy police sergeant remained upstairs with us, ponderously writing in a notebook.

"But why did you suspect Calvey?" Gilroy asked me, scowling at the tire grease that remained on his hands.

"I didn't really. Not at first. But I kept thinking about the entry in Teri's appointment book. Pietro Orenthro. Very unusual name. Then when I phoned the police and asked for P.O. Calvey, it made me wonder. What if the P.O. didn't stand for Police Officer? What if he was using his real initials in his byline all along?"

"P.O. Calvey," mused Mr. Carr, "for Pietro Orenthro Calvey. He's been writing for us for years, and even I never knew him as anything other than Police Officer Calvey. Good theory, Hackerstein, but unsubstantiated, yes?"

"Yes," I admitted. "It was just a hunch until I asked two follow-up questions, and Sergeant Salem told me Calvey's full name and that he smoked Winston cigarettes. Then I knew. In a small town like this, how many Winston-smoking Pietro Orenthros can there be?"

"Too bad," said Mr. Carr. "I liked both Teri and Calvey. Why did he do it?"

The sergeant spoke up. "Calvey claims he came here to make out with the victim but during the visit she told him she was through with him. Lost his temper. Crime of passion. Not premeditated. He's confessed, says he'll cooperate fully. He'll be charged with either second-degree murder or manslaughter. That's up to the D.A."

"I wonder," said Gilroy. "If he gets that one phone call you're always seeing on TV, will he call a lawyer, or a Hollywood press agent?"

He and I started to exit but Mr. Carr called me back.

"Hackerstein!"

"Yes, sir?"

"Good work. Now write up the murder and arrest and have it ready for typesetting in the morning."

* * *

Our next issue contained my story—quite a scoop for our little newspaper. For which Mr. Carr handed me a twenty-dollar bill—the largest bonus ever given out at the paper. I had it framed.

When my internship ended, Mr. Carr gave me a huge key ring, with an ashtray as its hub, as a souvenir.

On my first day back at school in September, a teacher saw my new key ring and called the principal, who suspended me for two weeks. Our zero-tolerance policy includes all images of weapons, drugs, and related paraphernalia. Since cigarettes are not allowed, I was told, neither are ashtrays. Or depictions of them. Seems like a dumb rule to me.

I debated during that suspension whether to keep bringing that key ring to school. After all, it's just a key ring...isn't it?

WISTERIA COTTAGE

By M. H. Callway

"Disgusting! Stafford's at it again." Verna trained her opera glasses on her neighbor's garden. "And him a married man!"

The binoculars were her favorite pair. Brass-rimmed and inlaid with mother-of-pearl, they'd once been her Great Aunt Betty's prized possession.

"Please, Verna! He'll hear you," Alison whispered.

* * *

Until now she and Verna had been enjoying a reasonably peaceful breakfast of croissants and coffee in the back garden. Trust Stafford and his predilection for young women cyclists to put a blot on this lovely August morning.

"Really, Stafford's private life is none of our business," Alison went on, knowing it was futile.

"Ah-ha! Look at her run."

A young woman with a blue backpack scurried through Stafford's garden. Verna tracked her step by step until she slipped through Stafford's back gate into the alley behind their houses. Clearly she'd spent the night.

Verna sighed with satisfaction and continued scanning Stafford's property; her hawk nose and helmet of gray hair enhanced her predatory image.

"Not 25 if she's a day. What on earth does she see in that old goat?" she

299

declared. At which point Stafford, balding with a cyclist's stream-lined muscles, appeared on his back porch.

"Now he did hear you," Alison said, cringing.

"I don't bloody well care," Verna shot back loudly, her British accent stronger than ever. "He should stick to riding that $10,000 carbon-fiber bike of his instead of female cyclists half his age."

Stafford threw them a smug smile and waved.

Great, Alison thought. Small wonder he'd called her and Verna nosy old witches—even though all three of them were in their mid-fifties.

Her ears still burned from hearing Stafford's rant to his bike buddies last week. Five men, all clones of one another, downing beers on Stafford's back patio after pedaling some no-doubt heart-exploding mileage. MAMILS—middle-aged men in Lycra—that's what George, her late husband, had liked to call them.

How she missed George! He'd skewer a self-satisfied twerp like Stafford with a zinger. Mind you, he'd reserved a few choice put-downs for his sister, Verna, too.

"Are you going to finish your coffee or not?" Verna's voice broke through Alison's thoughts. "Mustn't waste, you know."

Alison quickly drained her cold coffee. Anything to restore the morning's peace. Be patient, she reminded herself. You owe Verna a lot. She gave you a safe place to heal after losing George.

And, for the past 12 months, she and Verna had gotten on as housemates. Except for the upheaval over Alison's dog, Nicky. That had nearly proved disastrous. And lately, to be honest, Verna's eccentricities grated more and more on Alison's nerves. Topping her list of annoyances was Verna's pseudo-British accent.

Verna and George had grown up in Oshawa in the shadow of the Ford car plant where their parents sweated it out on the assembly line. George, despite his pharmacy degree, loved to call himself "your typical Canadian trailer park boy"—and he'd delighted in puncturing his sister's snootiness.

Throughout their 25-year marriage, Alison had urged George to be kinder to his sister. After all, they had no other family. Not to mention that Verna handled his pharmacy's accounts for very little money. Perhaps the put-on accent was simply a tribute to Verna's love of all things British, Alison would argue. After all, Verna *had* lived in England with their Aunt Betty.

Verna's closeness to Betty had irritated George, Alison knew. In her letters, Betty always called Verna a studious and serious girl, while referring to George as "that scamp" or "that silly flibbertigibbet." Hardly a fair assessment of George's character, and the spiteful way she'd cut him out of her will...

Alison glanced at her watch. Fifteen minutes till her bereavement group began. Five minutes to relax, five minutes to spar with Verna about it and five minutes to walk over to the cathedral.

First, relax! She breathed in the fragrance wafting from her herb garden: sage and lavender contained by a border of clean white lake stones. Taking up gardening had been a new experience for her. When she'd first moved in, Verna's backyard had consisted of nothing but a bleak, dried-out lawn and a wisteria vine growing rampant over an ancient potting shed. Mind you, the wisteria produced such a profusion of graceful mauve blossoms that it more resembled a surreal painting than a living organism. Now it fitted in beautifully with the cosmos, hydrangeas, and rose bushes Alison had planted.

One evening, in an uncharacteristic burst of sentimentality, Verna had confided that she'd grown it from the seeds of Betty's original vine in England. She'd even named her heritage limestone house "Wisteria Cottage" in Betty's memory—the house she'd bought with the money Betty left her.

Alison's five minutes of bliss gazing at the garden were nearly up. Restoring Verna's garden had been welcome therapy but also a convenient excuse. She hadn't written a word since George died. Her literary agent had nearly given up on her. If her writer's block persisted, her dog detective books would fade into oblivion—and soon.

But she missed Nicky so much...

Nicky, the inspiration of her cozy mystery series. How she loved that silly old dog! Despite his bad habit of eating almost anything—even socks—with the inevitable regurgitation and carpet soiling. Losing him and George felt too much to bear at times, but Nicky had gone to a better place. If she kept telling herself that often enough, maybe she'd believe it.

The bereavement group at the cathedral had saved her. Shortly after moving in with Verna, she'd spotted the brochure on the back table one Sunday after communion.

Knowing Verna's low opinion of support groups, she'd waited to pick up the pamphlet until Verna was busy chatting up the bishop. And she'd kept her attendance a secret. But one Sunday the bishop mentioned it in passing just as she and Verna were leaving church—as a widower he led the group. Verna had flown into a snit. She'd accused Alison of lying, calling her "a limp biscuit" and "a New Age wet."

Then the Nicky disaster happened. And now this silly spying on Stafford.

Never mind, time to go. Alison stood up, brushing croissant crumbs off her dog-patterned top and fitted jeans.

"I saw you checking your watch," Verna said. "Off to indulge in another tears and follies session, are we?"

"Oh, come on." To ward off Verna's grumpiness, Alison asked, "Is Stafford really married?"

"Of course, he bloody is," Verna said with relish. "I told you that when you moved in with me. Your memory's going, really it is."

Alison took a breath. "So where's Stafford's wife? I've never seen her."

"She's in Boston. They live apart, by mutual agreement, ha-ha. To further their brilliant law careers. As if. Bloody convenient for him, wouldn't you say?"

Verna raised her opera glasses, but Stafford had vanished back into his house.

Alison took the opportunity to escape through Verna's back gate. Halfway to the cathedral, she realized that she'd forgotten her house key. No worries, Verna devoted every Saturday morning to scrutinizing their household accounts. She'd be sure to be home later.

* * *

After group, Alison and her friend Norma headed for their favorite coffee spot, The Blue Dragon Café, across from the cathedral. They'd connected immediately when they met: Norma had lost her wife, Ava, to an aneurysm, as suddenly and devastatingly as Alison had lost George. Over time, they discovered that they both loved dogs and books. Not to mention the maple lattes brewed by The Blue Dragon's warm-hearted hipster owner, Wendy.

"Is he here?" Alison asked, pointing to the café's sunlit back patio.

"Of course." Norma threw her a conspiratorial smile. "Wendy's with him out back. You go ahead, I'll bring our lattes."

Alison rushed outside—and heard a bark of joy. The next instant a large golden retriever nearly bowled her over.

"Nicky, oh Nicky. Down boy." She managed to calm him. A treat from her back pocket helped. "Thanks so much, Wendy."

"No problem. Happy to help my dog fam. He behaved perfectly while you two were at your meet." Wendy winked and slipped back into the cafe.

"That's out of character, Nicky. What mischief did you get up to with Norma this week?" Alison asked.

"Nothing too serious." Norma set down their lattes on the cast iron patio table. "But my buds on the force would say I've gone soft now that I'm retired." Norma had been the first woman police officer accepted into Kingston's canine unit.

They sat down while Nicky settled down on the patio stones by their feet. Alison stroked his soft fur. If only he hadn't ruined Verna's living room carpet—not that it had taken much effort on his part. What was it George had called Verna's décor? Oh, yes, "Buried by Beige."

"So how goes the battle this week?" Norma asked.

Alison sighed. "We had words again about my wasting money in The Blue Dragon Café. Coffee brewed at home is so much cheaper, you see."

Norma shook her head. "Ask Verna to join us next Saturday. Find out what she's missing."

"Oh, I have, many times. But she says she prefers her own company." When Norma pulled a face, Alison quickly added: "I think it's because she's always lived on her own. Except for that year she spent with Betty in

England."

"I guess they prefer tea over there."

"Maybe." Alison smiled. "George used to say that Verna squeezed a nickel so hard the beaver on the backside screamed."

"That's an old one." Norma couldn't help laughing. "But Verna doesn't need to worry about money. She's high up at the insurance company, right?"

"Yes, she's an actuary. According to George, she didn't have the personality to be an accountant. That was mean of him, I know."

"No kidding."

"I used to get after George about the way he teased Verna," Alison went on. "He thought he was just being funny, you know, older brother, younger sister stuff. Strange how they grew up to become such different people. George was the dreamer who loved to take risks. Verna lives by rules and routine."

"She needs to feel in control, I guess." Norma gave Nicky a pat. "So what was her Aunt Betty like?"

"George used to call her The Old Dragon." Alison thought back. "I only met her once. We were on our honeymoon in England. George wanted me to meet his one and only British relative. Betty lived in a lovely little village in the Cotswolds. It had such a strange name. Middle Slaughter, can you imagine?"

"Sounds like something out of an Agatha Christie mystery."

"It really was! Her cottage was so quaint, all overgrown with ivy and wisteria. And Betty herself with her wild gray hair and briar walking stick. At first, I thought she was a character, but she turned out to be not at all nice."

"How's that?"

"We could hardly see inside her cottage, it was so dark. She kept all her curtains drawn because she was at war with her neighbors. They'd accused her of poisoning their dog. They'd even gone to the police about it, but luckily their dog got better."

"Wow!"

"She denied everything, of course. But she did go on and on about how much the dog barked and what a nuisance he was. Anyway, we'd booked a table at the pub for lunch, but she refused to go. She didn't want to walk past the neighbors, because they were outside in their garden, you see. Instead she served us tea and a plate of stale digestive biscuits. I only ate one out of politeness. She got mad at George because he helped himself to a second cookie."

"And I bet George said something."

"Better than that. He couldn't help being mischievous." Alison smiled, remembering. "He took a bite out of his second cookie, said 'sorry,' and put it back on her serving plate. Betty looked like a cobra about to strike. According to Verna, that's why Betty cut George out of her will and left everything to her."

"You've got to be kidding! How did George take that?"

"Like a big joke! Let Verna have the money, he said. She'd earned it kissing the old bat's butt for a year until she croaked. He just wished he'd taken a bite out of each and every one of her mangy cookies."

"Good for George!" Norma said. "You have to put Betty and that awful tea party in your next mystery."

Alison stared into her half-finished latte. "Oh, Norma, I've hardly written a word. Nothing's working. And with George gone, my dog mysteries feel, well, silly and trivial."

Norma set down her mug. "I don't think your books are trivial. Or silly. And neither do you, right, Nicky?" The dog thumped his tail. "We all need more cozy mysteries, especially these days. Don't you see? Your readers want to feel that justice is done. Did you know that my wife, Ava, was a big fan of your books? She got me reading your series, too. Yes, this old retired cop is a fan of yours. Does that surprise you?"

"Yes!"

"Look, I'll bet you ten maple lattes that once you get probate for George's will and you have your own place, your writer's block will vanish just like that." Norma thought for a moment. "If things get too tense with Verna, you're welcome to sleep on my sofa."

Alison shook her head. "No, I've imposed enough on you already. I owe you the world for taking Nicky." She took a breath. "I decided something during our group meditation today. It's been a year. I'm not waiting around for probate any longer. I'm going to find a job."

"Great! Ask the bishop. I heard he needs help at the cathedral office."

"Oh, no, that would make Verna furious."

"Why?"

"She's got a thing for him."

"No way!" Norma burst out laughing. "Well, I'm not into men, but I have to say he's pretty good looking—for a 75-year-old guy!"

Alison couldn't help laughing, too. "Funny thing, George used to call Verna his sexless maiden aunt. Like Betty in England. But I think he got that wrong."

"Everyone has a sex life," Norma said. "After what I saw on the job, I can guarantee it." She leaned over to pat Nicky who was getting restless. "By the way, does your vet have any new ideas about what Nicky ate?"

Alison shivered, remembering that terrible Saturday six months ago when she'd returned home from group to find him so ill. How the vet had barely managed to save his life...

"He did ask me once if Nicky ate plants. Apparently many garden flowers are poisonous. Like those hydrangeas I planted, for instance. But I didn't put them in until after Nicky got sick."

"Too bad you can't tell us, eh, Nicky?" Norma said to the dog who certainly enjoyed the attention he was getting.

Across the street, the clock on the cathedral tower chimed noon.

"Oh, no, I'm late for lunch." Alison stood up. "I must run. Literally. Peace in our time and all that." She crouched down and cuddled Nicky.

"My offer still stands," Norma said.

"Thanks! You're the best!"

* * *

Out of breath from running, Alison slowed to a brisk walk. If only she'd made more money as a writer. If only George hadn't taken such ridiculous risks with their money.

His last venture, *George's Foraging Tea*, had turned out to be a bottomless pit. He'd been so convinced that millennials would adore his organic, locally grown herbal concoction. But he'd died before his tea could go into production.

To clear their debts, she'd been forced to sell George's pharmacy and their house. Once the dust settled, his estate amounted to $50,000. So little to show for their 25 years of hard work, but as the bishop said, the past is done. One must move forward.

Turning into Verna's street, she stumbled over a heap of clothes strewn over the sidewalk.

The clothes were moving. A flash of blue.

The blue backpack! Stafford's girlfriend was being violently sick over the pavement.

"Oh, I'm so sorry! I didn't see you." Alison kneeled down beside her. "Do you need help?"

The girl shook her head but she was pale as a sheet of paper. Foamy yellow vomit leaked from her lips.

This was an emergency! Alison rushed up to Verna's front door. Locked!

"Verna!" She banged on the door.

No answer. She knocked and shouted again. Still no answer. Why today of all days had she forgotten her key?

"Don't...don't," a faint voice croaked. The girl held a cell phone in her trembling hand.

Alison grabbed the phone from her. Fortunately, it didn't need a password. She punched out 911.

The ambulance arrived in minutes, its siren blaring and lights flashing. By the time the paramedics had loaded the girl onto a stretcher, she'd gone limp and unresponsive. They asked Alison if she was family.

Dazed, she shook her head. "She's a friend of John Stafford, our neighbor next door." She pointed to the house. The paramedics noted down Stafford's name and address.

The ambulance left. The street fell as silent as a Sunday morning. Alison slumped down on Verna's front steps. Now what?

She realized that she was still holding the girl's cell phone. She keyed in Verna's landline. From where she sat on the front steps, she could hear the phone ringing inside. One, two...ten. No one picked up.

Verna must have gone out. Probably peeved because Alison was late for lunch.

No point waiting around, Alison decided. She'd walk over to the hospital, find out how the poor kid was doing.

* * *

Fortunately the hospital's emergency department wasn't busy. Alison told the young man behind the reception desk what had happened. He checked his computer.

"Yes, the paramedics just brought her in," he said, eyes on his screen. "She's in ICU."

"ICU?" Alison echoed.

"Are you a family member?"

"No, I found her. I called the ambulance." She repeated what she'd told the paramedics about Stafford.

"Yes, we've been in touch with Mr. Stafford," the receptionist said.

"I still have her phone."

"Why don't you hang on to it for now?" he said. "Just leave me your name and phone number."

Alison gave him her information and stumbled outside into the summer heat. If she hadn't found that girl, she might have died. She might still die.

She cut through the hospital parking lot, heading for home. Footsteps crashed up behind her.

"You!" a harsh voice shouted.

Stafford loomed over her, his face red with rage. "You gave the hospital my name! How dare you interfere!"

Alison found her voice. "I–I was only trying to help."

"Do you have any idea what you've done?" Stafford seized her by the shoulders. She gasped, too shocked to defend herself.

"Ma'am, is there a problem?" A security guard was striding past the parked cars toward them.

"Yes, yes, there's a problem!" Alison shouted.

Stafford released her so quickly that she staggered. He swore and marched into the hospital, the security guard close behind him.

Alison willed her legs to move. Heart churning, she ran out of the parking lot onto the main street.

The world was spinning out of control. She needed to think, a quiet place to decide what to do. She ran for the one place she felt safe: The Blue Dragon Café.

* * *

The sun was setting by the time Alison returned to Wisteria Cottage. She tried Verna's front door. Still locked and still no answer. And no house lights were on.

Where was Verna? What had she been doing all day?

Frustrated, Alison made her way to the back of Wisteria Cottage and let herself in through the garden gate. A faint light glimmered through the gaps between the rough boards of the potting shed. Someone was rustling about inside.

It had to be Verna.

Something held her back from calling out Verna's name. She crossed softly over the grass, passing the flower beds and the herb garden, to the patio behind the house. Betty's mother-of-pearl opera glasses still rested on the ornamental iron table where she and Verna had eaten breakfast together. In the deepening dusk, she felt the chill bite of fall in the air.

The door to the shed creaked open. Verna stepped out. Her gardening gloves and pink Crocs clashed with her tailored beige pantsuit.

In the fading light, Alison watched Verna approach. "Where were you all day?" she asked.

"I could ask you the same question," Verna replied.

"What were you doing in the shed?"

"None of your business." Verna tossed a sharp kitchen knife onto the patio table, pulled out a chair, and sat down.

Alison joined her. How to begin? She took a deep breath. "When I came back from group, I found Stafford's girlfriend collapsed on the sidewalk outside," she said. "I had to call an ambulance."

"Do tell." Verna peeled off her black-stained gardening gloves.

"The girl's in ICU. She's deathly ill." When Verna didn't react, Alison said, "Please tell me you had nothing to do with it."

"Are you mad? Why would I hurt Stafford's baby cyclist?"

"Because Stafford annoys you."

"You really *are* losing your marbles."

"We need to talk, Verna."

"Oh, is that why you've staged this dramatic confrontation? Like the final chapter in one of your canine cozies for the credulous?"

"Fine, despise my books," Alison said. "I spent the afternoon at The Blue Dragon Café. I borrowed my friend Wendy's laptop and searched the internet."

"Wasting time as usual."

"Not at all. That girl had foamy yellow vomit. It's a classic symptom of wisteria poisoning. Wisteria seeds are especially toxic. You were getting rid of those seeds in the shed, weren't you? Hiding the evidence."

"Don't be ridiculous."

"I can tell by the stains on your gloves," Alison went on. "Nicky had the same yellow vomit when he got sick. You fed him those nasty black wisteria seeds while I was at group. Don't try to deny it. Poisoning him was easy because he'd eat anything. But that girl—how did you do it?"

"No ideas? A clever mystery writer like you?" Verna toyed with her gardening gloves. "Theoretically speaking, a kind neighbor might—and I mean *might*—offer tea and sympathy to a young woman crying her eyes out after her married boyfriend's chucked her."

Alison's mouth went dry. "You put them in her tea!"

Verna threw her a cold smile. "Millennials love to down locally sourced

310

organic teas just to feel spiritually pure, no matter how filthy the taste. Why they might even drink George's precious foraging tea." She didn't bother hiding her sneer. "That silly little girl."

"How could you!" Alison's mouth went dry. "You hurt her just to get back at Stafford. That—that's evil!"

"Don't be a fool." Verna sighed. "I didn't do it for myself."

"I don't understand."

"Stafford *begged* me to do it. That's where I've been all day. Holding his hand."

"What!" Alison stared at her. "You two hate each other! Why in heaven's name would you do anything for him?"

"Why do you think?"

"But, but...You can't be serious. You and *Stafford*?"

"Oh, I know what you want to say," Verna said with a flash of real anger. "That I'm too old for Stafford to fancy me. Well, he's old, too. Though he is in good shape. Rather a bonus for what I want."

Alison could hardly breathe. "But why the theater? Why lie about it?"

"The lie suits us both. We like the sex and neither of us wants attachments. I value my privacy and Stafford values his wife's money. She doesn't suspect a thing about us. But he really buggered things up this time. The girl fell in love with him. She threatened to tell his wife. Stafford's terrified his wife will divorce him. Too many past indiscretions, you see. Yes, love and money, the motives you overuse in your pathetic dog detective stories."

"Verna, this isn't a novel. You and Stafford tried to *murder* that girl."

"How observant of you." Verna flicked a spot of dirt off her jacket.

Alison couldn't believe she was having this conversation. "Did you...did you kill your Aunt Betty? To get her money?"

"Of course not! I loved Betty. She taught me how to be free. How to rid myself of, shall we say, unpleasant obstacles."

"Like her neighbor's dog. With wisteria seeds."

Alison felt a deep chill. She thought back to the long, lonely night she'd spent waiting for George to return home to Toronto after he'd driven down to Kingston to visit Verna. The police eventually found his car by the side of the highway. George was inside. Death undetermined, the coroner said. Now she knew the truth.

"You killed George, didn't you?" She could barely get the words out.

Verna said nothing.

"What did you do?" Alison demanded, her fury rising. "Brew him a new recipe for *George's Foraging Tea*?"

"Maybe."

"He was your *brother*."

"Yeah, some brother." Verna's British accent vanished. "Putting me down every chance he got, while I worked for him for nothing. He fails at every one of his businesses and calls *me* stupid? He blew up at me because I wouldn't use Betty's money to bail out his *Foraging Tea* disaster. Last straw, I guess."

Alison felt ill. "Why did you ask me to move in with you?"

"I felt sorry for you after George died. You've always been nice to me. And when George's will clears probate, you're going to hand over that $50,000. To me. Payment for the money George owes me and for letting you live here at Wisteria Cottage."

"You've got a damn nerve! I'll tell the police everything."

"Go ahead. Stafford will swear that you're obsessed with him. That you spy on him every chance you get. That you poisoned his girlfriend out of jealousy. And I—very reluctantly since you're my only family—will back him up."

"I'll tell the police you and Stafford are lovers."

"They won't believe you."

"You fed Stafford's girlfriend the tea! The police will believe *her*."

"Yes, from a box of *George's Foraging Tea*. I had no idea what was in it. You've had ample opportunity to doctor it. You're the big mystery writer. You know all about poisons. Or ought to." Verna leaned back in her chair. "You can't prove a damn thing. Checkmate!"

Alison pushed back her chair and stood up.

"Where are you going?" Verna jumped up, rocking the table. The opera glasses tipped over.

They stared at each other. Then Verna picked up the knife.

"Are you out of your mind?" Alison said.

Verna upended the table. The opera glasses crashed onto the patio stones.

Alison turned and ran for the back gate. Her foot hit a rock. She tumbled head first into the herb garden. Verna crashed down on top of her.

She bucked and twisted as Verna tried to hold her down. She caught hold of Verna's wrist. But Verna was too strong. Alison felt her grip slipping. Desperate, she shouted for help.

"No one can hear you," Verna panted. She wrenched her arm free. Towering over Alison, she raised the knife.

Alison seized a border stone. Threw it blindly. And heard a satisfying cry of pain.

Verna hunched over, hugging her chest. Alison struggled out from under her weight. And staggered to her feet.

But so did Verna. She still had the knife. She came toward her.

A dark shape shot out of the shadows. It blindsided Verna, knocking her down. She shrieked in fear.

"Nicky!" Alison cried. He had pinned Verna to the ground.

The knife! She snatched up another border stone. "Drop the knife, Verna. Or I'll break your arm! I swear I will!"

Verna opened her fingers. The knife fell to the ground. Alison kicked it away from her.

"Alison! Are you okay?" a familiar voice shouted behind her.

"Norma!" Alison sagged with relief. Her friend stood by the garden gate. "Thank heaven, you're here."

Norma ran through the garden to join her. "I saw Verna attack you!"

"She tried to stab me." Alison pointed to the knife.

"Leave it there. That's evidence." Norma looked down to where Verna was struggling under Nicky's forepaws.

"Alison attacked *me*. I was defending myself," Verna said.

"Shut up! I saw what happened," Norma said to her.

"Get your bloody dog off me! You told me he was dead. You lied!" Verna shouted.

"To protect him," Alison said, realizing it as she spoke. "From you."

"Good dog, Nicky. Keep holding." Norma pulled out her phone. "Wendy called me. She said you looked upset at the café this afternoon. So Nicky and I decided to check in on you. Good thing we did."

Alison could no longer hold back her tears. "Oh, Norma, Verna killed George."

"What!"

"And she poisoned that girl in hospital. She and her neighbour, John Stafford. They did it together."

"You're a damn liar!" Verna shouted.

"Don't engage her," Norma said. "The police will sort her out. And that Stafford person, too."

For the second time that day, flashing lights and sirens filled Verna's street. Alison hugged Nicky as the police led Verna away.

"You're a real hero," she whispered. She'd make him the star of her next book, non-fiction this time.

Verna's opera glasses lay where they'd fallen, a galaxy of broken glass and metal.

KILLER CUPCAKES

By Shawn Reilly Simmons

Penelope slid her fingers along the wall, searching for the light switch. The cinder blocks were rough under her fingers and had a slightly oily feel to them.

"Crap," she muttered under her breath.

Penelope was sure she had seen the thick black light switches right there by the back door the day before when she had asked to borrow this kitchen. She was completely in the dark after the restaurant's heavy back door had swung closed against the purplish early morning sky. Her messenger bag, overloaded with all of her personal items plus her work files and a big heavy cookbook, jerked down from her shoulder into the crook of her elbow, throwing her off balance.

Her fingers crept further along the wall and then slipped into a nest of worms.

"Ack!" Penelope jerked her hand back, clenching it into a fist that she held tightly to her chest. "What the hell?"

Blowing out a loud sigh, she straightened her other arm, setting her bag on the floor between her feet. Shaking out her clenched fist, she knelt down to the floor, feeling around blindly in her bag for her phone, cursing herself for just throwing everything into it that morning in a mad rush to get out the door.

Finally feeling the smooth edges of the phone underneath the heavy cookbook, she yanked it out of the bag, letting the other contents spill out onto the floor. Her fingers found the button to illuminate the screen, and she swiped the phone to life, shining the light against the wall. The electrical panel with the industrial black switches was up higher on the wall than she'd remembered, and she'd been blindly feeling for them in the wrong place. She had, however found a cluster of wires that led to the box, or what her brain had determined was a bunch of worms.

Penelope flipped all of the switches to the on position, and the fluorescent lights overhead hummed slowly to life. She squinted for a minute, adjusting her eyes to the artificial light.

She looked down at the floor and sighed again. She bent down to scoop up the contents of her bag and placed everything that had spilled out on the stainless-steel counter that ran against the far wall of the kitchen.

Glancing at her phone, Penelope noticed she had a new text. A slow smile spread across her lips when she read it. "Miss you already. Have a great day." It was from Joey. She had been disorganized and rushing that morning because she had stayed the night before at his place after he'd cooked her a particularly delicious dinner, which they enjoyed with a nice bottle of pinot noir.

Penelope turned on the oven, rotating the temperature dial to 350 degrees. She always loved being the first one in the kitchen. Even though this wasn't her kitchen and she was unfamiliar with it, they all had that quiet, cool, humming tension to them at the beginning of the day. New and clean, the faint scent of lemon hanging in the air. Soon more cooks would arrive, more food would be prepared, and the quiet of the morning would be replaced with sounds of chopping, pans banging on iron stove coils, and chefs and cooks shouting orders at each other. The cool morning feeling of the kitchen would be replaced by electric heat and frenzied activity in a matter of hours.

A sharp knock on the back entrance jerked Penelope back to the present. She made her way to the door and pressed the long bar that released the lock, swinging it open.

A tall, thin woman in a stiff white chef coat stood just outside, a backpack strapped tightly to her shoulders. She craned her neck to peer behind Penelope into the kitchen.

"Are you Penelope Sutherland?" the woman asked.

"That's me," Penelope said. She stepped aside and swept her arm towards the kitchen behind her.

"I'm Samantha Blankenship, here for the interview?" A quick smile etched its way onto her face, then disappeared.

"Yes, Samantha. Nice to meet you," Penelope said. "Thanks for contacting me about the position." She smiled encouragingly at the young chef and moved over to the steel table to retrieve her files, pulling her resume from the stack. "You're a junior pastry chef at Le Gateau. That's impressive."

"Yes. It's my first job since school. I graduated at the top of my class, so I had my choice of places to work," Samantha said. She began to shrug her backpack from her shoulders, then hesitated, glancing at Penelope.

"Go ahead and put it there," Penelope said, nodding at the table.

"Thanks," Samantha said, removing the heavy pack and setting it down. She twisted her long fingers together as Penelope continued to read her resume.

"What made you want to become a pastry chef?" she asked, glancing up from the paper.

"Um...I think it's because I loved sweets as a kid," Samantha said quietly. "And I like making pretty things from just flour and sugar. Yeah. That's why," she said, nodding confidently.

"Great, well, I'm looking for someone who can come on part-time, or on a freelance basis. Our situation is unique because we're a traveling crew, and we don't need upscale desserts every day. But sometimes we do, and I can't always spare a member of my crew to bake when we're trying to get dinner ready. Logistically it makes sense to bring someone on that can handle that aspect...when we need them to."

"Okay, well, I'd be happy to be considered for the job. I'm flexible and—"

A loud rap at the back door interrupted her.

"Hang on a second," Penelope said. She pointed to the table against the far wall. "Why don't you get set up over there?"

Samantha nodded and picked up her bag, making her way to the table.

The back door whooshed open again to reveal a short, stocky man with silver hair and a tan face. He smiled generously, and his hand shot out towards Penelope. "Burt Salazar. We spoke on the phone. It's nice to meet you in person," he said, vigorously shaking her hand.

"Hi, Burt. Thanks for coming," Penelope said, nodding at the table. "Go ahead and get set up. That's Samantha."

Samantha smiled tightly at Burt and then went back to pulling items out of her backpack and setting them on the table. Burt eased up beside her and began setting up next to her, placing different containers of icing and decorative sugars on the table.

"Okay, guys. Make me some cupcakes," Penelope said.

"Want one?" Burt noisily opened a small cellophane-wrapped tray lined with bright blue marshmallow birds and waved it at Samantha.

"Um, no thanks," she said, her nose wrinkling the tiniest bit.

"You sure? They're good. You don't like spring peepers?" He chuckled and plucked out a little bird with his thick fingers. He waved the tray in Penelope's direction.

Penelope laughed and said, "I don't think I've had one of those since I was a kid at Easter." She took one and popped it in her mouth. "Yep," she said after she swallowed the peeper, "just like I remembered. A hard, sweet marshmallow."

"I love them," Burt said, munching on another bird. "Any color. They're all good."

Just then, Penelope's phone chirped from the other side of the room, and she left the two chefs to their work.

About a half hour later, Burt said, "All done, chef."

Penelope had been typing away on her tablet in the corner of the kitchen, answering emails and planning menus for the upcoming week. The smell of chocolate hung in the air around them. She had glanced up a few times as the two chefs worked, their backs to her. Burt liked to hum while he worked, swaying on his feet to his own internal music. Samantha worked quickly and quietly, her movements economical and precise.

She walked over to where they stood, their creations next to each other on the table. Burt looked at Penelope hopefully while Samantha stood with her hands clasped behind her back, quietly confident.

"These both look great," Penelope said. Samantha's cupcake was topped with an elaborate pink flower sculpted out of sugary fondant icing. Burt had painted his cupcake with a thin blue icing in the shape of a bird that looked a lot like his beloved spring peepers. Penelope picked up Samantha's first, taking a small bite of the cake portion.

"Wow. Really good chocolate flavor," she said to Samantha.

"Thank you, chef," Samantha said.

"Mine's red velvet," Burt said, nodding at his.

Penelope took a bite of Burt's cupcake. "This one is great, too, Burt. Nice flavor. Both of you have done a great job. So, let me think about it, and I'll be in touch."

Penelope watched the chefs re-pack their bags. Samantha finished first and turned to shake Penelope's hand.

"Nice meeting you," Penelope said. "I'll call you tomorrow to let you know my decision."

Samantha nodded and pushed her way out the door, squinting into the now bright morning sun.

"Thanks for the opportunity, Chef," Burt said, gripping Penelope's hand tightly in a handshake.

"You're welcome, Burt. I do have one question for you," Penelope said. "There is a two-year gap on your resume where you don't have anything listed. I see that you worked in restaurants before that...were you in school during that time?"

A brief shadow crossed over his face, and his smile faltered for the first time that morning.

"Um, no, miss," he said. "Well, in a way, I was."

Penelope nodded. "Well, you can put that down on your resume—"

"No, it wasn't that kind of school. I did take a class...the truth is I was in prison."

Penelope blushed. "Prison? What for?"

"Robbery."

"Oh. I see," Penelope said, shifting her weight to her back foot.

"They offered courses for us to take if we wanted to," Burt pressed on, "you know, how to cook, get your GED, different stuff like that."

"Well, that's good," Penelope said. "You learned how to bake in prison?"

"I had baked before, you know, working in all of those kitchens. But now I have the certificate to back me up. I officially know it, you know?"

"Yeah. So...robbery?"

"Yeah. The messed up thing is I didn't even know I was doing a robbery. I gave a ride home to my friend from work, and he asks me to make a stop. Next thing I know, he's running out of a store, telling me to go go go...the police show up at my door, and I'm aiding and abetting." Burt spoke quickly, and Penelope got the feeling he had told this story many times before.

Burt glanced down at his feet, then back up at Penelope. "I know you don't know me, and I understand if you don't want to take a chance. But I promise you won't have any trouble from me if you give me a shot."

Penelope smiled and shrugged. "I have a good feeling about you, Burt. Your work is beautiful. And anyone who likes spring peepers as much as you do can't be bad."

Burt laughed. "Wait, are you giving me the job?"

"Yep. Actually, I'm giving both of you the job. Since it's a revolving, freelance type of deal, I think having more than one person available to me is the best idea. We'll have plenty of work for both of you, I'm sure."

"Oh great. Thanks for the chance. I really appreciate it," Burt said.

Penelope walked him to the door. Burt smiled and nodded happily at her, thanking her again as he pushed through the door.

"See you soon," he said as he walked out into the new day.

"Yep. Very soon," Penelope said, closing the door behind him.

THE BIG PAYOFF

By Karen Dent

Ray Smart worked hard at being invisible. Good for his PI business. Until his partner Frank got killed and the cops blamed him. Enemy number-one wasn't what he wanted for his future. He also didn't want his partner dead. Lucky for Ray, before the coppers tried to finger him he was tipped to the setup and avoided the rabid hand of justice in time to scram. Enough time to stake out someone who could give him a lead to who done it and why.

Ray's mind kept going over the events of Fat Thursday: Chinese food, Mai Tai's and the cryptic riddles Frank dropped while he drank his dinner. That night kept spinning through Ray's mind like the old Victrola his grandfather used to play over and over. Fat Thursday was the last time he saw his partner without bullet holes pumped through his body.

* * *

"So listen," Frank slurred, "if something happens to me, you need to know stuff."

"I already told you," Ray said, mouth around a sparerib, "I don't want anything to do with your side shit."

"Listen, ya stupid mook, just knowing me can get you tagged. Better you should know the score and have ammo if you need it."

Ray looked up from chowing down. "What're you saying, Franko? You in trouble?"

"Nothing I can't handle." Frank carefully checked the customers before he turned back. "Just remember, if you find yourself wrapped up, I got proof down from heaven."

"Listen, stupid bastard." Ray put his chopsticks down, "Don't die on me. I got bills to pay, paperwork to finish."

Frank laughed and held up his glass. "To staying alive."

* * *

The fact that Frank drank his dinner that night should have alerted Ray to something major being on the wrong side of right. But his partner was always a bit squirrelly when he discovered something new on someone big.

Frank's motto: 'Always best to figure out how important it is to keep your info on the QT or let it leak just enough so's they know you know. Two ways you stay alive, but if you don't get it right, the daisy patch could be calling your name.'

Ray already missed seeing his partner's crooked teeth gleam and his soft brown eyes glitter with humor. Fact is, Franko loved drama. Loved the danger and always believed he could calculate the odds in his favor.

Too bad he misjudged this time.

* * *

Street noises brought Ray back to the present. At three a.m. in lower Manhattan, there weren't many except the bark of a dog and tonight, the splash of car tires as they sluiced through the wet, black street. A city boy, Ray enjoyed the smell of wet pavement and breathed in deeply. It reminded him of hot summer months, tar and the fire hydrant spray he dashed through barefoot and screaming from the cold.

A police cruiser headed down the narrow street and Ray folded himself deeper into the black-shadowed doorway of a tenement building.

When the car passed, he continued surveillance of the couple seated in the all-night diner across the street. They were at the counter trying hard to ignore each other and doing a lousy job of it.

Ray tightened his lips around the homemade cigarette nestled in the corner of his mouth. Smoking was a habit he'd given up years ago, but it was an old friend and he enjoyed the companionship. He didn't light up, but habits die hard; like falling for the wrong dame. He kept the cigarettes but ditched the flame and gave up both the smoke and dolls like Madelaine. He kept away from both until she got killed along with Frank and he got framed for both. His thoughts skittered back to the morgue.

* * *

Charlie let him in and showed him the slab. His throat closed up and he felt a deep sadness pass through him. Madelaine's raven black hair was still matted with blood and brains, her beautiful perfection marred by the brutal force of a machine gun, close range.

"Whoever did it," Charlie said, "they wanted to annihilate her. Nothing left of face, chest, hands. Figured she tried to protect herself and they just shot the shit outta her."

He shook his head to rid himself of the memory.

* * *

The curtain of rain was hard to see through but it was enough. The woman, Cricket Bouffey, finished her cup of joe and prepared to leave. She stopped at the coat tree, threw on her raincoat, and picked up her umbrella. She also palmed the money-sized paper package left for her in the pocket of the coat hung next to hers. Smooth and light-fingered as always, she headed out into the night.

The man Ray knew as Sasquatch Marvin ordered another greasy-spoon special and flipped open his newspaper. Ray smiled. Knowing Marvin wasn't planning to play protection for Cricket, he relaxed. He didn't relish being snuck up on and nabbed from behind. As big as Sasquatch was, boxing made him light on his feet but sadly soft in the head. The big guy's idea of being gentle was making sure you ended up wearing a full body cast and not cadaver weeds.

Ray tossed the sodden cigarette, pulled his fedora down further, and carefully followed Cricket. He held the advantage since no one knew he skippered before the coppers descended on him tonight.

He had a whole evening to find things out thanks to Pete Kelly. He worked the 10th squad downtown and gave Ray the heads-up with enough time to scram up the fire escape onto his roof and disappear.

Ray already knew where Cricket was going. Back to Benny's with his big payoff burning a hole in her pocket and a little extra scratch for her. She was hoofing it pretty good and making a big show of checking for shadows, so he kept close but not too close.

Ray knew people. Sometimes better'n they knew themselves. If he wasn't mistaken, Cricket was going to figure out the dough in her pocket could show up a little lighter than it left the diner. She'd need to count it to see by how much. Another short uptown block and—

Cricket's steps slowed. Leisurely she fell into a stroll and stopped in front of a closed store and pretended to window shop.

Across the street, Ray melted into a puddle of dark cast by a humpbacked Chevy. He wasn't surprised she used the old glass-mirror trick to check the street and sidewalks before she finally ducked into an alley. She was smart and had been around long enough to know the score.

He allowed enough time for her to carefully slit open the package and begin to count the dough before he emerged from the shadows, ready to ask questions. Two thugs appeared at the mouth of the alley. Light glanced off the shiny metal of their guns. Ray heard two sounds.

A whimpered "No," then the soft pop pop pop from silencers. Like synchronized swimmers, the two killers turned and hot-footed down the street and out of sight.

Ray dashed across the street to the entrance of the alley. He bent over Cricket and felt her pulse. Her china-blue eyes were wide open. Surprised and definitely dead. The opened package spilled plain note paper cut like dollar bills. The cheap paper began to soak up her blood.

* * *

Ray walked around to think things through. Frank's murder wasn't a big surprise but Cricket's was. Ray's partner had his fingers in a lot of dirty pies. Still, Frank had standards and if he gave his word, he kept it. He just couldn't let a golden opportunity pass him by.

"What's the use of fighting it, RayRay? Everybody's got an angle. Might as well get a little something for our efforts. If we can make both sides work for us, why not?"

Stupid Mook. 'Why not' was what got him killed. From the get-go, Ray let everyone know he played it straight. No bribes, no muscle work, no deals. On the other hand, everybody knew Magpie Frank collected things. Used to say it was good leverage. Better than coin. He never understood leverage couldn't resurrect a corpse.

Ray knew Frank was onto something big but couldn't figure where Cricket fit in enough to get her dead. He thought back to Thursday and Frank's boast.

* * *

"This one's complicated, pal. Audacious. And if I play my cards right, a big payday just to play mouse."

Ray figured keeping quiet this time was probably what got him killed. Knowing Frank kept his trap shut, someone decided it best to keep it that way. And just to be sure Magpie was on the up-and-up and didn't spill to his partner, they had to get rid of him, too. Just in case.

What no one knew was Franko had his own 'Just in Case.' A place he kept all his who, why's, and where's.

"You'd be surprised," he bragged, *"there's lots of reason's I'm worth murderizing."* He laughed. *"But everybody knows my word's good when I promise to zip my lip."*

In the nine years they were partners, Frank didn't squeal anything about anybody. What he did tell Ray was where his hiding place was.

Heaven was a drop down to a hidey-hole in Benny's office no one knew about. Not even Benny. A complicated twist, push, and yank inside an old bookcase Frank discovered. A pleasant surprise when he was unexpectedly left all alone in Benny's office a few years ago while the fat man was hauled downtown to talk to the cops. Forgotten and nosy, he did what he does best.

"Don't ask why I was there," he told him, "but the gods love a good joke. I checked out the space. Found the perfect spot."

People were always hunting for Frank's stash. The office and his flat were burgled more times than their cleaning lady came in to straighten up. Once Frank found his piece of heaven, he used his new hidey-hole whenever Benny was out.

"Okay," Ray bit, "you just walk into Benny's and ask if you can cool your heels in his office while he's out?"

"Use your noodle, smart guy."

Ray shrugged, "Don't care."

"You better. You need to know in case the bad guys win." He took a breath. "I drop down from Heaven. Get it? Heaven."

* * *

Yeah, Ray got it. The roof. The building was an old speakeasy transformed into a bar with living quarters upstairs and a big basement with tunnels that led who knew where. Ray was thankful the stash wasn't in the bowels of Hell. As it was, getting to Heaven then down into Benny's office was not going to be easy.

* * *

Ray called Pete and told him where to find Cricket's body, who he thought ordered the hit, and why.

"Someone's tightening their circle of need-to-knows. Frank knew Cricket was Benny's connection to a few politicians. Kiss and tell stuff. Palsy-walsy with the inner circle because she volunteered to work their campaign, then managed to work her magic in other ways."

"No one believes you killed Frank. Stay low for a while—"

"Not going to happen. Listen, I'm going over to Benny's—"

"Are you nuts?'

"I've got a plan—"

"To die? Listen knucklehead, I didn't tip you off so you could get yourself killed."

"Meet me. Back alley. No sirens, okay?"

Silence.

"Pete, they killed Frank, Madeline, and now Cricket. I think I know where to find out why. Just trust me, okay? An hour. Don't be late."

There's a lot to be said about knowing things, acting on them, and being smart. Frank was smart but he miscalculated. He liked to play the odds, and one thing was certain, this secret was big. Three murders so far. If Ray didn't figure this out soon, probably four.

He headed for Heaven and offered up a prayer to Frank's gods.

* * *

The roof of Benny's still sported a few dirty skylights. Originally it gave people more ways to escape a raid if necessary. Now they were a convenience to let out smoke and the odor of stale beer and whiskey. Not so convenient for the poor slobs who lived next to the bar. No amount of complaining to the City Mayor or Councilmen ever got anybody anything except a bloody nose and some broken bones.

Ray was in luck. The skylight above Benny's office was cracked open. He hunkered down and peeked in. The two trigger guys lounged on a couch while Benny, like a bloated frog, sat at his large mahogany desk.

"So you done it?" Benny asked. "What about Pureboy?"

"He's probably still squealing 'I didn't do nothing.'" The two Trigger guys laughed.

Benny glared. "Heard he wasn't home when they called. Scarpered before they could nab him." No one made a sound. "Pureboy's out there. Might know things. Did anybody see you two tonight?" They both shook their heads while Benny continued, "Frankie's partner isn't stupid. He's gonna figure out who framed him and why." The goons looked nervous. "Fallout can be dangerous," Benny added softly, "for everyone."

The trigger guys, nicknamed Weasel and Rat Face, pulled their guns and walked to the windows. Weasel spread the curtain with the tip of his gun, "If he comes around here, it'll be more bad for him," Rat Face grunted.

Benny struggled out of his chair, "Listen, boys, stake out downstairs. Shoot first, question later. We don't need him poking around finding stuff."

The three of them left. Lights out, the office was stone-cold empty. Ray sat back and wondered if it was a set up. Would they know he'd show and try to get into Benny's office? Did they know where Frank stored his stuff? He sat thinking about all the angles until he saw the office door below him slowly inch open.

Painted red nails on a delicate hand held the door ajar before a body slipped in. It was dim, too dim to see who it was. The sound of doors opening and closing, the rattle of pens, paper being pushed aside floated up and out onto the roof.

The lights snapped on and Benny waddled in, Weasel right behind him. "Well, well, well," Benny said. "Lookee what we got here. I thought I told you to lay low until we needed you."

Ray almost fell through the skylight. Beautiful, alive Madelaine stood in the middle of the room. Her breathy voice purred, "I can't do it, Ben. It's cold and damp down there. Besides, no one recognizes me this way."

Gone was her long, raven-black hair, replaced with a blonde cap of curls. Her violet eyes sported big round tinted glasses and her languid grace was now sharp with movement. She was a good actress, but Ray recognized her between his heartbeats. Disguised in another person's skin, she still looked like Madelaine to him, but oddly familiar, too. Like someone else Ray knew.

"I'm going nuts, Benny. No one to talk to, waiting for the switch and studying my part. I need time to inhale something other than rank basement air."

Frank's drunken rant Thursday night came back in vivid detail.

* * *

"Politicians suck," he slurred. "Would serve the bastard right. Such a pompous—"

"Who are you talking about now?" Ray spooned rice onto his plate.

"Who?" Frank's blood-shot eyes focused, then he got cagey. "Never mind. But this is big buddy boy." He sat back and muttered, "Can't figure what to do. Allow the switcheroo or blow the whistle?"

Ray stared at his partner. Frank wanted to share. Needed solid advice and knew Ray would never muscle in on his score. But it was against his nature to spill something valuable if he thought he could use it. Whatever Frank was into, it was more dangerous than usual if he considered exposing profitable information.

"You've got a gift for spinning gold out of straw, Franko, but this one smells. I never heard you think of blabbing to the cops."

Frank just laughed and clammed up. Maybe if he'd told he'd still be alive. Or maybe they would both be dead.

* * *

The light below clicked off. The room was empty again. Ray now knew where he'd seen the blond that Madeline had morphed into. No longer round in all the right places, Madelaine was sharp edges with nervous hands that ran through her curls. She was good, academy award good. She had become the spitting image of Joseph Clifford Sterling's daughter. The restless thoroughbred that stole the heart of America and helped get her father elected Mayor. Delilah Sterling.

Ray yanked the skylight open and dropped down into the room. He needed enough time to find and pocket Frank's stash before fat man and trigger boys returned. He began his search and ignored the burning itch to rush down and confront Madelaine. Why did she fake her own death and whose body was stretched out on the cold slab downtown?

Methodical, Ray searched the bookcase. No secret jog, no little lip to flip.

Frustrated he stepped back and stared at the haphazard wall of books.

Frank's voice floated up from his memory. *"Trust your eyes, buddy boy. I laid a clue for ya, just in case."*

A heavy tread in the hall approached the office. Ray ducked beneath the desk as Benny waddled in, Rat Face behind him. With a wheeze, Benny flopped down on the couch while his henchman paced the office.

"I don't like it," Rat said. "He could be anywhere."

"He's not our main concern right now," Benny growled. "Sit down, you're makin' me nervous." Rat sat on the edge of the desk, a leg dangling in front of Ray. "Mister high and mighty's takin' too long to agree. He's stonewalling."

"Says he wants to see his precious daughter first. Make sure she's all right."

"Tough. Either he cooperates and signs on the dotted line, or he gets nothing and his little darling starts to squeal."

Rat chuckled. "Yeah, dirty little secrets from her lying pretty mouth will sink him faster than anything we could do. Good thing you figured out a way to make that happen."

"He either signs those land deals, or she shows up dead with daddy's fingerprints all over her. He's screwed either way."

The groan of the sofa and shuffling feet announced departure.

"Hey, boss, what'll we do with the copy once we get what we want?"

"Don't worry about her." Benny's soft voice added, "Loose threads get cut so's they don't tangle anything up." Their chuckles echoed down the hall.

Ray slowly slid out from under the desk. Facing the bookcase, he stared at it, thinking about what he heard. Everything fell into place and he knew Benny's master plan.

Frank's clue floated into focus. Right there in plain sight. Weathered, cracked, and ripped, book spines on a lower shelf spelled out 'Franks Heaven.'

Ray needed solid proof. He pulled the books out and worked the small space. His fingertips caressed the old wood as thoroughly as he would a lover. Talented, the secret drawer opened. He pocketed four notebooks, three photos, and one folded map.

The itch to get to Madelaine was now a raging fire. Stupid dame, her cham wouldn't get her out of this jam. She was greedy, but he bet she didn't know about the dead kid murdered in her place or the plans Benny had after his trap was sprung.

* * *

Ray slowly opened the door and peeked out. Empty. He skulked through the upper hallway and saw no one. It was several hours before opening so no one was around except the twiddledee brothers and they were localized downstairs. He opened a small closet and took out a hat and overcoat, same shape and color as Weasel's. He hoped in the dim light anyone he encountered would assume who it was, and he slipped downstairs. Rat Face stood with his back to him, staring out the front. Ray moved quickly to the basement door.

"Hey!" Rat Face called out, "Benny don't want you down there anymore. She's starting to—"

Ray shrugged, opened the door, and headed down. He counted on Rat not challenging his partner. Weasel was the brains of their two-pack and Rat expected him to do whatever the hell he wanted.

Ray stopped and listened for sounds of being followed. Nothing. Stealthy, he continued down the rickety wooden steps and stepped into a wide, earthen-floored basement. Shiny gold hair was in one corner pacing. In another was a hospital bed with a sleeping form on it. Dirty gold hair spread out on a pillow.

"Hi ya, Maddie," Ray said quietly.

Madelaine spun around. Her eyes, no longer camouflaged behind glasses, glittered. "RayRay." She rushed him and buried her face in his chest and clung. "They said you were dead. Both you and Frank."

He peeled her off, "We gotta get outta here, Maddie."

"What? No. Not yet, I—"

"Listen kid, in a few hours you're going to be fish food."

"Don't be ridiculous. Benny promised—"

Ray realized his quick exit was not going to be easy. "Sorry, doll." Ray socked her in the jaw. She went down soft, like a rag doll. He tossed her over his shoulder, turned, and put one foot on the stairs before the door at the top opened. Light spilled down. He had enough time to twist and melt under the stairs and into shadow.

Rat's whine floated down, "Yeah, I heard you the first time but I'm telling ya I saw you—"

"It wasn't me, idiot, you're imagining things again. Come on, Benny wants to talk to us."

The light went out and the door slammed shut. Ray gently laid Madelaine down and went over to the girl on the bed. An IV hooked up to her bruised arm dripped knock-out juice. Her face was gray. Ray pulled out the IV and slapped her a couple of times. Color began to mottle her cheeks.

He quickly inspected the basement. Two small tunnels were carved out of the rock wall in the back. They curved down into black and blew icy breath that stank of river water.

He tossed his hat by one of the tunnels and went back to sit by Madelaine. Hidden beneath the stairs and shrouded in shadow, he squatted down, removed his gun, and waited. If the two murderers came down to find Madelaine missing, they might think a rival gang got wind of Benny's master plan and muscled in to steal his key player. Perfect exit through one of the tunnels without anyone being the wiser.

If Ray was lucky, both morons might rush the tunnels and be cornered. He'd shoot if he had to, but if Pete shows like he's supposed to, Ray would rather the killers rot in a tiny, damp cell, not unlike the present surroundings.

Ray heard a slight rustle behind him. His gun got kicked out of his hand. It clattered across the floor as Madelaine shoved him onto his ass, stepped over him, and shouted, "Help! Benn—"

Ray grabbed her ankle and yanked. She fell to her knees and he clamped a callused hand over her mouth. He whispered, "Are you nuts? I'm trying to—Oww!"

Madelaine bit down hard and crabbed backward. "Me nuts? You stupid, meddling fool. This is my one big payday. My one chance to get the hell out of this lousy town. We got plans, Ben and me. You could be a part of them if you don't ruin everything."

Ray grabbed her. "Plans? Frank's dead. Some girl passed off like you is dead and now Cricket's dead. Who else—"

"What?" She stopped moving. "Cricket's—?"

"Murdered." He halted. "Wait, you knew about the other girl?"

"They did Cricket?"

"Focus, Maddie. They're getting rid of anyone involved in this scam. You included."

"But Benny told me—"

"What you wanted him to. A sweet payoff where no one gets hurt. So who's the poor kid lying in the morgue?"

Madelaine's expression got a frosty look that Ray didn't like. "No one special."

Disappointment clouded his eyes. "You knew."

She straightened, "Yeah I knew, so what? She was the perfect patsy. Always wanting to be me. Be important. So I let her. Benny said it worked out great."

"Yeah, if great means you're so shot up you don't even have a face." Ray heard movement upstairs, turned, and popped her again. Down for the second time, Ray was free to wait for the boys.

"Too bad," Rat Face whispered on his way down. "I thought the original was real polite like."

"Yeah. Now we have to play nice-nice with the bitch."

They laughed as they descended the stairs.

"Hey, Prima Donna," Weasal called. Silence. At the bottom of the stairs he gave a quick eye roll around the room. "What the hell?"

"Maybe she's upstairs takin' a piss," Rat Face offered.

"Did you see her walk by you, stupid? We were standin' right there."

"Maybe she's hiding." They looked at each other and both bolted to the tunnels.

Ray stepped out. "Hello boys."

* * *

Pete was good as his word. Just a few cracked heads, a knuckle sandwich, and Benny's trigger boys were escorted out and into a patrol car. Benny was nowhere to be found. Pete called in an ambulance and Delilah Sterling was on a gurney and on her way to a hospital.

It hurt Ray to hand Madelaine over to the cops. Especially when she pulled her helpless 'I didn't know, I'm just a victim' routine. He'd fallen for that too many times to believe it now.

Ray laid it out for Pete. "The big play was Mayor Sterling couldn't be blackmailed."

"So then what did Frank have that blew this up so big?"

"Sterling had a major land deal to sign off on. Big business to get the contract, or farming and community living. Benny wanted that contract, but Sterling was for the people."

Pete shook his head. "And?"

Ray walked Pete to his car while organizing his thoughts. "It's an election year. While most of his constituents might forgive a peccadillo—"

"Enter Cricket," Pete said.

"Exactly, but Sterling didn't care. Benny knew he had one Achilles heel, his daughter. A convoluted and effective plot sprang from Benny's marbled brain, like Zeus's progeny."

Pete nodded. "I get it. Find someone who looked like Sterling's daughter, talked like his daughter, and use her to smear his good name and lie, lie, lie." Pete got into his car. "Scary good. America's sweetheart denouncing her own father."

"And endorsing another candidate," Ray added.

"Brilliant. I didn't think Benny had it in him."

Ray paused before he added quietly, "Pretty sure he had help."

"Oh?"

"Except for the third act of the ugly scenario, which is pure Benny. Daughter exposes father, father kills daughter and ends up committing suicide. Neat and sweet."

* * *

Ray sat alone in Fat Thursdays. He lifted his Mai Tai, "Frank, thanks to you good has triumphed and evil has been thwarted."

On the table before him was one of Frank's notebooks, written in code. Ray struggled with guessing the key. He already had a piece of the papyrus. Like the Rosetta Stone, deciphering the particulars rested in how Frank outlined Benny's master plan in the book.

Within that story and other entries of misdeeds and schemes were scattered words: Spare, Mai, and R. In fact, Ray found those exact three words in each scribbled entry, with dates.

"Frank, you dirty bastard!"

Each date corresponded to their dinners on Fat Thursday. There would be clues in what Frank said those nights, too.

Now Ray just had to remember what they talked about and apply the key.

HELL HATH NO FURY

By Eve Elliot

MILLIONAIRE PLAYBOY JULIAN DAVENPORT SETS SAIL WITH NEW BRIDE!

Two months after his scandalous divorce from actress Imogen Carter, the dashing heir to the Davenport mining fortune has taken a new bride in the person of Angeline Sutton, eighteen-year-old daughter of industrial tycoon Hiram Sutton. The glamorous newlyweds have embarked on a sailing honeymoon to the south of France aboard a 300-foot luxury yacht, *The Erinyes*, a wedding present from the bride's father. Rumour has it the sailing party includes several associates of Mr. Davenport—among them, astonishingly, are Miss Carter and her new husband, Dr. Arthur Chenoweth...

Society Eye Column, *London Gazette*, 12 August 1938

"You're quite a curious fellow, Dr. Chenoweth."

The man seated to my left, a Mr. Perry according to the place card before him, leaned in to whisper as we seated ourselves at the lavish dining table aboard Julian Davenport's floating palace.

White-gloved staff poured wine as the rest of the party took their seats, including the newlyweds themselves. Only one guest was missing, and I felt her absence keenly.

"How so?" I asked, without much interest.

"Well, I shouldn't like to be on honeymoon with my wife's former husband and his new wife," he returned. "I wonder what possessed Davenport to invite her along."

"He didn't," I said. "It was her idea."

My companion laughed. "These young women today, they certainly know their own minds. My hat's off to you then, for being a jolly good sport about it."

"I'd do anything for her," I said, because it was true.

"What about *Davenport,* though?" he chuckled. "After such a vicious divorce I wonder he doesn't fear for his life. Hell hath no fury, et cetera. It's a wonder he even allowed her to set foot on board."

"She's the more famous of them," I said. "He knows how to attract press attention when he wants it."

"You know, I'm rather reminded of that new Christie book, what is it... *Death on the Nile*, that's it. Ripping good read, a woman scorned and all that. Although," he paused, his amusement growing, "she'd be a fool to exact her revenge on Davenport with Chief Inspector Thorpe aboard as well."

My eyes went to Thorpe, who was accepting a glass of Burgundy from one of the staff. Florid, rotund, sitting back against his chair like Alexander surveying Palestine. Insufferable man. I'd always detested him as the head of Scotland Yard—for he often publicly insulted the psychiatric profession whenever there were newspaper fellows about—and my animosity had only grown since his retirement. He was Davenport's uncle, and now spent his leisure penning ghastly detective novels, the culprits in which were invariably the mentally ill.

Who else had joined this unorthodox honeymoon? My eyes scanned the table, recognising only a few faces. Eustace Grant, a medical man I knew slightly, was now Davenport's personal physician. Anthony Fraser—now there was an eye-raiser; he was an enormous, hulking young fellow and the son of a shipping tycoon Davenport had allegedly ruined. Marjorie Hunt, a gossip columnist whom Davenport had successfully sued, made another startling addition to the entourage. And of course my absent wife, perhaps the most surprising guest of all.

A substantial matron took the empty chair to my right, having found the place card with the name Mrs. Williams. I had rather hoped to be seated with my wife, but I saw immediately that doing so would have been to her disadvantage. Clearly her place was directly opposite Davenport and his new bride. I remained content to anchor the end of the table with my gregarious new acquaintance and the portly dowager.

And then, as if an angel had alit on earth, my eyes caught the only sight I ever cared to see. My wife, Imogen, had entered the dining saloon.

She was startlingly beautiful. So lithe and elegant, such lustrous skin, such glittering dark eyes and shining ebony hair. She'd triumphed as Cleopatra in Drury Lane last year and had inhabited the role so thoroughly she'd collapsed from exhaustion on closing night. She was exquisite and alluring, and like the more famous Cleopatra, utterly irresistible.

All eyes were drawn to her as she entered. She gifted her smile to several of Davenport's guests, touching their shoulders with her slender fingers before gliding to her seat. Her smile was all beneficence and grace, and my heart thumped pitifully just watching her.

"Shame she went through that spell of trouble," Perry said, *sotto voce.* "What a beauty."

Imogen slid gracefully into her seat and accepted a glass of wine. She downed it quickly, and held the darkly-stained glass aloft to be refilled. The startled server hesitated only a moment before pouring her another, spurred to action by her upturned face and brilliant smile. The wine had tinted her lips a dark, lurid red, which suited her complexion beautifully.

Oh, she was a magnificent creature, holding her head high, daring anyone to pity her, flashing her radiant smile and narrowing her onyx eyes across the table at her ex-husband as she swirled wine around her glass in slow, mesmerising circles.

Davenport, still dashing at nearly fifty, still debonair with his slicked back hair and his elegant moustache, still trim and broad-shouldered beneath his pristine white dinner jacket, studiously avoided her gaze.

"I propose a toast to our gracious hosts," she said then, her voice so rich and sultry it stilled the room. All conversation stopped as she raised her glass towards Davenport, who sat back and regarded her with a cautious expression. "Here's to Mr. and Mrs. Davenport. The second Mrs. Davenport, that is."

The pale and lovely Angeline blushed a furious pink, and looked down.

"Hear hear," voices around the table chimed in, although in somewhat muted tones.

"May you find happiness with this woman for many months to come, until you find someone else to take her place."

"Imogen."

Julian Davenport's handsome face was frowning now, flashing a warning at his former wife.

"Now, darling," she cooed. "Let's not pretend this marriage will last any longer than ours did."

Who could help but fall in love with that mellifluous voice? What a fool Davenport had been to break his marriage vows to such a woman.

"I say, Miss Carter... I beg your pardon, *Mrs. Chenoweth*," Thorpe said gruffly. "Let's enjoy this magnificent meal, shall we? Let bygones be bygones, as it were?"

Murmurs of agreement swept the table.

"He will leave you, you know." Imogen turned her attention to Angeline. "He will tire of you and seek out other women. You must know this."

"Imogen, that's quite enough," Davenport said. "You promised me you were fully recovered from your...your..."

Breakdown, I mentally filled in the word for him. *The nervous collapse* **you** *caused when your scandalous affair and plans to divorce her were publicly revealed.*

"...from your *difficulties*," Davenport went on. "And I hope it's the truth."

"The truth?" she echoed, ending on a tinkling laugh. "Who are *you* to speak of promises and truth?"

The tension around the table grew. Imogen glanced at each of the perturbed faces and addressed them.

"You know he only married this little tramp because she's pregnant, don't you?" She blinked, feigning surprise. "Otherwise he'd have tossed her away by now, as he does all his women."

"Imogen!" Davenport barked.

It was perhaps the only time I'd ever seen the sophisticate tremble with anger.

"I told you it would be dreadful having her here!" Angeline erupted then, her thin, girlish voice breaking. "Oh, Julian, she's vile and vicious and utterly insane, you said so yourself!"

I'd rarely seen a more delightful tableau than the one before me. The mighty Davenport, caught between his furious wives, publicly embarrassed by the women he thought he could abuse with impunity. He tried to placate his new wife, all the while glaring back at his former wife with barely contained rage.

"Pull yourself together, Angie," he was saying, though she shook her head and began to cry.

"Everyone will know soon enough, dear," Imogen said with an elegant shrug. "Why, you're already showing."

"Ladies and gentlemen." Davenport lifted his chin and addressed the room, the very picture of dignity. "Do please excuse us. I should like to speak with Mrs. Chenoweth privately."

"No!"

The voice was Imogen's but the ferocity in it was like nothing I'd heard before. All eyes stared at her as she rose and planted both hands on the table with a defiant *bang* that made the tableware rattle.

"I beg your pardon," Davenport challenged her, rising as well. The former spouses stared at each other, eyes glittering with animosity.

"You can't hide from this," she lashed out. "I will see that the world knows what a filthy cheat you are."

"You're insane," he growled. "They never should have let you out of that...that...*asylum* you belong in."

"You can't silence me any longer, Julian, I won't allow it." She looked around the table at the stricken faces. "He wanted to bring another woman into our bed, did you know that? More than one—two, three, as many as he could. He wanted to have an orgy and—"

"Enough of this nonsense!" Davenport straightened up. "You're out of your mind, you need…"

A wail broke through Davenport's words, and everyone turned to Angeline, who was now red-faced and weeping. She pushed back her chair, threw down the napkin she'd been twisting, and fled from the table, nearly crashing into a bewildered waiter.

"Angeline, wait!" Davenport called out. Casting a vicious glance at Imogen, he turned and followed his new wife, his plaintive calls echoing down the narrow corridors towards the back of the yacht.

When I turned to look at Imogen, her eyes were dancing.

Dinner was a subdued affair, and the only conversation to be had was delivered in hushed tones. Each new subject was extinguished quickly, presumably because no one wished to be too loud or too gay. A little after ten, Imogen rose smoothly from her chair.

"This is simply too boring. Goodnight."

"Shall I join you, dearest?" I half-rose from my own chair.

But she was beyond hearing me. All eyes silently watched her retreating back, lushly sinuous in her deep-cut backless gown. As the silence around the table grew ever more uncomfortable, I cleared my throat and finished the last of my wine.

"If you'll excuse me, I shall join my wife."

I doubt anyone was anything but relieved to see me go. I passed through the saloon and down the narrow corridor towards the berths and paused before the polished burled oak door to Imogen's cabin. I lingered there, touching the cool surface for a moment, hesitating, before turning to enter my own cabin directly opposite.

At three a.m, I was startled awake by a scream.

* * *

I threw on my dressing gown and hurried to Davenport's cabin, which I had determined to be the source of the scream. Presently I was joined by several of the other gentlemen, hastily attired in pyjamas and dressing gowns, crowding the corridor outside his door. Even Marjorie Hunt arrived, her hair pinned up in curlers, her face a greenish mask of night cream.

"Make way, let me through," I commanded, with the full authority of my medical degree. Bodies jostled and flattened against the panelling as I prised my way into the master cabin.

The sight before me was gruesome. Julian Davenport, still dressed for dinner, lay face up on the bed, a knife protruding from the dark red stain in the centre of his chest.

Kneeling on the bed beside him, his new wife Angeline was wailing, clutching his cold hand in both of hers.

My heart went out to the poor child. I wished I could say something to soothe her, but instead I dutifully examined the body and checked for a pulse. Finding none, I straightened up and shook my head. "Miss Hunt, would you be kind enough to take Mrs. Davenport to the galley and have the cook give her some brandy?"

"Yes, come with me, dear," Marjorie Hunt said, guiding the weeping girl off the bed. "You've had a terrible shock."

"What happened?" Perry appeared, looking disheveled and confused.

"Someone killed him!" Angeline cried as Marjorie led her from the room. "I came in and found him like this! Oh my poor Julian!"

"I say, Chenoweth, what should we do?" This was Fraser, looking ashen. "Someone has gone to rouse Dr. Grant, but what can be done?"

"We must return to England, of course," I said. "You there," I pointed at Perry. "Advise the Captain that we must reverse course immediately. Where is Inspector Thorpe, has anyone woken—"

"Here I am, Chenoweth," came the gruffly sleepy voice of the man himself, who pushed his bulk into the room, tying the belt of his dressing gown about his belly. "What the devil is—"

He broke off when he saw his nephew's body, and his face paled.

"Lord have mercy," he whispered.

"Inspector, I'm afraid this situation calls for your expertise. With your permission, I'll place a ship-to-shore call to the police in Cornwall as soon as we're in range. I know the Inspector there quite well, he's a good chap. In the meantime, I suggest you secure this room and start questioning everyone on board."

"Yes, of course," he mumbled, his stare fixed on Davenport.

Just then a piercing shriek shattered our nerves anew, only this time it did not belong to Angeline.

"Imogen!" I cried, and tore from the room.

"Dear God, what is happening on this boat!" Perry exclaimed, and he and Fraser followed me down the corridor.

My heart pounding, scarcely able to draw breath, I stopped at Imogen's door and tried the handle. It was locked, but I kept rattling it, uselessly. Her shrieking sobs assailed us from within, and I slammed my impotent fists against the door in an agony of desperation to get inside.

"Mrs. Chenoweth!" Fraser called out. "Open the door!"

"Break it down, man!" I cried, and the brute obliged, flinging himself against the door again and again until the latch broke and we three tumbled in. I scanned the room, frantic, but it appeared untouched, not even the coverlet on the bed had been disturbed.

"Imogen! My love, where are you?"

A whimper from the tiny closet beside the door mobilised us, and in seconds the sliding door was thrown aside and I sank to my knees, felled by the sight of my beautiful wife cowering in the depths. Her knees were drawn up to her chin, her eyes wide with terror.

"There now, my love," I cooed, smoothing her wayward hair out of her eyes. She was slick with sweat and shaking, frail as a leaf. "It's alright, darling, I'm here."

It was then that I noticed the spray of dried blood spattered across her dressing gown.

All three of us noticed it. Her wild eyes darted between Fraser and Perry, and when her gaze met mine, she opened her mouth and screamed.

* * *

By eight a.m, as the yacht motored smoothly towards Cornwall, a gloomy quietude had befallen the sailing party. The staff offered to serve breakfast, but no one had the appetite for it. We gathered forlornly in the ship's lounge to await we knew not what.

I paced before the great glass panes that overlooked the bow, until commotion from the outer hallway made all heads turn towards the door. Inspector Thorpe entered, followed by Dr. Grant, who guided Imogen delicately toward a narrow bench by the door. Imogen blinked, uncomprehending, until Grant helped her take a seat.

The dreadful events of only a few hours ago immediately returned to me in full force. I had allowed myself to be pushed aside by Thorpe and Grant when they had followed Imogen's scream and crowded into her cabin. I had been overcome with emotion, I am not proud to admit, and hadn't the wherewithal to assert myself in the matter. Shocked by the intensity of her distress, I had performed only a cursory examination to determine that the blood was not her own, and had then allowed Mrs. Williams to bustle me and the other gentlemen out of the room.

I'd passed a dreadful few hours, not knowing what was taking place behind my wife's closed cabin door. Seeing her now, in a clean shift and dressing gown that were both too large for her, and likely the property of Mrs. Williams, my heart surged with the tenderest love and concern. Imogen looked so frail and vulnerable, swathed in yards of white cotton, the look of a startled doe upon her beautiful face.

I made a move to go to her, but upon seeing my advance she began to fret, her agitation so wretched it stopped me short.

"Perhaps you ought to leave off, doctor," Grant said to me discreetly. "She's calm now, let's not disturb her. Don't you agree?"

I could only nod, a lump in my throat preventing speech. She looked so childlike and confused, so much like she had after her exhausting run as the Egyptian queen. I had been able to care for her then, but now I was utterly useless.

At length, everyone who had been witness to the evening's misadventure arrived in the lounge, all wearing grim expressions. Everyone took a seat, and looked to Thorpe for what to expect next.

Thorpe stood in the centre of the room, and cleared his throat. "Good morning, ladies and gentlemen. No doubt you are anxious for further details of last night's...incident."

"How is Mrs. Davenport?" asked Mrs. Williams. "She was in a frightful state."

"Mrs. Davenport is resting in her cabin," Thorpe said, with avuncular reassurance. He tipped his chin at Grant. "Dr. Grant has been tending to her since the event."

"Do we know what happened?" Fraser's voice cut through the murmurs. "And do we know *who*..."

"Yes, I'm afraid so. As many of you saw, my nephew was..."—Thorpe paused to clear his throat—"...stabbed through the heart with a knife from the galley. He would have died almost immediately, according to Dr. Grant."

I did not take offence at Thorpe's reliance on Grant over myself. Knowing Thorpe's distaste for my profession, I was not surprised at being excluded.

"The Captain has reversed course and we are now roughly two hours from Penzance," Thorpe said, consulting his watch. He looked up and gestured to me. "Dr. Chenoweth, being a native of those parts, was good enough to contact the local constabulary via ship-to-shore radio, and assures me that police officers will meet us as soon as we drop anchor."

"Why did you let *him* make the call?" Perry asked. "I say, given the circumstances, wouldn't it have been wiser to contact your own colleagues, Inspector Thorpe?"

Thorpe cleared his throat again. "Yes, well, the Davenport family would appreciate discretion in these terrible circumstances. I discussed it with the Captain, Dr. Grant, and Mrs. Davenport, and it was agreed that we should return to England with as little unwanted attention as possible. Dr. Chenoweth's personal connection in Penzance affords us a more discreet arrival than we might have enjoyed otherwise."

Everyone turned to me and I smiled weakly. "I was able to reach the Chief Inspector, and advised him we would be returning with Mr. Davenport's body. He assures us the press won't be alerted. The Captain heard the entire conversation, if you doubt me."

Thorpe nodded. "Very good, thank you, doctor. I assume you also communicated instructions regarding..."

He trailed off, with a subtle flick of his head toward Imogen.

"Regarding what?"

His bushy eyebrows rose. "Mrs. Chenoweth, of course. In her current state, and given the violence of her outbursts, I suggest she be placed under arrest discreetly, before arranging for the removal of my nephew's remains."

"Under arrest?" I sputtered. "What the devil do you mean? I informed the police of the murder, yes, but I requested an escort for her to St. Lawrence's asylum in Bodmin, where she can receive the care she needs. I said nothing to them of her being involved in his death. That's preposterous!"

Thorpe rocked back on his heels and sighed, looking about the room for confirmation of support in what he was about to say. Evidently finding it, he came toward me with slow, purposeful steps, folding his hands behind his back.

"Doctor, I am not alone in the belief that the crime was indeed committed by your wife. In light of the blood stains on her—"

"Don't be absurd!" I cried. "Isn't it obvious what happened? Imogen must have come upon him before Mrs. Davenport did, saw that he had been stabbed, and bloodied her gown whilst leaning over him to try to rouse him."

"Really, Dr. Chenoweth—"

"You saw her in her cabin," I challenged. "She was virtually catatonic. Fraser, Perry, you were with me when we discovered her," I appealed to them, but they looked away. I returned to Thorpe. "She was out of her senses with shock. If she'd had the presence of mind to murder the man, she wouldn't have then run to the closet to have a mental collapse."

"I rather think that's precisely what happened," Thorpe said.

"Nonsense! You're making a mistake, Inspector, and I urge you to rethink your conclusions. There is a murderer loose on board, and you're content to lay the blame on an innocent woman, one who clearly lacks the capacity to even understand what has happened."

"Who among us do you believe is a murderer, then?" This time it was Marjorie Hunt, glaring at me from her perch beside Perry.

"You, for instance," I said desperately, gratified by the shock that lit her face as I pointed at her. "Davenport sued you for libel, he ruined your career at the *London Gazette*. Why should you not be considered suspect?"

"Because he invited me aboard to discuss writing his autobiography, you fool," Marjorie snapped. "He wanted us to forget the past and collaborate. He said he'd always *adored* my writing."

I pivoted and faced Fraser. "What about you? He ruined your father, we all know that. You could have been planning your revenge for years!"

Fraser laughed bitterly. "Revenge? Hardly. My father had no head for business. He didn't need any help from Davenport to run the firm into the ground, I assure you. And as for me, I was invited aboard to meet Mrs. Davenport, and discuss a business opportunity involving her father."

My heart began to pound. I could feel the sweat beading on my forehead. I was the centre of attention, and what I said next could mean everything to Imogen.

"Anyone on this vessel could have done it," I said, my tone controlled and quiet. "Mrs. Davenport, for example. She was discovered with the body, covered in blood. She'd been so angry with him at dinner, we all saw it. Perhaps they'd continued to fight, and in a passion she stabbed him."

"Mrs. Chenoweth was also angry with him at dinner," Mrs. Williams put in.

Nods of agreement and murmurs circled the room.

"I was with Mrs. Davenport all evening. Ask Dr. Grant." Marjorie Hunt lifted her chin imperiously. "I was consoling the poor child, she was in such a state after your wife's outrageous display."

"It could have been any member of the staff," I said, hearing my own voice falter. "It could have been you, Inspector Thorpe, or me for that matter. You simply can't assume—"

"I killed him."

The whispered voice cut through my words. I turned to stare at the

347

speaker.

She was looking down, hiding her luminous dark eyes.

"Imogen, no!"

I crossed the room and dropped to my knees in front of her, searching her face. She seemed less afraid of me now, and only blinked at me with dull eyes.

"I did it," she said calmly. "I killed him. I admit it."

"What have you done to her?" I demanded, surging to my feet again to face Grant. "Why was I not allowed to see her last night? What did you give her, a barbiturate?"

"She was given nothing, doctor."

I whirled back to Imogen. "My darling, listen to me. You don't know what you're saying. You've had another break, like last time, do you remember? After you played Cleopatra? You're not well, my love, but I will take care of you, I promise." I fell to my knees again. "Only don't admit to this terrible thing, you don't know what you're saying."

"But I do," she reached out and caressed my face with her hand. I closed my eyes to savour the sensation of her hand against my cheek. "He betrayed me, and then threw me away. He deserved to die. And so I killed him."

"Imogen," I said, as tears spilled down my cheeks. "I love you so very much."

Her eyes grew wary then, and her beautiful features contorted into a grimace. She lifted her hand and slapped me viciously.

"Get away from me, Julian!" she howled. "You can't be here, I killed you! I killed you! You can't be here, *I killed you!*"

She began to strike me then, shrieking and screaming, arms flailing as I took the blows and tried to calm her. Thorpe and Fraser were there immediately, restraining her.

I sat back on my haunches, helpless, as Grant approached and deftly slid a hypodermic needle into her arm. She crumpled at once, her long black eyelashes fluttering closed.

* * *

Two hours later, *The Erinyes* dropped anchor off the south pier of the sheltered harbour at Penzance. A small craft was lowered from the outer decks, and being that only Grant, Thorpe, Imogen, and myself were going ashore, it was discreet enough not to draw curious eyes away from the behemoth that was the yacht.

Thorpe had agreed, after my impassioned pleas, to allow the police to escort Imogen to St. Lawrence's first, before subjecting her to their interrogations. It was a mercy, and I knew it, and my dislike of the man softened somewhat.

A sleek black car awaited us at the end of the jetty, emerging from the swirling morning mist as the small craft approached. Inspector Thorpe stepped onto the dock as soon as the vessel was secured, and I followed behind, wearily.

Two gentlemen stepped from the car to greet us, the taller of the two shaking Thorpe's hand and introducing himself as Inspector Penrose, sent by the Chief Inspector to assist. Penrose introduced his companion as Constable Evans, and when I was introduced, both men's faces pinched into expressions of sympathy as they avoided my eyes.

Dr. Grant stepped onto the dock then, Imogen beside him. I should have been at her side, would have given anything to be at her side, but it was agreed I should avoid upsetting her delicate mental balance any more than I already had.

"Have you arranged for her to be taken to hospital?" I inquired of Penrose. "The Chief Inspector is a personal friend. He assured me she would be seen by a physician before being interviewed."

"Indeed, sir," Penrose said. "They're expecting us at St. Lawrence's."

"I should like to come with you," I said. "And to the station, when she is able."

"Of course, sir. This way, if you please."

Imogen was helped into the back of the car. As Penrose took a seat beside her, she cast a panicked look at us through the window and splayed her fingers against the glass. My darling girl looked absolutely terrified, and my heart nearly broke.

I took the front passenger seat, and at length, Constable Evans started the engine and pulled away.

The dock grew farther and farther away through the rear window, the figures of Grant and Thorpe fading into indistinct swaths of colour in the gray morning mist. I adjusted the rear view mirror, and met Imogen's gaze.

There was a tight, uncomfortable silence throughout the car, as though we were all holding our breath. And then, as though we'd all exhaled at once, the tension broke.

"Oh, you were *marvellous*, Arthur!" Imogen cried, throwing her head back with a lusty laugh. "Simply marvellous! And *you*, Jerry..." She turned to the man beside her and kissed him. "You never should have left the stage, you convinced even me!"

"My finest performance yet," the erstwhile Penrose said. "For my finest leading lady."

"My Marc Antony," she cooed. "Come darling, kiss your queen."

They embraced, and sank into a violently passionate kiss.

The fellow who had assumed the role of Constable Evans turned to me as he steered the car out of town, towards the motorway that led to Southampton.

"Mind if I ask you something, doctor?"

"Hmm?" I stared at the mirror, unable to take my eyes off my beautiful wife, feeling the pangs I always did when she carried on with one of her lovers.

"Wasn't she your patient? At the Broadmoor asylum?"

"Yes," I said, fondly recalling our first days together, when I was the only one who'd cared for her, the only one who'd understood.

"And you married her?"

"The moment I could. I was sacked, naturally, but after the inquiry I didn't waste a minute making her my bride."

"So..." He gestured to the back seat. "Why'd you go along with this?"

"Everyone thinks she's been taken away by the police, you see." I turned to him, exceedingly proud of her brilliant plan. "No one will alert the real police. We can sail for Argentina tonight and—"

"I understand that bit," he said. "And you've paid us well enough so it's no skin off my nose...but don't you mind them carrying on like that? Her being your wife and all?"

I gazed into the mirror at my beautiful girl, and my heart swelled with love.

"I'd do anything for her," I said, because it was true.

THE SKI LESSON

By Carolyn Eichhorn

"Again!" Becca called, adjusting her grip on the cushioned handle. She willed herself to concentrate on her balance better than the last five times. The engine roared and she tensed her legs against the push of the water. It plumed on either side of the ski until she rose to the surface, tentatively straightening her legs a bit until she was standing, no—hurtling—across the quiet water of the cove. The speed and seeming hardness of the water beneath her wobbly slalom ski fueled a panic that Becca remembered from the previous summer and then she was down hard. She sputtered and righted herself, quickly checking that nothing embarrassing had happened to her bathing suit before her dad got the boat turned around and close enough for cousins to see her yanking at the inevitable wedgie. Her ski had come off and floated several yards away. Wearily, Becca held her hand above her head to let her dad and Uncle Joe know that she was okay before paddling after it.

"You had it, Beck! That was really great!" Her uncle sounded sincerely proud of her so Becca managed a smile, though she felt ridiculous. Her ski vest from the previous summer no longer fit now that she had boobs, so she was wearing her aunt's vest which rode up in the water next to her ears even though it was cinched in as tight as it would go.

"What do you say, honey? Wanna go again or are you getting tired?" Becca's dad asked.

"I think I've got one more," Becca said. She had nearly gotten up and stayed on a single slalom ski that time and she didn't want to lose her momentum, though her arms ached and her legs shook.

"Good girl!"

Her dad circled the boat around behind her slowly so the tow rope would come to Becca in the water. She watched it get closer as she tucked her right foot into the rear binding of the ski. The braided rope slid across her fingers until the handle was close enough to grasp. Becca let the boat pull her through the water slowly, making sure to keep the tip of the ski centered and just out of the water. Exhaust from the boat engine mixed with the smell of the lake and the wet rubber of the ski vest. It felt familiar and not unpleasant. She took a deep breath before shouting "Okay!" to the boat.

The power and sound of the engine always surprised her, but she bit down her fear and pushed herself up and out of the water. Once again, she skimmed across the surface. Cheers erupted from the boat, but she was too far out in the cove for her mother to see from the pier. Uncle Joe's lake house was two thirds of the way up one of the many small coves on Lake Gaston. Vacation rentals and weekend houses clustered these idyllic offshoots from the busy main lake. It was early in the season and a Wednesday, so Becca was the only skier on the cove that morning, though the main lake was always crowded with fisherman, jet skis, and even some stand up paddleboarders. The problem was that the boat had to go somewhere so Becca was soon out of the quiet cove though her dad stayed relatively close to the shore.

Becca was feeling her feet start to cramp when she realized that her dad had started a wide turn which meant that she was going to cross her own wake. She'd not yet survived this hurdle on one ski, unable to maintain her balance in the chop. She adjusted her grip and held tight against the centrifugal force. Her cousins would have let the momentum swing them wide so they could lean in and send up a spray of water but they'd been skiing almost since birth. Becca had gotten up on two skis for the first time the previous summer when she was fourteen. A late bloomer.

The churning water directly behind the boat felt hard beneath her ski, like a rocky path centered between flanking wakes. Outside these barriers, the water was glassy. To get there, Becca had to cross out and over the boat wake. She had only moments before her dad completed the loop and they crossed the waves they'd made coming out of the cove. Becca decided if she was going to wipe out, she'd rather do it in the softer water so she pulled to the right and hoped for the best. With a few scary wobbles, she slid over the water ridge and hung to the right rear of the boat, between the shore and the boat wake. The water felt much softer here, though she sank a bit lower. The waves came but Becca handled them easily, letting out a whoop of relief. Her dad steered back into the cove and Becca stayed on the inside of the turn so she slowed a little too much, struggling to stay on the surface. She was still hugging the shoreline though she stayed at least a dozen yards out from the piers and boathouses so she wouldn't collide with any swimmers in their vicinity.

Becca's legs shook and her hands could barely maintain their grip on the tow handle, but she was determined to ski close enough to Uncle Joe's pier for her mom to get a good picture before she tossed down the rope and sank gracefully like her cousins did. She'd get that up on Instagram before settling on her beach towel for some sunbathing. Melissa back home was going to absolutely die with jealousy! Too late, Becca saw the bundle of cloth just before she hit it and flew forward, the tip of her ski catching her just below her right eye. Only when she'd face-planted in the water did she remember to release the tow rope. The impact knocked the air from her lungs but the vest righted her in the water immediately. Becca leaned back, struggling for her breath and gently tested her limbs for injury. Her face had taken the worst of it as far as she could tell from the throbbing cheek. She touched the skin with her fingers before raising her hand to let the boat know she was okay as she'd done a dozen times before. This time, her dad wasn't encouraging her from above when she squinted in the bright sun. Becca's dad had stopped the boat before completing the loop that would bring the tow rope to her. It idled about twenty yards away, its occupants engaged with something on the far side. They weren't even looking at Becca. As if they had forgotten she was there.

Annoyed, she looked for her ski and found it floating a few yards to her left. Becca paddled over, grabbed the ski, and pushed it ahead as she kicked her way toward the swim platform on the back of the boat. The lake water was always a bit cloudy, preventing Becca from seeing her own feet which made her a little anxious, especially out in the main lake. The surface of the water was warmer than the unseen depths where her toes dangled. Becca forced her arms to push her a little faster toward the boat. Still, no one looked over at her for more than a second or two. Becca let the ski bump the side of boat, but still they ignored her. With a dramatic sigh, Becca hoisted herself on the platform before pulling the long slalom ski from the water. The ski was heavy and she struggled with the awkward weight of it, trying not to bang it against her uncle's boat or herself. Eventually, Becca placed the ski in the back of the boat before climbing over the stern and dropping into the sun-warmed vinyl seat. Still she shivered.

"Don't mind me," she started when she saw that her dad was on his cell phone and her uncle had his arms around her younger cousin's shoulders. Something wasn't right. She pushed herself up onto her exhausted legs, steadying herself in the rolling boat. When she got to the bow, she saw the bundle of cloth that had caused her fall. Only the bundle of cloth was a set of clothes and those clothes had a person in them and that person was dead.

* * *

Spring had been a trying time for Harold, though he still found solace in the early morning routine around the house he'd shared with Louise these last 27 years. He still managed the basic upkeep of his boathouse and pier, though lately the maintenance of the house had required the services of a local handyman who would drive over from Littleton every other week to tackle gutter cleanouts and dripping faucets. Louise still took care of the yard, or she had anyway, before the incident. Harold gripped his coffee mug with the familiar rising anger, but the gentle breeze from the water soothed him as it always had. Mornings were his quiet time, his personal relationship with the lake. He knew it better than most after all these years. He and Louise had purchased their lot early on, before the crush of out-of-state money and opportunistic developers crowded the shoreline

355

with enormous vacation houses with wide wrapping porches and multi-leveled boathouses. Smaller homes like his were getting squeezed between structures that looked like resorts, or worse—the original houses were torn down altogether and replaced with seven-bedroom monsters that lived on vacation rental websites. Strangers flocked in with their noisy, ill-behaved children, their drunken parties, and lack of respect for the lake and its real residents, the year-round caretakers.

Harold sipped his now lukewarm coffee as he swung the hose nozzle back and forth until his pier was rinsed clean of bird poo. The herons had been by before dawn, but at least it wasn't otters. Harold accepted the chore as part of life on the lake. There was a stillness before 7, even during peak season, that Harold needed more than he needed coffee. A far-away boat engine could be heard from the main lake, but no traffic was visible yet from the cove. The occasional fisherman silently glided past, casting lines across the glassy surface into the pockets near the shore between piers. Their trolling motors nudged them gently past the NO WAKE signs and boats on their lifts. Harold could still hear the call of the herons and the occasional splash as turtles eyed him briefly before submerging again to the cloudy depths.

Harold coiled his hose neatly and gave a wave to his neighbor across the cove. It was Wednesday, so Jim had arrived to mow and trim the immaculate yard he no longer enjoyed every day. He'd moved into town the previous spring to be closer to his ailing father and now rented his home to a different group of noisy strangers every week. Against Harold's advice, Jim had even left the ski boat for the use of his guests, though it was obvious that few understood the rules of the lake or even in some cases, how to operate a motorboat properly. One day, one of those idiots would run into a paddleboarder or a kayaker and then Jim would get it.

Harold inspected the boat hook affixed to the support column for his boathouse roof. One of the rubber tips was now missing. He cursed under his breath, feeling the anger rise again. It would be useless until he replaced the tip that protected against marring the fiberglass surface of any craft. Quickly, he scanned the pier, but it was as tidy as ever and still glistening with the rinse he'd completed. Harold scanned the lake for activity, but saw none aside from Jim who now navigated his yard in large loops on his fancy riding mower, his head protected by a hat, wrap-around sunglasses, and a pair of enormous ear muffs. The mower was fast, but Jim knew every rock and tree and could expertly maneuver through his yard and the common areas around the access road in about an hour. He'd offered to cut Harold's yard a few times, but Louise wouldn't have it. Even after 45 years of marriage, Louise still didn't even trust Harold to trim without damaging her plants and flowers. She trimmed and weeded by hand, almost every day. Even now, she was bent over a bed of Hostas on the other side of the house. Harold winced at the trampled Black-eyed Susans that had previously brightened up the lot line, nearly down to the water. He hadn't noticed them in the dark and Louise showed no sign that she had seen them either. Lately, when she got upset, Harold struggled to calm her. She hardly slept these days, restlessly moving about the house at all hours. Sometimes she would get startled when Harold called her back to bed as if she'd forgotten why she was up. Lately, she'd been waking even before he did, sometimes making her way down to the water. Harold raked the river stones along the steps leading from the house so slipper-soled feet wouldn't bruise or trip. Even so, he worried, wondering how long the two of them could safely stay in their home.

* * *

Becca held the towel tightly around her shoulders and watched her dad and Uncle Joe talk with the sheriff. They were back on Uncle Joe's pier finally. It had taken the police almost 40 minutes to find them out on the lake after Uncle Joe called about the— Becca didn't know what to call it. The body? The man they'd found drifting like any other debris washed down after the afternoon rains? The police had placed it in a metal basket of sorts to lift him from the water and then into a zippered black bag. Becca's dad told her not to look, but she couldn't help herself. The man's shirt and swim shorts were ripped or cut in places and skin showed beneath which was also torn. He wore one shoe and his bare foot had something wrapping his ankle. He wasn't bloody or anything as far she could tell, but she still shivered, feeling both sorry for the man and grateful that she hadn't touched him when she'd fallen. They also collected any floating debris nearby, even some twigs and a bit of plastic, dutifully cataloging and photographing as they went. It took forever.

Her mother had been hysterical and had tried to shuffle Becca back into the house as soon as the boat returned to the pier, but the Sheriff had questions for all of them. Dad and Uncle Joe promised to keep an eye on her. Becca's cousins went inside, though. They were pale with shock and fear, even Joe Jr., but Becca thought some of it was due to her mother's visible distress. Becca tried to remain calm and listen as the officers carefully wrapped the ski and then combed over Uncle Joe's boat from front to back. *Bow to stern*, Becca thought. They snapped photos of the hull and the prop and several police boats moved slowly through the cove and the main lake near where they'd found him. A whoop came from the far end of the cove, where the water was choked with grasses and the sheriff talked into a radio while looking that direction for a moment before returning his attention to Uncle Joe. It was too shallow there for boats, so no houses stood on those lots, only trees. Uncle Joe Jr. had tried to tell her that the collection of sticks and logs was a beaver dam, but Becca could tell by Uncle Joe's smile that her cousin made it up. Joe Jr. was always making up stories about a lake monster named Gassie, whole towns underwater upriver where they'd dammed the reservoir, and even ghosts moving about at night on the far side of the cove next to the party house. He was a year younger than Becca, but a prankster like his dad, so everything he said was suspect. Except about skiing. Joe Jr. and even nine-year-old Nathan were great at watersports, though the boys preferred wakeboarding to skiing. Still, they encouraged Becca, giving her the confidence to keep trying, though when midmorning hit, the cove was already too crowded for her to focus. People from the big house across the cove would be out around 11, tanning on towels or floating loungers.

The people in the party house were *loud*. They stayed up real late every night laughing and talking on the deck above the boathouse. Uncle Joe said that visitors often didn't understand how sound travels easily across the water, even for long distances. She'd heard them last night singing and arguing and splashing around as late as three a.m. Becca's mom and dad had muttered about it at breakfast and Uncle Joe had laughed and said this was nothing compared to the upcoming holiday weekend chaos. Busy times meant extra power boats, kayaks, floaties, and jet skis, and quite often, drinking operators of all of the above. And sometimes, there were accidents.

The sheriff's boat at the end of the cove moved slowly toward Uncle Joe's pier with a large inflatable lounge and a stand-up paddleboard that looked like Uncle Joe's, except it was red instead of blue and white. The officer gestured to the back end of the board and Becca could see the tether was broken. Just as Becca was about to ask her dad why the police were excited by this, her mother called her inside and away from the investigation.

* * *

Louise was dicing sweet pickles for tuna salad when Harold returned from the hardware store in Warrenton. She scraped the pickles and some chopped celery into the bowl with the edge of the knife across the cutting board, which set Harold's teeth on edge. He turned away and pulled a cold beer from the fridge. Louise would disapprove of his drinking so early in the day, but Harold had earned it. He sank into a chair on the deck and gazed out to the lake as he drained the bottle. The tension that had gripped his chest and shoulders started to recede slightly, so he went for another, pausing to scoop up the sandwich Louise had made for him without meeting her eyes. He ate in silence, his eyes on the police boats as they made their exit to the main lake and back to wherever they'd come in from, maybe Eaton's Ferry. When he returned his plate to the sink, Harold confirmed that his wife had settled in the living room with her television shows before grabbing a third beer from the fridge and the small bag from the hardware store. He took them both down to the boathouse.

The police were gone. Some kids were outside a few houses down, but not in or near the water. One figure stood on the pier next door surveying the debris from the night before. Bottles lined the upper railing alongside red plastic cups and at least one bikini top. They'd been at it for hours again last night, completely oblivious to everyone else. The drunk girls on the giant float didn't bother to tie it when they went back to the house and it blew off the pier and became wedged under Harold's pier during the night. Even now, the wet squeaking sound echoed in Harold's ears. He set his beer down and got to work replacing the tip on the boat hook.

* * *

"There are no such things as ghosts," Becca told Joe Jr.

"Is so," he said which wasn't very scientific. Becca required more detail. She'd seen *Ghost Hunters* on TV.

"Tell me exactly what you saw," she said.

Later, Becca brought her uncle's binoculars out to the deck while her dad got the grill started. She scanned the houses across the cove. The party house was unusually quiet, though she could see a couple in the rope hammock. They appeared to be sleeping, not making out like Joe Jr. had insisted. A guy was picking up trash and filling a black plastic bag and another dragged a suitcase to a car parked beside the house. Two more sat up at the house on the back deck while a third seemed to be looking at something out toward the main lake. To the left, the old guy was fiddling with a long metal pole on his dock and then hosing everything down again. He'd been hosing the deck down when they went out in the boat that morning, too.

Nothing else was happening. No ghosts, no Gassie, nothing. Gentle waves lapped at the shore, no doubt from passing boats out on the main lake. The presence of the police must have dampened the spirit in the cove. She placed the binoculars on the patio table and stood next to her dad.

"How are you, honey?" he asked.

"Fine," Becca said quietly as her dad put a reassuring hand on her shoulder. "That man," Becca started, "from before. What happened to him?"

"An accident probably," her dad replied. "The Sheriff thinks he fell off his paddleboard and maybe drowned before getting hit by a boat overnight."

"Those long cuts?"

"Yeah, honey. That could be a boat prop."

Becca thought about that. Not a lake monster, just a boat. It seemed possible; after all, she'd hit him with her ski. She'd been afraid that those wounds had been her fault, that she'd sliced him with the metal fin on the underside of the slalom ski that helped to stabilize her in the water. Back home in Maryland, her dad worked for a law firm, so Becca knew that he'd tell her the truth. A sort of parent-daughter privilege. He wasn't a lawyer, though. More of a lawyer's helper. He helped them find out the truth before trials and stuff.

"Dad?"

"Yes, honey?"

"Maybe Xbox would be better tomorrow."

* * *

She was up again. Harold quickly found his shoes and searched the house. As he passed through the kitchen, he glimpsed her white nightdress in the backyard close to the riprap along the water's edge. She nearly glowed in the moonlight, tall and flowing, her white hair loose and moving in the breeze. He hurried down the steps, his heart beating at an unsafe rate. He resisted the impulse to call out to her. She held something in her right hand, but it was obscured in the folds of her nightdress which seemed to glow in the moonlight. She was cutting the weeds along the rocks which protected the shore from boat wakes. The machete swung in wide arcs from side to side, just as it had when he'd found her out there the night before. Harold's stomach lurched at the sound the blade had made in the dark, slicing through the damp grass into the wet sandy clay. And then striking bone.

Louise had not remembered it in the morning. Not the man stumbling into their yard through her flowerbed or Harold hustling her back inside and changing her out of the blood-soaked nightgown, nothing. She'd wept at the trampled plants where the man had stomped through while chasing the stupid runaway float. Harold had gotten her back into bed with a sleeping pill and then returned to the dark yard. Ironically, the man had died quietly after the endless racket all week. His face had been in the water and he hadn't moved. He wore swim shorts and a tee shirt which gave Harold the idea. He'd crept over to the silent house next door in the darkness and pushed the paddleboard off the edge of their pier. He walked it carefully through the shallows to where the man sprawled near the rocks and tugged the body through the water to rest partially on the board. He'd fastened the tether to the man's ankle. The man was heavy and the board kept getting caught on the bottom, so Harold used the boat hook. He pulled at the tether from the pier until it was free of the shore but the line broke and the board bumped at the dock pilings and drifted under it joining the escaped water float the man had been trying to retrieve from under Harold's pier. Panicked, Harold had pushed at the body frantically with the end of the boat hook until the board floated out into the cove. He tugged the float free as well, giving it a push to the open water. He then rinsed the machete and the boat hook before returning to the house. For good measure, he'd also turned on Louise's irrigation system. Nothing left to do but pray.

* * *

Becca couldn't believe her eyes. Right where Joe Jr. said. There was a pale figure among the trees. And then it was gone. Becca's stomach flipped with fear and excitement. She peered through the binoculars again and saw the figure close to the house over there. The ghost seemed to carry something in one hand, swinging it back and forth. Becca strained to see, fiddling with the focus and holding her breath. The moon was out, but it was hard to see among the pines and plants. When it got dark here at the lake it was *dark dark*. Like that time she visited Luray Caverns with her parents and the guide turned off the light for a moment. Becca struggled to stay calm. In a moment, the figure reappeared, standing briefly in the clearing where

Becca could see the swinging object glint in the moonlight. It was a long, shining knife. Becca dropped the binoculars and went to wake her dad.

* * *

When the police came in the morning, Harold was almost relieved. Exhausted, he sat on a patio chair, his shoulders slumped and his head down. He'd not slept in a long time, not really. Louise was confused and then indignant, eventually shrieking at top volume as they escorted her to a waiting car. The sound tore at his soul. He'd failed her. For a moment, his anger was back at the unfairness of it all, the stupid renters, the decline he'd mourned as they grew older, and just the impossibility of everything that had once been so simple and right. Harold watched as the police inspected the waterfront and the pier, even the crumpled flowerbed. When he heard one officer call out that he'd found blood on the rocks by the shore, he closed his eyes. When the deputies unlatched the gardening shed door, he knew it was all over. He hoped it would be quieter wherever they were taking him. He needed some quiet.

* * *

"Are you sure, honey?" Becca's dad asked.

"Yeah. Let's go again. Hit it!" Becca gripped the towrope against the pull of the boat and rose confidently to glide across the lake's surface. Xbox seemed lame compared to catching a murderer, so Becca went for the lean in her turns, earning that plume spray and the photo to prove it.

DEATH IN THE ROSE GARDEN

By Susan Thibadeau

Caroline Kent put the newspaper down and sipped her tea. The article she'd just read wouldn't have been such a surprise if Ginny were still alive. Even though Caroline had been halfway around the world, Ginny would have called and told her Thomas Finchley had been murdered. But that was wrong. Ginny would have been with her. Therefore no one would have told her about the murder.

A knock interrupted Caroline's reverie.

"Auntie, are you decent?" Caroline's nephew, Alex, poked his head around the door. When he saw her at the table, he smiled and stepped into the kitchen carrying a box of produce—lettuce and tomatoes and other things. "Welcome home. I picked this up at the farm stand. Knew you wouldn't have had time to get there yet."

Caroline took the box to the counter and started unpacking. "You are such a dear."

Alex helped himself to a cup of coffee and carried it to the table, where he pointed to the article Caroline had been reading. "That case has been a can of worms for the investigators." "Oh, is Vicki working on it?" Caroline's nephew was married to a Pennsylvania state trooper.

"Part of the team. Yes." He pointed at Thomas Finchley's photo in the paper. "I don't suppose you knew him?"

Posed at a desk, a sparsely filled bookshelf behind him, the man in the photo looked smug and self-important. Well-coiffed gray hair and an obvious salon tan told the story of a man who had spent his life catering to only himself. "Why do you ask, dear?"

"Everybody knows everybody in this town," Alex said.

"Yes, that's true." Caroline smiled at her nephew. "And, yes, I did know him. A long time ago. We were in high school together. We even went out on a few dates." She noted Alex's contained excitement at her disclosure.

"What was he like?" he asked.

Caroline considered the question. Back then, Thomas Finchley was part of the popular crowd. Rich and good-looking, he was on all the varsity sports teams. Football in the fall. Baseball in the spring. The star of both teams, Thomas had no shortage of girls to date. It was a surprise, then, when he asked her to the homecoming dance in their junior year. It was a surprise, also, that he was a perfect gentleman on that date. Caroline had heard rumors about the popular kids' drinking and drug use, but that night Thomas had been almost shy in his courtliness. That's what made it so much more disappointing when, a week later, he brought a bottle of scotch along on their second date. Caroline ended up driving him home and walking the three miles back to her house. He apologized, and she gave him another chance. A mistake, though, for she'd had to walk home once again.

"He was a troubled young man," Caroline offered. There was no point dredging up the past now that he was dead. Near the end of junior year, he and his friends, the popular kids, celebrated their baseball team's playoff victory with a few bottles of scotch at his family's country retreat. He'd been too drunk to drive, but he'd done it anyway. After the inevitable accident, Caroline heard whispers a man had died, leaving behind a young wife and a daughter named Daisy.

Caroline was surprised she still remembered the girl's name. Maybe it was because of the book she'd had to read for English class at the end of that school year. *Daisy Miller*. It was sad how Daisy Miller's money couldn't protect her from her tragic fate. Thomas Finchley's wealthy parents had been able to shield him, though. Soon after the accident, Thomas's parents took him to a private school somewhere in New England, far away from rumors and repercussions. He'd remained in that region for the bulk of his life. She hadn't seen him again until two years ago, soon after he'd moved back to western Pennsylvania when he'd given the welcoming speech for a local arts festival. He'd walked right past her that day, and Caroline remembered thinking that was alright. She didn't need to relive every little thing in her past.

And, besides, it was then, that summer, that Ginny had started to feel so very tired. Caroline pushed vitamins and herbs on her dear friend. Nothing worked. And, finally, they found out why.

"Auntie, did you like him?"

"I suppose," Caroline answered. "But, as I said, he was a troubled young man." She changed the subject. "The article said he was at the family's country retreat when he was killed."

"Vicki said it's more like a castle."

"Is that so? I didn't know it was quite so grand." Caroline said. "I believe it's been in the family for several generations,"

"Finchley's fiancé, Elena, will be very well off. Just the country house alone should set her up for life."

Caroline thought the name "Elena" was lovely, evoking memories of her recent Mediterranean travels. She wondered where Thomas would have chosen to honeymoon. How terrible for Elena to lose him before their wedding. "She inherits even though she wasn't married to Thomas yet? What about the rest of the family?" Caroline knew Thomas hadn't had any children, but she remembered he had a much older brother. And maybe a sister as well.

"Finchley had just changed his will, giving Elena everything and cutting out his only living relative, a nephew. She'll be wealthy, and that's a very strong motive for murder."

Caroline sat down at the table. "The article said Thomas had been found in the rose garden. It said he'd been hit with a blunt object early that morning. It's unusual that so much information would have been released."

"Not really. They didn't describe just how vicious the attack had been. Apparently, it was a gory sight. Anyway, I think they're hoping to arrest Elena very soon."

Caroline wondered why the investigators were so focused on Thomas's fiancé. "Was anyone else—"

A knock interrupted Caroline's question. Alex opened the kitchen door.

"Aunt Caroline, welcome home," Vicki said, swooping in with a bouquet of flowers. She kissed her husband on the cheek as she walked past him to pull a vase out from underneath the sink. "I just wanted to stop and welcome you home on my way to work." She placed the filled vase on the kitchen table. "I loved all the photos of your trip you posted online."

"Thank you, dear." Caroline motioned for Vicki to sit. Those photos had been of the places Ginny had especially wanted to see, places they'd planned to visit one day, places Ginny made her promise to see for her. The Blue Mosque. The Bosporus strait. Ephesus. And then onward to Athens. And, finally, to Rome.

"Auntie, you were asking a question," Alex said.

Caroline regathered her thoughts. "Yes, dear." She turned to Vicki. "Alex said you're working on Thomas Finchley's murder. Was anyone else at the estate, besides Thomas and his fiancé, when he was killed?"

"Yes. His administrative assistant, his housekeeper...and his nephew, John."

Caroline noted Vicki's slight hesitation. "Is there something about the nephew?"

"Not really...only that he would have inherited if not for the change in the will."

"You don't think he could kill someone, though, do you, Vic?" Alex asked his wife.

Vicki agreed, then added, "And, anyway, he was out golfing with a friend. He left before dawn to make it to their early tee time."

"But he has a strong motive," Alex challenged. "Maybe he didn't know about the change in the will, and he expected to inherit."

"He says he knew Finchley had changed his will," Vicki argued.

"Then maybe he was so angry that, in a fit of passion, he killed his uncle," Alex said. "I think he's the more logical choice for the killer, given how brutal the attack was."

Caroline had been following the verbal sparring of the young married couple. They were so perfectly suited for one another, their love so obvious. As always, Caroline felt buoyed by that love, freed to wonder and question. "Has the time of death been established?" she asked.

"Sometime that morning," Vicki said. "Of course, they don't have the exact time, but—"

"You see," Alex interrupted, "the nephew could have done it before he left for the golf course!"

"Elena, Finchley's fiancé, claims Thomas brought her coffee in bed at about eight-thirty that morning," Vicki said. "And if she's telling the truth, then it can't have been the nephew who killed him."

"Might the administrative assistant have seen Thomas that morning, too?" Caroline asked. "Surely, Thomas wouldn't have had the assistant staying at the house if he wasn't expecting to do work every day."

"No, Aunt Caroline." Vicki took one of the muffins Caroline offered. "She says she didn't see him at all."

"From what I've heard," Alex added, "the poor woman was probably grateful to be left alone."

"But why, dear?"

"Auntie, I thought I'd do a little snooping, you know, just because I was curious about Finchley's investment firm," Alex explained. "Turns out, he was a hard man to work for. And he was especially hard on Marilyn Jennings—that's the assistant."

Caroline suppressed a smile. Marilyn was such a delicious name. Scenes from old-time movies she and Ginny both loved flashed across her mind's eye. Marilyn Monroe aboard ship in *Gentlemen Prefer Blondes*. And on a train in *Some Like it Hot*. Monroe's characters almost always managed to overcome obstacles and achieve their goals. Perhaps Marilyn Jennings had sought to do the same, in her own way. "How, exactly, was it hard on her, Alex?"

"A friend who worked at Finchley's firm said he demanded long hours. And that wasn't all. Apparently, he thought nothing of interrupting his assistant's days off by calling her into the office for trivial tasks. And my friend heard Finchley yell at her lots of times, for things that weren't her fault. He sounded like a nightmare boss. I wouldn't blame her if she did kill him," Alex answered.

"But, honestly, Aunt Caroline, I just don't see her for it," Vicki said.

Alex nodded. "Then again, if a person is pushed too far, they might do things they wouldn't normally imagine doing."

That was true. Until Ginny's all-consuming pain, Caroline would never have imagined screaming at nurses to give her friend the shot they were late with. The memory of Ginny's agony haunted her dreams still. She would have killed to get that pain medication if she could have.

"But as motives go, Marilyn Jennings' motive is still pretty weak," Vicki persisted. "After all, she's probably out of a job now."

"You say she didn't see Thomas that morning," Caroline said. "Where was she? What was she doing?"

"She was in the study from eight in the morning on. There's a coffee machine in the study and a powder room off of it. She said she brewed a pot of coffee, then hunkered down at her desk and never left."

"And Thomas never went into the study? How odd," Caroline said. "What about the housekeeper? Did the housekeeper see Thomas that morning?"

"She was in the kitchen the whole morning, wasn't she, Vic?" Alex finished the last muffin.

Vicki agreed. "And Finchley didn't go into the kitchen at all, according to the housekeeper."

"This all seems so odd," Caroline reiterated. "How did Thomas bring his fiancé coffee if he hadn't been to the study or to the kitchen?"

"Precisely! The fiancé is lying. He didn't bring her coffee." Vicki started to get up from the table.

"Which means the nephew could have killed Finchley before he left for the golf course," Alex said triumphantly.

Vicki frowned at her husband. "But then, why would Elena lie about having coffee brought to her in bed?"

"I don't know. Maybe they're in it together."

Caroline smiled at Alex's persistence, one of his many wonderful qualities.

He and Vicki had been such steady support throughout Ginny's illness, especially after Ginny moved into Caroline's house. Alex and Vicki were both there for her, tending to the housework so she could tend to her friend. "Who is this housekeeper?" Caroline asked.

Vicki sank back into her seat. "Peggy West. She's worked there for almost a year. She's a local woman. Twice divorced. Lived in the area her whole life. Very active in her church."

Caroline had always loved the name Peggy. It reminded her of a time when the jazz singer Peggy Lee ruled the charts and optimism flourished. At least for some.

"Auntie, you look miles away," Alex said.

"Not at all, dear. I wonder, what if Thomas's fiancé isn't lying?"

"It all comes down to motive and opportunity," Vicki said. "Elena had the strongest motive and, like everyone else, she had opportunity."

"And you don't believe she loved Thomas?" Caroline asked.

"Elena was much younger than Finchley," Vicki held up her hands, "and before you say that's not proof of anything, both the assistant and the housekeeper independently said they suspected Elena was cheating on him."

"With the nephew, I bet," Alex said. "No one has found any proof, though."

Vicki frowned. "But their suspicions seem more plausible given Elena's response to Finchley's death. She says she's grief-stricken, but would a grief-stricken woman go out and purchase a whole new wardrobe and book a trip to Cabo?"

Caroline supposed there were an infinite number of ways to grieve. Elena's shopping might not have been any different than Caroline's incessant novel-reading in those days after Ginny died. It might have been a way to anesthetize. It might have been the only way to keep going on, even when you felt you couldn't.

"You said that the bludgeoning was brutal," Caroline said to Alex. "What did the killer use?"

Vicki answered for her husband. "Thomas Finchley's old baseball bat. We know because his high school teammates had all signed it."

"Did he keep it in the house?"

"In his game room," Vicki said, leaning forward. "Someone had to go into the game room and take the bat out to the rose garden, where they killed Finchley. We found it next to the body."

Caroline visualized the rose garden. There would be red roses or, perhaps, white. She couldn't imagine Thomas Finchley with pink roses, but red and white, that Thomas would approve. Perhaps he'd been hovering at a flower, drinking in its scent. And someone crept up behind him, and then there would be blood. So much blood. Such a different death from dear Ginny's. But just as awfully final.

"Auntie, are you cold? Do you need me to fetch a sweater?"

"No, dear." Caroline patted Alex's hand. "Did Thomas usually spend time in the rose garden?"

"Only once in a while, to snip a rose or two for Elena," Vicki said. "But his wife spent a lot of time there. And we think she lured him into the heart of the garden, which is sheltered from view, and she killed him there."

Caroline thought "heart of the garden" was a nice phrase. A garden was, after all, a living thing and the idea of it having a heart tickled her. She was sure Ginny would have been as delighted as she was with the idea. She didn't think it would have amused Thomas Finchley at all.

"Was anything else found near Thomas besides the bat?" Caroline asked.

"Just a rose clipper," Vicki answered. "Near his right hand."

It was hard to believe the homecoming dance was almost forty-four years ago. Yes, Thomas was right-handed. Caroline was sure of it. She remembered how his right hand shook, pinning on the corsage he'd brought her. Little red roses and baby's breath and a silver bow. She'd looked into his eyes when he was done and thanked him. She'd told him that it was her first corsage ever. And he'd nodded then, gravely. A sweet young man. When he wasn't drinking.

"Elena lured him out to the garden by asking him to help cut some roses, and then, while he was busy, she pulled out the bat and clubbed him to death," Alex said. A moment later, he frowned. "Or maybe his nephew talked him into clipping a few roses, and then he snuck up on him." Alex's frown deepened. "Or they were in on it together, like I said. In any case, one or both of them expected to inherit a lot of money."

"If you think, my dears, that the motive for murder was money," Caroline said, "then, I agree, that would lead you to think of the fiancé. And, possibly, the nephew."

Vicki agreed, adding, "Money is the root of all evil, after all."

There were people who did, indeed, value money above all else. Caroline remembered how old Mrs. Franklin, who lived the next block over, almost cheated her house cleaner out of her pay. And how cruel Martin McNulty, her cousin's ex, sued her cousin for her property and almost won with forged documents. Their crimes were perpetrated coldly. Dispassionately. Wouldn't killing someone for money be done with equal precision and without passion?

"There seems to be an overwhelming rage involved in poor Thomas's murder," Caroline said. "Did either the fiancé or the nephew seem capable of that?"

"No," Vicki said. "And that's been troubling me."

"Finchley's fiancé had a strong motive though, Vic," Alex insisted, picking up the book on Caroline's table, *Endless Night*, and holding it up. "Just like in this book. The murderer meticulously planned meeting and marrying his wife and then killing her for her money."

"Dear, the murder in that book didn't involve a brutal attack. It was, as you said, very coldly planned out. The pursuit of money and what money could buy drove the murderer. And the act of murder didn't entail rage," Caroline said.

"Then, maybe it's the administrative assistant who did it." Alex put the book down. "Or maybe the housekeeper." He grinned. "Maybe Finchley criticized her cooking one too many times, and it drove her into a homicidal rage."

Vicki shook her head at her husband. "The baseball bat. The baseball bat wasn't just lying around in the rose garden. Someone went into the game room and took it out to the rose garden. That does indicate some kind of planning, doesn't it, Aunt Caroline?"

"Yes, Vicki."

"And that would mean someone had planned the murder out."

"Yes," Caroline agreed. "But remember, along with the planning, the murderer's rage was so strong that they bludgeoned poor Thomas mercilessly."

Vicki looked at her watch and stood. "I'd better be getting along."

Caroline sensed Vicki's disappointment. There had been times, in the past, when Caroline had been able to offer insight into a case Vicki was working on. Caroline took some pride in that. Ginny had toasted her friend after each of the cases was solved and the murderer arrested. They'd shared a strong sense of justice, a need for order. But any sense of order had been obliterated for Caroline when her dear friend died. Caroline had been taken aback by the anger she felt even as she was perplexed because it had no target. Still, in the early morning hours, she wished there was someone she could blame. Someone she could punish for her loss.

"You know," Caroline said as she walked Vicki to the door, "Thomas was in an auto accident when he was a teenager. The whole thing was hushed up, and Thomas was sent away."

"Yes, Aunt Caroline," Vicki said.

Caroline put her hand on Vicki's arm. "Tell me, about how old are the assistant and the housekeeper?"

When Vicki told her, Caroline said, "I do believe you need to look into the housekeeper's background further, my darling. I can't be sure, but yes, it all seems to point to the housekeeper."

* * *

Two days later, Caroline joined Vicki and Alex for an early dinner at their favorite restaurant. She'd managed to catch up on sleep. A double-edged sword, exhaustion's dissipation making room for anger and grief to flourish.

"You look more rested, Auntie," Alex said.

Caroline smiled at the young couple's contained excitement. "What is it, my darlings?" For a moment, Caroline hoped a baby was on the way.

"How did you know, Aunt Caroline?" Vicki asked.

Caroline searched Alex and Vicki's faces. "Know what?"

"How did you know the housekeeper did it and not the fiancé?" Alex asked.

"Oh, Thomas's murder." Caroline's smile faded. "Oh, yes. The first thing was the motive, you see. What would be a motive for such a brutal killing? What had Thomas done, and to whom, that would warrant such retribution? Thomas had killed a man. And that man's daughter would have been the housekeeper's age."

"That's all?" Alex asked.

Caroline's smile returned. That wasn't all, of course. "Well, it was the baseball bat, too. Thomas had gotten drunk and caused the accident while celebrating his baseball team's victory. Killing him with his own baseball bat—and I'll bet the murder took place on the very same date as the accident so many years before—would have seemed like poetic justice to the dead man's daughter."

"Still seems a leap, Auntie."

"Yes, dear," Caroline agreed. "But then, what cements it all is the name was the same."

"The name, Auntie?"

"Yes, the little girl who lost her father in Thomas's accident was called Daisy. At least that's what I remembered."

Alex sighed. "Auntie, the housekeeper's name is Peggy, not Daisy."

"Yes, dear. But both of those names are nicknames for Margaret."

"I get Peggy—the whole Margaret, Meg, Peg thing—but how is Daisy a nickname for Margaret?" Alex asked.

"Marguerite is the French name for Margaret. It's also the French word for daisy, dear," Caroline said.

Vicki frowned. "We'd never done anything more than a cursory check on the housekeeper. She might have gotten away with it if not for you, Aunt Caroline."

"But now you have her," Alex comforted his wife. "I just don't see how she could have held on to so much anger for all these years, Auntie."

Caroline agreed with her nephew.

But that night, after Caroline had returned home, she thought perhaps they'd both been wrong. It was only anger that kept Caroline from drowning in grief. But it was a diffuse anger—at fate, at cancer, at everything all at once—and Caroline sensed there was danger, it would slowly fade. If she had the option, perhaps she too would choose to cling to a more focused anger, one that could rage across the decades, keeping grief at bay forever.

THE PROBLEM OF THE PRICKED BALLOON

By Tom Mead

Hester Queeg was slicing sandwiches for the picnic when the first balloon went by. She was in her kitchen in the San Franciscan suburb of Walnut Creek, looking out on the busy street, when an immense ovoid shadow fell across the family station wagon.

With the last chicken and mayo concoction stowed in her little boy's Buck Rogers lunchbox, Hester headed for the back door. 'Okay, picnic's ready! Let's get going.' And the kids cheered and charged through the house and out to the car.

As they drove down to the cove, where Finneran's Bluff had been taken over by hot dog vendors, a Ferris wheel, and all the trappings of the 1961 summer fair, a silent and ghostly pair of hot-air balloons loomed above them. Believe it or not, it was an old-fashioned balloon race, like something out of Jules Verne.

Before we get into what happened, I need to tell you a thing or two about these balloonists. To call them competitive is to demean the notion of competition. These men were stone-cold predators. The first, Carter Wentworth, had got the ballooning bug from his grandfather, the paper mill tycoon. For Carter, the open sky evoked a sense of freedom he just couldn't find in the boardroom. He lived for it. If he could, he would have funnelled every cent of his immeasurable family legacy into it. He was dressed like some kind of WWI flying ace, complete with jodhpurs, goggles, and pilot's cap. At first sight of him, you would not know whether to laugh or surrender.

And hot on Carter's heels was his bête noire, his greatest foe, who also happened to be his closest friend. This was Otto Phipps. Where Carter was sprightly and eccentric, Otto was smooth and calm. His was the business brain that handled all of Carter's various interests. But like Carter, he was a flying fanatic.

It was precisely one fifty-nine (about an hour ahead of schedule) when the incident occurred. From where she stood on the Bluff, all Hester could see was the underside of the baskets. Two balloons, neck and neck. But then something happened. The underside of Otto's basket gave an audible creak, followed by a crack and splinter. Then it buckled.

There were screams from the crowd as Otto tumbled feet-first toward earth. He plummeted in front of several hundred paralysed bystanders, vanishing over the cliff and down into the cove.

With her right hand, Hester covered her little girl's eyes. With her left hand, she gently guided her boy away by the elbow. Needless to say, there was nothing the kids wanted more than a glimpse of Otto Phipps's mangled corpse. Seizing her children by the hands, Hester managed to find her friend Lucy, who sat at a picnic table eating a hot dog and had no idea what had just happened.

'Lucy,' Hester said, panting slightly, 'can you do me a favour?' Lucy, her cheeks bulging with processed sausage meat, looked down at the two beaming kids.

* * *

Now that she had an impromptu babysitter, Hester was free to indulge her morbid curiosity. Peeping over the edge of the cliff, she saw the outline of Otto Phipps, face-down in the sand, limbs horribly twisted and still. A couple of thin trails, like bicycle tyre tracks, stretched away from him across the sand.

Her acquaintance Detective Ed Kemble, who'd ditched his raspberry ripple at the first sign of trouble, caught her eye and came over.

'Pretty messy, huh,' he said.

Hester nodded slowly, lips pinched tight.

'What is it? You look like you're thinking about something.'

'I'm just wondering what the odds are of an accident like that happening in front of so many people.'

'Yeah, pretty slim. And you know what's worse? A couple of feet further to the left, he might have survived. If he'd hit the water instead of the sand, this may have been a different story.'

'A lot of unfortunate coincidences.'

Kemble narrowed his eyes. 'What are you thinking?'

'Nothing,' said Hester with the hint of a smile, 'nothing at all. And don't forget to examine those tracks in the sand.'

'What tracks?'

'A pair of tracks leading away from the body. I saw them from up on the Bluff.'

'Well they're not there now.'

A small crease appeared between Hester's brows and she peered once more over the edge of the cliff. The tracks were gone.

Once they realised there was nothing more to see, the crowds began to disperse. An ambulance arrived, and the coroner—a lithe, bald little man with bruise-coloured bags of sleep deprivation under his eyes—descended slowly and cautiously between the rocks. From her vantage point, Hester watched him begin to examine the corpse. She noticed a sudden jolt in the coroner's body language, as though he had just received a startling shock.

He straightened up and gradually wended his way back along the coastal path. Hester saw him converse with Detective Kemble, a twang of agitation in his voice. Slowly, with practiced casualness, she sidled closer.

'Damnedest thing I've seen,' said the coroner, 'are you *sure* he didn't hit the water?'

'Of course, I'm sure,' snapped Kemble, 'I got eyes, don't I?'

'Then you're not going to like what I'm about to tell you.' Hester craned her neck to listen. 'That man down there—I don't care if he's a millionaire or a pauper or the Dalai Lama—wasn't killed by a fall. That man died by drowning.'

* * *

Eventually, the ghostly unoccupied balloon bumped down to earth, where it was immediately seized by the uniformed officers. There was nothing to see—just an empty basket with its frayed and ripped floor through which Otto had plunged.

'Well, what the hell do you make of *that*?' Kemble demanded.

'Drowned...' Hester repeated, rolling the word round on her tongue like a jawbreaker.

'Well, there's only one thing for it,' said Kemble. 'He must have been dead before he hit the ground.'

'But how? I saw him climb into that basket this morning. He was alive and well.'

'How do you know?'

'On the television. They showed the launch on the news programme.'

'Must have missed it,' Kemble mumbled.

'Well, they showed both men climbing into their baskets and taking off. And Otto Phipps was very much alive.'

'So let me get this straight,' said Kemble, collapsing against a rock, 'the case we're dealing with is a man drowned in mid-air?'

The coroner shrugged his shoulders and scuttled away. Kemble looked at Hester. 'I need a cigarette,' he said.

* * *

Somehow—and don't ask me how—Hester managed to convince Detective Kemble to take her with him when he interviewed Carter Wentworth. Lucy, thankfully, was willing to take care of the kids for a while, so Hester was free for a few hours to visit the illustrious Grosvenor Hotel.

Wentworth was in the honeymoon suite; his limo had taken him straight there from the scene of the calamity. He was holed up far away from prying eyes on the top floor. But he wasn't alone when they arrived—the door was answered by a squat, bulldog-like fellow in a black suit.

'I'm Lou Brody,' the man said, 'I look after Mr Wentworth.' He said it almost like a threat.

He led the unlikely pair of Detective Kemble and Hester Queeg through to a little salon where Wentworth himself lay in an armchair with one leg propped on a footstool. Beside him sat a middle-aged woman, evidently a secretary of some kind.

Wentworth immediately leapt to his feet and began pouring out drinks. It was like some kind of strange cocktail party happening only in the head of the bewildered billionaire. A sad sight, really, this little fellow shuffling around and bumping into things.

'I just don't know,' he said, 'who would want to do something like that to old Otto.'

'You were old friends?' Hester inquired.

'Friends, enemies, you name it. We were everything to each other.'

'Mr Wentworth is speaking rhetorically,' said Miss Jensen. She had stood and leapt to her employer's defence. Hester noticed that the very top of the old man's head scarcely reached his secretary's shoulders.

'Damn it Miss Jensen, will you let me talk?'

Miss Jensen immediately clasped her hands together, as though in penance.

'What can you tell us about what happened today?' said Detective Kemble gently.

Wentworth thought for a moment. 'I want to know if you've considered something. I want to know if you've thought about the idea that maybe Otto did himself in?'

'Suicide?'

'That's what I mean.'

'What makes you say that, sir?'

The old man cocked his head. 'Well, he was pretty morbid lately. Talking about life and death and loneliness and what-have-you.'

'Did he have any other close relationships? Any lady friends?'

'Only Miss Jensen. And can you really call Miss Jensen a friend?' he gave Miss Jensen a cursory half-glance. 'You don't know what it's like to be alone in the world.'

Hester looked across at Miss Jensen, whose gaze was downturned and solemn. The poor secretary must be accustomed to this kind of abuse and self-pity. It wasn't long before Carter dozed off, practically mid-sentence. Miss Jensen dismissed Lou Brody with a curt nod. Then she composed herself and escorted Hester and Detective Kemble to the door.

'He's not a well man,' she said apologetically. 'He's been struggling for a long time. I'm starting to think his mind is slipping.'

'It's very sad,' said Hester.

'He can't do the things he used to. And, of course, he's completely cut up about Otto.'

'I notice that you call him "Mr Wentworth," but Otto is just Otto.'

'Otto was always very kind to me,' answered the secretary, 'I'm going to miss him a lot. He was a good man. Such a good man.' She looked to be tearing up slightly.

'Here you are, dear,' said Hester, offering a handkerchief.

Miss Jensen refused it politely. 'I'm quite all right thank you Mrs Queeg. Can you see yourself out?'

* * *

'I feel like the secretary knows something,' said Kemble as they drove away.

'I got the same impression,' said Hester. 'But *what?*'

'Something going on between Carter and Otto. They were rivals, then they were colleagues, then they were rivals again. Weird.'

Hester nodded hesitantly, 'You could be right. There was just something about the way she said Otto was a "good man." It was like she felt she had to defend him.'

Detective Kemble dropped Hester off home and then sped back to the station to write up his interview. A pity, for if he had hung around in Walnut

Creek a minute or two longer, he would have seen Hester clamber into her station wagon and immediately head back towards the Grosvenor Hotel.

She found Miss Jensen in the hotel bar, nursing what looked like a gin and tonic.

Discreetly, she sat beside her. 'Is there something you want to tell me, Miss Jensen?'

The middle-aged woman turned sharply on Hester. She was crying. 'I'm sorry,' she said. 'I know I shouldn't have lied to you and the detective.'

Hester looked around, checking there were no observers. 'It's all right,' she said. 'You have nothing to be afraid of.'

Sniffling, Miss Jensen went on: 'I hoped I wouldn't have to tell anyone. But I guess there's no harm now.' She paused, took a breath. 'Otto was stealing from the company. He had been for a long time. Funnelling pensions into his own bank account.'

Hester's eyebrows arched. 'How do you know?'

'I never confronted him about it. I never needed to. It was all there in the company finances, if you knew where to look. It's just, *I* was the only one who looked.' She sighed. 'He was a good man, Hester. He was.'

Hester didn't say anything.

* * *

The next morning, just after nine a.m., Detective Ed Kemble got a phone call at his office. It was Hester.

'I think...' she began, 'I think I need to watch the footage again.'

'What footage is that?'

'The balloon launch. Can we arrange that, do you think?'

Kemble had to pull a few strings, but he managed to get Hester in at the local TV station. He drove her over there in his VW Beetle (during the trip, she apprised him of her second encounter with Miss Jensen), and they sat side by side in a screening room while a sweaty and harried projectionist fumbled through a heap of film drums.

'So you want the Carter Wentworth balloon launch?' he said, his speech muffled by the fat cigar clenched between his brownish teeth.

'Right,' said Kemble.

'Okay,' said the projectionist, 'here we go.' And the projector flickered to life.

The footage was pretty much as she remembered. The clamour of reporters in the grounds of the Wentworth mansion. The two baskets, side by side.

First of all, Otto strode through the crowd and hopped into his basket. He wore the familiar old-school pilot's goggles and cap and waved cheerily to the crowd.

Next came Carter. He presented a hunched, sheepish figure as he approached the basket surrounded by bodyguards. It was almost comical—this little guy dwarfed by all those men in suits.

'Well?' said Detective Kemble when the film stuttered to a halt.

'Could I see it again, please?'

Kemble looked at the projectionist, who quickly reset the projector and fired up the film once more. Again, Hester watched Otto Phipps walk across the grass and leap up into his basket, all smiles. And then Carter Wentworth arrived with his retinue.

'Again?'

'Once more, please,' she answered.

She watched the footage a total of four times. When it was over, Detective Kemble had some difficulty gauging her reaction as they walked out of the studio. She didn't speak, and moved slowly.

'Well?' he finally asked.

'I just have one question,' she said. 'Do you happen to remember what the weather forecast was for the day of the fair?'

Kemble did not, but a quick detour took them to the TV station's meteorology department, where all the weather reports were recorded. Hester was provided a transcript of the report for two days ago. Kemble watched her read it and tried to decipher the expression on her face.

* * *

Next, they headed back to Finneran's Bluff. On the drive, Kemble caught Hester humming a snatch of a Bobby Darin tune. 'You seem happy,' he said.

'Well, I am, Detective Kemble,' she said, 'because now I know how Otto Phipps was killed.'

When they got to the Bluff, Hester made straight for the edge to peer down into the sandy cove. 'There,' she said, pointing.

Kemble looked. 'What is it?'

'Those lines. When I saw them the day of the fair, I thought they were tracks, like bicycle tyres or something. But they're not. They're shadows.'

Kemble squinted, but could scarcely make out the twin, narrow lines along the sand.

'You can understand why I was so puzzled when you pointed out that if there *had* been any tracks, they had gone. But of course, it was just the movement of clouds in front of the sun which obstructed those shadows; made the lines disappear.'

Kemble, shielding his eyes from the sun's glare with his hand, peered round and tried to work out where the shadows came from. He soon spotted an electric pylon a little further along the cove. Not invisible by any means, but of course, you had to *know* you were looking for it.

'What does that mean?' he said.

'Well, for one thing, it explains how Otto Phipps fell out of that balloon.'

'Oh yeah?'

Hester nodded. 'You see, I've been thinking a lot about baskets. Like for instance, how could a basket which is carrying a man eighty feet above ground suddenly give way? The answer, of course, is that it couldn't. Not without a catalyst. And those wires were part of the whole trick.

'Because that's what it was, you see. A magic trick. But a magic trick that went wrong. Let's get one thing out of the way first: Otto Phipps was not stealing money from Carter Wentworth.'

'How do you know?'

'Don't forget, he was the business brain. If he was stealing, he wouldn't have let someone like Miss Jensen find out about it. He would have covered his tracks perfectly. No, what happened was that somebody *framed* Otto.'

384

'Oh yeah? Why?'

'The intention was evidently to make it look like Otto was stealing and then to fire him. But I think by the time this plan was in motion, Otto had already turned the tables. He countered the attempt at a frame-up with some scheme of his own. Probably blackmail.'

'From what you're saying, that means the killer could only have been—'

'Carter Wentworth. Let's not forget, Otto was a lot cleverer than Carter. He must have realised that his old friend had got greedy—or *greedier*—and so he dug up a little dirt of his own. And where did that leave things? Stalemate.'

'None of that makes sense,' cut in Kemble. 'If these two men were bitter rivals, why were they in a balloon race together?'

Hester smiled. 'They weren't. It happened like this: sometime the day before the accident, Carter killed Otto. At a guess, I'd say he knocked him out and drowned him somewhere on his estate—the drowning was an essential part of Carter's plan.

'The idea then was to go ahead with the balloon race, which had been planned long in advance. But there was a difference: while two men would go up in the balloons, only one would come down alive.

'The dead body of Otto Phipps was quickly dressed in flying gear—I would imagine Lou Brody did this. After all, let's not forget that he "looks after Mr Wentworth." Then, the corpse was stowed in the basket. This must have happened before the press corps convened at the estate for the lift-off.

'It was a show for the cameras, you see. *Carter* was the Otto who climbed into the basket. He wouldn't need to be a master of disguise, what with the goggles and cap, not to mention the scarf that flapped over his mouth. All he really needed was some padding to alter his physique and some built-up shoes to make him taller.'

'If Carter played Otto, then who played Carter?'

'Look no further than Lou Brody once again. I noticed in the footage how Carter seemed sort of hunched over, whereas in the hotel, he stood ramrod straight but still barely reached Miss Jensen's shoulder. That gave me the idea that, on film, it was Lou trying to conceal the few extra inches he had on his boss.

'So, we have Carter in the basket with Otto, and Lou impersonating Carter in the second basket.'

'Then how,' Kemble demanded, 'did Lou end up on the ground? And how did Carter end up in the right basket again?'

'All it would take was a length of cable between Carter's balloon and Otto's, loosely tethering them together. What looked like a neck-and-neck race was, in fact, one balloon *towing* the other. Lou could have hopped out of the basket while still on Carter's property. He might simply drop onto the roof of the house, leaving Carter and Otto's cadaver in one balloon, pulling the empty basket behind them.

'Carter is an expert flyer, with a tendency to overplay his physical infirmity—as we saw at the hotel. But it would have taken a lot of nerve, all the same, to hop from one basket to the other. Maybe he used the cable to pull the basket in close, to allow him to clamber between the two in mid-air. Then he must have changed clothes.'

'That's fine and dandy,' said Kemble, 'but how did Otto's body wind up on the beach?'

Hester sighed. 'That's where the plan went wrong. The weather report predicted a north-easterly breeze. That would have taken the two flyers over the ocean—but the breeze never came. Carter's idea was for Otto's balloon to be lost at sea—hence the drowning. He intended to simply sever the cable and let the balloon carrying his dead friend float away, eventually dropping into the sea. Instead, the two balloons were carried inland. The cable got tangled in the wires between the pylons. And the basket containing Otto's body was wrenched open. And he fell.'

While Kemble went to radio his colleagues, Hester stood on the Bluff, looking down. She studied the sand where Otto Phipps had lain. And she studied the twin shadows, trails in the sand leading to nothing. Almost like a metaphor, she thought. Or maybe not.

BIRDS OF A FEATHER

By Gregory Meece

Since retiring from the police force, Alex Portman enjoyed relaxing near his breakfast room bay window, hopeful of spotting a new entry for his backyard bird list. He proudly recalled the morning when a busy blue-gray gnatcatcher stopped fluttering long enough to lounge on his garden fence. In doing so, it earned the singular honor of putting Alex's list over the half-century mark. Watching birds was definitely more relaxing than detective work—and a lot safer than watching criminals.

But Alex found that it was becoming increasingly difficult to grow his bird tally. Suburban habitats have their limits. When he saw an advertisement on the "Feathered Friends" website promoting east coast birding activities, he decided it was time to explore more diverse natural settings. A group of similarly enthused birders was heading to a wildlife refuge the weekend after Thanksgiving. Living on the mid-Atlantic coast afforded one an extensive variety of natural habitats to visit and enjoy. Just a couple of hours from Alex's home were brackish marshes, deep woods, and rolling meadows. In such venues one might find an array of raptors, waterfowl, and songbirds.

* * *

As he stepped into the Visitor Center, Alex was immediately greeted by Henry Biddleman, who introduced himself as the group leader. A 50-ish fellow, Biddleman dressed his part: cargo pants with deep pockets and belt loops to hold notebooks, a compass, mosquito spray, stow-away poncho, and other essential equipment; a broad-brimmed hat to keep out the sun; and a birding vest (for whatever function it is that a birding vest serves).

"Welcome birders," proclaimed Mr. Biddleman. "We here at the refuge prefer the term 'birders' to 'birdwatchers.' Some folks hear 'birdwatchers' and they immediately picture a peculiar breed of quirky social outcasts."

Looking at Mr. Biddleman, Alex thought to himself, "Gee, I wonder why?"

With the birding group assembled before him, Mr. Biddleman employed his usual icebreaker activity to help the birders get to know each other. "Let's go in a clockwise direction, starting with Carol over there," he said. "Miss O'Shaughnessy, can you tell us something about yourself and your birding goals?"

Carol O'Shaughnessy, an attractive woman who appeared to be in her 40s, introduced herself as a bookkeeper, and single. She explained how she began birding as a comforting activity. It took her mind off of unwanted thoughts. "Unfortunately, I had some bad times in my life," she explained. "The little birds I invite to my feeder cheer me up. I just cannot look at a bluebird or a goldfinch and feel down. On rainy days I really miss my little friends. I hope to add some songbirds to my list today."

"That's lovely, Carol," said Mr. Biddleman. "Birding is a great hobby for adding a little joy to one's life. There may be some particularly elusive songbirds out there waiting for you today. The ones that stay high up in trees are most challenging. I hope you have a strong pair of binoculars with you."

"I'm saving up for a better pair that will provide crisp details, even from a distance. It may help me compensate for a hearing deficiency I have had since my youth. Not being able to hear some high-pitched sounds, as you know, can present a real challenge in birding."

"Have you considered using a bird sound app?" asked Alex. "There are several available these days. Just press a button, record the sound, and up pops pictures of the most likely suspects."

"I don't know much about the new technology. Besides, that sounds like cheating." Carol giggled. "I like to 'earn' my bird sightings the old-fashioned way—by identifying their field marks."

"Ah, you make reference to our good friend Roger Tory Peterson," said Mr. Biddleman, referring to the American naturalist whose famous field guide to birds became the bible to many birding enthusiasts. Peterson's books are noted for their practical method for identifying birds and distinguishing them from their close relatives. Even amateur birders use "the Peterson System," a key feature of which is its use of "field marks" that accompany each bird portrait. Often, one tiny detail, such as the stoutness of the bill or a whitish eye-ring, is the only way to tell the difference between similar species.

"Eddie, you're next," said the leader. "Tell us a little about yourself, if you don't mind."

A young man, perhaps in his 20s, Eddie Toomey appeared to be jittery, as though he, in fact, really did mind talking about himself. Alex read his body language—not making eye contact when speaking, folding his arms as if to protect himself—as signaling an introverted type. "Nothing wrong with that," thought Alex, recalling his trepidation about speaking in front of a group when he was young.

"I'm an electrician by trade," said Eddie. "I hope to see some new birds today."

"Anything else you would like to share?" asked the group's leader. Seeing Eddie shake his head, Henry turned to Alex next. "Alex Portman, what got you into the world of ornithological endeavors?"

"My interest in birds began early," said Alex. "I guess it started when my parents surprised me with a kid-sized pair of binoculars they purchased at the secondhand store for my birthday. It was just in time to help me earn my Boy Scouts Bird Study merit badge. As the years moved on, I also moved on from canoeing, archery, and other merit badge quests, but birding took a hold as a lifetime hobby."

"Your parents really got their money's worth with that birthday gift," said Henry. "What do you do?"

Alex took the question to mean, "What is your occupation?" He told the group he was retired but left out the nature of his past career. It was a carryover from his active-duty days when he often found it prudent to keep a low profile in unfamiliar social settings. Not only did being in the company of a detective tend to make some folks uneasy, but a detective never knows when someone he meets might be involved in a future case.

To Alex's left was a rather tall man. Even seated, Alex figured the man had to be at least six and a half feet. He wore a charcoal gray, cloth jacket, threadbare at the elbows. Baggy denim pants. A pair of black oxfords that had seen better days. Alex thought it odd that the man kept his red wool cap on even though the room they were in was quite comfortable. He appeared to be at least 70, but still had a lot of vigor when he spoke, which was with a noticeable accent. Alex, who had become somewhat adept at matching accents with their places of origin, pegged it as Eastern European.

"My name is Danilo Melnyk. I am, how you say, 'newbie' to this hobby. Have not lived near countryside in long time. Many years I did like to look at the birds, but not many different kinds to see where I was—same ones almost every day. Seeing them soar so high gave me feeling of freedom. Sometimes, I wish I could join with them. Did not know how to call them, though."

"You mean using bird calls?" asked the leader.

"I think Mr. Melnyk means he wasn't familiar with the proper bird names," offered Alex. "Bird nomenclature."

"Yes. You are correct, Mr. Alex. I did not know a Teetmouse from a Noothatch," he replied.

Closing the circle of introductions was Marra Browne. She appeared to be a formidable woman who could take care of herself in the wilderness. Of all the birders present, Marra looked the most fit to take on the trails, even carrying her backpack, which appeared to be heavily loaded based on its bulging sides. Her shin-high angle boots might have been purchased at the Army Navy store. She wore a canvas, camo-patterned jacket with an olive drab hooded sweatshirt underneath.

"Maybe she figures her attire gives her an advantage in stealthily spying on the birds," Alex thought amusingly. "She could easily pass for a hunter (or is it 'huntress'?). I'll bet it would be challenging for a deer, or a human, for that matter, to spot her in the woods."

That is, until she spoke.

"I hear it's a damn good time to catch the end of the fall waterfowl migration!" she trumpeted. Alex noted how Eddie Toomey's body jerked, obviously startled by Ms. Browne's voice. "Hope to see ducks, ducks, and more ducks." Each time he heard the word "duck" Eddie twitched again. "There's one bird I hope I don't see. That stupid woodpecker that's been pokin' holes in the cedar shingles on my roof. I even resorted to getting my old man's pump-action shotgun—tried to blast him a few holes of his own! Ha! Ha!"

"My, my," said Mr. Biddleman, looking at a loss for what to say. Collecting himself, he turned to his laptop computer. After making a few quick keystrokes, the screen behind him lit up and the group saw an overhead picture of the wildlife refuge come into focus. "This short video will show key points of interest in the preserve as well as many of the different species that live here or visit the freshwater impoundments and adjacent salt marsh. Would someone please turn out the lights in back?"

A few minutes later the video projector shut itself off. Someone switched the lights back on. Mr. Biddleman stood and pointed to a ceramic bowl painted with holly and berries. In it were artfully arranged bags of alternating green and red colors. "My wife put together little gifts for you to take along. It's trail mix. You can tell my Mildred's already in the Christmas spirit by the bags' colors," he laughed. "The green bags don't have nuts in them, in case any of you have that food allergy. And here's an idea for your consideration. I know that dedicated birders challenge themselves by using lists to keep track of their sightings. Perhaps we can make our day even more fun. In addition to challenging ourselves to identify new birds, how about a friendly competition? The preserve's maps show its well-marked trails through the refuge. I will give each of you a copy. There are six trails and six of us. Just pick a trail and find your birds. When we reconvene at lunch, we'll compare lists. It's mostly for the honor of boasting that you spotted the greatest variety or added the most birds to your life list. What do you say if we all chip in to cover the lunch tab for whoever spots the rarest bird?"

After the group nodded, indicating its assent to the challenge, Mr. Biddleman distributed the trail maps, wished everyone good luck, and dismissed the birders to their separate adventures. As Alex received his trail map, he noticed Eddie quietly collecting his package of trail mix. He thought he might try to engage the shy boy. "Hey, Eddie, can you grab me a red bag? Maybe I'll run into some hungry squirrels out on the trail." Eddie's face remained blank despite Alex's attempt at humor. He handed Alex a bag and quickly left the room. The look on Alex's face showed his confusion.

Upon reaching the uppermost section of his three-mile walking trail, Alex lifted his binoculars. He adjusted the flywheel in the center of his 10x42 Bushnells to check the focus. "These should prove to be worth every penny I paid for them," he thought as he directed his binoculars to the grassy salt marsh below. His life list had several open boxes to check in the waterfowl section. He hoped to have a sporting chance of spotting a gadwall, green-winged teal, or a horned grebe. Grasping the barrels of his binoculars, he carefully adjusted the interpupillary distance and delicately fine-tuned the diopter adjustment while focusing on the expanse below. Something filled the viewing lenses, but it certainly was not the breast feathers of a merganser or the red eyes of a common loon. Something was lying face-down in the reeds. It appeared to be a body.

Alex scuttled down the embankment. When he reached the muck edging the marsh, he was able to crouch close enough to notice familiar clothing. Denim pants, gray jacket, red wool cap. The face was buried in the marsh grass. From the man's barely perceptible chest movements, it appeared that time may be running out. With excruciating slowness, the person lying there was able to turn his head to the side, searching for air. Now, Alex was certain who lay before him—Danilo Melnyk!

It was apparent, even from a side view of the face, that Melnyk had a horrific gash near the temple. Alex pulled up the side of the man's cap to ascertain the extent of the injury. Melnyk's eyelids fluttered as he attempted to focus them on the man leaning over him. Ever so slowly, his lips parted. He uttered, "Hit with rock. Why?" Those barely whispered four syllables would be his last.

* * *

As the police examiners in the field photographed the crime scene and collected evidence, the officer in charge spoke quietly with Alex. Lieutenant Davidson recognized Alex right away from his days on the force. Retired or not, Officer Davidson treated Alex as a colleague.

"We could use your help on this one," he told Alex. "According to the forensic examiner on the scene, the cause of death appears to be a cracked skull. Melnyk likely lost a lot of blood between the time he was struck and when he was spotted through your Bushnells. According to the report, the victim's wallet, cash, and watch were still on his person. His birding scope, tripod, sandwich wrapped in foil, unopened bottle of water, and a green plastic bag filled with trail mix were secure in his backpack. His binoculars were still looped by the straps around his neck."

"Whoever killed Melnyk is likely to still be in the preserve," said Alex.

"Each birder who signed the Visitor Center registry, including a dozen or so who were not part of your group, has been accounted for. The birders in Henry Biddleman's group are assembled in a meeting room in the rear of the Visitor Center. Let's join them."

When the two men entered the room, they immediately heard a raised voice. "Alright, young man, enough of the silence stuff!" Mr. Biddleman pointed his finger at Eddie Toomey.

"Leave him alone," shot back Mrs. Browne. "Just 'cause he's not a big talker don't make him guilty. Then, again, he did seem awfully nervous this morning. What's up, kid?"

With his head pointing toward the wall, Eddie slowly replied, "I'm just shy. I had nothing to do with what happened."

Using a skill developed from years of questioning reluctant witnesses, Alex knelt next to the boy, placed his hand softly on his arm. Using a gentle voice, he said. "Eddie, I believe you. But for everyone here to know that you are innocent, you need to tell the truth. You're not really an electrician, are you?"

"How did you know?"

"When I asked you for a red bag of trail mix, the kind with nuts, you looked right at them and handed me a green one. I thought, 'He must be color blind.' There's one thing I know that will keep you from getting a job as an electrician. Color blindness. Getting colored wires mixed up could wind up costing lives."

"Guess I picked the wrong fake job to have, said Eddie. "The bags looked like shades of gray to me. I figured it was 50-50. If you corrected me, then I would have acted like I grabbed the wrong one by mistake, and I would have given you one with the other shade."

"A birder who's color blind? That's rich," said Mr. Biddleman with a smirk.

Carol O'Shaughnessy, perhaps thinking of her own hearing issue, spoke up for the boy. "Mr. Biddleman, some of us aren't willing to let a personal challenge prevent us from living," she said.

"But why lie about being something you're not?" asked Alex.

"I don't have a job. I still live with my parents. Everyone here is older than me and I just was afraid of not belonging. I really do love birds, though. I thought I could learn some new things from all of your experience," Eddie said while looking up at the others for the first time.

"There. So, leave him alone," said Mrs. Browne, scowling at the group leader.

"Mrs. Browne, maybe we should be focusing on you," shot back Mr. Biddleman. "You come here dressed like you're hunting for something a lot bigger than birds. Maybe you are here on other pretenses. It sure isn't a love of birds. No true birder would make a remark about blasting one with a shotgun!"

Here Lieutenant Davidson chipped in. "My guys searched all of your backpacks. Mrs. Browne, can you explain why yours is the only one concealing a deadly weapon?"

"If you searched my backpack, you also undoubtedly found two wood decoys. I'm a carver. And I'm sure you checked my folding knife carefully, officer. It also has a straight gouge, chisel, V-tool, and hook knife on it—all for woodcarving. But Biddleman's right. I'm not here to check birds off some list. I'm a pretty good carver. Mostly caricatures. Won some blue ribbons at shows. But all the buyers want these days are duck decoys. You can't cash a blue ribbon at the bank, so I figured I'd start carving waterfowl. Hoped to get some good reference pictures on this little outing."

Carol O'Shaughnessy, though stoic during the tense series of accusations and counter accusations, turned to Alex and posed a question that no one else thought to ask. "Alex, why didn't you mention that you were a detective during the icebreaker activity?"

"Well, Carol, I guess nobody asked. I didn't mislead anyone. I simply told the group I was retired, which is true."

"But you were the only one there when the body was discovered. Doesn't that at least interest those conducting the investigation?"

The lieutenant addressed this point. "Ms. O'Shaughnessy, until the investigation has run its course, all of you, including Detective Portman—I mean, retired Detective,— are considered persons of interest." Just then, another officer came in and motioned for Lieutenant Davidson to step out of the room.

"Hey, I just thought of something," bellowed Marra Browne. "Am I the only one that thinks it's kind of weird that Biddleman had us take separate trails? If you ask me, the cops ought to follow that lead." Looking straight at the group leader she asked, "Ain't these little excursions usually done as a group? Otherwise, what's the point of doin' it? Unless, of course, you wanted that foreign guy to be all alone when you whacked him..."

Mr. Biddleman held up his hand to signal to Ms. Browne that it was time for her to stop talking. "You are absolutely correct. We birders learn from each other, and we enjoy the camaraderie that comes with the hobby. If you must know, the competition was not my idea. It came from someone else in the group." At this point, Mr. Biddleman silently turned to face one of the members of the group. The others in the room followed suit. With the room's attention directed toward her, Carol O'Shaughnessy began to speak.

"Well, um, yes. It was my suggestion. The idea came to me during the video presentation, and I shared it with Mr. Biddleman. I like the challenge of seeing how many birds I can identify. I thought a little competition would make it exciting if we..."

This time it was Alex's turn to interrupt. "Carol, perhaps it's time for you to tell us everything."

"What do you mean, Alex? I enjoy birding. As I told you all, it cheers me up when I'm not feeling so good."

"Because of what you described as a bad time in your life. My guess is that you were referring to the event that took place when you were just a little girl. Carol, you forget that I spent the last 40 years in the police department. The gunshot that killed your mother—I can't imagine your pain. The trauma is still with you, isn't it?"

Carol's gaze became unfocused, as if she were retreating to another place and time. Staring straight ahead, but at no one in particular, she began to speak in a monotone voice, absent emotion. "He shot her at point-blank range. She was holding me tightly. Protecting me. The gunshot damaged my hearing." After letting out a sigh, she added, "And it wrecked my life."

The group fell silent. Lieutenant Davidson was suddenly back in the room, whispering something to Alex. The group seemed to be collectively anticipating the next person to speak. It was Alex who broke the silence.

"When I asked about computer apps to identify the bird calls, you said you didn't know much about new technology, Carol. Perhaps that's why you didn't identify Mr. Melnyk's binoculars as the type with an integrated digital camera. Melnyk's last words were that he was struck by a rock. That means he saw what was coming. He saw you as he was falling. He couldn't tell us that. But the memory card in his binoculars could. When you landed your blow, the camera was activated. It shows everything that Melnyk saw."

Carol O'Shaughnessy put her hands over her face. For the first time, her emotions poured out. She looked up through her tears and said, "I only came today for a chance to enjoy birding with people who shared the same interest. But when I arrived, I thought I recognized in the group the man who killed my mom all those years ago. He murdered her and nearly destroyed me. I was a kid, but I never forgot that face, his height. Then, when he spoke, his accent made memories of that day come flooding back. I heard the name Melnyk, and it sounded so familiar. When he told everyone about not living near the countryside in a long time, seeing only the same kind of birds almost every day, it was because he was in prison! It was a minimum 40 years he received, which means he must have just gotten out. Oh, I was young then. But I remember him. That horrible face with the large birthmark on his forehead. When I hit him, it was a final blow for justice. It was vengeance."

"But you didn't see his forehead," said Alex. "He kept his wool hat on."

Lieutenant Davidson added, "Underneath his cap, you would not have found any birthmark. The person you killed was an innocent man. He was Melnyk's brother."

The murderer's face collapsed into her hands and her body shook uncontrollably. Someone in the group made a remark about field marks.

THE DEAD DONOR

By Michele Bazan Reed

Driving up Route 7 Friday afternoon, with the late-October breeze off Lake Champlain wafting the mingled aromas of dried leaves, cut hay, and cow manure through her car's open window, Hazel H. Baum thought that weekend's reunion might be the most boring thing she'd do all year. But on Saturday, after watching the college's biggest donor flop face-first into the cake honoring his birthday—frosting in Hitchcock College colors of purple and gold squishing out on either side of his face—she revised that opinion.

Members of the Class of 1955 screamed. College staff scurried around, one calling out for any doctors present, as another loosened the stricken man's tie and checked for a pulse. Rushing forward to see if she could help, Hazel arrived at the podium just as the alumni magazine editor turned, teetering on four-inch spike heels with a look of horror on her face, and shrieked, "He's dead!"

The party erupted into pandemonium. Hazel could see Emily Prince, the editor, was about to faint and led the poor girl over to a nearby table, grabbing a glass of punch for her. So, although staffers cleared the ballroom of guests rather quickly, Hazel was on hand when the police arrived.

"Who's in charge here?" asked Tim Avery, the first officer on the scene.

A tall, thin woman, elegantly dressed in a black skirt suit with a sequined top underneath, stepped forward. Pushing back her perfectly coiffed auburn hair, she gestured with a shaking hand to her embossed name tag: Mary Jean Dougherty, Major Gifts Officer.

"And the deceased is?" Avery's brows furrowed as he bent to peer at the face in the frosting.

Mary Jean was strangling a copy of the event program. Looking down as if surprised to see it, she dropped it on the table and took to wringing her hands instead. "His name is Calvin Lockwood III...of the class of 1955." There was a hint of reverence in her voice.

"Of the Lockwood Foundation Lockwoods?" Avery stopped writing in his notebook and looked at her over the top of his glasses.

"The very same. We were celebrating his 85th birthday." She waved absentmindedly at the cake, the gold and purple balloons. Her voice dropped to a whisper. "We were hoping the college would be the recipient of the birthday gift, though. He had hinted he was considering a substantial donation to fund science programs here at Hitchcock."

Officer Avery compressed his lips to bite back a comment. It seemed, judging by Mary Jean's chagrined look, that her sorrow was more about the loss of the big bucks than the dear donor.

"It looks like a heart attack or maybe a stroke of some kind. Why did you come, and so quickly?" she asked, a puzzled look on her face.

"Somebody posted a photo on Instagram with the hashtag #HitchcockCollegeHijinks. We get alerts when anything in this little corner of Vermont is tagged on social media. Usually a waste of time—but now and again..." Avery waved a hand in the direction of the dead man and shrugged.

"Oh great, just what we need. Bad publicity. I can just see the headlines in tomorrow's Burlington Free Press." The look on Mary Jean's face confirmed Avery's earlier assumption about her priorities.

By then the scene-of-crime team had arrived and Avery directed the police photographer to begin her work.

"I'll need a full list of everyone who attended the party and how to reach them. Make sure no one leaves campus until I say so," Avery told Mary Jean. "And flag anyone you know who came into direct contact with our victim."

At the sound of that last word, Hazel sucked in her breath. Victim. She felt a twinge of pity. Calvin was her classmate, although he wasn't the easiest person to get along with back then, and his wealth had made him even more unbearable, if that were possible. "I'm just glad Mabel wasn't here to see this," Hazel whispered to Emily.

"Who's Mabel?"

"Calvin's late wife. They met here at Hitchcock and married soon after graduation. She died just after the holidays. Heart attack."

Hazel knew the officer's next question even before she heard it.

"Do you know of anyone who would have a reason to want Mr. Lockwood dead?" Avery was asking Mary Jean.

"More like, who didn't," Emily, now revived by the punch, muttered to Hazel.

"Indeed. I guess his personality never improved with age, huh?" The octogenarian winked at Emily. The pair had bonded when the younger woman wrote a profile of Hazel for the alumni magazine the year before.

"I was writing a big piece about him for the next issue—the bosses always like to puff up potential donors with a cover story. But everyone I spoke to on campus had something negative to say...all off the record, of course." The editor rolled her eyes. "Seems he dangled the promise of that sciences grant like a carrot to allow himself access to all sorts of cutting-edge research, some of which he used in his company's businesses. Plus, he lorded it over the scientists to the point where they couldn't stand to see him coming."

"Yeah, he was pretty obnoxious as an undergrad." Hazel kept her voice low. "Had an eye for the ladies, too."

"Ha! Tell me about it," Emily said. "Pinched quite a few bottoms on his campus visits. Administration had to do some damage control so female professors didn't file harassment suits and jeopardize his promised giving." She took a sip of the punch. "I have to admit, he made me a little uncomfortable, kept edging closer during the interview. I was glad to have Chuck along as a bodyguard."

"He's a good guy." Hazel had grown fond of the lanky Charles Waggoner, *aka* Chuck, when he photographed her for Emily's magazine story.

"Do you think he'd have some photos of who approached Calvin during the reception? That might give us some suspects," she said.

"You always did love a mystery," Emily said. Hazel wouldn't admit it out loud but focusing on the puzzle kept her mind off the horror of seeing her classmate keel over dead.

"Oh, and maybe some of those people you interviewed, the ones who had negative things to say about Calvin?" Hazel added. "Maybe we could check into them, see if any match up with the people seen up close to him tonight."

"Fifty years in the classroom got you in the habit of giving out homework assignments, huh?" Emily's green eyes crinkled up with the smile she shot the retired teacher. "Sure, I can get those things. Will you be at the Golden Alumni luncheon tomorrow? I'll find you and we'll compare notes then."

"H-Bomb? Is that you? It's been ages!" A big bear of a man enveloped Hazel in a hug. Seeing Emily's puzzled look, he explained.

"When we were undergrads, Hazel Baum here earned the nickname H-Bomb for her, well, I guess you'd say 'explosive' personality." He winked in Hazel's direction.

"Oh, there was more to the nickname, Gus. Go ahead, tell her the whole story. I've got no secrets from Emily."

"Well, it was 1952, and the government was conducting tests on the hydrogen bomb out at the Bikini Atoll." He pronounced it AY-tall. Emily nodded. She'd learned that in her history classes. "And, at the same time, a va-va-voom actress name of Brigitte Bardot debuted a nifty little number called the bikini on the beaches at Cannes. Made bigger headlines than the bomb tests."

"So, when I decided to try out the new fashion for a dip in Lake Champlain, I earned the nickname H-Bomb, and it's followed me for six decades!" Hazel had a look in her eye like she'd do it all again in a heartbeat.

"Hazel, the bookstore's having a big sale on alumni sweatshirts. We're going to need them for the bonfire tonight. What say we go over? Maybe they'll have Vermont maple candies for my grandkids." Gus nodded in the direction of the campus store. With a wave to Emily, Hazel followed him out of the ballroom.

* * *

The next day at the luncheon, Emily slid into the empty seat next to Hazel.

"Hey, kiddo." The octogenarian flashed her a grin. "Whatcha got for me?"

"Plenty." Emily pushed a sheaf of papers over to Hazel. "First off, I was in Mary Jean's office today, getting my list of assignments for the rest of the weekend, and I heard her take a call from that Lieutenant Avery. She turned her back to me and tried to muffle her voice, but I'm a trained journalist—which is to say, a real snoop. I heard every word."

Emily looked down at her agenda of events and read some scratchings in the margin. "I heard her gasp, and then she said, maybe a little louder than she intended to, 'Poison? How could that happen at an alumni party?' I wrote down everything she said, old newshound's habit," Emily said with a wink.

"Lucky for me they're all used to seeing me scribbling in my reporter's notebook. When she turned around and narrowed her eyes at me writing, I just told her I was using the few quiet minutes to sketch out a list of photos for Chuck to take this afternoon." She giggled.

"That's great, Emily! Now we have a means. All we need are the motive and opportunity." Hazel read a lot of mystery books and liked to talk like a detective.

"Well, I've got more to report. Although if you hoped for a nice manageable list of suspects, you're out of luck. Mr. Lockwood had more enemies than dollars...if that's possible. And some of those antagonists were photographed in close proximity to him yesterday."

She flicked open her laptop, and with a few keystrokes, called up a file containing thumbnails of all of Chuck's shots from the birthday reception. "The great thing about Chuck is that he basically keeps his finger on the shutter, capturing shot after shot, then choosing only the best to present to me for publication." Emily told Hazel. "So when you look at his raw files quickly this way, it's almost like a movie."

"Who's this one?" asked Hazel, pointing to a photo of a tall, thin man wearing jeans, topped by a jacket and a tie with a colorful pattern of the Periodic Table of the Elements.

"That's Dr. Samuel Norris, head of the Chemistry Department. He applied for a Lockwood Foundation grant to patent a procedure to distill industrial solvents in half the time. Mr. Lockwood turned him down, and the next thing you know, Lockwood Industries patented it."

"Looks like they're having words," Hazel said.

"Yep, they sent me in to distract the scientist and get him out of there before he disrupted the party too much. When I walked up, I saw him shove Mr. Lockwood's outstretched hand away, and heard him say, 'You'll pay for stealing my patent, Lockwood. Just wait and see.'"

Hazel bet some of those solvents could be used as potent poisons. "I suppose he could have murdered him with some toxin smeared on his hand or a needle secreted up the sleeve of that jacket," she told Emily. Hazel filed that thought away for further investigation.

"How about this woman? With the stop-motion effect, it looks like she's waving her arms and her face is inches from Calvin's." Hazel grimaced. In her time, a young woman wouldn't be so confrontational. They were standing at the buffet table, and Calvin's plate was resting next to the woman's right hand.

"Sharon Seaver. Works at the library. She accused Mr. Lockwood of sexual harassment, but they say the administration tried to buy her off with a promotion. When she wouldn't back down, they threatened her job and she gave up, but it seems like she still held a grudge." Emily scrolled down to the next set of photos.

"Aww, there's Dr. Peterson, bringing Mr. Lockwood a cup of tea. How sweet." She started to scroll further.

"Seth Peterson?" Hazel sat upright and peered at the screen through her bifocals. "He was a classmate of ours. There was no love lost between those two, I can tell you that. Mabel was Seth's girl."

"Wait a minute. Are you saying Mr. Lockwood stole Dr. Peterson's sweetheart and married her? Now I really dislike him. Not to speak ill of the dead...or a donor." She glanced around to be sure no one had heard.

"Yes, Mabel and Seth were engaged to be married. In our senior year, when Seth went on a study-abroad trip to Costa Rica to gather biology specimens, Calvin wooed her. I guess his good looks, fast car, and family fortune won out over quiet, studious Seth."

"Well, judging by the smiles on their faces, and that cup of tea, I bet they decided to let bygones be bygones," Emily said. "Dr. Peterson's a world-renowned researcher now. He's been working hard to solve the bee crisis."

Hazel had read about how bee colonies were dying off all over the world. It was a mystery that needed to be solved, and quickly.

But as the college president droned on at the front of the room, Hazel's mind was buzzing with a mystery of another sort.

* * *

The next day, Hazel skipped the Farewell Breakfast to nose around a bit on campus. She stopped first at Dr. Norris' office.

"Excuse me, ma'am? May I help you?" A sharp-eyed secretary in a cardigan and sensible shoes came around the corner of her desk toward Hazel.

"Oh, I was just wondering if Dr. Norris was in? Someone told me yesterday at the Alumni Gala that he was doing some very important research. I, well, I'm looking for some opportunities to invest my retirement fund and..." She never got any further, as the secretary interrupted her.

"Just a minute, ma'am, I think he's at his lab on the other side of campus. I'll just give him a call."

She looked frustrated as she punched in the numbers on her cell phone. "It's coming up not available. I'll bet he forgot to plug it in again. Absent-minded professor and all that. I'll just take a quick run over to Chadwick Hall. We should be back in, oh, no more than about 10 minutes."

"That's sweet of you, dear. I'll wait right here. Don't worry about me. I'll find something to occupy my time." Hazel tried to look her age for once, and picked up a science magazine lying on the coffee table in the waiting area as she gingerly lowered herself into a guest chair.

When she heard the elevator ding as the secretary descended to the parking lot, Hazel went into action.

She tested the professor's door by opening it just a crack. The coast was clear. Hazel slipped inside and closed the latch ever so softly as she glanced at her watch. Nine and half minutes left.

She could see that this professor may have been absent-minded, but he was organized, at least where his grants were concerned. Maybe it was that nice secretary's doing, she thought.

Hazel riffled through a file drawer until she came to the L's. Sure enough, filed under Lockwood Foundation was Dr. Norris' application, including patent drawings and scientific formulae, followed by Calvin's rather curt letter of rejection.

The professor included clippings of Calvin's businesses putting his invention to use, including tear sheets of Lockwood Industries' stock evaluations. What she saw next caused her to suck in her breath.

Maybe Norris's threat to Lockwood had nothing to do with physical violence. He was planning to sue the wealthy industrialist for several million dollars for patent infringement. He and his lawyers had prepared a meticulous case and the folder included documents that showed the suit would be filed within days. Lockwood had vowed to fight it, and a letter from his law team threatened a countersuit. The wealthy industrialist planned to accuse the professor of plagiarism, a charge that could ruin his academic career.

If his suit was successful, Norris would have plenty of money for his research. So why would he kill this golden goose? Hazel wondered if he would be able to translate his suit to Calvin's estate under state law.

On the other hand, in the scientific world, a researcher's reputation meant everything. Even a hint of plagiarism could tarnish his name and make Norris an academic pariah. Calvin's threat could have spawned an overwhelming fear that drove the professor over the edge.

Just then Hazel heard the elevator bell again. She slipped out of the professor's office and sat down in the waiting room with the magazine on her lap, eyes closed and head lolling a bit to one side.

"Oh, ma'am. MA'AM." The secretary raised her voice in the hopes of not having to shake the sleeping octogenarian. "I tracked down Professor Norris and he's at a dentist appointment. He can be back in half an hour."

"What...what time is it?" asked Hazel. "I must have dozed off. Oh my goodness! Look at the time! I have a ride to catch in 10 minutes. Be a dear and just give me the professor's card and I'll call him when I get home."

* * *

Hazel's next stop was at Sharon Seaver's office in the library.

She thought about it on her way over, and considered the woman a likely suspect. In her work at the library she'd have plenty of access to books listing poisons that could kill. Even if she didn't search the scientific tomes, a mystery story would yield a likely murder weapon or two. Standing by Calvin's plate the way she was, she could have snuck some poison into the dish. Something colorless and odorless that Calvin would never notice.

Hazel truthfully introduced herself as an alumna visiting campus for the weekend. She asked questions about the library's set up and new acquisitions, focusing on research journals about toxicology and mystery books.

"Oh, I'm sorry, Miss Baum, but we specialize here in the library nowadays. My focus is on local Vermont lore. I can show you books about Champ, jack jumping, and shipwrecks on Lake Champlain. Not to mention ghost stories of course. We've got plenty of haunted B&Bs."

"Ooooh, none of that spooky stuff, please!" Hazel looked over shoulder and shuddered. "I'm a member of the class of 1955, and when my classmate Calvin Lockwood was so suddenly stricken yesterday, the last thing I want to think about is a visitation by you know...ghosts." The last word came out in a pathetic little squeak.

"He was a hateful man, and made my life a misery," Sharon said. "I tried to complain about his treatment of me and so many other women, and I almost lost my job over it."

She looked down at her hands, and Hazel could see the effort she made to calm their shaking.

Sharon sighed. "But now that he is dead, it's made me think about things differently, and I almost feel bad for him. All his money didn't help him live longer or better, did it? I'm going to forget all my anger. Life's too short." Sharon shook her head and shoulders as if to rid herself of the bad feelings. "Now would you like me to call a librarian who may have the information you're looking for?"

Hazel shook her head. "No, dear, I think you may be right. In the time I have left, I'll try to focus on more positive subjects." She gave her sweetest old-lady smile and doddered away.

Either Sharon was a consummate actress or she really meant her words. Hazel mulled it over as she left the building. Fifty years in a classroom with students cheating on homework assignments and forging permission slips gave her a kind of sixth sense about whether someone was lying or not. She wondered if it was still strong, or would fail her now.

When she was out of sight of Seaver's office, Hazel hustled for the campus shuttle to take her across the quad to the biology building. She'd pay a call on her old friend Seth Peterson.

* * *

"Hazel Baum! Well, I'll be!" Professor Peterson rose from behind his desk to envelop his classmate in a hug.

"Hello, Seth." Hazel glanced around the lab. "You've done pretty nicely for yourself, here at the old alma mater. I hear you're busy saving the bees?"

"Let me show you around. Here's my greenhouse where I grow the plants for the bees to forage on, and over there are the apiaries where my little darlings live. I hope my research will reverse the trend of hive death we're seeing all over the world and bring the bees back to do their job for planet Earth."

Hazel glanced around, looking impressed, and read the names of the plants in Peterson's little garden. "Oh! What are those little drawer thingies for?" She pointed at the hives.

While Seth faced the hives and droned on in a long-winded and totally academic discussion of the proper living conditions for various species of bees, Hazel plucked a leaf from a nearby plant using a couple of tissues she always kept handy. She stuck the lot in her jacket pocket.

"Terrible thing about our old classmate Calvin, eh?" Hazel said, when Seth had stopped pontificating.

"Well, he got my girl, but I got the last laugh," Seth said in a whisper.

Hazel looked up in alarm, but Seth was staring out over his hives. "He's dead, and I'm still here, saving the world, one bee at a time."

"Got to run," was all Hazel said as she backed out of the lab and headed straight to Lt. Avery's office.

* * *

"I can't believe dear old Dr. Peterson is a murderer," Emily said over coffee the next morning. "How did you figure it out? And who am I going to feature on the back page Faculty Profile in the next issue, now that he's in jail?"

"Well, he obviously had a motive, what with Calvin stealing Mabel away while he was on that research trip. It broke Seth's heart, and I knew he'd never forgive Cal." Hazel set down her mug and reached for another apple-maple muffin.

"But when Calvin died that way, a heart attack right at his birthday party? Just like Mabel died less than a year ago. Funny a husband and wife would die suddenly of the very same thing, eh?"

"Yeah, I guess so. But they do say old married couples become more and more alike as the years go on. Makes you wonder." Emily stared at Hazel, waiting for more.

"Well, I remembered a call from Mabel about a week before she died, saying how sweet it was that Seth had sent them a Christmas present of a teapot with a full tea caddy and a jar of homemade honey. She told me she thought Seth had moved on from losing her love those many years ago, and she was happy for him."

Hazel shook her head at her friend's naivete. "I guess she was the first to try the tea. I didn't think anything of it at the time, but when you showed me that picture of Seth handing a cup of tea to Calvin, I started to put two and two together.

"When I visited Seth's lab, I saw that he grew plants for the bees to forage on. Set aside from all the other plants in a separate enclosure was a patch of oleander, with a little hive of bees right in that patch. Oleander's leaves make a deadly tea and the honey from bees who forage on it can kill as well. I knew then that Seth's Christmas gift and his comforting cup of tea to the poor widower were nothing more than double-whammy lethal cocktails designed to stop the hearts that broke his."

Emily could only shake her head in admiration.

"I snuck an oleander leaf out of his lab and Lt. Avery said the toxicology report confirmed the presence of oleander toxins in Calvin's body. Confronted with the evidence, Seth confessed to killing both Calvin and Mabel, so he will face charges in her death, too."

Emily gave Hazel a hug. "Awww, I'm sorry your reunion turned into such a catastrophe."

"Catastrophe? It's the most fun I've had at a reunion in years!" Hazel winked as she raised her mug in a toast. "Here's to next year, kiddo!"

THE MISSING CASE OF BEER

By Rob McCartney

I banged my palms against the steering wheel as the traffic crept north on Highway 400 at a snail's pace.

It was all supposed to be smooth sailing. Book Friday off work, be on the road to cottage country by noon to beat the traffic and join Phil on the dock on Rebecca Lake by cocktail hour.

Apparently, half of Toronto had the same idea.

My Santa Fe SUV tires crept slowly along the hot pavement, with an endless, winding snake of cars ahead of it.

The SUV was loaded for bear, and I couldn't see out my rear window. Bags of fresh bedding, clothing, and groceries were piled to the roof. Two cases of beer lay buried somewhere in there. Everything my daughters and I needed for the next few days was squished into every possible nook and cranny. I was hell-bent on avoiding a disruptive mid-weekend trip into Dwight or Huntsville for supplies.

The upcoming Monday—the first in August—was a national Civic Holiday in Canada, and the Muskoka region of Ontario always turned into a cottage playground. I desperately needed these four days away from the office.

But I wasn't off to a good start.

In the back seat, my two daughters, Sam, fifteen, and Maggie, fourteen, seemed ambivalent to the traffic, tapping away on their cell phones and tablets. Maggie wore her earbuds and hummed to Katy Perry.

The girls had groaned about coming to the cottage this weekend. They wanted to stay in the city with their friends. But Phil and I had promised our wives we'd take the kids up north to give the women a break. Phil's my neighbor on Rebecca Lake, and he and his sixteen-year-old daughter Tammy had had the foresight to leave Toronto the previous night.

I veered off Highway 400 and onto Highway 11 at the fork just past Barrie. I white-knuckled it, repeatedly hitting the gas, then gasping as I slammed on the brakes to avoid smashing into the car screeching to a halt in front of me.

I told the girls we didn't have time to stop at Webers for burgers and fries. That led to a chorus of protest, and I caved in. I found myself standing in a lineup behind about one hundred hungry travelers.

Twenty minutes later, I was handed a cardboard box with our order. We sat down at a picnic table. I wolfed down my burger, but the girls took their sweet time. I realized I was gritting my teeth.

I remembered what my wife, Peggy, had told me. 'Watch your blood pressure, Gerry. Try to relax.' I took a few deep breaths and ran my fingers through my hair.

The girls finally stopped picking at their fries and dumped their wrappings in a nearby garbage can. I was ready to roll.

North of Gravenhurst, the traffic eased up. I made one final stop at a gas station to buy a few bags of ice. After that, my lead foot pushed heavy on the gas pedal, and we soared along Highway 60 to Limberlost Road. I sighed with relief when I turned onto Kells Bay Road, where our cottage awaited. Stones on the old road made metallic clinking sounds on the bottom of the SUV. Still buried in their electronics, the girls were indifferent to the beauty of the forests surrounding us.

I could almost taste an ice-cold beer hitting my lips.

"We're here," I pronounced as we pulled into our gravel driveway. The girls headed for Phil's place to see Tammy the second I put the SUV into park.

Left solo, I unpacked the SUV, determined to do the bare minimum so I could catch as much sun as possible. Our cottage faced west onto the lake. We would have about three more hours of sunlight, and I wanted to lap it all up.

I saddled myself with as many bags and knapsacks as I could carry and squeezed through the squeaky cottage screen door. I tossed the girls' bags in their room and unloaded whatever groceries needed to go into the refrigerator. I stuffed the ice into the beer fridge in the tool shed and stacked my two cases of beer on the cement floor. The weather was too good to waste time loading beer into the fridge.

Back in the cottage, I rifled through my travel bag and dug out my bathing suit and a T-shirt. I changed and quickly put the few clothes I'd brought into the dresser drawers.

I returned to the shed and dropped a bag of ice on the cement floor to break it up, and packed the chunks in a cooler with a dozen or so beers.

One thing was still bugging me—that squeaky screen door. I grabbed a can of WD-40 and sprayed the door's hinges. I opened and closed the door a few times, and it was no longer squeaking. With that behind me, I hit the narrow footpath leading through the trees to Phil's cottage.

"Gerry," he yelled from his dock as his Golden Retriever Millie ran to greet me, her tail wagging. "I told you to leave last night. You've missed most of this brilliant day."

"Well, I'm here now, so let's get this party started," I replied, scratching Millie's head.

The girls had worn their bathing suits under their clothes on the drive up and were already swimming when I set foot on Phil's dock. Phil gave me a bear hug, and we sank into his large, wooden Muskoka chairs.

The girls must have thought I had some contagious disease because as soon as I arrived, they plucked towels off deck chairs and disappeared into Phil's cottage.

Phil and I clinked beer bottles and cheered the official beginning of the weekend.

"So great to be out of the city," he said. "You can't beat this little slice of paradise."

The odd boat cruised by, but the lake was mostly peaceful. We breathed it all in and gossiped about who was at the lake for the weekend, who had violated building codes, and who had a beef with whom about property lines.

Cottages are a labor of love, so we also chatted about the work that was underway this summer. We both used the same handyman, a local named Donnie Gilbert, who earned his bread and butter doing jobs city slickers couldn't do ourselves.

Donnie specialized in building sheds and docks, landscaping, and laying stone slabs artfully for fire pits and pathways. When his excavator wasn't heaving boulders, he ran a logging company and loved his chainsaws almost as much as his wife, Deb. He was a bushman with sophistication. An expert angler and hunter, he was also a renowned chef and relished cooking for his buddies at hunt camp.

"Donnie's coming by tomorrow," Phil said. "Going to cut down those dead trees. Hope it's not too noisy. Shouldn't take long, knowing Donnie."

We sometimes worked alongside Donnie to keep costs down. Last summer, Donnie and I built a garage to store my four-by-four, boat trailer, and snowmobile. I held the nails, and he held the hammer. Owning a cottage means always tinkering. Our cottage was an old log cabin that used to be a hunting lodge. When we bought it, the cabin had been unused for years and was infested with mice. There was mouse poop everywhere. The cabin needed to be gutted, and Donnie had done the job.

I reached into my cooler for a fresh Steam Whistle and twisted off the cap. The silence was broken only by the odd loon call or a chirping bird. I finally started to unwind.

Then the serenity was split open like a wet oak log by a sharp axe.

Two thundering jet skis bombed across the lake, ruining the moment. The riders revved their engines and hooted and hollered. It was those damn McLaughlin twins—Terry and Max.

The teens came within fifty feet of Phil's dock and started doing donuts. The engines gurgled loudly as they circled, churning up the water which rocked Phil's dock and moored tinny and power boat.

I saw red and jumped to my feet, swinging a fist in the air. "Get out of here, you little buggers," I yelled. I doubt they could hear me, but they could obviously see me as Terry flipped me the bird. The twins laughed at us and raced off out of sight across the lake.

"Take it easy, Gerry," Phil said, putting his hand on my shoulder. "They're just kids."

"I know, but those damn jet skis just piss me off no end," I said. "And those McLaughlin kids are always stirring up trouble."

The truth was Terry and Max were the same age as my daughter Sam, and I rued the day they all started hanging out together. I didn't want my girls having anything to do with these jerks. When they weren't jet skiing, the twins were screaming their dirt bikes down our road, stirring up dust and scaring the hell out of Millie. Their father, Doug, was notorious for his boozing and often drove their water ski boat three sheets to the wind. He was a poor excuse for a father, and his kids were spoiled rotten. I didn't trust any of them as far as I could throw them.

I managed to calm down and reminded myself that I was here to unwind from my high-pressure job as an advertising rep that never left me time to smell the roses.

"Sorry for the outburst, Phil," I said.

"It's okay, buddy. I feel ya."

We watched the sun traverse across a blue sky spotted with white puffy clouds. I had my eye on one cloud that looked like a diving dragon when I heard someone holler hello from the lake. I spotted a canoe headed toward us.

It was Glenn Brown.

Three things about Glenn Brown. First, he was notoriously cheap. He made a habit of showing up uninvited without any beer or liquor, breaking cottage etiquette rule number one.

Second, he never shut up. Once he started weaving an irrelevant yarn, he'd talk your face off. Nobody could get a word in edgewise. He told the same tired glory day stories over and over again about girls he dated when he was sixteen or about some buddy who did something crazy. Secretly, Phil and I called him Mr. Anyways, because whenever someone else did get a chance to speak, he'd interrupt, saying, "Anyways, this guy I know...."

Third, Glen always showed up at the worst possible times, such as right before dinner. He didn't know when to take his cue to leave, either, and always overstayed his welcome.

I felt the tension in my chest grow as Glenn's canoe glided up and scratched along the sandy bottom of the shoreline. When he tied the canoe to a small tree, I knew he planned to stay.

True to form, Glenn asked for a beer, and Phil obliged. One beer turned into four, and for the life of me, I don't think I got a single word into the conversation. I was ready to burst when he finally got into his canoe a few hours later.

Once he was out of earshot, I let out an agitated sigh. "That's a relief. I thought he'd never leave," I said as he paddled off in the twilight.

"Ah, c'mon now, Gerry," Phil replied. "He's not all that bad. Just laugh it off."

The sun set behind the woodlands across the lake, and the sky lit up in bright sheets of orange and purple. I took a pull off my beer and tried to curb my anxiety to enjoy the moment.

I'd picked up a couple of eight-ounce rib eyes from Whole Foods back in the city, and we headed to my cottage to light the barbecue. The girls, who wanted nothing to do with us, were content to stay at Phil's and make Kraft Dinner.

I lit the propane, and the barbecue poofed to life. I was scraping the grill when I noticed Phil reach into his bathing suit pocket. He looked around to make sure the girls weren't around and pulled out a marijuana joint.

I have to confess I'd also brought a small vial of weed which I'd stashed in a roll of socks in my bedroom. We did say boys' weekend, after all.

Phil lit the joint with the barbecue lighter, inhaled, and coughed. We both laughed as he passed it to me. "Look at us," I said. "A couple of over-the-hill party boys."

"Well, you really need it, Gerry," Phil said. "You're so uptight. Just go with the flow, bro."

We got a bit high and threw the steaks on the grill along with some shucked corn on the cob. We ate outside at the patio table.

"Ahh, that was delicious," Phil said with a sigh of contentment. "But time for me to hit the hay. Busy day tomorrow." He meandered down the footpath with Millie in tow.

The weed and dinner had combined to make me a sleepy camper, and I looked forward to crawling into my cozy bed with the screened windows open. Being teenagers, the girls would be up for hours, but I felt they were safe. They were good girls who never got into serious trouble.

I walked to the front of the cottage and phoned Peggy to say good night. She was hosting a girl's evening, and I could hear bursts of laughter in the background.

"You sound a bit tipsy," I said.

"So do you," she replied.

"Well, maybe a little. Phil and I got into a few pops." I didn't mention the joint.

"Are you being a good boy?" Peggy asked.

"Better than those damn McLaughlin brats!"

"Now, Gerry, don't get worked up. We talked about that—"

"I know, I know. Sweet dreams, honey."

"Sweet dreams to you, my prince."

I hung up my cell phone, locked the tool shed, and went inside.

* * *

I was enjoying a freshly ground cup of coffee on my lakefront deck, looking out over the still, glass-like water. There was no breeze, and you could hear boat motors across the lake. I had a beach towel and was about to wade out into the shallow water when I heard rustling in the bushes.

Phil emerged from the footpath with his own cup of Joe.

"Hey, neighbor!" I chirped.

"Hey, Gerry," he said, somewhat somberly.

"Everything okay?" I asked.

Phil sat down on the cushion of a beach recliner and slapped his palms against his knees.

"Question...how much did I drink last night?"

"Not that much," I replied. "Unless you'd gotten going early before I arrived. Why?"

Phil scratched his head and wore a puzzled expression on his face.

"It's just that I was putting empties back into my beer case this morning out on the front porch, and there's a few empty slots where beer bottles should be. I wondered if maybe I left a few empties over here. I was a bit foggy after that joint..."

"No, you didn't bring any beer. We drank mine, as usual," I quipped.

"Hmm, that's odd."

"Maybe Glenn took the bottles for the deposit money," I joked. "I wouldn't worry about it."

Just then, we heard tires crunching gravel along Kells Bay Road. A pickup truck passed my cottage and pulled into Phil's driveway.

"That's Donnie," Phil said. "I better get back."

Phil stood up, wandered back down the path, and disappeared into the bush.

Phil's beer bottle enigma reminded me to stock some beers in the tool shed refrigerator so they'd be cold by the afternoon. I opened the sliding glass door heading into the back of our cottage and got the key for the shed. Outside, I turned the key in the lock and swung open the shed's big, wooden, barn-style doors.

On the floor was one case of Steam Whistle. The other case was missing.

In my haste to capture the remaining sunlight the previous evening, had I forgotten to bring in the other case from the car? I looked in the car, and it wasn't there.

Suddenly, I was not in my happy place. Someone had ripped me off.

It wasn't just that someone had stolen from me. Now I'd have to go into Dwight to buy another case of beer to get through the weekend. I had vowed that my SUV would remain parked right where it was until Monday evening.

It was about then that I heard a chainsaw fire up next door. Donnie, I thought. Would he? I'd had a key made for him so he could access the shed to do work while I was in the city. Would he steal from me?

I'd have to calm down before I approached him. He had about five inches and 60 pounds on me. I wouldn't want to provoke a punch from his hefty workman's meat paws. I put on my flip-flops and marched down the footpath.

Phil was watching Donnie take down a rotted-out oak tree that was threatening to fall on his cottage. Donnie wore his regular outfit—brown corduroy overalls with a T-shirt and steel-toed work boots. He also wore bulky protective earmuffs to cut down the sound.

"Donnie," I yelled over the noisy chainsaw. "Donnie!"

Donnie looked around, spotted me, and turned off his chainsaw. He lowered his earmuffs around his collar.

"Hey, Mr. Baldwin," he said. "What's up?"

I thought twice about accusing someone expert in the use of a chainsaw, and I soft-peddled my response.

"Donnie, you didn't happen to come by last night and borrow a case of beer out of my tool shed, did you?" I asked nervously.

"What are you talking about?" he asked, a confused look on his goateed face.

"Well, it's just that I had two cases of beer when I arrived yesterday, and one case is missing. I think Phil is missing a few beers, too, from the case he left on his front porch."

"What are you suggesting, Mr. Baldwin?"

"Nothing, I just thought you have the only other key to the shed and—"

"I hope you aren't implying that I stole from you," Donnie replied.

"Oh, steal is a strong word, Donnie. I just thought—"

Donnie took a few steps forward until he was a foot away, looking down at me.

"Look, Mr. Baldwin. I don't need to steal, and I don't drink beer. It's too fattening. I only drink vodka soda coolers. That's how I stay so lean. But I think I know what yer driving at."

Donnie reached into his pocket and retrieved a chain of keys. He removed the one for my tool shed and handed it to me.

"There you go, Mr. Baldwin. I don't think I'll need this anymore."

"Donnie, wait. I didn't mean—"

"I know what you meant," he interrupted. "I'm suddenly booked on jobs until November, so I won't be needing no shed key."

What had I done? I'd just lost my irreplaceable handyman—over one lousy case of beer. Donnie turned away, pulled the cord on his chain saw, and got back to work as if I wasn't there. Phil stood there, looking stunned.

Back at the cottage, the girls were still asleep. Not unusual for them to be in bed at noon. I tiptoed to the rocking chair in the living room and sat down. I was hot under the collar that someone had stolen my beer. I was also peeved that I'd just been dropped by my most valued employee. It made me even more resolved to find the beer thief.

Then I remembered something. I'd left the screen door unlocked overnight. Anyone who knew where I left the keys could have snuck into the cottage, taken the shed key off the rack, grabbed my beer, and replaced the key. If I hadn't oiled that damn screen door, I likely would have heard the intruder.

And maybe the thief hadn't needed a key. I'd left the shed door open until I'd gone to bed and hadn't bothered in my inebriated state to see how many cases of beer remained. It was possible someone stole the beer while I was on Phil's dock or while we were barbecuing out back. But who would have known we weren't near the shed?

Glenn Brown. That cheapskate.

I didn't care much for Glenn, and he probably sensed that. He could have easily walked down the road undetected in the dark. He would have seen Phil's beer case on his porch and could have grabbed a handful. Then he could have simply walked into my shed, stolen the beer, and gone home.

I got in my silver tinny and fired up the engine.

* * *

Glenn was standing on his dock and reached down to grab the side of my boat as I pulled in. He tugged the bow rope and tied it to a mooring cleat. I climbed out and tied the stern.

"How's it going, buddy?" he said, slapping me a high five.

Before I could answer, he'd launched into a story about going over to Ned Anderson's place for drinks the previous night and how they'd tied one on.

I waited impatiently for him to stop talking. It took him about ten minutes to relive his and Ned's drinking antics, but I jumped in when he stopped to breathe for about five seconds.

"Glenn, hush up a minute," I implored. "I've got something important to ask you."

He looked befuddled but complied. I explained to him how I was missing a case of beer and delicately backed into my accusation.

"You didn't happen to pop by and borrow it, did you?" I asked.

"What do you mean borrow it?"

"I wondered if you had taken some of Phil's beer off his porch and the case from my shed."

A look of sincere hurt spread across Glenn's face. "You think I'd do that?"

"Well, you, Phil, and I were the only ones on Kells Bay Road up last night, and I know it wasn't Phil."

Glenn's pained look turned to anger.

"You prick," he said. "You've got some nerve coming over here and accusing me of stealing from you!"

"I didn't say you stole it, it's just that—"

"I was at Ned's from the time I left your dock 'til three a.m. Just ask him. I was too drunk to steal your beer. I could barely find my dock with a flashlight when I canoed home."

I felt a lump in my throat. I believed him and didn't plan on making matters worse by checking out Glenn's story with Ned.

"Look, I'm sorry, Glenn—"

"I think you better get in your boat and split, man. And don't expect to see me pulling up at your dock anytime soon. I think we're done here."

Glenn untied the bowline of my tinny and threw the rope in the boat. Then he walked off the dock and inside his cottage. When someone at a cottage doesn't come out to greet you when you arrive in a boat, it means they don't want visitors. That's cottage etiquette rule number two.

It was time for me to go.

I puttered around the lake for a bit, trying to decide what to do next. I'd now alienated two people, and both of them were probably better friends than I deserved. Still, I couldn't seem to let it go. It was just a case of beer, and if I had to drive into town to buy a new one, it wouldn't kill me. But being stubborn is one of my faults.

I steered the boat in the direction of the McLaughlin cottage.

* * *

The McLaughlin's dock was jam-packed with watercraft, so I was careful not to bump into any expensive toys. I squeezed the tinny into a tight space between the jet skis and a water ski boat. I waited to see if anyone came out. A minute later, Doug McLaughlin walked down the dock looking perturbed. Doug wore work coveralls and held a paintbrush.

I got out of my tinny and stood up on the dock.

"What's up, Baldwin?" he asked. "Heard you were hollerin' at my boys yesterday. Something about their jet skis. You got a problem with that?"

Immediately intimidated, I went on the defensive.

"Oh, no, Doug," I said. "It's just sometimes they get a bit close to the shoreline—"

"I've got news for you, Baldwin. You don't own the lake. Now, what can I do you for?"

I second-guessed my decision to come here, but it was too late to turn back now.

"Doug, it seems like someone stole a case of beer out of my shed last night. I know boys will be boys, but as a fellow father, you don't think the twins would have had anything to do with that, do you?"

Doug scowled and stepped in close. I won't lie. I was frightened.

"First, you scream bloody murder at my boys, now you're accusing them of stealing beer? They're only fifteen years old!"

"Well, Doug, I just wondered if maybe you'd want to know if they did take it so you could, you know, discipline them. I mean, they do see you drinking all the time. Maybe they were curious—"

That comment ended the conversation. Doug McLaughlin wound up and punched me in the face for the first time since my playground days.

I stumbled backward, and he kept coming. "Wait, Doug, I don't think you understand," I whimpered.

"Oh, I understand just fine, Baldwin. Now crawl back into that piece of crap tinny and get off my property! And don't let me catch you picking on my boys again."

I leapt into the tinny, and my shaking hands untied the lines from the mooring cleats as quickly as I could. My right eye was throbbing and swelling shut. I pulled the engine cord, but the motor wouldn't turn over. I tried again. No luck.

"Git, git!" Doug yelled.

I grabbed an oar and pushed off from the dock, paddling furiously.

Doug stood with his hands on his hips, watching as I struggled to drift away.

I floated out to a safe distance and tried pulling the cord again. This time, the motor caught life, and I throttled off.

* * *

Back at the cottage, I pressed a cold beer bottle against my face and looked at my purple shiner in the mirror. How would I explain this to the guys at the office? I could hear them now. "Your wife hit you, Baldwin?" or "fall off your bar stool?"

The weekend had unraveled. And I still didn't know who stole my beer.

Flustered, defeated, and deflated, I opened my sock drawer. What the hell, I thought. I'm so uptight I might as well smoke a joint. The girls were nowhere in sight, and no one would ever be the wiser. I pulled out the balled-up blue socks where I'd stashed my weed.

But it was gone.

Someone had been in the cottage rummaging through my belongings and had stolen my marijuana! I stormed out of the cottage. I felt violated. I decided to walk up Kells Bay Road to blow off some steam and think.

After about five minutes, I caught a familiar scent—the sweet aroma of marijuana. I sniffed the air like a bloodhound trying to determine its origin. Then I heard giggling.

I left the road and went into the forest, trying not to step on any branches. In a clearing, Maggie, Sam, and Tammy were sitting on piles of granite slabs. They were passing around a joint and sipping on beers.

On the ground was my missing case of Steam Whistle.

I charged into the clearing. "Girls!" I yelled.

They all jumped, and Maggie vomited on my flip-flops.

I had some apologizing to do around Rebecca Lake.